ONE YEAR OF UGLY

ONE YEAR OF UGLY

A NOVEL

CAROLINE MACKENZIE

37INK

SIMON & SCHUSTER

New York   London   Toronto   Sydney   New Delhi

37INK

SIMON &
SCHUSTER

An Imprint of Simon & Schuster, Inc.
1230 Avenue of the Americas
New York, NY 10020

This book is a work of fiction. Any references to historical events, real people, or real places are used fictitiously. Other names, characters, places, and events are products of the author's imagination, and any resemblance to actual events or places or persons, living or dead, is entirely coincidental.

First 37 INK/Simon & Schuster hardcover edition July 2020

37 INK/ SIMON & SCHUSTER and colophon are trademarks of Simon & Schuster, Inc.

For information about special discounts for bulk purchases, please contact Simon & Schuster Special Sales at 1-866-506-1949 or business@simonandschuster.com.

The Simon & Schuster Speakers Bureau can bring authors to your live event. For more information or to book an event, contact the Simon & Schuster Speakers Bureau at 1-866-248-3049 or visit our website at www.simonspeakers.com.

Interior design by Erika Genova

Manufactured in the United States of America

10 9 8 7 6 5 4 3 2 1

Library of Congress Cataloging-in-Publication Data has been applied for.

ISBN 978-1-9821-2891-3
ISBN 978-1-9821-2893-7 (ebook)

For my parents, who put stars in my eyes; my husband, who helped me reach out and grab those stars; and Caeleb, my very own little star.

UGLY

It was Aunt Celia who got us into the whole mess. The entire Palacios family thrust smack into the middle of a crime ring because of Aunt Celia and her financial wizardry. What a circus. And after everything we did to get out of that socialist cesspit and make a better life in this cracked and broken Promised Land—Trinidad.

Take it from me: greener grass is always a mirage.

———

Lucky for Aunt Celia, she was dead by the time the shit hit the fan. Or I guess the shit only hit the fan *because* she was dead. Don't get me wrong—that miserable bitch Aunt Celia was hands-down my favorite relative. My favorite person, even. In the many weeks since she'd dropped dead of a heart attack, a day hadn't gone by that I didn't miss her acid humor and mordant insights, her cocaine-dazzled disco tales of the eighties. Her wit was lethal as a syringe of cyanide. No one could ever replace her. But in the present moment, shivering with cold sweat under a stark Trinidadian sun while some lunatic held us all to ransom, well, there was only one person to blame for it.

1

Crank the clock back only fifteen minutes or so and we'd been en-joying our first Palacios Sunday barbecue since Aunt Celia died. Things were feeling almost back to normal after the shock of that late-night phone call when Mauricio, Aunt Celia's ex-husband-cum-common-law-partner, told us he'd found her white-lipped and cold on the kitchen floor. We felt it in our bones, the insidious guilt of regularity creeping in. And saw it in the weather—at the time of Aunt Celia's death the rainy season had soaked the earth, driving the vio-lently vivid green of new life to spread across hills and coastlines and sprout from gutters and pavement cracks like an untameable verdant pestilence, while our own deluge of grief had forced new emotion to sprout from unexpected places in us. Vines of regret, blossoms of nos-talgia. But now the rainy season was over. Ours and the island's. The downpours had dried up, and all that aggressive green overgrowing everything was drawing back from the landscape like the sea pull-ing back from the shoreline. We were drying out too. The fauna of grief was withering up in us, had stopped suffocating us like parasitic strangleweeds. Life was rolling ahead, as it does, and there we were at Aunt Celia's house—Mauricio's house—drinking and barbecuing like any old Sunday. Even Aunt Celia's daughters, Ava and Alejandra, were back to wearing their beauty-pageant makeup and gossiping over boys and tawdry tabloid magazines. They were Irish twins—seventeen and eighteen—but everyone thought of them as actual twins since they were so identically big-breasted, wide-hipped, and large-assed, with the same swishy black hair down to their teeny-weeny waists. I watched them flicking their Princess Jasmine manes, cooing over their half brother Fidel, a rosy-cheeked one-year-old. My younger sis-ter Zulema tittered and cooed with them, poking Fidel's round belly. Zulema was twenty-two, but huddled up with the twins, they could easily pass for triplets. Same high-pitched squeals, same cleavage, same air of a Miss Universe hopeful.

My brother Sancho jabbed my arm with the meat prongs, pulling my attention back to the smoking barbecue pit.

"*¿Qué te pasa?*" I rubbed the spot where he'd poked me. "What's your problem?"

"Mmmo barb . . . cue sau."

Christ, slurring already. I'd noticed the glassy eyes, the dark curls plastered to his forehead with liquor sweats—but hadn't realized we'd already got to slurring. Sancho moved quick.

"Do you mean more barbecue sauce?"

"*Claro, coño.*"

I squirted sauce over the rows of patties, trying to think of a way to get Sancho to relinquish barbecuing duty before he burned the meat or blew up the gas grill or accidentally impaled himself on the prongs.

While I slathered the burgers, Sancho slung an arm around my shoulder. Here we go.

"You 'member Uncle Rubio, Yola? You 'member his barbecues back in Caracas? *Verga*, Uncle Rubio knew how to party. You 'member?"

Sancho, like most people after they've had a few, loved to whip out tales of all our dead relatives, especially his two personal favorites: Uncle Rubio and Uncle Ignacio, legendary for their drinking prowess, imperviousness to hangovers, and acts of unparalleled inebriated lunacy. Sancho thought of them like a blushing young novice thinks of Mother Teresa: with pure doe-eyed aspiration. I thought of them like what they were: a couple of alcoholic pricks.

"Yeah, yeah," I said. "Like the time Uncle Rubio thought it would be a riot to shoot Aunt Milagros's parrot and stick it on the grill? Like *that* family barbecue?"

"Ha!" Sancho doubled over to smack his knees. I winced, half-expecting the prongs to drive into his femur. "That was a barbecue for the books! Pedro the Parrot—tasted like chicken!"

"Yeah. Hilarious. Listen, let me watch the burgers. You go drink some water, go eat a hot dog or something."

"Know what was so great about Uncle Ignacio and Uncle Rubio, Yola?"

"What?"

"They knew how to party."

"Yeah, they partied themselves right off a cliff."

This was true. Uncles Ignacio and Rubio's spectacular double demise had been the culmination of an all-night drunken bender with Rubio at the wheel. I pictured them sailing over the edge of that cliff like Thelma and Louise, hands clasped, their matching gold chains rippling in the slipstream while they slurped the final dregs of rum from their flasks.

"They knew it's better to leave the party early than hang around until the end when you're *cagando* in your pants and pissing in a bag!" He was properly shouting now, beer bottle aloft like a torch. "Aunt Celia knew it too. I'm telling you, better to get out early while the party's still pumping!"

"Sancho, shut up and go drink some water."

"Don't think I dunno what you're tryna do, Yola."

"I'm not trying to do anything. It's hot and you've been out here at the grill for hours, you need to hydrate. . . ."

And then a moment like when you're shouting into your friend's ear at a club and the music suddenly cuts off. The whole backyard, full of the cacophony of an extended Venezuelan family only a second before, went abruptly silent. Sancho was squinting over my head toward the house. I turned to follow his gaze. A skinny man with a chinstrap beard was standing at the far end of the yard just in front of the back porch, wearing this bizarre getup—white patent cowboy boots, snug snakeskin trousers, and a billowing purple-and-black striped silk shirt. All he needed was a lick of eyeliner and some mousse and he'd fit right in with an eighties rock band. Had he been anywhere else but standing oh-so-casually in my family barbecue, I'd have laughed. But there was something about the casualness that was far from reassuring. He had a right to be there, that's what his stance said. *Just you try to kick my ass out.* That, the way he looked around with an oil-slick glint in his eye, not moving, not explaining himself—it all made me uneasy. Gave me that sick stomach flip like when you see a man walking toward you on a dark, lonely street. You tell yourself it's just a man walking on a street, nothing to be afraid of. But that visceral instinct warns you anyhow: this could be trouble.

Then I saw the gun in his hand.

I took a step backward, the urge to run immediately kicking in, even with my family all around me. Another step back and I knocked into my father without meaning to. I hadn't even realized he'd been walking up behind me. He kept going, brushing past me. As I looked back, my eyes fell on the picnic table. Zulema and the twins were like mannequins, staring goggle-eyed at the intruder. But where was Fidel? My heart skipped. I scanned the yard behind me, all the empty arms. Who had the baby?

The same way that silence had thudded onto us like a cartoon anvil, a sudden whooshing intake of breath from everyone at the exact same second made me spin around to see what the hell had happened.

While we'd all been distracted by this David Bowie–inspired stranger in our midst, Fidel had barreled across the yard with all the amphetamine-grade energy of a toddler newly confident on his feet, and had launched himself at the man's snakeskin-clad legs. It was your proverbial slow car crash, watching Fidel tug at the edge of those patent boots to get the man's attention. And before anyone could move to stop it, Fidel was in the man's arms, propped on his hip. Gun in one hand, baby in the other.

Fidel had only been in our lives a few weeks, a cherubic worm that wriggled out of the woodwork after Aunt Celia died. A Filipina servant for an affluent Syrian family had shown up looking for Mauricio to babysit because her employers said they were paying her to watch *their* kids, not her own. (We didn't doubt the kid was Mauricio's. Only a real political genius like him, with his Communist sympathies despite everything we'd been through in Caracas, would name his kid after Fidel Castro.)

Watching the man holding our newly discovered family baby, it was like gravity had gotten stronger. My limbs just couldn't move. I waited for flight or fight to kick in, for some base instinct to carry me blazing across the yard in a Lara Croft–inspired burst of badassery to wrestle Fidel off this armed stranger's hip. But nothing happened. No one moved a fucking muscle. We were pillars of salt.

Thankfully my father's made of sturdier stuff than most and my brother is perpetually brimming with drunken fighting gusto. So while the man bounced a giggling Fidel on his hip like a kindly uncle, my father crossed the yard in indignant strides, shoulders thrown back, while Sancho followed (only swaying very slightly) to stand at *Papá*'s side, gripping the meat prongs. Now, my father has the gentle heart of whatever Taino blood still lingers in his DNA, but the height and wiry brawn of a genocidal Castilian conquistador. Sancho—even drunk—has the same thing going for him, except what he lacks in muscularity he makes up for in soft yet intimidating beefiness. But they might as well have been a couple of ballerinas twirling across the lawn in pink tutus—the guy didn't look ruffled by the pair of them in the least. In fact, he looked downright amused as he watched them approaching. He was having the time of his life, slowly corkscrewing fear into us.

A wordless standoff ensued, the kind where Clint Eastwood would be standing there squinting hard, chewing intimidatingly on a toothpick. A dusty tumbleweed rolling by wouldn't have looked out of place as we all watched on, breathless, the stranger's lupine grin stretching wider as the tension curdled. In my periphery I saw my mother, normally poised, graceful, and emotionless as a ceramic figurine, digging her French-manicured nails into my sister's arm. Her hand was trembling. This alarmed me almost as much as the stranger's gun.

Finally my father broke the standoff. He took a step forward. "Brother man, give me the child," he said, arms outstretched. "Best you explain what you doing at my brother-in-law house, man, before *crapaud* smoke your pipe."

(As a school driver for the two years we'd been in Trinidad, *Papá* listened to Trini talk radio for hours on the road and had picked up more local proverbs and creole dialect than the rest of us. He always whipped it out at inappropriate times, like some absurd nervous tic.)

The man threw his head back and gave such a vaudevillian *ha-ha-ha* of a laugh that it made little Fidel jump and whimper. "You talk like a real Trini, man! Better than Celia. Celia never knew no Trini lingo at all."

My father's arms dropped to his sides. This guy knew Aunt Celia? That one had shocked *Papá* just as much as me. But he caught himself quick. "How you know my sister?"

The man scratched the side of his head with the gun barrel as though pondering the question, then gave an exaggerated shrug.

"Give me the baby," *Papá* repeated.

The man continued ignoring him, smiling down at Fidel, whose plump, pink lower lip was quivering, about to break into a wail.

Papá was begging now: "Please, what you doing this for, man? Take anything you want. Don't hurt the child."

Just then, Mauricio walked out into the yard from the house. Approaching the stranger from behind, he paused in his stride to belch and give the man's snakeskin-and-silk getup a derisive once-over. "Who's this *maricón*—Boy George?"

The man swung around to grin at Mauricio. At the portrait of man, gun, and baby, Mauricio let out a string of *vergas* and stuck his hands up—as if the man would give a shit whether Mauricio was armed or not. He had a baby and a gun. What threat could middle-aged, slack-bellied Mauricio possibly pose?

"Ah, Mauricio! Is you self I waiting on!"

Fidel reached his arms out toward Mauricio, babbling at him.

"Mauricio, Mauricio," the man continued. "Celia tell me so much about you that I recognize you easy. Maybe I even know your face already from a passport photo. Yes, man, heard a lot about you. And I can't lie—not all good! But you know Celia a'ready. She was like Angostura—*bitters*! I take everything she say about you with a pinch of salt, don't worry, man."

Mauricio hadn't moved. Fresh sweat shone on his forehead.

The man gestured with his gun for Mauricio to stand beside my father, which he did, hands still in the air. Then the man surveyed the yard, his gaze steamrolling us all. When his eyes landed on me, he said my name—"Yo-la"—slow and sensuous, like it was a truffle he was rolling around on his tongue. My eyes stayed downcast as I heard him identify the twins, my sister, my mother, and my father's youngest sister, Aunt Milagros, with the same lecherous precision.

"Now that I see everybody here," he said, "I would like to introduce myself. My name is Ugly. You know—*Feo*? Some people call me Mr. Ugly, but seeing as how me and Celia was good friends before she die, all-you could call me Ugly."

Fidel was crying now, wriggling in Ugly's arms, grasping at the air for Mauricio with sausagey little fingers. Ugly bounced him on his hip. "What happen, small man? Eh? What you crying for?" He sucked his teeth. "Look, go by your damn father."

He motioned Mauricio over with the gun. Mauricio didn't move. "Come nah, man, Mauricio, I said take this blasted chile! Slobbering all over me." He wiped the gun barrel across a stream of dribble on Fidel's chin, but Mauricio still didn't move, hands raised like he was in a stickup, mouth hanging open. That's Mauricio for you, the classic chauvinist—always running his mouth about how women "should stay on their backs in the bedroom and on their feet in the kitchen and leave the rest of it to the men," but those big bulging machista balls are the first to shrivel at any sign of trouble.

Clocking Mauricio's uselessness, my father took a few slow steps forward to take Fidel from Ugly. The second *Papá* had the baby, Ugly took two quick strides to place the gun at the center of Mauricio's forehead. Mauricio blinked—once, twice—as the metal made contact, like he'd been jarred out of a daydream.

"Mauricio, you going to join me inside for a chat. Celia had a few outstanding business affairs with me when she die. We going to see how we could rectify that. Sound good?"

Mauricio just stared up at the gun barrel, going cross-eyed. When he still hadn't said anything, Ugly lowered the gun. For a split second I was lured into relief, until Ugly struck Mauricio a blow to the jaw. Whimpering, Mauricio cupped his mouth. Thick blood dribbled through his fingers.

"I said—*Sound good?* People answer me when I ask a question, Mauricio, even people who so ignorant they think a man with style look like Boy George."

Then Mauricio was nodding quick and frightened. "Sound good," he said. The words were a gurgle. Blood ran down his chin. He spat weakly onto the grass.

"Nice, man. Let we go inside."

Ugly threw an arm around his shoulders, laughing with all the cheer of a homicidal Santa Claus. Mauricio jumped as the arm clamped around him. His skin was gray, bloodless as Aunt Celia's had been in the coffin. Something about the way Ugly then guided loping, tongue-tied Mauricio toward the house with the gun aimed at his ribs made me think of a circus ringleader cajoling a ketamine-doped gorilla into its cage.

"Hector!" Ugly called over his shoulder. "You come too. Leave that chile."

My father handed the baby to my brother. Drawn to his full six feet, he looked every bit the dignified alpha male. This wasn't a comfort. I didn't want my father in there puffing his chest out, facing off with some psychopath. Let Mauricio deal with it! Let Mauricio get a bullet in the head! My mother shared my sentiments. As *Papá* began following Mauricio and Ugly, she ran across the yard to clutch the back of my father's shirt. "Hector!" She couldn't get anything more out than that. Ugly stopped to waggle the gun at her.

"*Señora* Palacios, I recommend you don't mix up yourself in my business. I need to speak with Mauricio *and* Hector." He lifted his chin toward the barbecue pit. "Best you go flip them burgers like a good little *señorita*. They smelling burnt."

My father gently twisted himself out of *Mamá*'s grip, kissed the top of her head. "*No te preocupes.* I'll be fine."

At the porch door, Ugly turned once more. "No *policía*, people! Any *policía* and there go be two sets of brains splattered on the wall in there. If I so much as hear a fucking siren or see a car pull into that driveway, I ain't asking questions first. Understand? Bang *uno* and bang *dos*." He pointed the gun back and forth from Mauricio to my father.

Then they went into the house and all we could do was wait.

———

When *Papá* and Mauricio eventually came out again, my father wore a curious expression, like he was trying to work out a particularly difficult math equation. Still ashen, Mauricio was running a hand over his stubbled chin, murmuring to himself. Ugly emerged from the house behind them, stopping to stand on the porch, a finger running along the gun barrel until we'd all turned, a captive audience in the most literal sense, to face him. When he saw he had our full attention, he waved brightly.

"Nice to meet all you Palacios in the flesh! I go be seeing you again very soon. That a promise from me to you." He flashed sterling teeth. "And I does never break a promise."

THE COCKROACH
FAIRY TALE

That was our first visit from Ugly.

That was also the afternoon we found out just how Aunt Celia had gone about securing fraudulent residency permits for herself, Mauricio, and the twins.

Now, let me be straight with you: the residency permits came as a total surprise to me and the rest of the family. Because none of us, not even fanatically Catholic, shit-scared-of-everything Aunt Milagros, had bothered with residency permits, fraudulent or otherwise. We'd all moseyed across the seven-and-a-half miles of ocean separating Trinidad from Venezuela in fishing boats in the dead of night—my immediate family first, the pioneers of the Palacios exodus if you will, then Aunt Celia with Mauricio and the twins, followed by Aunt Milagros not long after. Who the hell needs residency permits when you know a guy with a boat?

Plus none of us needed false papers to get work. Aunt Milagros worked at an Opus Dei charity that turned a blind eye to her immigration status, *Papá* had his school driver gig, *Mamá* ran a nail parlor out of an annex next to our house, I was a freelance translator working from home, Sancho and Mauricio worked under the table at a casino, and Zulema slotted herself into the local Color Me Beautiful spa without so much as presenting a résumé. In fact, her illustrious "qualification" as a Color Me Beautiful image consultant was all we'd been waiting on to get the hell out of Caracas.

But it turned out Aunt Celia had to get falsified papers for the twins to finish secondary school in Port of Spain. Luckily they'd gone to glamorous English-speaking expat schools their whole lives or else no fake papers in the world could've salvaged their educations. Anyway, papers were what Aunt Celia needed for her girls—and that was where Ugly came in.

He'd provided Aunt Celia with his illicit relocation services that included sourcing a man with a zippy boat, making sure no *guardia* or Coast Guard showed up, getting the falsified residency permits, and even enrolling the twins at one of the island's best public secondary schools. Not hard to imagine that his fee, payable in twelve oh-so-convenient yet virtually impossible installments, would've been sky high. When I heard the amount, I couldn't help whistling. I knew Aunt Celia and Mauricio had been well off in Venezuela, but this was big money for people coming from a crumbling economy. We're talking sell-a-kidney money. So—surprise, surprise—Aunt Celia had missed the last two payment deadlines, and seven installments were still outstanding.

Papá told us all this after gathering everyone in Mauricio's living room once Ugly had left. When Mauricio spoke for the first time, wincing because of his bruised jaw and busted lip, he had to pause twice to wipe his leaking eyes. "We owe Ugly nearly six hundred thousand TT dollars," he said. "*Six hundred thousand!* We'll never be able to pay."

That was for shit sure.

He slouched forward, pressing the heels of his palms into his eyes. His body shook. So much for all his usual macho bluster. Ava, sitting on the arm of his chair, draped herself across her father's hunched

back, hugging him. *Papá* continued, stone-faced at Mauricio's cultur-
ally uncharacteristic display of emotion: "This debt doesn't only affect
Mauricio and the twins." My stomach was knotted so hard it hurt. "If
the money isn't paid, Ugly is going to make us all suffer."

"*What?*" *Mamá*'s jaw muscles were twitching, neck stiff as an iron
rod. There was that razor-sharp edge of hers, gift-wrapped in pearls
and pencil skirts, but forever simmering beneath the svelte veneer.
Her eyes were on Mauricio. He was lucky she thought violence was an
unattractive trait in a woman or I'm sure she would've gone straight
for his jugular.

Papá shot her a look and went on. "Since we obviously can't raise
the money, we all have to work off Celia's debt." He exhaled and ran
both hands over his hair. "Ugly will be back again in one week. We're
to wait here for him—all of us—next Sunday, to find out the details."

He looked around the room gravely. "It goes without saying that
we can't contact the police. We're illegal residents in this country.
There's no one who can help us besides ourselves. And even if the
police wouldn't immediately ship us back to Venezuela, Ugly has made
it clear that if anyone makes any anonymous reports or any attempt at
involving law enforcement, we'll all be shot. Not just the perpetrator—
all of us. We have no choice but to follow his instructions."

My mother was doing this thing where she steadily pounds her fist
against her chest. She did it for hours without stopping after she found
out her mother died a couple years back, and when we were teenagers
she'd do it if she caught us sneaking out or whenever we came home
shit-faced from some house party. When she walked in on Zulema
getting it doggy-style from her high-school boyfriend, I thought she'd
have a crater above her heart from all the pounding. And here it was
again, that ominous drumbeat gnawing at my nerves.

"So he's blackmailing us," I said.

"Yes," said my father.

I don't even know why I was surprised. Our immigrant story is as
classic and unchanging as any Hans Christian Andersen fairy tale—the

tale of the illegal refugees who risked it all to live like cockroaches, hiding in the dank cracks of an unknown society where they hope no one will find them, antennae forever twitching, listening for the heavy boot of National Security, only to discover that the strange new place they call home has all the ugliness of the world they left behind, except worse, because here you're stripped of rights, dignity, person-hood. Anyone can crush you under their heel, splatter your little roach innards, just like Ugly was doing to us.

Mauricio was swearing under his breath and sniveling while Ava rubbed his back. I wanted to yank him up by the hair and tell him he had no goddamned right to cry. We had nothing to do with Aunt Celia's deals with some flamboyantly dressed Trinidadian criminal. Mauricio should've been the one paying off the debt or working as Ugly's pawn, not us. Ugly could stick Mauricio in thigh-highs and a wig and put him on a street corner to work off the debt as far as I was concerned.

Unable to tolerate the sight of Mauricio crumbling in on himself, I fixed my eyes to the dining table where Aunt Celia and I had had so many long lunches together. She'd never said a word about Ugly or about getting fake permits—had she? I skipped through the last times I'd sat with her at that table. True, she'd mentioned she was making jewelry to sell at artisanal fairs, which I'd found strange because she always seemed to revel in the luxury of housewifedom, but I'd had the impression that the jewelry thing was because she wanted a hobby, not because of any financial problems. I trawled through all of those final conversations, each a vivid snapshot, like I was thumbing through a picture book, searching for some clue of Aunt Celia's secret, until I came to the lunch we'd had just before she died. My very last conver-sation with Aunt Celia and it had been so stupid.

"I don't have any girlfriends here, *Tía*. You expect me to go out clubbing alone? How pathetic."

"You know what's pathetic? When in a few years you're blowing out the candles on your thirtieth birthday cake with your cats. Life is short, *bruja.* You're twenty-four—get out there, fuck a few frogs, kiss a couple princes, then you'll hit two birds with one stone."

"What two birds?"

She'd counted them out on her fingers. "You won't waste your youth on pointless fucking chastity, and you'll find yourself a husband in the process."

"Jesus, give it a rest with the husband thing."

"Listen, Milagros has enough spinster bitterness to last our family a lifetime. Can't have you winding up like that tragedy."

"*¡Verga!* Poor Aunt Milagros."

"Oh, she fucking looked for it. She's had her legs superglued shut since her *quinceañera*, always more concerned about finding Jesus than finding a man, *la gran idiota.* Let me tell you something, Yola. Life is not some box of chocolates like they say in that movie. Life is a big piece of sugarcane."

"Sugarcane?"

"Yes, a *maldito* sugarcane! You have to bite down hard and suck as much sweetness out of it as you can. Don't be afraid to sink your teeth in, *chama*, it's the only way you'll ever draw out the sugar."

I should've told her what she meant to me right then. I should've said, "Aunt Celia, you're the most entertaining, insightful, foul-mouthed bitch I know, and I love you for it."

But I'd never say that. We never say the things we feel. We keep our mouths shut until the only option is regret. Maybe if I'd have opened up more to her, she would've told me about her debt to Ugly.

My attention was wrenched back to the present by a thudding on the front door. All heads whipped around—Ugly back already? Mauricio peered up at the door through his fingers. Though it was his house, he didn't move from his chair, a quaking six-year-old hiding under his bed from the bogeyman. Rolling his eyes at Mauricio in exasperation, my father motioned for all of us to stay seated, then went to open up.

"Yes?"

To my—and everyone else's—surprise, a girl's voice answered from the front step in Venezuelan-accented Spanish.

"Does Mauricio Benitez live here?"

"*Sí.*" *Papá* opened the door fully and stepped aside.

The girl came in, pulling a suitcase behind her. Color flushed her cheeks as she saw the room full of people staring at her. She looked like she was in her late teens, with free-flowing dark curls and almond eyes. Her denim jumpsuit showcased a nipped-in waist, hips that called to mind African fertility carvings, and bra cups that spillethed over. Her eyes found Mauricio instantly. He stood up, gray-faced.

"¿Vanessa, *qué carajo?* What the hell are you doing here?"

"I came to live with you."

We watched on in confusion as Mauricio went to stand beside the girl. Like a mood ring, his face had gone from gray to deep vermilion.

"Everyone, this is Vanessa." His eyes were on his feet. "My daughter."

As if our family didn't have enough bullshit to deal with.

NAVIGATING THE BULLSHIT

Here was the story with Vanessa, Mauricio's first kid on the side and illegitimate little Fidel's predecessor by seventeen years in the potentially still-unraveling yarn of Mauricio's evidently long history of infidelity. As we eventually found out, she was the product of an extramarital fling Mauricio'd had while visiting his parents in the rural hamlet of Isla de Gato . Ever since Vanessa was born, he'd been visiting annually and regularly sending money to Vanessa's mother, entirely unbeknownst to Aunt Celia, of course. So when, through the ever-active Venezuelan gossip network, word filtered all the way back to Isla de Gato that Aunt Celia and her formidable bitchiness were out of the picture for good, Vanessa decided it was time to make a better life for herself with her dear old daddio. She found a man with a boat all on her own, and made her way to Trinidad, then up to Port of Spain, relying on her outstanding physical attributes and a wardrobe consisting primarily of Lycra to get free transport and food along the way.

The bulk of this information would be gathered the following day when *Mamá*, under the guise of the Kindly Aunt, invited the twins over to her nail spa in our annex for free after-school mani-pedis in a transparent bid to plumb them for intel on Vanessa.

Since I share my mother's proclivity for family gossip, I was also waiting on the twins to turn up that afternoon, grappling with that same incredulous hangover feeling like when you can't quite believe what went down the drunken night before. *Did I really do nine Jägerbombs? Did I really kiss/sleep with/get finger-banged on the dance floor by _____?* Had Ugly really happened? Were we really being blackmailed? Had yet another of Mauricio's side kids actually manifested in our lives?

I was standing at the kitchen window, lulled by the drone of a heavy downpour on our roof as I brewed coffee and mused on what Ugly might expect us to do. Though it was obviously a surreal situation to be in, I felt relatively sanguine about the whole thing. We hadn't even discussed it when we got home from the fiasco of Mauricio's barbecue-turned-blackmail-bonanza the night before. I'd overheard my parents speaking in hushed tones, *Papá* saying that he'd told Ugly flat-out that no daughter of his was going to be prostituted to clear Celia's debts if that's what he was thinking, that Ugly would have to kill him first. "He said killing me could be easily arranged but I'm off the hook because he's a 'mogul' of the relocation business, not the prostitution industry. That's all he said. He wouldn't tell me what we have to do." Anyway, with my instinctual fear of sex slavery mercifully off the table, I felt no need to panic. Or who knows, maybe it was just emotional shock and my brain had numbed itself to the reality of what it actually meant to be blackmailed by a criminal.

Just then, what had been Aunt Celia's car came tearing through the rain to stop in our driveway, Ava at the wheel. She and Alejandra tumbled out in their school uniforms, running toward the annex and squealing at the rain. I took my coffee, grabbed an umbrella, and ventured out, holding the mug close to breathe in the steam while my flip-flops squelched through the sodden grass, flecking my calves with mud.

In the annex, the twins' muddied sneakers and socks were heaped at the door. Ava was already seated at *Mamá's* table, having her nails filed.

Pornographically wet in her uniform, Alejandra was draped across the couch like a lounging Cleopatra, wriggling her newly liberated feet and pointing her toes like a ballerina warming up. When they all turned to see me, I was met by a chorus of "*¡Hola*, Yola!" which no one ever got fed up of singing at me anytime I walked into a room.

My mother arched an eyebrow at me. "You're not expecting any freebies this afternoon too, I hope? You know that everyone who walks into my spa is a paying customer—I don't care if you're my *mamá* resurrected from the dead. This is just an extra-special treat for the girls."

Treat my ass. What she wanted was the inside scoop. But I did too, so helped speed things along. I joined Alejandra where she was stretched across the couch. "So," I said, smacking my lips at a bitter sip of black coffee, "what's she like?"

I waited eagerly for the onslaught of bitching at how much they hated their unfaithful father and this unwelcome interloper in their home. But instead: "Oh my gosh, Yola, I know it's such a mess, but Vanessa is *such* a sweetheart."

Mamá and I shared a confused glance.

"She really is sweet," added Ava, nodding earnestly at my mother. "We freaked out yesterday when she turned up—I mean *freaked* . . ." Alejandra was even laughing. "But *Papá* told us that it was this big mistake, the only time he'd *ever* slipped up, right after *Mamá* told him she was getting a divorce."

"He was heartbroken, you know," said Ava.

"Was he heartbroken when Fidel was conceived too?" I asked.

"It really took a toll when *Mamá* got a lawyer and everything. She even kicked him out for a while. He said it totally crushed him," chirruped Alejandra, ignoring me. "And of course, whatever *Papi* did isn't Vanessa's fault. It was his mistake. Vanessa's always wanted to meet us. She's never had a real family, just her on her own with her mother in Isla de Gato."

"And she really is just so sweet," added Ava.

"*Verga*, we get it, she's sweet," I said. "But you seriously like her? How can you when . . ."

19

Mamá was glaring at me. Eyes like an owl on speed. I knew what that look meant: drop it. But if anyone had to stick up for Aunt Celia, it was me.

"Sorry, *chama*, I don't see how you can be okay with everything..." I started, but Ava interrupted me.

"I guess we realized that you really never know how long you'll be around. You could die at any second of any day. That's what *Mamá's* last lesson was to us. All that matters is love and family. And Vanessa's our half sister. We *want* to know her and love her."

"That's a beautiful attitude to have," beamed Mamá, who'd been nothing if not vocal about her dislike of Aunt Celia, so couldn't give two shits about whether Mauricio ever cheated on her or not. She was just tickled at having new gossip fodder for her and Zulema to discuss over their pink zinfandels when they had "girly nights." But as much as I wanted to call my mother out for her hypocrisy (Think *she'd* want to "get to know family" if family constituted a Shakira-shaped teen *Papá* had fathered in the early days of their marriage? Bitch, please.) and as much as I wanted to cajole the twins into ripping Mauricio a new one, I realized it wouldn't be worth my while. The twins were gonna stick by Mauricio's asinine story of heartbreak-fueled adultery no matter what, because nothing I said could ever shift the female impulse to forgive and justify the picaresque wanderings of the male member. Maybe we all have the natural compulsion to make excuses for men, or else the world would descend into anarchy as wives, girlfriends, and daughters mass-murdered all the cheating husbands, boyfriends, and baby daddies out there.

So I boarded the denial canoe alongside the twins and picked up my oar. "You're right, guys. Mistakes do happen in marriage. Your attitude is great." Because when your family members are cruising along a river of bullshit, sometimes it's best not to tell them how to navigate. The only thing to do is help them paddle ahead into clearer waters and leave the bullshit behind.

UNAVOIDABLE CLICHES

S even a.m. the following Sunday morning, our day of reckoning. We didn't have to be at Mauricio's house for our meeting with Ugly until midday, so I was indulging in my morning ritual: reading on a beach chair in the backyard wearing my favorite pajamas, a threadbare Rolling Stones T-shirt stolen from an ex back in Caracas.

I was just tipping the mug over my tongue to get the last drops of coffee when a loud burst of knocking echoed through the house. I turned to look through the open porch doors. You could see straight through to the living room, past the dining table to the front door. Figuring it was Sancho or Mauricio come to strategize with *Papá* before our tête-à-tête with Ugly, I flipped back to the page I'd been reading.

Another round of knocks and my father shouting "Hang on! I'm coming!" then the creak of hinges desperate for WD-40 as *Papá* opened up.

"*¡Buenos días*, Hector! Nice to see you up and about at this bright and early hour of the day of our Lord."

Ugly.

I looked over my shoulder so fast I nearly snapped a vertebra. My father, in bleach-splattered boxer shorts, was blocking the open door-way. I turned back to look down at my legs, bare right up to the white triangle of my underwear. Christ, why did we have to be a naked house? No one was ever fully clothed unless we had guests. I craned my neck around again to see if there was any possible way I could dart into the house and across the living room to the bedroom hallway without being noticed.

(There wasn't.)

I tried pulling the T-shirt down lower—pointless—and settled for tucking my legs up against me, sinking down low in the beach chair, and praying Ugly wouldn't notice the back of my head if he happened to look through the French doors leading to the porch and backyard.

That sociopathically cheerful voice: "What happen, Hector, you not inviting us in?"

Us?

Heavy footsteps and the door slamming shut.

"Now, now, Hector, no need for slamming doors. Best you remember to keep your cool. Román don't have the same patience as me. He who slam the door in the wrong man's face is he who get his hand chop off so he cannot slam any door again! That not how the saying does go, Román?"

Who the hell was Román? My neck twitched with how badly I wanted to look behind me, but I stayed put. If Ugly saw me in this T-shirt and panties, I'd have to burn them both. Something about the way he looked at you made you feel like his tongue had run over your body instead of his eyes.

"What I can do for you, Ugly?" sighed my father, not hiding his exasperation. You had to hand it to him, *Papá* had *huevos*.

"I said to myself, why wait till lunchtime to come and talk to my new Palacios friends? I thought, why I don't pay everybody a visit at they house with my right-hand man?" He whistled. "Boy, Milagros nearly wet she-self she was so frighten when we gone to see she!"

"*Hijo de puta*, you better not have fucking done anything to Milag—"

Papá sputtered, choked. Hearing him gasping for air, I leapt up instinctively from the chair—to do what, I have no idea, but you hear your father being choked, you fucking do something. A man, taller and much younger than *Papá*, had him lifted by the throat. The tips of my father's toes grazed the tiles.

"STOP!"

Ugly started at my scream, and the younger man's eyes flicked toward me as his hand instantly unclamped itself from around my father's neck. *Papá* rubbed at his throat, gulping air, but the look he gave me could've razed whole cities to the ground.

"Well, well, you should have tell us we have company, Hector!" I stood there, hands over my crotch. What now? Ugly was making his way across the living room toward the porch doors, my father and the younger guy trailing him. *Verga.* I dropped back down into the beach chair and pulled the edges of my T-shirt down as far as I could, managing to at least cover my underwear. And then the three of them were standing over me: my father, livid and glowering; Ugly grinning with a demented malevolence. But this other man, he was looking me over like someone contemplating a painting, with a sort of curious appreciation. I felt the pink hit my cheeks the second my eyes connected with his—two live wires sparking as their tips touched. Now that he was standing directly in front of me, I could see that he was *some*thing. Rich olive skin, tousled dark hair—pretty-boy features—but on a lightweight boxer's broad-shouldered, sinewy frame, with exceptionally vascular forearms that gave the effect of having been used to land many a jaw-cracking, nose-breaking blow in scrappy street fights. Other hints at a less than savory past: the scars on his forearms and knuckles—a constellation of marks, all different sizes and shapes, some with the rippling sheen of old burns, others that looked like they'd been roughly carved into his skin with the tip of a blade, and round pocks that could be souvenirs of chickenpox or the wrong end of a lit cigarette. There was a whole history of rough living etched into his arms and fists. He smiled at me, showing protruding canines that overrode otherwise flawless dentition. The scars, the fang-like teeth, the wiry strength—they gave him a predatory something, made my pulse quicken. I caught his eyes dart down the length of my legs, sending a current of cold air running from my chin to the tips of my toes and back up again. It was only at a wolf whistle from Ugly that we unlocked our eyes.

"All you Palacios women really something special to see, boy. Román, you see this girl? I know she lanky, not like her cousins, but she have a nice ass on her, boy. Wait and see when she get up."

Without taking his eyes off me, Román stepped forward and extended a hand. "*Encantado. Un placer*, Yola, *de veras*."

I was taken aback. He was Venezuelan. I took the hand, felt the rough calluses on his palm, the intentional lingering of his fingers as our hands slowly slid apart, the contact stirring something visceral and hungry in me.

"Meet Román," said Ugly, clapping him on the back. "He handling you Palacios for me. Keeping all-you in line, making sure everything run nice and smooth."

"And this," said Román in lightly accented English, "is, of course, Yola. Yola Encarnación Palacios Suárez. English degree from La Universidad Central. Master's in technical translation. Amateur fiction writer. Short-listed for the *Concurso Latinoamericano de Cuento*, the Fernández Lema Prize, the *Honor de Miranda* short story prize."

My skin rippled with goose bumps. I was so private about my writing that I'd only talked to Aunt Celia about it. And I'd never even told her about those short lists.

Román watched me evenly, but there was none of Ugly's malice in his face. "You're a very talented woman," he said. There was a smooth sense of control in the way he spoke that put me on edge.

Ugly whooped, took his gun out of its holster, and twirled it deftly on his index finger. "Talented? But she never win a single one of them prizes you call out! Sound like a loser to me." He cackled and holstered the gun. "Don't look so shock, Miss Yola. Román here know everything about everybody. You ain't hear I tell you he my right hand? He have a file fat so . . ." He gestured to show that the file was apparently two feet thick. ". . . on every one of all-you. He know everybody skeleton and which cupboard to look for it in. Don't try no fuckery with Román—he know what you doing before you even think to do it."

He shoved my father's shoulder. "Come, Hector, enough niceties." *Papá*'s cheeks were flecked with red, the vein running along his forehead thick as a tree root, turgid with rage. "Important business to discuss!"

Ugly led my father away, but Román lingered, staring at me with a glimmer of a smile. I stared right back, affronted at how entitled he was to just stand there and drink me in. Affronted but sort of flattered.

Now, I know what you're thinking—*This guy's a criminal who was just choking your father, you horny bitch!* All I can say is: forbidden fruit is the original aphrodisiac.

And then there was the other thing. You hear about it all the time—cheesy clichés about thunderclaps and fireworks—but when it happens to you, you realize those clichés came about for a reason. During that sexually charged stare-down, I felt all those stale old clichés. I had the sensation of being incredibly alive and invigorated, like I'd just slipped beneath the cool ocean on a hot day, like I'd just jumped out of a plane with the clouds rushing up to meet me. I felt every delicious, sentient thing I'd ever seen, smelled, touched, tasted, like a syringe of adrenaline had been rammed into my chest. It was lust. Pure wet, messy, make-your-toes-curl lust. The kind that makes you do stupid things like sleep with dangerous men.

Still, there are limits. I wasn't going to take things a step further and actually have a conversation with the guy. So I got up from the beach chair and turned on my heel, not caring that my underwear was exposed now that Ugly was inside. I tossed my hair over my shoulder, grateful for my financially unsustainable addiction to lavish hair products that kept it lush and glossy. And I walked away, mentally patting myself on the back for my self-control, but so weak in the knees I must've looked like a newborn foal as I tottered back to the house.

Only at the porch doors did I let myself look back. He was watching me with a half smile, like he'd been waiting for me to do exactly that.

THE FUCKED-UP YEARS: A FINAL HIT

It's a testament to the kind of parent my father is that when Ugly and Román left our house after moseying by for a Sunday morning visit peppered with violence and threats, he didn't knock back a few tranquilizing rums or seek out my mother for a conciliatory quickie to make him feel better about being choked. Instead he came, features softened with paternal concern, to ask me why I'd never told him about the literary short lists. "I didn't even know you were that into the writing thing. I wish you'd told us, *gordita*, I'd love to read your stories."

I exhaled by way of a weak laugh. "I never won. There was nothing to tell." That was a lie. I'd never won anything, but I'd had short stories published in a smattering of literary journals all over Latin America. Plus there was the novel I'd been drafting for over a year back in Caracas, that I fantasized compulsively about getting published if only I could get my shit together and finish the thing.

I couldn't put my finger on why I'd never shared any of it, especially not the novel that I'd worked on for so long. Maybe it was because so much of my writing was inadvertently about my family.

Or maybe it was because I felt I needed something as concrete as a competition win or a book deal to be taken seriously when I publicly declared myself a writer—so I wouldn't have to tack the word *aspiring* onto it.

"*Por favor*, as if we'd care about winning," said *Papá*. "You put too much pressure on yourself." He shook his head. "You're so much like Celia, you know that?"

"I do."

Which was why I'd only talked with her about my writing and even then I kept my secrets. I had only told her about the novel and the published short stories, never the short lists. She'd only respect a win.

"Anyway, you'll tell us next time you enter a contest, won't you?"

"I will," I lied. "Definitely."

Fatherly concerns dealt with, he went on to tell me that we'd still be having family lunch together as originally planned, but that everyone would be coming to our house instead of Mauricio's. "There's a lot to discuss," he said. "And I don't want to talk about it somewhere my shoes are sticking to the floors and there isn't a crumb in the house. Mauricio needs to get a damn housekeeper."

"Let him pay Vanessa to cook and clean. Isn't she here looking for work?"

Papá stifled a smile but didn't indulge me. "Everyone's coming over for twelve," he said. "And cut Vanessa some slack. If I can be okay with her, so can you."

"I know, I know. The twins are on board with her as well, so who am I to stay up on my high horse. But it's not as easy as you think."

"Well, like I said, you're like Celia. Being on a high horse comes natural."

I gave a mock laugh and stuck my tongue out at him before turning back to my laptop and the translation job I'd been working on. But *Papá* lingered at the door until I looked up from the screen.

"What's up?" I asked.

"I really do see so much of Celia in you now. It was never as notice-able to me until after she was gone."

I smiled, my cockles warmed by the power of good old genetics that allowed familial traits of bitchiness to transcend even death.

By lunchtime, the family was gathered at our house, lounging around the living room and the backyard while Zulema and I helped my mother in the kitchen. Whacking the knife against the cutting board as she sliced a cucumber, Zulema leaned in to whisper to me.

"Who was that man with Ugly?"

"Román. He's Ugly's muscle or something. Gets intel on everyone. He's Venezuelan too."

"*Really?*"

She said it like I'd just told her the most eligible bachelor in town was newly available. A flare of proprietary jealousy took me by surprise.

"How'd you see him anyway?" I asked.

"Out the window. *Duh.*"

I'd forgotten that her bedroom window looked out onto the front yard and the street. She must've seen when they came and left.

"Oh." I hoped she couldn't tell that just the thought of Román was having an effect on me. I could picture his eyes, feel the roughness of his hand, hear the steady control in his voice. My cheeks flushed. I chanted it in my head, a mantra: *He's a criminal. He's a criminal. He's a criminal.*

"He was pretty freaking gorgeous," giggled Zulema.

I gave her a once-over out of the corner of my eye. My sister and I have the same slim, leggy build, same long Amerindian hair, but with different key assets. She has the tits, I have the ass. I looked at the porn star–perky boobs trembling while she chopped, then down to the unimpressive slope of her backside. Hoped Román was an ass man. *He's a criminal. He's a criminal. He's a criminal.*

"Girls, let's put everything on the table now." *Mamá* was taking an immense lasagna out of the oven, eyeing my sister and me suspiciously, like she always did when we were whispering. "Yola, hurry up with that salad. You haven't even chopped the tomatoes yet."

"I can do the tomatoes!" Zulema dumped the plastic tub of cherry tomatoes onto the cutting board. *Whack! Whack! Whack!* I eyeballed her cleavage. *Shake! Shake! Shake!*

There we all were: one big, happy family coming together for Sunday lunch and to review the details of our collective blackmail. Even little Fidel was there, doing his gooey adorable baby thing. We'd all grown so attached to him that his mother, Camille, dropped him off sometimes on Sundays, her only day off, so she could take a much-needed break from round-the-clock servitude. Now he was bouncing on Vanessa's knee while she fed him a bowl of mashed pawpaw. Another attempt, I'd noticed, at trying to make herself useful, along with offering to lay the table and help with whatever *Mamá* needed. I clung harder to my grudge on Aunt Celia's posthumous behalf. With the twins and everyone else already welcoming her with open arms, I was the only one left who seemed to remember that Vanessa was Mauricio's seventeen-year-old secret. It might've been a flagging, irrational cause to keep up my dislike of her—the girl's ass-kissing did seem pretty sincere—but it was the last candle I could burn for Aunt Celia.

Plus there was the other thing that was getting under my skin: her shameless flirting with my brother, who clearly wasn't hampered by any Celia-inspired guilt. Notoriously unscrupulous in matters of the crotch, Sancho was perched on the arm of the couch next to Vanessa, tight curls spilling into eyes that peered straight down the bottomless crevice of her cleavage. Since she was Mauricio's daughter, not Aunt Celia's, and therefore not a blood relative, I strongly suspected Sancho was trying to sleep with her. Never mind he was twenty-nine and she was seventeen, and that Sancho had been dating a Trini girl, Megan, who doted on him, for the past year. I thought of all the time

I'd invested in small talk with poor old Megan, all those hours I'd never get back—always a waste of time getting to know anyone from Sancho's ephemeral relationships.

Christmas was a month away, so parang music, Trinidad's peppy tropical equivalent of carols, was playing on the radio, making us all grit our teeth at the atrociously pronounced and often nonsensical Spanish lyrics. And though the house was undecorated out of respect for Aunt Celia, any outsider who'd seen us all gathered together, the parang setting the seasonally jovial atmosphere, would've thought our family lunch was downright festive. But we could all sense the subtle tension. No one ranting about Venezuelan politics, no playful banter, none of Sancho's inappropriate blue jokes or Aunt Milagros's depressing stories from the Opus Dei charity—just stilted chitchat about nothing at all.

When everyone had eaten, *Mamá* announced that she was going to tidy up the kitchen. She found discussing money to be in poor taste, so I knew the whole issue of Aunt Celia's, and now our, debt was painfully uncomfortable for her. That kitchen was her only escape.

My father walked to the center of the living room, tacitly calling us all to order. He scanned the room. "Where are Sancho and Vanessa?"

Eyes skipped nervously from the ceiling to the floor to cuticles, all avoiding my father. Clearly I wasn't the only one who'd noticed Vanessa and my brother flirting earlier.

A second later, *Papá* spotted them by the mango tree at the far end of our yard. Vanessa was backed up against the trunk, batting her eyelashes and tittering while Sancho regaled her with some presumably riveting tale. My father hollered for them to come inside; then, without further ado, our blackmail briefing began.

I said I wasn't panicked about the whole thing, and I still wasn't.

But anxiety and panic aren't one and the same, and now the anxiety was really kicking in. What were we going to be forced into doing? I'd never found myself in a position before where I had no choice—none whatsoever—but to obey someone's orders on pain of death or deportation. It was surreal. It was scary.

31

Looking around, you could see that everyone felt the same. Features had hardened suddenly. Mouths were stark lines. Nails had been chewed clean off. Mauricio looked the worst out of everyone. Eyes red and unblinking, he looked like he hadn't slept in years. I didn't care. I blamed him for everything, even more than Aunt Celia. Why had he left her out on a limb doing deals with Ugly on her own when he'd always been the breadwinner in their household? I couldn't understand it.

Aunt Milagros wasn't too far behind Mauricio in terms of appearance. She looked like she'd forgotten a hairbrush even existed. Though she was only in her late forties, she'd let her herself go completely gray—"So those uncouth Trini men will stop harassing me in the streets!"—and now her hair looked like a silver storm cloud electrified by lightning. I'd never seen curls stand on end before. It gave her a sort of Einstein look. The visit from Ugly that morning must've scared her senseless. I even thought I'd smelled the lingering stink of cigarette smoke on her paisley blouse when I'd kissed her hello earlier, evidence of a nerve-induced nicotine fix. Which was especially concerning given that Aunt Milagros wouldn't even drink Coke because she said its origins lay in the "evils of the coca leaf," far less indulge in a proven carcinogen for anxiety relief.

"So," my father began, "Ugly and his colleague Román spoke with Mauricio, Milagros, Sancho, and me this morning, as you all know. But not all of you know what was discussed. Essentially, we've been given the terms of our 'deal' with Ugly, if you want to call it that. It's the only option we have to clear Celia's debt. We're all going to be involved— even you girls." He gave the twins a nod. They were sitting side by side, mirror images in matching pink gym gear, ponytails streaming behind them, chewing their bottom lips.

Then *Papá* laid out the terms under which we'd all avoid having our throats cut and tongues pulled through the slit like neckties. (To stress the importance of us not going to the police or talking to anyone about our situation, *Papá* felt the need to quote Ugly word for word.) But first, my father explained how Ugly's operation worked: Ugly brought illegal Venezuelan immigrants into the country for certain (extortionate) fees. He arranged the pickups in Venezuela and the drop-offs in various fishing villages in South Trinidad. As part of his "relocation packages," he sorted housing, forged documentation, under-the-table employment, and whatever else was necessary for the migrants to start a whole new life, just like he'd done for Aunt Celia. It was a massive operation, presumably involving an extensive network of bribed government and police contacts, which, according to Ugly's bragging, had allowed him to bring thousands of Venezuelans across the slim strip of ocean separating the South American continent from Trinidad.

And where would the Palacios family fit into all this?

"Ugly will be using our homes as safe houses for the Venezuelans coming in." There was no missing the bitterness in *Papá*'s voice.

"Families, people on their own, groups . . . however Ugly wants to configure things is up to him, but Román will be doing the drop-offs. We deal with him only, never Ugly. We just have to be standing by at all times to receive and accommodate whoever Román brings. We'll be providing comfortable shelter and food, at our expense. They'll stay for as long as necessary until Ugly is ready for them to be moved. Then Román will collect them again."

"And it's *all* of us doing this? Every household?" I asked. My father nodded.

"I, like, totally cannot believe this is happening," moaned Zulema, twisting the silky rope of her hair like it could turn back time to before we were living at Ugly's mercy. "How long will we have to do it?"

"For as long as Ugly feels it will take for Celia's debt to be paid."

"But that could be years, Uncle Hector," said Ava. "What if he sends strangers into our houses for like a decade?"

"We have no choice in any of this. Ugly is not a man to make empty threats, trust me. And Román is equally dangerous." He rubbed his neck and I knew he was remembering Román's hand around it. A twinge of guilt tugged at me.

"Whatever Ugly and Román want us to do," *Papá* continued, "we just have to suck it up and do it. There's no alternative. Keep your heads down and we'll all get through this."

"So we have no way out?" Alejandra was incredulous.

"No, none! NONE!" Voice cracking, Mauricio clutched at his hair and threw his head back.

I scoffed. "Cool it, Scarlett O'Hara."

Mauricio looked at me, bewildered. "Who?"

My father motioned impatiently for us both to shut up. "Listen," he said, "I know this is a mess, but at least Ugly has given us a way to work off the debt. Sooner or later this will all be over."

"But these are *illegal* people we'll be sheltering!" Aunt Milagros was wild-eyed, her silver curls demented in their disarray. "What if the police find out?"

We all turned at the sound of a hoarse laugh from my mother, standing in the kitchen doorway. "*We* are illegal, Milagros. *¿Se te olvidó?*"

That shut everyone up. It was true. We were all criminals living in a country without permission, without the protection of the police or government. Snails without a shell, totally exposed.

"Yasmin is right," said my father, after a long silence. "We're in no position to judge anyone. We have to look at this as an opportunity to help our countrymen find a better life like we all did. We have to be positive. We are going to clear Celia's debt, and we'll be standing by our Venezuelan people. It's our turn to be the Good Samaritan."

A murmur of agreement rippled through the room. Nothing appealed to a pack of wayward Catholics like a Good Samaritan reference.

"How will we know when people are coming?" asked Vanessa.

"I don't know," said my father. "We have to be ready to receive them whenever."

I looked around the living room. Our house was comfortable enough for my parents, Zulema, and me, but even when Sancho had briefly lived with us when we first moved in, things had felt cramped. The couch was also a pull-out bed, and there were a couple of unhung hammocks heaped in a corner of the porch, but that would only be enough if a few people stayed with us at a time. How many people would Ugly be sending our way? Would it be whole families, whole cargoes of people crammed into our home? I had so many questions but could see my father was stressed, even as he forced a smile. I stayed quiet. No use asking anything anyway, not when *Papá* had no control over any of it. Ugly was the one pulling the strings—Ugly and Román.

Papá resumed his pep talk. "For now, all we can do is wait until the first people are sent. Just remember, these are *our* people. They're going to be desperate, frightened, and alone. Let's treat them with Palacios hospitality."

Everyone nodded and mumbled that yes, of course, we would welcome them, but no one bought into my father's spurious enthusiasm. How could we? Ugly could be sending anyone—drug dealers, thieves, murderers, rapists. There was no way of screening who'd be living with us, no way of knowing if we'd be safe in our own homes. A morose silence hung over us, a gray smog, until *Mamá* said she had a headache and was going to lie down. Then Aunt Milagros said she was going to her second Mass for the day, and Mauricio, maudlin as ever, said he'd go with her. The twins stayed behind, playing with Fidel in the garden while Zulema, Sancho, and Vanessa took out the dusty Scrabble set, I guess for something to take their minds off Ugly. Seeing Sancho and Vanessa giggling and finding excuses to touch each other while an oblivious Zulema concentrated on her first batch of letters, I decided to call it a day. But as I was heading to my room, *Papá* pulled me into the kitchen.

"I have something for you." He handed me a large brown envelope. "It belonged to Celia. Mauricio said he thought you should have it—Celia once told him you two used to talk about writing and books a lot."

My throat tightened. I took the envelope and pulled out a fat sheaf of pages, all typed up in an old-fashioned font. I remembered the antique Underwood No. 5 typewriter Aunt Celia had inherited from my *abuela* when she died. I thought Aunt Celia had kept it as an ornament, not for actual writing. The several hundred pages held together with a large binder clip proved otherwise.

At the very top of the cover page was a title in capital letters: *LOS AÑOS JODIDOS DE MI VIDA*. That was Aunt Celia's foul mouth all right.

I slid the pages back into the envelope and hugged it to my chest, a little piece of Aunt Celia in my arms.

"Where'd Mauricio find this? Is it a memoir?"

"It was in her desk drawer. Mauricio said it would be too painful to read anything she wrote so he hasn't even looked at it. He guessed it might be a novel, but with a title like *The Fucked-up Years of My Life,* my money's on it being a memoir. You read it and find out for us." He chuckled. "That Celia and her mouth. Your *abuela* used to make her gargle soapy water at least once a day, but that only made her swear even more, to prove a point."

Papá and I stayed in the kitchen remembering some of Aunt Celia's finer moments until I couldn't stifle my curiosity any longer with the heft of Aunt Celia's consciousness in black-and-white print weighing heavy in my arms. Whether it was a diary, a memoir, a novel, I didn't care—I hadn't realized how addicted I'd been to that signature Celia vitriol until her death had cut me off cold turkey, left me sick with withdrawal. So like Tony Montana burying his face into that iconic last-hurrah pile of blow, I couldn't wait a second longer before diving headfirst into my final unexpected hit of Aunt Celia.

A TURD WON'T GROW
TAIL FEATHERS
(AND OTHER INSIGHTS)

I sat cross-legged on my bed, Aunt Celia's manuscript in my hands. More than anticipation, I was mostly shocked that Aunt Celia had written this. Not once in the countless conversations we'd had about books and my writing had she ever mentioned that she was also a writer. Or at the very least, that she was writing something. It all made sense now that she'd been so kind in critiquing my work over the years. What else did I not know about the aunt I thought I'd been so close to? First the whole business with Ugly. Now this.

It didn't matter. All that mattered was that I'd get to hear her voice again on the page. Holding the manuscript, I imagined that I could feel the warmth of her hands still on the paper, pictured her sliding each sheet into the ancient typewriter, her red-lacquered fingernails clacking noisily across the keys. I exhaled and removed the binder clip, placed the cover page facedown on the bed.

The first chapter was titled *"La Llegada Sagrada"* and contained the full account of Aunt Celia's birth—her sacred arrival, as she'd not-so-humbly dubbed it—which had been family lore since as far back as I could remember, because when little Celia was born, she came out weighing exactly thirteen pounds and with a fully grown tooth. With the baby's unlucky weight and precocious tooth, *Abuela* was convinced that Celia was destined to be the Antichrist, or at the very least, one of his minions. So she persuaded my *abuelo* to give Celia up to an orphanage run by nuns. As the story goes, *Abuela* changed her mind a month later and returned to the orphanage racked with remorse to retrieve Celia, much to the nuns' relief (turned out Celia was just as bitchy and loudmouthed during her first month of life as when she was an adult).

It was no surprise that Aunt Celia's memoir or autobiography or whatever it was should start off with her brief stint as an orphan, because as the manuscript went on to confirm, she'd never let my grandparents forget that they'd abandoned her:

I'm sitting there at family dinner number one hundred and fucking sixty-two for the year. As if I really need to see Tía Ramona's mustache more than once a year at Christmas. The men are all outside, smoking cigars and drinking, swapping stories of who has the most mistresses, tugging on their ball sacks to see whose hangs the lowest, and I'm stuck in the kitchen with the women—Milagros plus all those musty old aunts and my mother, radiant with self-satisfaction at another dinner where she successfully made her sisters feel like big fat fucking failures in comparison to her. They're flapping their gums and respective mustaches, everyone bragging about the usual bullshit, when I hear Tía Mabel telling Mamá she just wishes she could've had kids as well raised as us. "I've always been dedicated to my children," breathes Mamá, beaming and bashful.

"Always dedicated, Mamá? You mean except in the case of a helpless infant who's committed the blasphemy of being born with a tooth, of course." I couldn't help myself. She'd fucking asked for it.

Mamá's looking at me like she wishes she'd clothes-hangered my former fetal self long before she had a chance to squeeze me out with that unholy tooth.

"Your mother is a good mother, Celia," whimpers Tía Mabel, the brown-noser.

"Ha! A good mother who dumps her newborn with a bunch of sexually repressed religious fanatics who think they're married to the protagonist of a two-thousand-year-old storybook? Good mother my ass. Tía, let me tell you something—you can call a turd a peacock, but it still won't grow tail feathers."

Mamá wouldn't leave her room for two days after that, and I was banned from attending the next four family events. Win-win.

I kept reading voraciously. The writing was sharp, witty, and merciless, just like Aunt Celia. And written in the present tense with a neatly crafted linear narrative, it read like an intimate diary, but one that was juicier than fiction. Only when a stack of pages were facedown beside me and the stripes of light falling through the louvers were the hazy pink of sunset did I put the manuscript down, wanting to ration the rest of it as long as I could. It was strange, reading her writing. I was hooked, but at the same time, the more I read, the more I felt the hole in my chest widening—I hated that I couldn't call Aunt Celia right then to tell her what I thought of her work.

The only way to ease the ache of that hole, a raw and ragged-edged wound newly opened by the discovery of her writing, was to keep reading.

In the wee hours of that morning, I finally forced myself to stop. I'd followed Aunt Celia from that dank orphanage to my *abuelos'* rural ranch, and was now smack in the drama of her wild teenage years. I stopped myself there even though there was so much more to read, just a few more chapters until her debauched twenties, which I was already so fondly familiar with thanks to the many stories she'd told me. But I made myself resist the magnetism of the manuscript—this was my last fix of Celia so I had to eke it out.

I tucked the manuscript into my nightstand drawer, still thrumming with the energy surge from reading good writing, and I knew then how I'd keep Aunt Celia's memory alive. I'd prove to her, dead or not, that all our conversations about reading, writing, books we loved, books we hated, authors we couldn't live without, authors we thought could eat shit, all of that talk hadn't been for nothing. If she could secretly pen a bona fide tome without ever making a single claim to being a writer, I had no excuse not to finish my own opus. I'd show Aunt Celia I could write.

————————

The next morning I was charged, ready to put pen to paper. It was time to forge ahead with the novel draft. Before our departure from Caracas, I'd been working doggedly on it for nearly a year while grappling with the usual procrastination pitfalls—trawling social media, color-coordinating my wardrobe, staring at my cuticles, Googling how to stop procrastinating—and I had only a few chapters left to write, along with a few plot holes to fill. But then came our upheaval to Trinidad and it was all too easy to put the book on the back burner. Now, though, Aunt Celia's memoir had given me exactly the jolt of inspiration I needed to get back to the literary grindstone. There were her classic Celia-esque insights for starters:

> Spotting a good catch is about numerology. A good man should always be tied to two crucial numbers: 6 and 0. Six represents the minimum of figures that should be coming into his bank account every month (in US dólares, claro), and the number of inches his cock should exceed to make him worth your while. Zero represents the ideal number of living parents, siblings, children, and former marriages attached to any prospective husband worth considering.

Not to mention the wild anecdotes that served as ample fodder for fiction:

It was a night made of magic ingredients—hairspray, disco balls, and rich boys. How was I to know it'd end in the worst kinds of shots (tequila, gun, mug)?

I was amped. Fingers hovering over the keyboard, I wet my lips, waiting for the first line of the next chapter to come to me, the one that would blow people's minds, have the Cervantes Prize judges creaming themselves. But the cursor just blinked at me on the screen (judgmentally, if cursors can be judgmental) as my hands stayed poised above the keys. I was stumped. I tried putting a few lines onto the page, but anything I wrote sounded contrived and flat, nothing that would leave any literary award judge gagging for more.

I opted for procrastination in a bid to get the juices flowing. Started browsing the Internet for local writing workshops. Now that I knew Aunt Celia the Clandestine Literary Wonder had been offering shrewd writing advice all along, it was time to find some other, equally useful source of writing camaraderie. To my surprise, I discovered that there were lots of literary events going on locally, and in San Fernando, the island's southern capital, the annual Bocas Lit Festival was under way. Scrolling through the festival website, I found myself getting nervous. I only wrote in Spanish, and the thought of attempting to write in my second language, far less read aloud my attempts at English prose, had always deterred me from doing any due diligence on Trinidad's literary scene, if there was a scene at all. I'd always felt that my intellect knocked itself down a few pegs when I expressed myself in my second language, and I wasn't willing to make myself that vulnerable when it came to writing. My words were my guts spewed onto a page, intestines laid out in rows of black and white. I couldn't chance laying those guts out with a language in which l was anything less than native-level flawless. But now Aunt Celia was gone and I needed writer folk for feedback.

After combing through the festival program, I settled on a lecture by a London-based literary agent—no workshopping my writing or reading anything aloud to strangers. An easy way to dip my toe into unknown waters. I registered for the lecture, already jittery about interacting with other writers. Trini culture was warm and hospitable, but the social scene was cliquish—I imagined the sphere of the local literati being even worse.

A few minutes after registering, a little *ping!* on my cell phone told me I'd gotten a confirmation email from the festival. I looked at the email on the phone screen, then went back into the inbox and scrolled down until I came to the last email I'd gotten from Aunt Celia. Sent three days before she died, telling me I needed to pick up a copy of *Middlesex* by Jeffrey Eugenides.

> *About a hermaphrodite! Why don't you write about one of these transgender people? Everybody's eating that shit up right now. Nothing gets people going like someone fucking around with their genitals. Write about it, Yola! Go get yourself a man-made penis for research ja ja! Then maybe you'll win yourself a Pulitzer like Eugenides.*

I'd written back a one-liner:

> *You have to be American to win a Pulitzer.*

It made me sick to look at my final, dry email reply. But I still read it every other day.

Feeling that familiar dull throb of missing her, I was tempted to take another read of the manuscript. But then I remembered why the manuscript had inspired me in the first place. Not just because of the writing, but because I had to put some quality shit on paper too, to prove myself to Aunt Celia if nothing else. I closed my novel manuscript and opened a blank Word document. A quick short story would stir the creative pot. Sensing that intangible something that sends the words flooding out of you, I wrote the first line:

She did it to prove something.

It was like putting your toe onto the edge of a slide greased with olive oil. With those few words, I slipped down the chute, tumbling down the creative rabbit hole in an avalanche of words. A couple hours later, a first draft of a pretty decent short story was on paper. Thus recharged, I returned to my novel, and wrote chapter after chapter, reconnecting with my characters, falling in love with the story all over again. I only broke focus when the outdoor security light came on in a series of staccato blinks, telling me it was dusk. The bulb of the light had been fading for ages, and would strobe fluorescently into my room for fifteen minutes every day at nightfall before it finally glowed steadily. I went to the window to pull the curtain shut, but something caught my eye. I peered through the louvers—was I seeing right? I leaned into the window, squinted through the slats at two shadowy forms at the far end of the backyard.

There they were. Sancho and Vanessa up against the mango tree, mouths locked, Vanessa on her tiptoes, Sancho with his hand jammed down the front of her jeans.

And just like that, I was struck by a great first line for a second novel:

He was too stupid to know he'd made a huge mistake.

————

I'm not even going to get into the Vanessa-Sancho thing. Setting aside my own mixed feelings toward her, the girl was seventeen years old. Sancho was pushing thirty, had a girlfriend and a blatant drinking problem, and was nothing if not rapaciously promiscuous, with or without said girlfriend. I was tempted to warn Vanessa, but what did I owe her anyway? She'd been playing up to him from day one, and I'd already been magnanimous enough to temper my frigidity toward her in spite of my Aunt Celia loyalties. I wasn't getting involved now if she and Sancho wanted to start up some sordid dalliance. So my reaction to catching them at it was like witnessing a Mafia hit—omertà: say nothing to anyone. In any case, we all had too much on our minds to grapple with that Nabokov-styled romance. The entire family was gripped by a pervasive nervous energy as we awaited our first batch of "guests." It was like waiting for an atomic bomb. The landline ringing was as good as an air raid siren. We had no idea when the blitzkrieg of illegal migrants was coming—we assumed, or hoped, that it would at least be preceded by a warning phone call, but who knew? Maybe Román would just kick the door in and send streams of illegals flooding into our living room. We had no idea what to expect.

But one, then several, days passed and nothing happened. The phone kept ringing with no one on the other end besides my widowed *abuelo* begging *Papá* to go back to Venezuela and incite a revolution—*"If Castro could do it with some beatniks and a few dinghies, why can't you?"*—and vehemently refusing to join us in Trinidad: *"Venezuela is where I was born and where I will die. What the hell will I do after I'm dead in Trinidad? Where will my spirit roam around? I won't have a damn clue where to go!"* And *Mamá*'s family still languishing in Caracas, calling to say there was no toilet paper, no medicine, no vaccines, nothing but canned food, newborns mewling like wrinkled kittens in cardboard boxes at the hospitals, brawls in the street between the *Opositores* and the *Maduristas*, newly ordained prostitutes in droves at the borders, young women cutting out their fallopian tubes because where can they get birth control and who can feed a baby. A whole nation rattling its cage, seething with resentment, demanding to know why the hell it couldn't do socialism Scandinavian-style, with high taxes but pristine streets, a bottomless supply of more high-grade dairy products than even the most robust intestinal tract could possibly handle, and minimum-wage workers still coining enough to go on Mediterranean cruises once a year, the kind of socialism that made El

Che nod his benevolent, CIA-executed head in approval and say, *Yes, compadres, you got exactly what I was going for*. But our malnourished, rage-filled relatives knew they'd got the shitty end of the socialist stick. Granted not as shitty as the socialism of *Nationalsozialistische* but shitty enough to prove that not all socialist idealism is created equal.

Whoever picked up the phone would listen and let our family members vent, wishing we could tell them we were rattling with nerves and resentment in our own cage, thank you very much, that we'd hauled ass all the way to Trinidad just to fall victim to Ugly, yet another megalomaniacal prick. But we stayed mum—because no matter what we were going through, at least we could buy Panadol for our stress migraines and toilet paper for our anxiety-induced diarrhea and groceries for our comfort eating. Maybe the grass here *was* greener, just fertilized with an equally pungent brand of horseshit.

A PERCEPTIVE MOTHERFUCKER

Trinidad likes to tout itself as this cosmopolitan melting pot, swirling with all the flavors of the race rainbow. But in fact, if you're not one of, or a blend of, the two majority races on the island, a pall of Otherness follows you like a lingering fart that won't waft away, the stench manifesting itself in relentless catcalls, the unshakable instinct that you should always keep your eyes on the pavement, and a keen awareness that you are constantly being watched. For Latinas, a relatively novel addition to the local ethnic pot, this Otherness is exacerbated by a label far brighter, more neon-hued, tinsel-bedecked, and eye-catching than any other: whore. Trinidadian public opinion deems us all, each and every one, a stripper, a hooker, an aspiring trophy wife, or a sneaky conniving slut. No room for the Madonna dichotomy when it comes to "Venes" here. So with my dual labels of Other and Whore firmly affixed the second I stepped outside, I thought it best to opt for the most neutral, innocuous clothing possible when I dressed that Saturday morning for the Lit Fest seminar: black T-shirt and black jeans. (Though granted, I couldn't fight the Latin grooming impulse that left my hair sleekly blown out and my nails freshly French-tipped.)

With my all-black armor donned, feet shod in intentionally unsexy Converse, I turned the key in the beat-up Datsun that Zulema and I shared, and tried to ignore the clamminess of my palms. Then I put on the audiobook of *Middlesex* for the drive, hoping it might ease my nerves. I'd bought it right after Aunt Celia died, thinking it would be easier to listen to High Literature in English rather than read it. But by the time I hit the highway for the long journey down to San Fernando, Eugenides's intricate prose had only made me more self-conscious about my own literary English. I killed the volume and drove on in silence, but *Middlesex* also had another unexpected side effect—I couldn't think of anything but the person who'd recommended it to me. It helped my anxiety to think of her, though: Aunt Celia had never been intimidated by anyone or anything. Maybe I could slip into her badass attitude like it was a superhero costume, equipped with a utility belt that shot laser-like bitch looks and stun guns that radiated scathing put-downs. She wouldn't have cared what a bunch of literary types thought of her English prose or if they automatically assumed she was some Vene whore. As I'd learned from the manuscript's account of her teenage years, Celia had an indefatigable ability to bounce back from any situation, no matter how embarrassing, an indestructibly elastic rubber band:

> *Who would've thought César Velásquez would've been the one to pop this cherry. Sure, he can kick a ball clear across a football field and hit a home run like no one else at school, but the guy's so dyslexic he can barely spell his own first name. Lucky for him, I'm already seventeen— how much longer was I gonna wait before doing the deed? Not like I'm Milagros who's probably already sewn her chocha shut and shaved her pubic hair into a likeness of the Santa Virgen.*
>
> *Well, joke's on me—two years of tolerating Semi-Literate César all because of his superstar athlete status at school and guess who gets dumped two hours after spattering his Spiderman sheets with the remnants of her hymen?*

Think that first disastrous sexual escapade put Celia off sex, men, or erotic adventurism? *No le importó un carajo.* In fact, seventeen-year-old Celia decided it was time to take her loins out on the town. She was determined to make up for that one disappointing notch in her belt. *If Milagros is going to be the Virgin Mary of the family, then I'll be its Mary Magdalene—before Magdalene gave up hooking.*

Maybe *Abuela* was right after all to think that thirteen-pound, tooth-endowed Baby Celia might have been the Antichrist.

Aunt Celia got a kick out of homing in on her targets at parties, en-snaring them with a come-hither stare and a shimmy of her legendary tits, then bedding them by the end of the night. It was shameless sexual adventurism, all about collecting experiences like she could stick them in a stamp book. That's not to say she wasn't aware of the risks of her libertine adolescent sexuality. She even shared one of the tricks she used to stop herself getting pregnant, the Prophylactic Pineapple.

> *All you have to do, according to Catalina del Valle, is eat three whole pineapples in one go if you get into trouble. Being the proactive young woman I am, I figure if I have half a pineapple a day, I'll keep up a steady enough level of whatever pineapple magic keeps the bambinos away. Sounds like basic biology to me. And Milagros always says I'm no good at science—pfft.*

Remembering Aunt Celia's account of her pineapple bingeing (which eventually led to chronic diarrhea) and her many scandalous conquests, my nerves were quelled, the drive went by quicker than expected, and before I knew it I was at San Fernando Hill, the hub of the Lit Festival. When I found my way to the right room, the other attendees were pretty much what I'd expected: artsy locals who eyed me in a way that said, *We see those labels stuck to your forehead,* a few old folk grasping at their last possible opportunity to realize their literary dreams, and then a handful of wanderers like me. I call us wanderers because we all had the slightly confused, wholly insecure look of an illiterate who's just wandered into a room full of highbrow writer types with high-strung attitudes to match.

An hour later, surprisingly satisfied with the lecture despite not quite grasping everything the British agent said because of her sharp nasal accent, so different from the lilting, singsong Trini intonation I was used to, I stood skimming the parking lot for the Datsun. How is it that there are things as wondrous as stem cell cloning and artificial intelligence, but no one has figured out whatever cerebral hiccup is responsible for you invariably forgetting where the hell you've parked your car?

I shaded my eyes with my hand, sweat patches blooming on my mercilessly heat-absorbent black T-shirt, and slowly scanned the rows of secondhand Japanese cars. No Datsun. Still no Datsun. Then, as my gaze fell straight ahead of me: no Datsun. But Román.

He was leaning against a black Jeep wearing a gray T-shirt and blue jeans, looking at me from behind dark sunglasses. For a couple of seconds I was too stunned by the sight of him to move. Suddenly the sun felt hotter. I was more aware of everything. The sound of my own breath, the moisture on my upper lip, the sweat slowly slipping down the hollow of my lower back, the smell of brakes and hot concrete. I was having the same reaction as I would in the guy-walking-toward-you-on-a-dark-street scenario, but if the guy was, say, Brad Pitt (circa 2001).

The moment stretched itself out as endlessly as silly putty, Román looking at me silently with an unreadable expression, not a bead of sweat or an armpit stain on him to dilute his James Dean cool, until I got my shit together and made my way over, channeling Celia in a bid to keep any hint of blushing, hip-sashaying damsel at bay.

I came to stand in front of him. "What are you doing here?"

Amused, he tilted his head slightly at my question, a cat smiling at an interrogative mouse. "Someone in the family leaves Port of Spain, I have to make sure they're not up to some kind of mischief, like popping into the San Fernando police station, for instance."

Why did I want to smile back so badly? I tried holding my breath, anything to stop his pheromones working their chemical magic.

"As you can see, I didn't go to any police station, so you can trot on back to your boss now." Aunt Celia would've been proud of how convincingly bitchy I sounded. "Or maybe you should be scurrying off to check up on someone else in my family. How do you know *they're* not all at police stations right now?"

Román wasn't fazed. He started counting out my family members on his fingers. "Your father's at the dentist having a root canal. Zulema's at the beach with her colleague from the Color Me Beautiful spa." He went on to say what each and every person was doing that day, rounding it off with: "And Alejandra told her father she's going to a movie with a friend, but really she's with Mikey Stollmeyer, who she's been seeing after school for the last five days instead of going to her friend Rebecca's house to study."

He flashed his palms at me and shrugged: *That's my job, what can ya do?*

I was horrified. But I'd be lying if I said I wasn't impressed.

"Fine," I said, playing nonchalant. "Then you must've known I was at a lecture and not going to the police."

"I did know. A lecture with Lizzie Atherton, an agent at W&W."

I swallowed, every heartbeat a horse's hoof to my rib cage.

He pushed his sunglasses up onto his head. His pupils shrank in the bright light, and I saw that his eyes were a mossy hazel. Of course. Couldn't just be standard dirt-brown like more than 50 percent of the global population.

"I came here to have a word with you," he said.

"About?"

"You're interesting to me." That unnervingly cool, even tone. "And I know I'm interesting to you."

He took a step away from the car, lessening the space between us.

We were close enough that if we'd been in a Harlequin romance, I'd have said he smelled of sandalwood and leather. (He didn't.)

I scoffed, shifting my weight and adjusting the strap on my laptop bag. But under his stare I was frost melting into wet, glistening dew.

"Obviously perception isn't one of your stronger skills," I bluffed. "Nothing about you is interesting to me."

But he only laughed, a laugh that was unexpectedly genuine, warm. It took me off guard. Something about him—the laugh, his easy languidness—made me feel like a teenager flirting with a harmless bad-boy crush. Like I was still in control.

He took another step forward. We were much too close. The tension between us suddenly swelled into something so palpable it felt almost natural, like our respective roles of blackmail enforcer and blackmailee had slipped off us to land in crumpled heaps on the concrete, leaving us in a bare state of unsheathed mutual attraction. I didn't flinch when he reached a hand out to push my hair away from my face with the knuckle of his index finger. I even found myself fighting the urge to lean into it. The knuckle slowly grazed my jaw until it stopped beneath the center of my chin and tilted my face upward. Keeping my chin lifted, Román pressed his thumb against my bottom lip, almost imperceptibly pulling my lips apart.

"You have a perfect mouth."

The heat of his thumb sent my dopamine levels skyrocketing, potent as a hit of Molly straight into my bloodstream.

Only the *beep beep!* of a nearby car alarm cracked that moment between us. I turned to see a sweaty man opening his car door as Román took a step back, shoving his hands into his pockets. My lip burned where his thumb had been. I ran my tongue over the spot, wishing he'd touch it again.

This was not good. I knew nothing about Román other than the fact that he'd assaulted my father and was implementing Ugly's blackmail. And still, I was caving. I had to get outta there.

But as I rounded on my heel to walk away, he grabbed my arm.

I twisted myself out of his grip, glaring. "*¡Carajo!* What are you, an animal?"

"I told you I came here to have a word." The imperturbable tone of Al Pacino in *The Godfather* telling Diane Keaton to chill with her upper-middle-class moralist neuroses. "I don't believe in beating around the bush, Yola. We're intrigued by each other. I felt it the other day, so did you. And I feel it now. So do you. But I want to make it clear that I'm not in a position to give in to that intrigue. Ugly doesn't believe in mixing business with pleasure, do you understand?"

I whipped my head back in disbelief. Who was that brazenly direct? Immediately I wanted to knock his ego down a few pegs. "You seriously came all the way here to tell me that? Well, let *me* make it clear: I am not intrigued by you. You're just some scumbag working for Ugly. Trust me, we won't have a problem."

Infuriatingly, he dipped his head and smiled, flashing his canines. Something about their prominence made me want to feel them pressing into my skin.

"Yola." He reached out to brush my cheek. I jerked my head away and he laughed. "You might not be intrigued by me." He turned to open the door of the Jeep, then looked back. "But you do want me."

He got in, started the engine, and peeled away, leaving me fuming at his arrogance and mortified by his accuracy. Motherfucker had seen right through me.

LESSONS IN PROMISCUITY

I learned from the little elves at Google, working tirelessly to bring us all the information we could ever need, regardless of factual accuracy, thanks to the advent of search engine optimization, that insomnia can be due to myriad causes. Such as anxiety (at feeling a searing and highly inappropriate lust for a man whose living relies on the ability to intimidate people, specifically people comprising your family). Anger and resentment (at said man pinpointing your lust and calling you out on it). Or mental excitement (and we're back to the lust). It therefore shouldn't come as a shock that I couldn't sleep for days after that encounter with Román. The guilt of feeling that shame-tinged longing metastasizing in me was the proverbial pea under my mattress. I mean, a bad report from Román could spell the difference between life and death for us, between busted kneecaps and intact kneecaps. Not even the Memory Foam mattresses advertised on four a.m. infomercials and supposedly invented by NASA-funded researchers (bet NASA was thrilled by the outcome of *that* investment) would be able to get me a night of untormented rest.

Right after Ugly told us random illegals would be invading our homes, there'd been a few nights when no one in my house had been able to sleep. Zulema and I had stayed up until three in the morning playing cards and waiting for exhaustion to kick in, while my parents spent their all-nighters watching cheesy eighties movies till they eventually passed out on the couch. But those insomnolent nights were *finito* now that so much time had gone by without any illegals being delivered. Everyone's nerves had steadied. We could almost pretend there wasn't some crime lord holding a six-hundred-grand debt over us.

I was now the family's lone insomniac. And while I lay there, enraged at my inability to sleep, I drew on Aunt Celia's manuscript as my only source of counsel, reading on into the heyday of her twenties in Panama City and Miami, interpreting every salacious anecdote as Aunt Celia giving advice from the Great Promiscuous Beyond. If those chapters of the manuscript proved anything, it was that she would've told me to bed Román immediately, then write about it and get some goddamned sleep. When she was even younger than me, freshly released from the grips of my *abuelo*s, she hadn't cared who the hell she was sleeping with.

Twenty-one years old and my yellow brick road has finally led me out of Venezuela to Oz: Panama City. Life is a beautiful thing here. Me and the girls, we go out on a couple modeling gigs, get easy cash to blow on sequined everything—then nothing else to do but DANCE! And the men! We're devouring them. We're a fucking wolf pack in this Emerald City. They could be anything—drug barons, politicians, priests, princes, no nos importa, we could care less. If they're cute, know the right lines, and have a big polla, we'll take them for a spin. Doesn't hurt if they have a few bucks to spend on cocktails and cocaine either. I've never felt so free, wild, and beautiful in my life.

Obviously I wasn't going to follow her "advice" to a T and start coke-bingeing and blowing a million different guys for the heck of it. But I did think to myself, lying there sleepless night after sleepless night, that it couldn't hurt to take a leaf out of Aunt Celia's book. I needed to slut it up a little, distract myself with another man who'd take my mind off Román. Someone who could stop me compulsively picking apart every moment of what had gone down in the parking lot, help me forget the warm spot on my lip where Román's thumb had been.

So the next morning: "Zulema, what're you doing tonight?"

My sister eyed me. "Why?"

It was early on a Friday. Zulema was touching up her red-carpet makeup with a pocket mirror before heading to work.

I shrugged, blew into my coffee mug. "I need a good night out, so if you're doing anything . . ."

Zulema squealed. I jumped, sloshing coffee onto myself. "*¿Qué carajo*, Zulema?" I pulled the hot, wet patch away from my skin, tenting the T-shirt.

"You *actually* want to go out, Yola! Finally! I'm always like, *Yola, let's go here* and *Yola, let's go there*, and you're always like, *Oh, I'm busy* and *Oh, I don't feel like it*. And now you actually want to go out! Ohmygosh ohmygosh, can I do your makeup? Ooh! I can dress you too! You *have* to wear a dress, Yola. And heels! You can't go out in jeans on a Friday night, *bruja*."

I laughed, though already regretting the decision to socialize with my sister, thus committing myself to a makeover of *Miss Congeniality* proportions. "I'm not sold on the heels and the dress, but count me in for whatever you guys have planned for tonight."

"Ohmygosh, I'm *soooooo* excited!"

———

Later that night we were at Buzz Bar, on a nightlife strip built as part of a luxury condo complex. Very Miami. Very swank. With all the bougie condo residents living only an elevator ride away, the strip was a hot spot for well-to-do patrons. Here, there were none of the usual nighttime sounds of frogs and crickets. Wildlife was drowned out by Prosecco corks popping, ambient electro-house music, and the tinkling laughter of the financially secure. The place was mobbed, people swarming around the single bar like flies fighting for a spot on a turd. Zulema and I wove our way through the tightly packed bodies on our five-inch stilts (she'd won me over on the outfit), scanning the place for her Color Me Beautiful work friends. Finally, we pushed our way through to a table ringed with girls I recognized from social media as Zulema's friends: all honey-hued blondes and glossy brunettes. The only specks of brown skin at that table were the freckles spattering all their shoulders. (Here's a tip: if you ever want to discern a white creole from a tourist, look for the freckles on the shoulders. You can't grow up white in Trinidad without the sun leaving that mark of authenticity. Like the etching on wallets that says "genuine leather" to show it's the real deal.) At the center of their table were two ice buckets bearing bottles of Prosecco, smartphones laid out around the buckets, every girl keeping a beady eye on her phone to avoid the utter catastrophe of a missed call.

As we approached, they all greeted Zulema perkily with chirps of "Zu-Zu!" and they all smiled while I was introduced, then applauded our gene pool and noted how much Zulema and I looked alike. I could tell off the bat that these were girls adept at social niceties, raised on the fringes of parents' dinner parties and cocktail nights, skilled in the art of pointless conversation and empty compliments.

"The hubbies are coming later," a brunette explained to Zulema after the initial pleasantries had wrapped up. "They're at ye old Yacht Club."

"Like they are *every* Friday," moaned a swishy-haired blonde, rolling her eyes. The others sighed in agreement, signaling that they too shared the burden of hubbies who drank at ye old Yacht Club every Friday.

Most of Zulema's work friends were older than both of us, in their late twenties. Even so, I couldn't believe they were all married.

People obviously got hitched young in Trinidad. One girl even had three kids—*three*! She was the only one who didn't work at the spa. She used to, but now she didn't work at all. Another shocker for me. Housewives were supposed to be old, matronly, boring, or from the fifties. Not hip twenty-somethings in faux-leather midi-dresses and spiked heels. I'd have been less thrown if Zulema said her friend was a sea monkey with three pet dragons. Even more bizarre was how the others reacted when Zulema introduced the girl as a housewife with three sons. They all swooped in, as if to her rescue, with comments like:

"God, that's a job I could never handle!"

"She's really more like a chef, a doctor, and a nanny who's always on call!"

"Hardest job in the world!"

At these accolades, Housewife shook her head modestly. "Tell me about it. I really *am* a full-time doctor and chef!"

I wondered if a real doctor or chef would agree. But like any woman, I masked my true feelings and chipped in with a totally false, totally supportive comment. "That must be so rewarding!" And then a misstep: "Is that what you've always wanted to be?"

I recognized the awkward, unified lifting of champagne flutes to mouths while gazes were uncomfortably averted. But Housewife held her own. This wasn't her first rodeo.

"Of course! I mean, it's very challenging and it really is a twenty-four-hour job. No sick leave for Mummy! But it's so rewarding too. Just you wait till your time comes, you have *no idea* until you're a mother. NO IDEA."

Relieved at Housewife's adept navigation of my question, the group laughed, heads tilted in sympathy for the domestic veteran in their midst. The things she must have seen. The things she must have been through!

I laughed too, and I continued laughing while the conversation went on to reveal that Housewife had a driver (like *Papá*) who collected her kids from school and daycare, and that she had a live-in housekeeper (like Fidel's mother, Camille) who did all the cooking, cleaning, and after-school child care. Twenty-four-hour job my ass.

As the night wore on, I endured the superficial middle-class chatter with the stoicism of wartime Winston Churchill, laughing and nodding and giving eye-rolls of solidarity on cue, and to make it all a tad easier, I pounded the Prosecco *hard*. Sancho and my deceased alcoholic uncles would've been proud.

———

I'd just come back from another protracted trip to the bar, a G&T in either hand, when I saw that Zulema's friends had been joined by their respective hubbies. The hubbies had also brought along a few stragglers from the Yacht Club, one of whom instantly caught my eye, mostly because he looked so out of place. Though he sounded and dressed like a local, he looked like a character straight out of an Irish folk tale: thick red hair and a jaw aflame with a wiry red beard. Then, of course, there were the startling green eyes, the fair skin. Usual ginger package.

Now, I know what you're thinking: A ginger stud? *Really?*

Yes—*really*. This guy was an absolute Goliath. So instead of the gingerness giving him the dweeby look of most redheaded guys, it made him look like a Celtic warlord who should be in a loincloth astride a black stallion.

His eyes were on me the second I walked up. Zulema began a round of introductions. I shook all the hubbies' hands, smiled, forgot their names as soon as I heard them.

"And who's this?" asked the Pseudo-Celt before Zulema had gotten to his intro. I was shaking the hand of Hubby #5. I eyed Pseudo-Celt. He gave me a cheesy wink.

"Yola, my big sister." Zulema swept her hand in front of me like I was a brooch she was presenting on the Home Shopping Network.

"Lola?" he said, extending a hand.

"*Yola*," I corrected, letting his hand engulf mine in its pink-skinned, freckled hugeness.

Our hands lingered the same way Román's and mine had when we met. And I'll be honest, I was attracted. But fireworks? Not even the snap, crackle, pop of Rice Krispies.

While we shook hands, Zulema introduced him as Ben Brown. The name left me a little underwhelmed. I'd expected a Gaston or a Thor, or at least a more riveting alliteration along the lines of Hulk Hogan.

Anyway, this Ben character and I got to talking, and with five Proseccos and two gin and tonics under my belt, I had a whole lot to say. We talked until it was well after two in the morning. My head was spinning. I hadn't even noticed when Zulema left. When I blearily checked my phone, I had a message from her telling me to get a lift home with Ben, along with a row of emojis: smiley faces sticking their tongues out beside several phallic eggplants.

I was reading that message just as Ben ran a hand down the back of my bare arm. We were still at the table, now empty except for the two of us and an ice bucket holding a bouquet of upturned Prosecco bottles.

"You ready to go, baby? Hmm?" He'd become greasier the drunker he'd gotten, his fingers insistent on the back of my arm.

I hesitated. "Um." Stalling for time, I drained the dregs of my glass.

With maudlin drunken longing, I ached for Román's thumb on my lip. But Román wasn't there. He was out somewhere stalking my family members, choking people who gave Ugly back-talk. Maybe he was there, stalking me right then. And that's what made me decide to leave with Ben. My drunk logic was: if Román was there watching, he'd see me leave with Ben and he'd get jealous. If Román *wasn't* there, then I'd leave with Ben and maybe he'd turn out to be the love of my life and I'd forget all about Román forever. Seemed like I couldn't lose.

So Ben and I went back to his place and went at it with all the fervor and clumsiness of two very, very drunk people. Was it good? Who knows. From what I can dredge out of that alcohol-soaked corner of my memory, it was as fun as a drunken hookup can be—

orgasmless (for me) and more worthwhile as an anecdote than anything else.

The second he finished, Ben tugged on his jeans and said he'd drop me home. Outside my house twenty minutes later, he left me with a kiss that actually made me squirm. The final proof that my social experiment was a flop. Babbling and boozing with a bunch of women wouldn't distract me from Román, and sleeping around with randoms obviously wouldn't do the trick either. Because as I hurled myself into bed—fully clothed, makeup smeared, hair in tangles—I knew that all I'd be thinking of, until I drifted into a stale-drunk slumber, was him.

INVASIONS

Luckily, just after my hookup with Ben, I was pulled back from the precipice of endless Román-obsessing: the illegal invasion struck.

It was a hot, sunshiny day typical of a Trinidadian December. Christmas was less than three weeks away. Proving the power of American neo-imperialism, Trinidad was aglow with wintry fairy lights and bedecked with plastic pine trees covered in fake snow, while carols of Jack Frost and chestnuts roasting on open fires rang throughout the tropical days and nights. To its credit, though, the island also had a rich Christmas culture all its own: seasonal sorrel juice, highly alcoholic eggnog called punch ah crème, pastelles made of cornmeal and minced meat (almost exactly like the *hallacas* we ate in Venezuela at Christmas), that catchy Spanish parang music, and of course, soca parang sung in English that was chockful of sexual innuendos about pork.

It was during this usual Trini Christmas bonanza, while I continued to languish with Román-induced sleep deprivation, that our first "guests" from the motherland arrived. As we'd always feared, it was a knock on the door that heralded the four horsemen of our apocalypse. And there were, funnily enough, four men on our front step. Not horsemen, but cattle farmers (close enough).

I was the first one to meet them. *Papá* was out doing school pick-ups, *Mamá* was working in the annex, and Zulema was at the spa coloring people beautiful. I was translating a radiology report at my desk when the knock on the front door came. I waited a few moments, knowing the FedEx guy would call on the landline if it was him. The phone didn't ring, but just as I relaxed enough to start typing again, more knocking, this time three loud, precise raps. At the exact same moment, making me jump out of my skin, my cell phone started ringing. I picked it up. Blocked number. "Hello?"

"I have a drop-off." Román.

Shit—a drop-off meant illegals.

I went to the front door, nervous sweat prickling my forehead as I held the knob. I didn't know if it was Román's voice or the prospect of welcoming a pack of strangers into our home that had me quaking as I opened the door, but when I did: no Román. Just four grim men carrying two heavy black garbage bags apiece. One was about my age. The others appeared to be well over fifty. They were dressed in button-down shirts and trousers, like they'd been told to walk with their best clothes on their backs. All were thin, dark-skinned, and somber. I felt racist for thinking it, but the older men looked almost identical. Perhaps I'd been living away from Venezuela too long and was only used to the Trinidadian race rainbow now.

Thinking these marginally racist thoughts, I smiled as wide as I could manage. "*Bienvenidos*," I said, motioning for them to come inside. As they filed past me, mumbling hello, I dashed out the door toward the annex. It was a slightly adolescent move—running for *Mamá* instead of handling the men myself—but if there's one thing every girl has embedded in her brain from the second she has any kind of cognitive function, it's don't invite strange men into your home and lock the door behind you (because then it's *your* fault for whatever happens next, *right*?). So with no patriarchal hero figure around, the next best thing was *Mamá*—what's sisterhood all about if not dragging a fellow woman into a potential hive of rapists to protect your ass?

Ever since Sancho had started dating Megan, who he was still seeing despite whatever the hell was going on with him and Vanessa, my mother's business had been booming. Megan had put all her friends onto *Mamá*, and if I thought us Latinas liked to groom, the whites and Arabs of Trinidad put us to shame.

Well, almost.

Mamá was booked up weeks in advance now, not just thanks to Megan's friends, but thanks to *Mamá's* own Machiavellian marketing strategy. In Venezuela, *Mamá* had never done waxing. Her thing had always been nails. But demand for epilation was *hot, hot, hot* in Trinidad thanks to year-round warm weather. So my mother, ever the shrewd businesswoman, began pitching herself as the best waxer in Caracas. "Peoples use to come from all parts of Venezuela to see me for waxing," she bragged, lying through her teeth. "Appointments from six months in advance to book! Ask anybody and they tell you."

While spouting her false propaganda, she quietly invested in all the waxing apparatus she needed and YouTubed how to wax any and every body part. Then hey presto, *Mamá* became the most in-demand waxer in West Trinidad.

So, as per usual, the pavement in front of our house was lined with SUVs, CRVs, and other bright 'n' shiny automotive behemoths whose owners were in the annex waiting to have their lips, legs, chins, underarms, forearms, taints, and vaginas stripped bare. As I burst through the wreath-bedecked annex door, *Mamá* shot me a sharp look. "*Momentito, hija,*" she warned, brushing seasonal red polish onto a broad-backed woman's nails.

The room was full up: full of Christmas figurines and potted poinsettias, full of shelves stocked with every beauty product known to man, and full of women tapping away on smartphones and flipping through tabloid magazines.

I widened my eyes at *Mamá*: *The illegal invasion is underway!*

She widened her eyes back at me: *I don't know what you're trying to tell me, but wait until I'm done!*

Finally, my mother finished with the woman's nails, stood, and wiped her hands on the pink apron she wore to work every day, perpetually dusted with other people's nail shavings. "*Señoras,* my daughter needs me to check something. I will be only a minute." One woman tutted and pointedly raised her Rolex to the level of her oversized Gucci sunglasses. *Mamá* ignored her and followed me back to the house.

Inside, the men were still holding their garbage bags, standing awkwardly in the living room. *Mamá* welcomed them like distant family. "*¡Bienvenidos!* Please, make yourself at home. How was your trip over? Any trouble with the Coast Guard? *Ay,* you poor *señores,* please, sit. Are you hungry? Yola, fix a jug of ice water and bring some glasses while our guests decide what they want to eat."

It was only while I was filling the pitcher at the faucet that I noticed the parked Jeep through the window. Román was in the driver's seat, talking on his cell phone. A stab of annoyance cut into me. Why had he just left me alone with these potentially dangerous men? I mentally kicked myself: *Román is a dangerous man, dummy.* Why the hell should I expect him to care about my safety?

I took the pitcher out to the living room. When I went back to the kitchen for four glasses, I didn't bother looking out the window again.

Mamá, after chatting with the men for less than five minutes, seemed fully assured that they wouldn't attack me if left alone, so returned to her waiting clients. I sat with the men uncomfortably while they drank their water.

"What kind of sandwiches would you like?"

They smiled. The younger one shook his head. "We don't want you to go to any trouble, miss."

"Yola, please," I said. "And really, it's no problem. *Hallacas* maybe?"

The younger one shook his head again. "We don't want to put you out." The older ones mumbled similar things, all smiling kindly.

I could tell, though, that they were only feeling bad to ask for food on top of everything else. It was the sort of thing polite people did, and it softened me up. So despite their protests, I brought them a heaped plate of reheated Jamaican patties from our freezer, and was unsurprised when they tucked right in. After they'd eaten, I showed them around, told them to make themselves at home, and excused myself to get back to work.

———————

I shut my bedroom door softly, some inane compulsion for politeness making me consider the men's feelings if I were to noisily lock the door, betraying that I still suspected them capable of being a pack of sexual predators.

Just as I'd managed to turn the lock slowly enough to mute the telltale click, a throat cleared behind me. I spun around to flatten myself against the door, the breath sucked straight out of me.

"¡*Verga!* How the hell did you get in here?" I slumped over with relief before quickly snapping myself back upright, realizing the situation I was now in: alone in my bedroom with Román.

He was sitting on my desk chair, facing me. The way the room was laid out, I couldn't see the desk until I was inside with the door shut. And I'd been so focused on surreptitiously locking myself in that I hadn't even noticed him there.

"Sorry," he said, standing. "I didn't mean to scare you."

"How'd you think I was going to react? Nearly gave me a heart attack." I wasn't lying. It felt like a rodeo bull was bucking wildly in my chest—but I knew that was just the Román effect more than anything else.

"Again—sorry," he laughed. "I want your heart to be nothing but safe."

He walked over in slow strides to stand over me. I would've stepped backward, away from him, but there was nothing behind me but the locked door—and if I'm totally honest, I didn't want to move away from him at all. That rodeo bull in my chest was really going apeshit now. Blood was thudding in my ears.

"I came in through the back," he said.

"I'm not worried about how you came in. I want to know *why* you came in."

He rocked back on his heels and shrugged. There was a boyish something about him, even with the gun I'd already spotted sticking out of the back of his jeans.

"Ever heard that English saying, curiosity killed the cat?" he asked, raising an eyebrow.

"So you're in here because you're curious? But I thought you couldn't—how did you put it again—give in to *intrigue*? That's what you said in the parking lot if I remember correctly."

He didn't bother to answer. "I read your work, you know."

I frowned, instantly self-conscious. "My writing? What for?"

"Part of gathering intel."

"What does my writing have to do with intel?"

He waggled a finger at me. "As a writer, you of all people should know that someone's art is the clearest reflection of who they are. The better I know my subjects, the better I can keep them in line. If I were tracking a writer like, say, Echeverría, I'd know to keep my gun locked and loaded. Someone who's more of a Neruda, I'd know not to worry."

Esteban Echeverría and Pablo Neruda? I hid my surprise and snorted. "So you go rifling through the twins' diaries to find out whether or not you should arm yourself around them too?"

He laughed. "I only read what you'd been short-listed for. That's the magic of this newfangled Internet thing. Everything just a click away."

Ignoring his sarcasm, I fought the impulse to ask what he thought of my work, and again, sought out my bitchy spirit animal: Aunt Celia. "I'm surprised. Who knew ignorant thugs like you could read."

I'd said it teasingly but his smile was gone.

"You shouldn't be so quick to judge," he said, quietly restrained. "Take it from someone who knows the danger of misjudgment." Though he hadn't moved, he seemed to have inched somehow closer to me. We were separated by the width of a feather, my neck arched almost painfully back to look up at him. So close that I noticed then for the first time that there was a thin, barely visible scar that ran across his mouth diagonally like a fine, silvery seam someone had sewn across it. Seeing it felt like I'd uncovered some intimate glimpse of his past, like I should reach out and touch it, ask how it had happened. I could smell the soap on his skin, his spearmint mouthwash, the lingering scent of his laundry detergent. All of it humanized him and emboldened me. Or maybe I was just fucking nuts like Celia, because I wasn't even a little bit afraid of him.

"You're really trying to tell me you're not a thug? I saw you choke my father with my own eyes."

"What you saw was me doing my job."

"Exactly—your job as a thug."

"It's not in your interest to condescend to me, Yola. I don't think you understand the position you and your family are in."

"I understand that we're in this position because of what you do for Ugly."

His eyes flashed but I held them firm. We were just a guy and a girl doing a tango. Current crackled between us like static. He wasn't going to hurt me and I knew it.

Like he'd done in the parking lot, he took my chin between his thumb and the knuckle of his index finger. "You're a piece of work," he said, and I could tell I'd struck a nerve. It made me laugh. Imagine—an armed criminal, and I'd gotten under his skin by teasing him about being illiterate. Why did he care so much?

The laugh had barely come out before his mouth was on mine. I didn't pull away. He crushed himself against me, his hardened palms pushing my arms up above my head, clasping my hands, his mouth hot and hungry, the length of our bodies against each other. Pent-up lust rushed through me, and in the blinding white heat of that moment, the whole world and everything in it was Román and me and nothing else mattered. Not Ugly's disapproval of mixing business with pleasure. Not the well-being of my family's kneecaps. Not. A. Fucking. Thing.

It was over as quick as it happened. Like forked lightning illuminating the night for one violently electrified moment before it all goes dark again. He pulled back and that was it—he was gone and I was alone, panting like I'd just leapt out of an airplane and found myself shaky-legged on solid ground again.

As I caught my breath, I felt no guilt for the first time since the unexpected parking-lot tryst. If Aunt Celia could sleep with married men and shame-riddled seminarians and half of Panama City . . . if people could screw their best friends' wives and their first cousins . . . if the whole world could carry on fucking as it pleased, why should I be any different?

GHOSTED

My father was born for safe-housing illegal migrants. Fresh from his afternoon school run and having clearly been given a heads-up from *Mamá*, he fell upon our new houseguests with all the bonhomie of a Sandals Resort manager, bearing three buckets of fried chicken and a bottle of rum. From the confines of my bedroom, where I was still starry-eyed, giddily recovering from Román and making a half-assed attempt at a translation, I heard *Papá*'s booming good cheer as he came through the front door. "Welcome, gentlemen! I brought food! You rum drinkers?" A pause. "Ha ha! Good man! I needed a stiff rum myself when we made our journey over, let me tell you. . . ."

As the afternoon went by, the men's chatter with my father grew warmer and louder. Soon the talk of our despised president, Nicolás Maduro, and *la Patria* was so loud I had to switch on the noisy AC unit just to drown it all out. By the time I'd finished work that evening, the atmosphere in the house was positively jovial. When I joined everyone, Zulema was back from work, talking with the youngest of the men, and my parents were in gales of laughter at some anecdote one of the older guys had just finished telling.

It turned out that the men were, as I mentioned, cattle farmers. It also turned out that I wasn't racist, because the three older men were in fact *triplets*—not identical, but pretty damn close. The younger man was a son of one of the triplets. Their names were José, Jorge, Joaquin, and Javier. The young one was Javier. The older men I still couldn't tell apart, and neither could anyone else, so that same night we ended up calling them the Jotas.

For our first family dinner with Javier and the Jotas, Papá inserted the extra leaves into the dining table and we all ate together, minus Sancho, who'd also received a couple of illegals of his own that afternoon. *Mamá*, with the help of Javier, who was apparently hoping to become a chef, prepared a feast to rival a Christmas luncheon. At dinner, one of the Jotas presented *Papá* with a bottle of expensive Venezuelan rum as a thank-you, which my parents found touching. All I thought was that the Jota had come here all the way from Venezuela with nothing but two garbage bags of his belongings, yet he'd still managed to prioritize *rum*.

The bottle was cracked open at the table and the rum drunk out of tumblers, straight. By the end of the dinner, there wasn't a single one of us who wasn't properly drunk. We all said good night like the best of friends.

But after I'd gone to bed, when I heard my doorknob turning with a creak, I jolted upright, all goodwill instantly evaporated. The Jotas! Come to rape and pillage!

The door opened. It was *Papá*. He sat on the edge of my bed. "*Gordita*, I know Javier and the Jotas are good people, but lock that bedroom door day and night whenever you're in here." He spoke softly, as though ashamed of himself for not trusting these men we'd known for all of a few hours.

"Of course," I said.

"Good girl. Sleep well."

I knew I would, Jotas or not—my guilt over Román had finally been expunged by the temporary satiation of my need for him, and my insomnia was gone along with it. I slept like the dead that night, dreams of Román dancing in my head.

Javier and the Jotas turned out to be excellent houseguests. They had warm, simple country manners, were considerate and helpful, cleaning the common areas of the house until everything shone, even folding the laundry that my mother perpetually left in the dryer, which was used as a communal closet between loads. In the evenings, Javier cooked dinner with *Mamá* and the three Jotas drank with *Papá* out on the back porch. They even cheerfully succumbed to Zulema's insistence that she do their colors for free, as a gift. Javier actually wore the flamboyantly teal button-down she bought him because "you, like, *need* at least one teal item in your wardrobe as a Spring, Javi." After a few days, it felt like they really were distant relatives who'd dropped in for a visit.

In the other Palacios households, it seemed their first batches of illegals were equally pleasant for the most part. Sancho had a young married couple, both university students who'd been beaten and tear-gassed during a protest and decided that spearheading the people's revolution against Maduro wasn't really their cup of tea.

Aunt Milagros had a family of five: two unwed parents and their three small children. Though she vehemently lamented their living and reproducing in sin, they were harmless enough.

Mauricio had the worst deal out of everyone, and for this I was secretly grateful to Román. Why shouldn't Mauricio have the worst deal seeing as he'd dumped all of us into his mess?

They had *nine* men staying with them—a bunch of guys looking for a better life, for adventure, for something to dull the boredom. Who knows.

As Mauricio complained to my father, they were messy, flirted relentlessly with the twins and Vanessa, and ate more than Mauricio could afford to feed them. Disaster!

But deserved (for Mauricio anyway).

The more time passed, the more I blamed Mauricio for everything. He had the casino job after all, so there was no reason for Aunt Celia to have been left indebted to a criminal, out on a ledge all alone with no help. Mauricio claimed he hadn't known about any of it, but that was no excuse as far as I was concerned and also reeked of bullshit. How'd he think the girls were able to go to public school without some strings being pulled? Whatever the real story, it still boiled down to Mauricio driving Aunt Celia to take desperate action to take care of the twins, though she had no financial means of her own. Whether he knew what went down or not, he was still accountable.

What I couldn't work out, though, was *why* Aunt Celia had embroiled herself with Ugly, with or without Mauricio's knowledge. Why stick her neck out to someone like Ugly if she couldn't possibly pay him back? Why shoulder the burden alone?

I knew I'd never know the answers, but the questions were still a lump in my throat I couldn't seem to swallow.

Meanwhile, in the week since Javier and the Jotas' arrival, there was no sign of Román. Total anticlimax.

I started looking for excuses to leave the house as often as possible, in the hope that he might turn up somewhere like he had at the Lit Fest. I went to the gym every day, lingered outside the grocery store and the mall, pretending to fumble with my keys, hoping that the black Jeep would appear.

Nothing.

I wasn't sick about it or crying into my pillow at night, but the guy was on my mind. A lot. I threw myself into work as a distraction. I blazed through translation projects, cranked out pages for my novel draft (most of which were shit but at least shit could be edited later), and turned to Aunt Celia's Panama City excursions for inspiration and entertainment.

Mr. CEO's playing big and bad, walking me to my car after all night pressed up against me on the dance floor, asking how does he know I'm

*worth the trouble. I say, "You tell me if I'm worth the trouble." I lean up
against the car and pull my dress up to my hips, give him a good glimpse
of what all the fuss is about, then flick my cigarette onto his fancy shoes,
get in the car, and leave, don't return a single one of his phone calls for
two weeks. Fucker's sent so many roses since then I could go into the
potpourri business. That's how you handle rich men with big egos—just
show 'em something shiny then take it away. They're all yours after that.*

If those snippets of her early twenties proved anything, it was that
Aunt Celia would never have pined over some guy or wondered why
he was MIA. If she wanted to fuck a guy, she'd fuck him. And if he
didn't give her the time of day, it was on to the next. Feelings were
never hurt, neuroses never hatched. The only sleepless nights she had
were the ones fueled by blow and amphetamines under the metallic
glimmer of a disco ball, the Bee Gees ringing in her ears and vibrating
in her platform heels.

That manuscript was my therapy. I drank it in and did my best to
switch off whatever emotions Román's kiss had stirred. No good could
come of starting up with our blackmailer's strong arm anyway.

———

Nearly two weeks into Javier and the Jotas' stay, and still with no further
contact from Román, I found the dining table laid with our version of
fancy tableware and my parents' silver candlesticks, one of the few
luxuries they'd smuggled over from Caracas. I joined everyone at the
table, where *Papá* was carving a joint of roast beef. Javier was passing
a bowl of mashed yams to Zulema, and the Jotas were helping themselves to beans and fried plantain. I pulled back a chair and sat. "What's
the occasion?"

Mamá gave a dramatic sigh as she twisted the cork out of a bottle
of red wine. "Javier and the Jotas are off tomorrow. Román called your
father to say their permanent housing is ready."

"It's gonna be, like, *so* weird without you guys around," whined

Zulema while *Mamá* swept around the table in her pumps and a silk dress, pouring wine into everyone's glass, bemoaning the loss of Javier as her sous-chef, *Papá* interrupting with a toast to the best drinking buddies he'd ever had. Even I felt nostalgic—they'd popped our safe-housing cherry, after all. That had to count for something?

The next morning, we sent Javier and the Jotas off with bacon-and-egg sandwiches and a thermos of coffee, like they were going on a camping trip. Lots of hugging, clapping on the back, and promises to stay in touch. *Mamá* was given a book of Colombian poetry and *Papá* another bottle of rum. These tokens were a relief to everyone: proof that Javier and the Jotas weren't that badly off if these were the kinds of things they still had floating around in their garbage bags.

When all the well-wishing was finally over, they got into a waiting taxi and our very first illegals were gone. Only when one of the Jotas leaned out the back window, waving goodbye, did I notice the rich ocher hue of his shirt—unmistakably Autumn. I guess we'd left as much of a mark on them as they'd left on us, even if it was just by way of getting them through their new lives in Trinidad in the best possible colors for their complexions.

BEHIND EVERY CRAZY BITCH

Reports rolled in that all the other Palacios households had been emptied that day as well. So to commemorate our collective first round of safe-housing, Aunt Milagros invited everyone over for dinner. Standing on her doorstep, we could already hear the rest of the family around the back, more boisterous than they'd been since Aunt Celia's death and Ugly's subsequent overhaul of our lives.

Aunt Milagros opened the door. Though her hair was still bizarrely unbrushed and dense with grease at the roots, she had gone out on a festive limb and was wearing deep pink lipstick, the boldest she'd ever dare! No doubt about it, this was going to be a night for celebration, though of what I wasn't sure—that we hadn't been killed in our sleep by the strangers we'd been forced to let into our homes? Good enough, I guess.

"¡Hola hola!" Aunt Milagros stained all our cheeks with pink and led us through the house.

Aunt Milagros's home was everything you'd imagine of a Catholic spinster's house. Covering every shelf were figurines of *Nuestra Señora del Valle, Nuestra Señora del Rosario, Nuestra Señora de* you name it. The mournful eyes of Christ were ubiquitous, staring down from crucifixes and framed paintings. And of course, there was the mandatory spinster's cat. A raggedy, green-eyed thing with ginger fur and white socks. Aunt Milagros didn't pay it any attention. I don't even think it had a name. Never saw food bowls or a litter box either. Maybe cats just manifested where there were lonely women.

Out on the porch, the overwhelming sense of Christian martyrdom dissipated and gave way to bright Peruvian wall hangings, potted bougainvillea, and other décor that was markedly less guilt-inducing than the house's interior. My family and I were greeted with a collective "*¡Holaaaa!*" and then we went our separate ways: *Papá* to sit with Mauricio; Zulema to the bathroom to reapply lipstick or mascara or whatever; and *Mamá* to the kitchen with Aunt Milagros. Sancho was at his usual post by the grill, prodding sausages and swaying with a glass of something undiluted and amber in his hand. Catastrophe waiting to happen. The girlfriend, Megan, was at his side, stuffed into a size-too-small floral dress, eyes flitting constantly to Vanessa, who was playing a noisy game of cards with the twins and wearing a painted-on romper with a zipper that started at her cleavage and ran right down to her crotch. Good luck, Meg.

I went back into the house to see if *Mamá* and Aunt Milagros needed help in the kitchen.

"Just a dream," Aunt Milagros was saying while removing the foil wrapping from a baked potato. "To finally have my house back to myself with my safety intact."

"*Ay*, Milagros, but what harm could a sweet family with three little children cause? We thought our illegals were great—those Jotas and that Javier, always so helpful around the house. Javier was a good catch for our Yola. Wants to be a chef, you know. But she didn't even give the boy a chance. Just locks herself in that bedroom all the time. One of these days she's going to—"

"Going to what?"

My mother jumped at the sound of my voice. "Yola! Don't sneak up on people like that!"

"One of these days I'm going to *what*?"

Mamá tutted and continued unwrapping the potato in her hand. "One of these days you're going to find yourself all alone and you'll want to know why, and it's because all you do is stay locked up in that damn room!"

"I'm *working, Mamá*. I *work* from home. You want me to translate on a table in the front yard like I'm selling lemonade?"

"Don't be so touchy, honey," said Aunt Milagros. "Your mother is just concerned. She wants you to meet a nice boy."

"*You* never met a nice boy and you're perfectly fine."

Aunt Milagros sniffed. "We're talking about you, not me." She brought her thumb to her mouth and tore off a hangnail. I noticed then that all her nails were ragged and short—which wasn't like Aunt Milagros, who usually kept her nails carefully manicured in the same soft pink she claimed Queen Elizabeth wore, her one act of Latina vanity. I'd have asked her about it, but she and my mother were doing this classic woman thing where they didn't say a word but were doing everything with passive-aggressive force, slicing into baked potatoes like they were disemboweling torture victims, launching balled-up foil into the garbage with the undue force of an Olympian hurling a discus.

I left them to their wordless seething and went back out to the porch, joining the twins and Vanessa at the picnic table where they were still at it with the cards.

"Can I join?" I asked.

"Sure! Take my hand." Vanessa jumped up and gave me her cards, tugging at the edges of her romper in a failed attempt to stop her ass cheeks peeking out. "I'm fed up of playing anyway."

I took the cards and sat while Vanessa tripped off to Sancho's side, curls, tits, and ass bouncing with every step.

Aside from *Mamá* and Aunt Milagros being cold with me the rest of the night, and Megan looking like she was on the brink of tears when Vanessa usurped her position next to Sancho at the table, the dinner went off without any hiccups. Everyone was in good spirits, especially Aunt Milagros, who raised her glass to merrily toast that she could finally get a full night's sleep now that there weren't "possible sadists, Peeping Toms, and murderers" under her roof (which seemed a tad dramatic given that the kids who'd stayed with her were all under age eight and their parents were schoolteachers). Weird toasts and all, the mood stayed buoyant, even when Sancho, drunk, tried sitting in the porch hammock only to flip the thing right over and land facedown on the tiles, breaking his front tooth. We all had a good laugh, in fact—especially when we saw how insane Sancho looked with his drunken leer and half a front tooth missing. The only one who didn't laugh was Megan, but this could've been as much from Vanessa running to Sancho's aid as from the spectacle of Sancho himself.

Home later, with a bottle of wine in me, I felt pretty good. Familial bonds had been renewed, I'd had a laugh at Sancho's expense, and I'd successfully forgotten about Román for a few hours—no easy feat since his ongoing absence had been a persistent snag in my mood.

I undressed and got into bed. My head felt light as a bubble with all the wine, but my eyes weren't heavy. Román was creeping into my mind again, tempting me to remember the spearminty taste of him, sliding my imagination into a spiraling Mills-and-Boon narrative punctuated by scar-dappled burnished skin, rough hands, heavy breath, mossy eyes, and a warm thumb on my lip. Frustrated, I kicked off the blanket and padded out to the kitchen, hoping a cold beer would be an effective nightcap.

Papá had beaten me to it. He was leaning against the kitchen counter, a beer to his lips. Seeing me, he lowered the bottle. "Couldn't sleep?"

I took a beer out of the fridge, cracked it open, and took a few glugs. "Have a lot on my mind," I said.

Papá's eyebrows were drawn together, his expression soft. It reminded me of the way he'd look at me when I was a kid if I'd scraped my knee or had a nightmare.

"I know this whole thing with Ugly must be hard on you," he said. "It's a real upheaval on top of everything else you're already dealing with."

"Everything else?" He couldn't possibly know about Román . . .

"You know, Aunt Celia's passing. She must be on your mind a lot. You know you can talk to me about it, right?" He hesitated almost shyly. "And about your writing stuff too. I'm not a big reader, but I'm always interested to hear about whatever you girls are into."

I took another slug of my beer, then kissed him on the cheek. "Don't you worry, *Papá*. I'm fine, and remember, I told you if there's anything worth telling about writing, I'll tell you."

"Or about anything else, *gordita*. I know you and Zulema are grown, but I'm always here if you need me."

For *Papá*, a little bit drunk usually equated to a lot mushy.

"I know." I clinked my bottle to his and said good night.

———

Propped up against my pillows, sucking on the beer, I wondered how my father would really react if he knew what was on my mind: how to make Román regret his little disappearing act. I pressed the bottle to my mouth, bubbles streaming upward as I drank, fantasizing about how aloof I'd be the next time I saw him. He'd try the old thumb-on-my-lip trick, the old dramatic kiss outta nowhere, and I'd roll my eyes. "*Control yourself*," I'd say. But even aloof seemed impossible. I was just so curious about him—curious, the same thing he'd said he felt about me—I wanted to know how he knew writers like Neruda and Echeverría, what he thought of my writing, where he'd gotten the faint scar across his mouth, why he was working for Ugly. I wished in that moment that I had Aunt Celia's hardness, that I could squelch that curiosity, forget what I'd felt when he left me shaken in my bedroom, or at the very least smother my licentious imagination that kept thrusting me into saxophone-soundtracked soft-porn reveries of him.

I reached into my nightstand for the manuscript, hoping that Aunt Celia's anecdotes would have their usual steeling effect, or at least distract my thoughts enough to be able to fall asleep. I'd finished the chapters on the bacchanalia of Panama City. Now Aunt Celia was in Miami, and I had come to the page that recalled the momentous event that would change her life forever: the night she met Mauricio.

1984, cocktail waitressing at Tuttles disco club. Twenty years old, tits up to my chin, a waist the width of a celery stick, and an ass like a shelf. The night I met the man who would be my downfall, I'm there at Tuttles doing my thing, mixing drinks, shaking the goods God gave me, and milking as much cash as I can from all the small-time drug runners flashing their firearms like the phallic compensations they are. It's just a half hour before closing when some guy leans over the bar and puts a hand on my wrist—heavy gold watch, bronzed hairy forearm. Unmistakably Latino. I look up and there's this slick motherfucker—wavy dark hair smoothed back from his face, white blazer, electric-blue V-neck, thick gold chain. I could see he was a jefe, a big boy.

"Do a shot with me?" he says—a Venezuelan, I hear the accent. I pour us a couple of Jose Cuervos and flash Big Boy a smile.

"Why not?"

We do a shot then a couple more waiting for the last of the cokeheads to traipse off the dance floor.

"Wanna go for a ride?" Big Boy asks at closing time.

He tells me his name is Mauricio, and a couple minutes later we're in his low, boxy sports car painted fire-engine red. That car knocks my socks off. I sink back into the bucket seats and think: This is a man to keep around.

Irony—gotta love it.

Now, seeing that this Mauricio has money and plenty of it, I don't lay a finger on him. I see the jeans bulging, the big hard outline, the blue balls in his eyes, and I say to myself—this one is for the long haul, the diamond—and so I actually let him date me. Fancy restaurants, snippy white maître d's with iron rods rammed up the rectum serving me like I'm the Queen of fucking Sheba. Hotel suites every weekend, champagne for breakfast, mountains of the purest blow on gold-edged mirrors, Mauricio hand-feeding me oysters, caviar, truffles, and all the other bullshit rich people are supposed to eat. That pussy power plays Mauricio like a fiddle. In two months I get the ring—a pink diamond—and I even cry when he gets down on one knee, like I'm really in love and not just off my face on Bollinger and class-A drugs.

Eyes finally heavy, I dropped the manuscript onto the floor and slid down beneath the duvet. So that's how it had all started—with a tequila shot. And Mauricio, once a big boy with money to throw around, with flash and attitude. What the hell had happened to him since then? And how depressing to bear witness to how a hot-and-heavy romance could, over a few decades, curdle into something as miserable as whatever Mauricio and Celia had by the end. Way less than a few decades actually—I remembered Aunt Celia once telling me, over an especially wine-soaked lunch, about what a shit husband Mauricio had been before they'd even had kids:

"There I was, Yola, seven months pregnant with Ava. First kid. I should've been happy as hell, glowing and sitting on a lily pad being worshipped by Mauricio without a care or a stress. But let me tell you something about women's intuition. You can always tell when a man is sniffing around for trouble. I knew he hadn't done the deed yet—a woman can tell these things, Yolita—but I knew he was out there sniffing. Instead of rubbing my back and feeding me bonbons, the *hijo de puta* has me working around the clock like a private eye just to keep his *verga* out of holes where it doesn't belong."

"Aunt Celia, you sure you wanna be telling me this?"

"*Coño*, you're twenty-three now. Time you learned how marriage really works. Now shut up and absorb some pearls of wisdom. So Mauricio wants to play with fire, and you mightn't believe it, but back then my Mauricio was something to see. He had a body on him, *bruja*. And this one little troublemaker, María, a Miss Sucre who couldn't even rank at the Miss Venezuela competition on account of a badly timed cold-sore outbreak, I catch her eyeing Mauricio in the streets, licking her lips like there's not a whole hotbed of herp under there. Bitch has a hungry little pussycat and thinks my husband is just the one to feed it. So imagine my surprise—or lack thereof—when Mauricio has the *huevos* to turn up at our house parading María like a bouquet of roses he's brought to surprise me. The *pendejo* actually had the audacity to say: 'Meet the new nanny! Here to help when the baby comes!' I watch this bouncy-haired, big-toothed home wrecker grinning at me in the foyer, waiting for a hug and a doggy biscuit, and I tell her one thing and one thing only. It's the only thing you ever need to tell some bitch who comes up in your territory trying to take your man."

"And? What'd you say?"

"To get the fuck out."

I'd laughed. "And what'd you tell Mauricio?"

"Now here's the thing you need to know about men and marriage. Sometimes words aren't enough. Men aren't so cerebral, not so good with the verbal communication skills, you know? They respond better to actions. So let's just say I took action."

With very minimal effort I'd cajoled her into admitting she'd semi-accidentally split Mauricio's skull open by launching an ashtray at him.

"Ah well," she hooted, "you know what they say, honey: behind every crazy bitch is a man who made her that way."

It was the perfect example of Aunt Celia's hard-as-nails attitude when it came to men, and just the reminder I'd need to keep my resolve firm when it came to Román in the future: Palacios women are not to be fucked with.

WHERE'S THE GEWÜRZTRAMINER?

For days after Javier and the Jotas left, the house felt strangely empty. No Jotas helping around the house, sharing tales of cattle-rearing, no Javier prepping dinner in the kitchen while humming old Gloria Estefan hits. But with the fickleness inherent in human affection, we soon got over Javier and the Jotas as we slipped back into familiar routines. I went back to reading and guzzling coffee in the backyard beach chair at six a.m. wearing just an old T-shirt. Zulema resumed her forty-five-minute beauty ritual before work in our shared bathroom, and my parents went back to their habits too, walking around the house in various states of undress, screaming at American singing competitions on TV while the poor amateur singers warbled and flailed in front of celebrity judges. With Christmas only days away there was no time to think about long-lost illegals. Last-minute gifts had to be bought and wrapped, food purchased and prepped, Christmas outfits assembled.

We were even too busy to think about when the next batch of illegals would be deposited on our doorstep. When the phone rang, we all assumed it was Venezuela calling with a mix of seasonal well-wishers and complainers. When there was a rap on the door, everyone hollered for Zulema, knowing it would be the FedEx guy delivering the gifts she'd ordered online. Life went on as though we'd never known Ugly at all, as if the only thing amiss was that this would be our first Christmas without Aunt Celia.

As for Román, I tried not to think about him. Whenever he popped into my head, I'd shove the thought out by writing or going for a run, until before I knew it, it was December 23, and our house and the whole damn island were in such a flurry of yuletide preparation that I actually *had* forgotten about Román. Gearing up for Christmas Day was tantamount to preparing for the apocalypse—so much urgency, so much stress, so much goddamned *traffic*. I'd just got back home from the mayhem of the mall after sitting in said traffic for hours, an outing I'd endured after realizing I hadn't bought anything for Zulema, a faux pas that could've brought a shit storm of passive aggression raining down on me till New Year's.

Drained as if I'd run a half marathon, I was making a pot of coffee to help me power through that afternoon's novel-writing session. While I waited for the pot to fill, I heard *Papá* in the backyard, singing along to parang playing through the tinny speakers of his wireless radio while he gave the gutters a fresh lick of paint. Every year since we'd all moved to Trinidad, Christmas lunch was held at our home on Christmas Day. (In an effort not to attract the attention of nosy or malicious neighbors, we celebrated Christmas with Anglo traditions.) Even though it meant replacing all the curtains and repainting every inch of the house, my father insisted on being the host as the patriarch of the Palacios in Trinidad. That meant he was also the host of family get-togethers at Easter, Corpus Christi, and every other religious holiday. In fact, we'd ended up adopting the Trini custom of celebrating all religious holidays regardless of our actual denomination. So last year, *Papá* had also been host to our family's Divali, Eid al-Fitr, and Shouter Baptist holiday luncheons.

But back to Christmas: my mother had been working fourteen-hour days to cater to all the clients clamoring for beauty appointments. At the Color Me Beautiful spa, Zulema was just as booked up. Apparently people needed to know exactly what hues of red and green would get them through Christmas with glowing complexions. So with all my family members occupied in their chores and workdays, I was yet again the only one who heard the three sharp raps at the front door. The same knock I'd heard the day Javier and the Jotas turned up.

I went to the window above the sink, throat constricting slightly with the expectation of seeing Román out there, like I was having a mild allergic reaction. If only there was an antihistamine to cure me of giving a shit about a man who I couldn't-shouldn't-*wouldn't* have.

Through the window I saw the black Jeep right where I'd expected it to be, but he wasn't in it.

Another three raps. He was at the door.

I took my time, drank from the faucet to cool my suddenly dry mouth, bifurcated by the dual hopes that he would and wouldn't be on the doorstep. But when I opened up, my heart dropped. Román was already pulling away in the Jeep. And our second shipment of illegals had arrived. *¡Feliz Navidad!*

———————

Vicente and Veneranda Manrique were well-to-do refugees, hoteliers who ran a four-star resort, the Tropical Dream Hotel, and who, on account of their substantial wealth, had a whole lot to lose, from first Chávez and then Maduro's socialist shenanigans. Way back when their hotel was a one-star motel, it'd seemed like a great idea for the rich to share with the poor, for everyone to be equal and entitled to the same rights and privileges. They only realized what a terrible idea socialism was when they had all the bright shiny privileges money bought. Then suddenly socialism seemed like a downright *awful* idea. Why should some politician get to force them to give away all their hard-earned dough? Why should they have to obey that horrendous new law that made them give big fat chunks of their profits to the rabble of their employees? So Vicente, ever the nationalist, took a stand, calling meetings of like-minded anti-socialist entrepreneurs. By the third meeting, the Manriques got word that they'd better stay on the right side of Maduro if they didn't want their Tropical Dream up in flames, the insurance policy mysteriously nonexistent.

They sold the hotel and tried to migrate, but hardly anywhere gave residency permits or even tourist visas to Venezuelans anymore, least of all a couple of Venezuelans who were almost retired and wouldn't be contributing squat in tax dollars. Hence, here they were in North-West Trinidad two days before Christmas, waiting on our doorstep like a pair of evangelical Mormons hoping to be invited in for tea.

I could see right away that Veneranda Manrique was a vain bitch. This was evident in the extravagant cockatoo coif of her hair, the lilac hue of her Chanel suit and matching lilac heels, and the glitz of the many fat rings on her equally fat fingers. Vicente Manrique seemed just as pompous, standing beside a full set of Louis Vuitton suitcases wearing a silk cravat and a cream linen suit. He had a stupid little mustache, a smug black ant trail above a deeply indented upper lip, a real *squiggle* of a lip that turned my stomach. When I opened the door to the pair of them, with their matching guts protruding toward me, I was instantly overcome by dislike.

Veneranda looked me up and down, a drawn-on eyebrow rising while her spurious smile stayed fixed.

"Good day," said Vicente, affecting the accent of an Argentine (deemed the snootiest of all Latin Americans, for those who don't know). "I presume you are one of our hosts?" He paused to look me over. "Or perhaps our hosts' help?"

I sighed and stepped aside, showing them in. "I'm Yola. Welcome. I'm not the help."

I went out to the backyard, leaving the Manriques sniffing with disdain at our furnishings. I found my father at the side of the house on a ladder. He was shirtless, white paint splattered all over his lean frame, hair poking out from beneath a beat-up old cap speckled with the paint of the last two Christmases. Seeing me, he paused to wipe his forehead, leaving an accidental white streak.

"What's up, Yolita?"

"Second leg of the invasion."

"Shit," said *Papá*. "Two days before Christmas? What was Román thinking?"

"How the hell should I know?" It had come out more bitter than I'd intended.

Papá didn't pick up on it. He dropped the paintbrush into a bucket of water and climbed down from the ladder. "Where are they?" he asked, removing his cap to run a hand over his hair.

I jabbed my thumb over my shoulder. "Living room. There's two of them."

Papá walked past me into the house. I heard him welcoming the Manriques and apologizing for his appearance, explaining that we hadn't been given notice of their arrival, but that they were most welcome nonetheless. Not even a hint of inconvenience in his tone. As I was crossing the backyard to head back inside, he popped his head out the porch door. "Listen," he hissed, "these people want *wine spritzers*. What the hell is a wine spritzer?"

"Don't worry, I'll sort that out," I said, laughing the oblivious laughter of the blissfully ignorant, not knowing that wine spritzers were just the beginning.

———————

We clocked on to the Manriques' extravagant expectations pretty quick after I fixed them wine spritzers, which they summarily criticized as flavorless and flat before asking if we didn't have a nice Gewürztraminer "lying around" instead. Shortly after that, I abandoned *Papá* and hid out in my room, using work as an excuse, and when I reemerged later that evening, it was to find Zulema in the kitchen, taking a tray of store-bought mini-quiches out of the oven and looking uncharacteristically frazzled—hair twisted up into a frizzy topknot, lipstick faded.

"Those people are, like, total nightmares," she whispered when she saw me. "They're asking for *cocktails and hors d'oeuvres*. They think they're staying at the freaking Marriott!"

"Why would they expect all that shit?" I said, reaching for a mini-quiche before she slapped my hand away. "It's ridiculous."

"I don't know, but *Papá* told me they've been dropping hints that if they're not satisfied, Román will be hearing about it."

"Oh yeah?"

"Yup. And that Román, *Papá* told me he's heard things about him. That he's, like, some big shot—works for *all* the drug barons and human traffickers over here. He's totally killed a bunch of people."

It felt like a boulder had been dropped from a hot air balloon straight into the pit of my stomach. Violent intimidation was one thing, but murder was another altogether.

"Where would *Papá* hear that?" I asked.

"Grapevine, duh."

"Grapevine of what people?"

"I don't know. Whatever. I mean, *look* at him. He just looks like a villain, don't you think? I didn't need anyone to tell me anything to know he's bad news." She looked at me sharply. "You don't think so?"

I shrugged. "I don't know a thing about the guy."

I went to the fridge and opened it just to stop Zulema scrutinizing my face. I told myself it was *pura paja*, just bullshit speculation. A man who had that effect on me couldn't have killed someone. Or at least I'd tell myself that until proven otherwise.

Dinner with the Manriques that night was nothing like our first dinner with Javier and the Jotas. Although Vicente stiffly recounted the story of why they'd left Venezuela, they dodged questions and stayed guarded despite both my parents' friendly overtures. They showed no interest in any of us, did not compliment the food, didn't thank us for our hospitality, and immediately after dinner, positioned themselves on the couch and demanded the remote. My parents handed it over bitterly, relinquishing a night of ridiculing wannabe pop stars.

No one wanted to stay up with the Manriques there on the couch, so we all turned in for the night, soured by our new illegals, missing Javier and the Jotas with renewed affection.

HOUDINI MAKES AN APPEARANCE

Mamá couldn't work all day on Christmas Eve, not with so many preparations to be made, so I'd offered to help out by driving her around to do last-minute errands that afternoon. At exactly midday, when I knew she'd have finished her last appointment, I went to the annex. The clients were finally all gone, but when I went in, I could see Mamá was stressed: she was tidying about as quietly as a toddler having a tantrum, flinging things in drawers, shoving past chairs, yanking all the singing elf figurines' plugs out of the wall like she was pulling out someone's fingernails. The toxic blend of Christmas stress, overwork, and the Manriques had definitely gotten to her.

"¿*Todo bien?*" I asked.

She gave a long exhale. "Everything's fine. I just need to get this place cleaned up. It's filthy from all those women traipsing through." She jabbed an accusing finger at the tiled floor. "Look at those dirt marks! You think any of those women use the welcome mat? You think they take a minute to scrape their royal shoes clean before they drag all their dirt and dog mess through my place of business?"

"Just leave it, *Mamá*. We can deal with it on Boxing Day. Zu and I will help."

"Ha!" She threw her hands up, glaring at me like I was shit smeared across one of her tiles. "You think on Boxing Day I won't be in here working? I must've forgot that we're millionaires who can afford not to work for weeks on end!"

"Would you relax? Let me give you a hand."

"Don't tell me to relax," she snapped, grabbing the broom. "Just go wait in the house till I'm done."

I left her there cleaning and muttering angrily to herself, but didn't go back into the house. I got into the Datsun, switched on the ignition, and cranked the AC right up. The car was a furnace, but I'd take the heat over listening to the Manriques haranguing my poor father from their permanent post on the couch. It'd only been twenty-four hours since their arrival, and already I was finding I couldn't get out enough. But it was my father who really had the brunt of it. He wasn't working, as it was the school holidays, so was left catering to the many whims of the Manriques—a tall order if ever there was one. Take, for example, an excerpt of a conversation between Veneranda and my father earlier that same morning:

"Oh . . . is that bacon you're cooking? Could we not have Greek yogurt and granola instead? Vicente and I are so very health-conscious, you see. We wouldn't dream of having all that fried pork fat for breakfast."

"I'm afraid there's no yogurt, Veneranda, but I've made you and Vicente some lovely vegetable omelettes here as well, see? You can just leave the bacon."

"Oh." A sniff. "I assume those eggs aren't free-range?"

"No, but unfortunately that's the only eggs we have."

"Hmm, yes, well, Vicente and I would go and buy some Greek yogurt and granola ourselves for breakfast, but with our situation it's best we lay low. Perhaps I ought to place a call to Román and see whether he can better attend to our needs? We really can't be eating caged eggs and pig fat. We are *so* health-conscious, you understand."

I'd imagined Veneranda patting her oil drum of a belly as she bleated about her health-consciousness.

Román was now a constant threat hanging over my father's head. That morning Vicente had even gotten *Papá* to upgrade our cable subscription by brandishing Román in his face. "Perhaps Román might know of some other host family more inclined to make their guests comfortable with suitable entertainment. We couldn't find a thing worth watching without the film channels last night. We need more cultural stimulation than basic television, Hector, I'm sure you can understand." An extravagant sigh. "But Román wouldn't be pleased to hear we want to move. That would be so much hassle for him. He wouldn't be pleased one bit, would he, Veneranda?"

"Oh no, Vicente, not pleased at all."

"And I wouldn't say Román is someone I'd want to upset. I certainly wouldn't want him to be upset with *me*, would you, Veneranda?"

"Oh no, Vicente, certainly not. Román is the absolute last person I'd want to upset."

There was nothing *Papá* could do but acquiesce. He'd only just managed to scrape his family out of Ugly's line of fire and wouldn't do anything to rock the boat now.

So that's why I chose to sit in the car for twenty-five minutes while *Mamá* cleaned up. When she did eventually come out, her hair was slicked back into a chignon, makeup had been freshly applied, and the nail shavings–covered apron had been discarded for a smart white cotton dress. Looked as though she'd never seen a day of stress in her life, like she'd been bathing in milk all morning long.

She got into the car and instantly flipped open her pocket mirror, examining her makeup for even the slightest slip.

"Ready to go?" I asked as I reversed out the driveway.

"Always ready, *mi niña*."

To look at her, you'd think that was actually true.

Later, lugging our purchases inside, I passed through the living room, behind the couch where the Manriques had been sitting since that morning. Veneranda's stockinged feet were up on the coffee table while she flicked through the newly added movie channels and Vicente snoozed next to her. They didn't turn when I came in, and I'd have been a moron to expect any offer of help with our bags.

The drone of the weed-whacker coming in through the open porch doors told me *Papá* was hiding in his gardening. Zulema was in the kitchen again, sourly spooning granola into heaped bowls of—you guessed it—Greek yogurt. She grunted by way of a hello while I started unpacking the groceries. I heard *Mamá* greet the Manriques coldly (no reply from them) as she followed me into the kitchen carrying the rest of the food bags. We'd had to pick up almost double the ingredients she'd already bought for Christmas lunch, plus two extra turkeys. Since each household had received its own Christmas bundle of illegals, we'd all decided to include them in our Anglo-style festivities. It seemed like the right thing to do. But for the time being, my mother had forgotten this spirit of charity and was scolding Zulema through clenched teeth.

"Why did you go out and buy that yogurt for them? Who do they think we are—their slaves?"

Zulema, annoyed but placid, sealed the bag of granola shut and covered the tub of yogurt. "*Papá* bought the yogurt. He just asked me to dish it out so he didn't have to."

"Disgusting people," spat *Mamá*. "We should call the police on them, get them carted back to their Tropical Dream Hotel to deal with Maduro."

"We can't call the police for them. The police would also want to get rid of *us*, remember?"

"You think I could forget, Zulema? Forget that we live like rats in a hole?" She carried on, spitting the words out while packing away the groceries as aggressively as possible, slamming every cabinet and tugging drawers open like limbs she was tearing off. Not wanting to get sucked into their spat, I mumbled that I was going for a run. I had to get away from the Manriques and the noxious mood they'd spread throughout the house like tear gas. I drove to my usual running haunt—the Savannah, a large, leafy park-cum-roundabout that's a sort of fitness hub. At any given time of day, there are outdoor boot-camp classes whipping potbellied women into shape, bare-backed fitness buffs stretching their hamstrings on the backs of benches, awkward-looking tourists with blue-veined legs strolling among the hordes of jogging and power-walking locals. The only downside to running the paved loop of the park is getting ogled by all the drivers cruising around the Savannah's perimeter, but the setting makes it worthwhile anyway: sprawling trees, grand old colonial homes, a backdrop of sloping green hills, fresh coconuts being sold from historic trucks. And right beside one of those very trucks is where Román appeared out of the motherfucking blue.

———————

I'd already run more than a mile when I saw him sitting on a bench in the near distance, scraping the jelly from inside a coconut with a shard of green coconut shell.

I stopped dead. I couldn't believe it was him: *Poof!* Right there before me. My very own Houdini. A gamut of emotion overtook me—surprise, anger, need. Then, once I'd managed to collect myself, there was nothing else for it but to walk on over.

I kept waiting for him to turn to me as I approached, but he continued his phlegmatic scraping at the coconut flesh while the runners, joggers, and pasty foreigners cruised by. He was as tranquil there with that coconut as an iguana lounging in the sun.

I was feet away. Nervous now. He still hadn't looked over. Did he know I was there? Was this really a Houdini-style reappearance or was I just running into him as a genuine coincidence? *Verga.* Maybe I should turn. Maybe I should run back the way I'd come. . . .

Too late. I was standing beside the bench, but he just kept looking straight ahead and eating the goddamned coconut jelly. I didn't know what else to do but say something.

"Getting a little stalking off your Christmas Eve to-do list?"

He kept eating. No reaction. Now my cheeks were more flushed from embarrassment than the exertion of running. I waited a few seconds, until I'd hit my limit for humiliation and was about to turn and jog away or possibly hurl myself into the moving traffic.

But: "You sure took your time strolling over here." Another casual scoop of jelly.

"I . . . I didn't think you saw me."

"You sure you get what a surveillance expert does, Yola?"

His head dipped so he was looking up at me from above his sunglasses. Then he raised his head again, tilted it as though he were examining the historic house directly opposite us on the other side of the road—a beautifully filigreed black-and-white mansion with a domed roof.

"Oh, I'm so sorry," I said. "I had no idea surveillance expert was your official job title. And you're surveying local architecture today? I'm surprised. I thought you had strict orders to keep an eye on us scheming Palacios at all times."

"What do you think I'm doing here, *flaca*? You're a Palacios. I'm hard at work." He rested the empty coconut husk on the bench, still looking straight ahead at the house as though he wasn't talking to me at all, but to himself.

More at ease now, I sat beside him. But the second I did that, he gave me a nod like I was a stranger he was politely acknowledging, then immediately stood. Confused, I went to stand up again.

"Sit," he said abruptly.

I stayed put, my temper sparking like kindling at his gruff order.

"Look straight ahead of you at the house. We shouldn't be seen talking." He feigned a sudden fascination with a jacaranda tree stretching into a purple-blossomed bouquet above us.

I did as he said, my stomach knotting. "Why's that?"

"Ugly's not a trusting man. It's always best to err on the side of caution—never know if he might have someone checking up on me." He made a move like he was cracking his neck, but something told me it was a more purposeful movement than that. "Let's say I've learned the value of caution in my line of work."

"Then why follow me here if we can't even talk properly because it's that dangerous?" Anger hit me sharp as a slap. What was his game? He'd stoked my fire so I had more pent-up heat in me than Krakatoa, and now he was telling me to snuff it out like it was a flame on a candlewick, that we couldn't so much as risk a conversation. What was the point of any of it? I was confused enough without him playing games then putting me in unnecessary danger to boot.

Without giving him a chance to answer, I got up from the bench to face him. A salty breeze sent the jacaranda's violet blossoms fluttering down around us. I reached out to yank his sunglasses off, so I could look him in the eye while I told him to fuck off with his noir intrigue and sinister warnings. But in a feline reflex, he snatched my wrist and lowered my hand to my side before I could do any of it.

"Have you lost your mind?" His voice was calm. I was not.

"Listen, Román, if you want to talk to me, then talk to me. And if you want to fuck me, then do it, but enough with the cloak-and-dagger bullshit. Obviously we both want the same thing, so let's just get it out of our systems and move on. Figure out how to make it happen, Surveillance Expert."

I wrenched my wrist out of his hand and strode away in the direction I'd come from, chin lifted, ponytail swinging indignantly behind me.

I didn't have to look back to know he was watching me walk away.

PAGAN TRADITIONS

Judging by the turnout at Mass that night with my family, Catholicism Inc. was booming in Trinidad. Everyone was decked out in red, green, and gold, singing lustily, smiling warmly at one another in acknowledgment of what upstanding blind papists they were.

As the Mass dragged on, I was pleasantly surprised that my mind didn't churn with muddled thoughts of Román as it had after our last couple interactions. I didn't pick apart a single snippet of our dialogue. I cruised through the homily and the singing and chanting and incense-swinging high on quiet confidence: I'd laid my cards on the table and knew now for certain that Román wanted me as much as I wanted him. Why else would he let me speak to him the way I had? Why would he have risked talking to me at all?

When it came time to put money in the collection basket, though, it wasn't Román I thought of but Aunt Celia. I remembered Christmas the year before, when she'd leaned into me while the little wicker baskets were making the rounds along the pews. *"Why should I have to pay for a bunch of priests to swan around with their noses in the air, giving people bullshit twelve-step plans for getting to heaven? Those false advertisers. Let them get their money from some other fool.*" Then she'd dropped a mint wrapper in the basket.

I wished I could lean in and whisper that to Zulema as she dropped in a ten-dollar bill. But she wouldn't get it. She'd put a finger to her glossy, cherry lips like a schoolteacher. She passed the basket to me. I added a five.

God, I missed Aunt Celia.

———

Back at the house, we ate our traditional *pan de jamón*, one of the few Venezuelan customs we kept up. We ate it every Christmas Eve after Mass with a pitcher of homemade punch ah crème strong enough to put everyone to bed well before St. Nick stuffed himself through the window (no chimneys in the tropics). The Manriques, claiming an entirely unsurprising gluten intolerance, didn't eat any *pan de jamón*, and were horrified at the caged eggs we'd used to make the punch ah crème. So they stayed inside watching reruns of *Friends* Christmas episodes with Spanish subtitles (so much for their high standards for rich cultural content) while we sat on the porch drinking and eating together, marveling at Sancho's ability to down the thick, creamy punch ah crème like it was lighter than water.

As he guzzled, Sancho told us about his illegals: a university professor and his blind common-law wife, who were incredibly dull, according to my brother. "I can't believe people that boring have the balls to sneak into another country," he chortled, crunching chipped-up ice between his back teeth.

We laughed, but were cut short by *Papá*: "It goes to show how bad things are. All the thinkers are leaving. That's what will break our nation. 'Brain drain,' they call it in English. No turning back now."

We went quiet, chastened, until *Mamá* raised her head from where it'd been tucked against *Papá*'s shoulder. "Should I bring the jug of punch ah crème out here?"

We nodded in unison. And to power through the somberness of

Papá's musing, we all hit that jug like we were in competition with Sancho. Within an hour we were good and drunk—too drunk to make it to midnight, when we usually toasted Christmas and opened gifts, another of our lingering Spanish traditions. So drunk even Sancho decided not to attempt the drive home and passed out facedown on an air mattress on my bedroom floor before I'd even had a chance to fully inflate it.

Zulema and I went to bed shortly after Sancho passed out, leaving my parents still drinking on the porch while the Manriques continued their *Friends* marathon, the laugh reel echoing late into the night, as comforting in its sitcom cheesiness as the red, green, and gold Rasta-themed Christmas lights twinkling in the street and the sight of my parents slow-dancing in the backyard, which I glimpsed just before shutting my curtains. Proof that although our Christmas was sullied by a dead family member, a violent blackmailer, and a pair of aristocratic assholes, consuming just the right amount of liquor could salvage any holiday.

I woke up at six a.m. on Christmas morning, head throbbing. Sancho was still splattered across the now completely deflated blow-up mattress, snoring loudly. I got up, the room out of focus, tongue like a wad of cotton in my mouth.

Water. I needed water.

I crawled off my bed, wishing there was a mute button for Sancho, and padded out of the room, overwhelmed by thirst. As I emerged from the bedroom hallway, I stumbled backward, taken aback by the scene in the living room.

No one in the family had decorated their homes, as a nod to the loss of Aunt Celia. Yet there was the Christmas tree, with all the trimmings, twinkling away. The coffee table and end tables held clusters of ceramic Santa Clauses *Mamá* had made during an artsy phase. The double doors to the porch were framed by green garlands with fairy lights twisted into them, glowing bright in the early morning grayness. Hanging beside the doors was another product of *Mamá*'s prolific artsy phase: hand-sewn Christmas stockings. The crèche had also been set up, with all the straw and stones *Mamá* usually added to give it a "lifelike effect." On either side of the crèche were two lit candles wafting artificial scents of gingerbread and apple-cinnamon, a serious fire hazard considering all the straw scattered around the Holy Family and their entourage. At the eye of this holiday hurricane were the Manriques, matching lumps on the fold-out couch.

My parents must have gotten utterly shit-faced and decorated. I pressed my fingers against my temples. Too much thinking and too little water. I dragged myself to the kitchen, keeping a hand against the wall to ease the vertigo.

Bent over the sink, slurping cold water from the faucet, I noticed that Christmas-colored curtains had been hung, the regular tea towels replaced with holiday towels showing seasonal icons prancing around in wintry scenes. I straightened up, nauseated by the excessive Christmas crap and too much water too quickly. Coffee and my beach chair. That'd do the trick.

I brewed myself an enormous mug of black coffee and headed through the Christmas cornucopia. As I was pulling the porch door softly shut behind me, I recognized Sancho's snores coming from the hammock strung up between two pillars. Except it wasn't Sancho, but *Papá*. I went to the edge of the hammock and peered in at my father in the swinging cocoon. His mouth was open, face slack and relaxed. I almost didn't want to wake him, but was too curious not to. I poked his shoulder until his eyes opened—a visible struggle. He tried wetting his lips, but it seemed he was having the same problem I'd had when I woke up: a tongue made of sandpaper.

"Merry Christmas," I said.

"Oh God." He squeezed his eyes shut. "Get me out of this thing."

I helped him climb awkwardly out of the hammock to plop himself into a low Morris chair.

"Coffee. Please."

I handed him the mug. He took two gulps, not caring or noticing that it was scalding hot, then handed it back to me before resting his head in his hands.

"What happened last night?" I asked.

"What do you mean?" he mumbled. "What happened with what?"

"Uhhh . . ." I pointed behind me. "With the *house*. It's like the North Pole in there."

Papá looked over his shoulder through the glass-paned doors. He slumped forward again, driving his fingers through his hair. "The Manriques."

"The two laziest human beings on the face of the Earth did all that?"

"No, no." *Papá* shook his head. "They came outside after you all went to bed. Venera-whatever-her-name-is started going on and on to your *Mamá* about the importance of traditions and being a good Christian, and oh God, she wouldn't shut her mouth."

"And you and *Mamá* were drunk enough to let it get to you, so you went crazy with the Christmas decorations." Even though my father looked like his head was being crushed beneath an invisible asphalt roller, I couldn't help laughing.

"Nope," he said. "*She* let it get to her, so *she* went on this Christmas rampage. Of course the Manriques went to sleep before she'd even finished putting up the Christmas tree. Man, those people can sleep—or they can fake it, anyway. Your mother only finished decorating around three a.m., and you know what she's like when she's mad—won't say a word but she'll make more goddamned noise than a bulldozer."

Papá reached a hand out for more coffee. I gave him the mug.

"Finish it," I said. "So why'd you sleep out here?"

"I wouldn't help so your mother told me I had to sleep outside. You know how she gets. But I just wasn't going to let those two fools guilt me into decorating. My little sister only died a few months ago, for godssake, and my whole family is being blackmailed. I'm not exactly in the Christmas spirit."

I realized then that his and *Mamá*'s binge might've been about more than just seasonal boozing.

Papá was swilling the coffee in his mouth, wincing at the burn.

"You know," I said, "I've never asked how *you're* doing with the Aunt Celia thing."

My father raised a wry eyebrow at me, then exhaled. "Celia might've been a pain in everyone's ass—she's *still* a pain in our asses with this Ugly mess—but she was my sister." He lowered his eyes, focused on sipping the coffee. "I'm doing how I'm doing," he added finally, voice uncharacteristically gruff.

I sat on the arm of the chair and leaned over to the side, touching my head to his at the temple. Our family wasn't big on physical affection, but we had our ways of showing we cared—a shoulder squeeze, ruffled hair, playful pinches, little ways to make contact and connect. *Papá* and I stayed with our heads touching for a moment before I stood again.

"Well, if you want to talk about it . . ." I said.

"*Tranquila*," he said, waving a hand at me. "It's Christmas, let's not focus on all that right now. Go get yourself a coffee and come tell me what you're writing these days. It'll help me get over the hangover—call it a Christmas present."

Papá and I sat out on the porch drinking a liter of black coffee each, and I actually did tell him about my novel draft. It was strange talking about my writing with someone who wasn't Aunt Celia, but I found myself almost rambling, desperate for an outlet. I talked and talked, until the rest of the household slowly woke up. Sancho wandered out into the living room first, stretching and belching and farting without a care in the world for the Manriques, who were also now awake. Zulema trotted out shortly after, a Christmas show pony if ever there was one, in a green sundress with a skinny red waist-belt and sparkly red costume jewelry. *Mamá* emerged last in an oxblood pencil dress and strappy stilettos, with Golden Globes makeup, hair swept into a chic updo. But even with all that, her face was, to use an expression of

Aunt Celia's, "as dark and pinched as a horse's asshole." I could see the hangover all over, even through the carefully applied glamour.

"*Mamá*, the house is, like, *magical!*" Zulema was twirling through the living room, bedazzled by all the Christmas crap. My mother scowled at her, snapping an earring into place, but Zulema didn't read the mood. "Totally a wonderful surprise!" Still twirling like a festive tumbleweed.

Mamá blinked at my sister, the kind of blink that hits you like a bullet. "Zulema, you're flashing everyone your damn underwear." From the safety of the porch, I listened to *Mamá*'s heels click to the kitchen, then the slamming of a cabinet and: "IS THERE NO FILTERED COFFEE IN THIS HOUSE?"

Zulema slumped outside, dejected.

"Don't worry, *linda*," said *Papá*. "You're not the reason she's so upset."

He explained about the Manriques' jibes and finished recounting the story in the nick of time, just as *Mamá* appeared in the open doorway. *Papá*, now slightly more recovered from his hangover, got up to try giving her a hug. She stood stiff with her hands by her sides. She was *pissed*. I think mostly at herself for caving to the Manriques.

Not long after, the Manriques came out to the porch as well, trussed up in matching gold-and-green regalia, and we all politely, if disingenuously, wished them a Merry Christmas. They, with equal insincerity, wished it right back.

"So what do you think, Veneranda?" *Mamá* swept her hand across the festive vista of the living room.

Vicente followed *Mamá*'s hand and blinked at the room with his piggy eyes as if only just noticing the decorations for the first time. He gave a sniff like he was checking a baby's diaper for poop. Veneranda didn't even look up at *Mamá*'s question. She was fiddling with an enormous ruby brooch that dangled from her bosom like a glittering, inflamed nipple. At last, she deigned to raise her head and survey the room.

"Very nice, Yasmin. Very nice indeed."

Mamá allowed herself a fleeting moment of triumph.

Until: "Such a silly waste to wait for Christmas Day to decorate, though. Just think, now you're going to have to take it all down again in a week's time. And that tree—*my goodness*, you must have had a lot to drink before you decorated it! We aren't drinkers, Vicente and I, as it's so dreadful for your health, but we can certainly recognize a drinker's handiwork."

She and Vicente chortled and patted their bellies.

We were all in the living room during this little exchange between my mother and Veneranda. *Mamá*'s eyes looked like they were about to pop out of her skull she was so angry. *Papá* put his arm around her shoulder, probably anticipating the need to physically restrain her. But Sancho, who'd already downed two strong Irish coffees, whistled long and loud.

"*Mamá*, you hear that? That's some disrespectful shit, man."

The Manriques shot him a dirty look, but Sancho only grinned at them, leaned to the side, and farted. As that interminable fart rippled through the room with what can only be described as panache, Vicente whipped his silk hanky from his pocket and covered his nose with a cry of "*¡Santa Virgen!*" while Veneranda yelped in horror. But the rest of us, even *Mamá*, burst out laughing, instantly recalibrating the sour mood of our first holiday as safe-housers. It would forever be fondly remembered as the fart that saved Christmas.

———

Thank God for Sancho's flatulence, because there was no room for sourness with the already precarious dynamic of the guest list for our Christmas lunch: myself, my parents, Zulema, and the Manriques were one household. Sancho returned home to get his two alleged dullards, the professor and his blind wife. Mauricio had lucked out, and instead of the cantankerous bunch he'd been assigned last time, he and his daughters came with a beret-wearing journalist who smoked hand-rolled cigarettes and said she went by the code name Simone, after de

Beauvoir herself, plus a guy in his twenties whom Mauricio introduced as being "highly educated and very cultured."

Aunt Milagros came with her second batch of illegals too: three "dancers" with ass, breast, and lip implants. It was clear to everyone but golden-hearted Aunt Milagros that the only thing these three women danced around was a pole, but she introduced them as "a troupe of professional dancers" like such a proud mother hen that no one wanted to tell her the truth. Plus she looked less on edge than usual, and she'd finally washed her hair, for the first time since Ugly came a-knocking (even if her nails were still ragged and there was still that odd smoke smell clinging to her clothes), so clearly the dancers were having a positive effect somehow.

Mauricio also brought little Fidel. The Moneybags family needed Camille to work that morning to help with their lavish Christmas buffet. Mrs. Moneybags didn't feel bad about this. Camille was contractually available to work twenty-four hours a day, six days a week, with Sundays off. This Christmas Day fell on a Thursday.

Tough luck, Camille!

With such an eclectic mix of people—hoteliers, dancers, the erudite, the blind, the flatulent, the vain, and the drunk—that Christmas lunch could've been an all-out catastrophe. But to my surprise, having so many different characters thrown into one pot turned out far better than expected, because we all had one thing in common: we all loved Venezuela and hated the man clinging to power at its helm. Any lull in conversation could readily be filled with "Have you heard about the latest riots in _____?" or "Do you know people are now paying as much as _____ to buy _____? *Imagínese*, just a few years ago that only cost _____!"

The conversation never stopped. Liquor flowed and sparkling-wine corks flew like confetti as bottle after bottle was consumed. We were having a whale of a time with our illegals, even the Manriques, who—despite Veneranda's claims that they weren't boozers—were actually sort of fun with a few drinks in them.

Or maybe we were all just drunk enough to find their pomposity more funny than annoying.

Now to highlight one of our esteemed guests: the supposedly oh-so-educated and cultured young man staying with Mauricio. His name was Kingsley De Oruña Willoughby and he insisted we call him by his alleged nickname, King.

No comment.

King was the sole penniless heir to a wealthy English rose (the Willoughby) and a high-born Spaniard (the Oruña), two love-struck Cambridge alumni who'd given their cold, aristocratic parents the finger by eloping to the backwaters of rural Venezuela just before completing their degrees, thereby forfeiting their inheritances in favor of near-annual cases of dengue fever and their little monarch, King.

He shared this curious backstory as a preface to why he'd joined the Venezuelan military in a desperate move to give himself a better future—and believe me, that preface was necessary for drumming up sympathy, because there wasn't a person present who would've applauded any member of the Venezuelan armed forces. King had been a soldier since he was eighteen, and now that he was in his mid-twenties, he said he just couldn't stomach being part of Maduro's strong arm anymore.

"The army was all I felt the world had to offer me. It presented me with a *luminous* future where I could protect the rights and liberties of our great Bolivarian Republic."

An intake of breath from Zulema, Vanessa, and the twins, chins propped in their hands, eyes swimming. Even *Mamá* and Aunt Milagros were swooning.

"I harbored aspirations of being a soldier akin to a knight of the highest order, defending our nation, our people, rescuing damsels in distress." A wink at the ladies.

I rolled my eyes.

"But then I saw that Maduro was using the army as a tool of *oppression*, a club with which he could bludgeon the nation. . . ."

To cut a long story short, he deserted, and that meant he had to find himself out of Venezuela ASAP. So King hopped aboard the Trinidad-bound pirogue parade. Despite his parents' Spanish and British nationalities, he'd only ever been registered as a Venezuelan citizen, so was hiding out in Trinidad illegally until Ugly or Román or whoever managed to get him a British passport, legit or otherwise.

And now here he was at our dining table, all bulging biceps and panty-dropping military stories. I didn't like the guy. The fact that he strutted around with his chest puffed out like a preening, arrogant rooster while forcing people to call him King had a lot to do with it. But I was the only one who felt that way. Everyone else was eating up the tales of King's army adventures. Especially Vanessa. She was laughing in that demented way women laugh when they're really into someone. Anything King said was met with squeals of "You didn't!" and bouts of wild giggles. There was also a whole lot of hair twirling, eyelash fluttering, the usual.

I wasn't the only one to notice Vanessa's sycophantic flirting.

King was obviously well aware—and so was Sancho.

My brother was unsurprisingly already drunk by the time King regaled us with the story of his parents' grand plan for rebellion gone awry. So when Sancho saw Vanessa throwing her head back to howl with laughter at every quip, stroking King's arm, shaking her prodigious tits at every opportunity, well, you can only imagine how hard he began pounding the drinks. By the time the sun set on that Christmas Day, Sancho was in extraordinary form, singing American carols and Trini parang and Venezuelan folk songs, and pretty much any other song, no matter how addled, that came into his head. He'd even dug out *Papá*'s old *cuatro* and was strumming it with all the flair of a rock-star guitarist, though he wasn't really making music, just adding to the general mayhem. Mauricio, the twins, Aunt Milagros, Zulema, the journalist, the professor and his wife, my parents, even the inebriated Manriques all cheered and clapped while Sancho performed for us. The strippers danced around him in a circle, not writhing on the ground with genitals splayed, but like folk dancers, clapping their hands above their heads, jiggling their silicone derrières, and yipping. Aunt Milagros beamed with pride and I clutched my stomach, eyes streaming with laughter at the chaos.

It was one of our best Christmases. The only thing missing was, of course, Aunt Celia.

I was sure everyone felt her absence in their own way. I felt it in sudden stabs that would catch me off guard—like when Mauricio's household arrived without Aunt Celia leading the way. Every Christmas, she would sweep into the room with all the devilish glamour of Cruella DeVil, always dressed in sumptuous reds, décolletage on spectacular display, diamonds flashing. It was an ongoing competition between her and *Mamá*—seeing who could one-up the other at family get-togethers—but at Christmas, my mother's Sophia Loren sophistication couldn't hold a candle to Aunt Celia. Aunt Celia was Zsa Zsa Gabor and Marilyn Monroe rolled into one. Even the Christmas tree would look dingy and grim compared to her. She'd fill the whole room up with her glitz and glam, her extravagantly wrapped gifts, the undiluted coarseness that seemed so incongruous amid all the seasonal good cheer. As full as our house was with family and illegals that day, the fizzle and pop of Aunt Celia was still noticeably absent—at least for me.

And then another stab—when I thought of how, ever since we were kids, she'd regale us with the real story of Christmas, told in a deliciously sarcastic tone of false wonderment—*"Long ago, there were these blue-eyed, blond-haired, generally unwashed people frolicking around a freezing cold land called Scandinavia. These people, called pagans, would celebrate Yule to commemorate the return of the sun and the end of the darkest days of winter . . ."*—with endless interruptions from Aunt Milagros, who would work herself into a frenzy listening to the blasphemous history of how various pagan traditions merged into the "commercialized, vulgar shit show that you kiddies know and love as the Birthday of your Lord and Savior Jesus Christ." It was hands-down my favorite tradition.

Although no one spoke about that missing chunk of our Christmas celebrations, and no one tried retelling the story, to Aunt Milagros's relief, I'm sure, I knew I caught a thickness in his voice when *Papá* pointed out that there were no Christmas crackers to pull at the table. Aunt Celia had taken an unexpected shine to this lingering British tradition in our adopted country, and had brought dozens of expensive crackers to our last two Christmas lunches in Trinidad. *"What, a whole childhood watching dubbed English Christmas specials on TV and you don't expect me to love this shit? That's how neo-imperialist brainwashing works,* coño, *I can't help it!"*

So there were no Christmas crackers or paper crowns, no pagan stories, and *Mamá* took the win for Best Dressed for the first time in our family history. Even so, I don't think for a second that Aunt Celia was forgotten. I think she was so present in all our minds that we didn't need to talk about her at all.

When the singing and dancing finally came to an end at God knows what time, the professor drove Sancho's car home with Sancho catatonic in the back. Everyone else slowly filtered out after that, my father insisting that Mauricio, who was drunkenly singing a teary-eyed ballad about being a widower at Christmastime, let one of his daughters drive them home. The Manriques passed out sitting upright on the couch, mouths hanging open like soggy, spitty caves, and soon it was just me, Zulema, and my parents in the porch, sipping the very last of the rum-infused sorrel juice, laughing over the antics and anecdotes of the day. Then suddenly *Mamá* jumped up from her chair, paused to get her balance, and ran into the house.

"What's with her?" slurred Zulema.

"¿Quién sabe?" said *Papá*, giving a little burp.

I had no idea either. A moment later, *Mamá* returned holding two small wrapped boxes.

"For my princesses," she said, flushed and sweaty from all the booze. With her pink, dewy cheeks, grinning from ear to ear, she was pretty as a schoolgirl.

We'd completely forgotten to exchange gifts amid all the hangovers, hectic preparation, and drunken festivities of the day. Zulema and I were about to hastily run inside to get our parents their gifts, but *Mamá* stopped us. "*Mañana, mañana.* I just wanted to give you these now, while it's still Christmas. Can't have a Christmas go by without a little something for my *princesitas.*"

Zulema and I opened our carefully wrapped boxes. Matching gold earrings. *Mamá* always got us matching jewelry. It was the closest she could get to forcing us into identical outfits like she used to do when we were kids.

We both pulled her into a group hug and *Papá* moved behind her to enfold all three of us in his arms as best he could.

That was how we ended that Christmas Day, all knotted together, not knowing where the tail end of the year might lead, but drunkenly confident that we could all get through it so long as we had each other.

NOW OR NEVER

I was woken by my cell phone vibrating on the nightstand. I cracked an eye, grabbed the phone. One a.m. Private number. Suddenly I was wide awake.

"Hello?"

"I'm outside."

A shiver ran through me at the sound of his voice, like a drop of ice water had rolled down my spine.

I faltered for a split second, unsure of what to say, how to play coy, then thought: fuck it. After all, I'm the one who told him to stop beating around the bush. It was now or never.

"I'm coming," I said, throwing off the duvet and lowering my feet to the shock of cold tile. I didn't even bother changing out of my oversized Ted Nugent T-shirt or putting on shoes. Knowing Román was outside waiting had hit me with a thousand-volt charge, set the tips of my fingers, lips, tongue tingling. All I wanted was to get to him, give in finally.

I tiptoed out to the living room, past the Manriques on the couch. My skin prickled with anticipation. I could feel the pink rising in my cheeks, my lips reddening, every sense heightened.

Hand on the doorknob, I was about to slip out the front door when a loud grunt stopped me dead. I swiveled my head around. It hadn't come

117

from the Manriques. They were perfectly still in their upright sleeping positions. And then I realized the porch doors were flung open. Through them, I saw my parents entwined around each other in the hammock, my mother's head on my father's chest. Another grunt from *Papá*, sliding into his usual thunderous drone of a snore. *Mamá*, who'd definitely been drunk off her ass to fall asleep in the hammock, didn't even flinch at the sound. Her face was soft, gentle for once in sleep.

Guilt, the party-pooping wet blanket that it is, cloaked itself over me. I let go of the doorknob. How could I sneak out to see Román when he was the threat hanging over my parents? I looked at them in that hammock and just couldn't do it. I let go of the doorknob and went back to my room, determined. Whatever was brewing between Román and me had to end.

I shut the bedroom door, leaned against it, closed my eyes. Tried not to think of him out there, waiting. An eternal minute passed. My feet twitched, every inch of my Román-charged skin urging me to turn and run out the door.

The phone vibrated again in my hand. I stared at it. Private number. I threw it on my bed, counting each time it buzzed. If I could make it through ignoring this call, I'd be okay. I'd have walked through the Valley of the Shadow of Lust and have come out the other side, guiltless, loyal to my family.

Finally the buzzing stopped. I slumped forward, resting my hands on my knees. I'd done it.

I pictured him frowning at the phone, confused. Putting the Jeep into gear, pulling away from the house, and never coming back except to deposit illegals. No more steamy bedroom rendezvous or surprise Savannah appearances. I'd never get a chance to discover any other faint or hidden scars, would never taste his mouth again, feel his hands gripping my waist, his body pressed into mine.

That was what broke me.

Never let anyone tell you that lust isn't the most potent of human motivators—or the most destructive.

Like a shot I was out of the bedroom and out the front door, praying he'd still be there.

And he was.

———————

"You took your time. And I see seventies rock T-shirts are a uniform of yours?"

I was in the passenger seat, Román's eyes running over me slow, muddling my senses so I felt hot and cold all at once, wanting to shiver while heat rose up like some serpentine, hungry thing from the pit of my stomach.

"I can't stay," I said, trying to convince myself that I really wasn't going to.

He gave a lopsided smile. "I wasn't planning on us staying." He shifted the Jeep into gear, but I put my hand on his, felt his knuckles broad and hard gripping the gearstick.

"No, I mean I can't stay out with you. I can't—I shouldn't do this. My family . . ."

He paused, wet his lips with the tip of his tongue, and exhaled, then shifted back into park and looked at me. Everything in me was dissolving with that look—my guilt, my resolve, everything but the need for him. He leaned in to me. My lips parted, mouth lifted up toward him, eyes fluttering shut. But he brought his mouth to my clavicle, bare where the T-shirt had slipped off my shoulder, and made his way slowly upward as my neck curved itself like a bough, pliant as the warmth of his mouth moved along my skin.

He could've done anything to me right then. I was all his. But he pulled back and grazed his thumb over my lip again—his custom now. "Your fucking mouth," he murmured, looking at it. If I didn't get out of the Jeep right then, that second, that would be it. I bit my lower lip where he'd touched it.

"I'm going back in. You know why I can't . . ."

"I know, *flaca*. Let me know when you can."

119

FIREWORKS

The Manriques left us during that limbo time between Christmas and New Year's. It should come as no surprise that we were glad to see the back of them. The day they left, *Papá* dumped all the Greek yogurt and granola in the garbage, like he was purging the house of any remnant of the Manriques' spirits.

New Year's came and went. In January, three batches of illegals came for a week apiece. Just your run-of-the-mill escapees—a mix of fleeing intellectuals, political refugees, impoverished asylum seekers, and a smattering of adventurers just looking for a new start. No one won us over like Javier and the Jotas, but no one repulsed us as much as the Manriques. The novelty was gone and it was all very humdrum. No choice but to suck it up and deal with the pain in the ass of having illegals wandering our home, rifling our fridge, and forcing us to cut corners however we could just so we could feed everyone—basic cable, no more air-conditioning except on the most unbearably humid nights, a backyard clothesline in lieu of the dryer, the introduction of "Meatless Mondays," "Canned Tuna Tuesdays," and myriad culinary reincarnations of corned beef.

When each new batch of illegals was dropped off, always in the daytime when I was the only one home, I never gave in to the urge to look out the doorway or peek between the kitchen curtains to see if the Jeep was there. Still, it was near impossible not to care that Román was never waiting for me in my room, even if he was only respecting my wishes. No matter how much I told myself that I'd made the right decision on Christmas night, the zing of anxiety would still hit me when I heard his three knocks on the front door, and I'd force myself to smother the intractable impulse prodding me to whip the door open and declare with husky Jessica Rabbit allure that I was ready to abandon my scruples and throw sexual prudence to the wind.

The salt in the wound was that through it all, I couldn't talk to Aunt Celia. Though she'd been dead for months, I realized then how much she'd been My Person. I'd confided in her, turned to her for every heartbreak, every romantic triumph. I found myself looking at her number in my cell phone. Just looking at it, letting the grief cut into me like I was slowly pressing the edge of a razor blade into my skin. In those moments I understood that just because you know someone's gone for good, it doesn't mean you stop needing them. The urge to call Aunt Celia would always be there, flaring up in times of need like emotional herpes.

The only cure for all of it was to keep busy. So I braved a few more trips to Buzz Bar with Zulema's spa crew and my gym buddies, made out with cute strangers for something to do, closed my eyes and pretended their eager, sloppy mouths were Román's—but it always felt like riding in a go-kart after driving a Lamborghini.

Mostly, I wrote like a motherfucker. The novel pages poured out of me, every character rapidly becoming more lovesick and horny and desperate than the last. I'd delete half the garbage I wrote the next day, but the catharsis of it was addictive. I even gave myself the added distraction of translating a few of my short stories into English, then sent them around to some competitions and journals.

The one saving grace that helped cement my resolve not to see

Román again was the fact that my family hated his guts. They bitched about him constantly, blamed him for everything: it was his name I heard when Zulema bemoaned the loss of her bathroom grooming time, when my parents could barely afford the sky-high grocery bills, when Sancho got a cockroach infestation because of two illegal kids dropping food between his couch cushions. And when Román broke Mauricio's right thumb after Mauricio pummeled an illegal caught stealing one of the twins' panties off the clothesline, the entire family started referring to Román as Beelzebub. It was the only salve I had, and even that didn't help much. Incredible—I barely even knew Román, but still I couldn't swallow good old logic. I'd listened to my conscience instead of my crotch—I should've felt strong, like I was a WO-MAN refusing to give in to the carnivorous wiles of a Bad Boy. Instead I was tangled up in a mess of regret. I didn't know what the hell was wrong with me.

Anyway, at least my distraction strategy of writing and translating at a manic pace worked. Worked so well, in fact, that a story I translated (on an especially remorse-tainted afternoon when I'd let myself peek through the kitchen window as Román made his way down our walkway back to the Jeep) actually got accepted into the *Paris Review*. Maybe the secret to artistic success really does lie in emotional torment.

———

In case you're not in the know, the *Paris Review* is kind of a momentously huge fucking deal. How that story of mine made it in there I have no clue—maybe Celia was up there with fluffy wings and a halo, wielding some kind of angel magic, I don't know. Seeing that congratulatory acceptance email was just what I needed to pull me out of my slump.

After telling my family the news of this literary coup (to which Zulema, Sancho, and my mother responded: "You write?" and which led *Mamá* to sulk over my "secretive disposition" for an entire afternoon), I took them all out for a fancy dinner to celebrate. We'd just gotten back home, and I was effervescent as the champagne bubbles in my bloodstream. The night had been a good one, everyone in that especially light mood we all felt during illegal-free spells when we could pretend life was normal again, when we had a little extra cash in hand. Looking forward to re-reading the *Paris Review* email for the fiftieth time, I wafted into my room, kicked off my heels, and was in the middle of peeling my dress off when I saw it.

Smack in the center of the bed: a single white anthurium.

I stared at it for a long moment, like it was a stick of dynamite rather than a flower, before picking it up by its long stem, admiring the single enormous petal. I sat heavily on the bed, the flower across my lap.

Román knew about the *Paris Review.* And with just that flower, all my concrete resolve turned to dust.

I had no way of contacting Román other than when he dropped off illegals, but the way Ugly's business was apparently thriving, I didn't have long to wait. A couple days after the anthurium's appearance, I heard the three knocks. I flew to the front door but wasn't quick enough to catch Román. There was just a twenty-something guy on the doorstep with a duffel bag over his shoulder. He tried telling me hello, but I blew past him, seeing the back of the Jeep pulling away from the curb on the opposite side of the road. I ran barefoot across the scorching asphalt until Román thankfully glimpsed me in the wing mirror and hit the brakes half a block from my house. When I got to the lowered driver's window, he watched me evenly from behind his sunglasses, his expression indecipherable as always. I was hopping from foot to foot, the balls of my feet raw on the sun-baked road.

"Thank you," I said, gripping the edge of the window, "for the flower."

"Don't ever risk talking to me out here in the open like this," he said tersely.

My hands fell away from the window. "Oh," I said, embarrassed at his dry response in the face of my girlish, barefooted gratitude. "I'm sorry, I just wanted to say thanks, and—but you're right, obviously. Sorry."

I turned to walk back to the house, but heard Román exhale hard. "Fuck it," he said. I looked back as he shot his arm out the window to grip my wrist, pulling me back to the Jeep.

Instantly that familiar heat unfurled in me, the blood in my arteries, veins, capillaries pulsing harder and hotter. I watched his lips part, splitting the gossamer-fine scar. He hesitated before speaking, exhaling again, as though uncertain of what he was about to say.

"Meet me outside. Two a.m.," he said finally.

I knew whatever I replied would be the fulcrum that would irrevocably pivot our relationship in one direction or the other. If I said no, he wouldn't try seeing me again. Román wasn't the desperate type to chase a girl after two rejections. If I agreed, I had no idea what would happen next. Nothing but trouble, most likely.

But I already knew I couldn't keep that exigent longing coiled up and contained in me any longer. I had to let it unspool itself, and I'd follow the thread wherever it took me.

"See you at two."

On my doorstep, wondering for the hundredth time if I'd completely lost my mind as I waited for the Jeep to appear. The night was dead quiet except for the croaking and creeping of nocturnal animals. The ambient sounds of my street—padlocks clicking shut, deadbolts being drawn, twanging foreign accents on blue-lit screens—had long faded away, but I couldn't help scanning my neighbors' houses to see if anyone was watching me. We lived on a safe street in a decent Port of Spain suburb, knowing we'd have to stay away from the shithole areas if we didn't want National Security to scoop us up like guppies in a fishnet alongside all the other illegals, but still there wasn't a single house that wasn't walled in by at least five feet of concrete, painted in bubblegum Caribbean hues that belied the pulsing fear all Trinis carry with them of "goontas," "gunmen," "grimers," "bad-johns," "Bad Man." As many words for criminals as Eskimos have for snow. Since living here, I'd forgotten what a window looked like without a grille of burglarproofing. And the fear had lodged itself in me too. Standing outside the padlocked, burglarproofed comfort of my own home, minutes away from two in the morning, every sense was keenly awake, listening not just for Román but for anything that might be lurking in the purple-black of the Trinidadian night.

At exactly two, the Jeep turned the corner. Up to that moment, I wasn't sure I could do it—the betrayal. But seeing him through the tinted glass, knowing what would come next, I was overwhelmed by the need that had been stewing, brewing, boiling in me for so long. The second the Jeep was in front of me, I pulled the driver's door open and climbed in, hungry to erase the space between us, smell his skin, taste him. Straddling him, I jammed my mouth against his so hard our teeth knocked, thrust my fingers in his hair, let his arms wrap around my waist to crush me into him, my knees banging into the hand brake and the gearshift and obscure car parts I couldn't name. His hands slid down my body, our hips ground into each other, fingertips dug into my skin through the sheer cotton of my camisole. There could've been a hundred hands on me. My body was one exposed pleasure-filled nerve, all my senses addled—I could smell his body temperature rising, taste his pulse as it quickened, touch his breath with the tip of my tongue, see the hot blood coursing through his body. We were in a world of billions of people but entirely alone, held in the snow globe of that Jeep, that quiet street.

When our lips came apart, we stared at each other, panting for a long moment before breaking into peals of laughter.

"Someone's happy to see me," he laughed.

I nodded and slumped against him, flopped my head onto his shoulder.

"So," I said, "where to?"

"I thought getting into the *Paris Review* called for fireworks."

I didn't bother asking how he'd found out about the *Paris Review*.

By now I knew Román was good at his job. I didn't ask where we were going either—just eased into my irresponsible decision, like the moment right after swallowing a Molly when you know there's no point fighting it now. Just go with it and let the chemicals run through your bloodstream, pump your neurons full of glitter and the warm-and-fuzzies until the inevitable bitter comedown.

We drove along deserted streets until we finally hit the winding North Coast Road, etched into a hillside several hundred feet above sea level. As we cruised along through mist tart with salt, I looked out over the cliff drops to our left, onto the never-ending black ocean smeared white with moonlight. To our right, the verdurous savagery of raw rainforest spilled onto the road: Jurassic ferns and balisier leaves, tangles of creepers and lianas, tall thickets of arched bamboo. All silent observers.

We traveled through sleeping villages, past tranquil bays and overturned fishing boats discarded on the sand, along roads flanked by trees crowned with dense yellow flowers. The quietly beautiful landscape had a soporific effect, lulling us into a comfortable silence as we drove, Román's hand firm on my bare thigh until he veered sharply onto a dirt track, startling my senses awake again. I braced myself against the seat as we bobbled along the potholed dirt to a small clearing where Román parked and switched off the headlights. Instantly we were swallowed up by darkness.

I heard his door open, saw the white beam of a flashlight as he pointed it to the ground. He came around to my side and took my hand, guiding me through the disorienting bush until the underbrush cleared and the ground began sloping downward, the air growing suddenly cooler, almost chilly. In the near distance: the sound of water plunging into water. Where the slant steepened, I slipped on moist leaves. Román's arm swooped behind me, a steadying bough. I brought myself upright and we moved farther downhill. In his other hand he held a machete, was using the flat side of the blade to push aside the leaves crisscrossing in front of us. I liked that he didn't hack them apart to clear a path. For all his proven violence, it said something that he used the machete how he did.

And then we were at the edge of the tree line looking onto a deep natural lagoon, glossy with the moon's reflection. A small waterfall gushed into the rippling water from high above, backed by raw rock face. It was beautiful. But that wasn't what he'd brought me to see.

All around us and above the pool, the air shifted with flashing sparks of light. Hundreds of fireflies winking in the dark. A soft, silent firework display, a sheet of lightning shattered into a million scintillating splinters.

"*Increíble*," I breathed.

Román turned to me so we were facing one another, and then pulled me against him. I looked up. Fireflies, like starry snow flurries, floated around him, and again I felt like there was no one but us in the world.

"Thank you," I said, "for showing me this."

"It's nothing."

We followed the edge of the pool to a cluster of rocks, damp from the light waterfall spray, climbed atop the largest rock, and sat side by side. And we talked. Román was cagey about how he'd ended up working for Ugly, but we talked about other things. For starters, I wanted to know how a guy from Ugly's underworld happened to have an affinity for literature. It still baffled me that he'd bothered to read my work at all, even with his supposed explanation about getting to know his "subjects" from the inside out.

"Listen," he said, prickling slightly. "I grew up rough in Caracas. No TV, no cash for the cinema. I could probably build the Tower of Babel out of all the library books I stole."

"So that's it? Books were easily accessible entertainment?"

"I always liked reading and yeah, books were more accessible to someone with no money and my natural . . . skill set." He laughed and I was relieved that his tone had lightened. "Frankly, I'm a little offended that you think I'm too ignorant to pick up a book."

"You just don't think of someone who strangles people and breaks people's fingers as much of a reader. No offense."

"What I do for a living has nothing to do with who I am."

"Doesn't it have *everything* to do with who you are?"

He'd been leaning back on his elbows on the rock but now straightened up. He looked more pensive than irked by my needling. "Sometimes people have limited choices. Ugly presented me with an opportunity to get out of a life that gave me *no* choices. You should know a thing or two about that yourself. You're a criminal too, you know, living and working here illegally. We all have to make choices we wish we didn't have to, and we can only hope we won't be judged too harshly for it. You had to make a choice to get out of Caracas. Now you're a criminal, whether you want to see it that way or not, and I'm sure you wouldn't want anyone thinking you were some Vene stripper here to seduce a rich Trini, or that you didn't have the ability to be an author just because the choice you felt compelled to make turned you into a criminal."

He was right. And far more eloquent than I'd expected.

The conversation ran on seamlessly. We talked about Venezuela's fall from grace, about living on an island we'd once seen as an inconsequential blip compared to the colossus of Venezuela, but where our people were now automatically pegged as a substratum of society suited solely to menial jobs and/or the sex trade, about the caustic irony of being treated this way in a country whose nationals were subject to even worse prejudices when they managed to claw their way through the immigration labyrinth to live in North America and the UK. We talked about the scars on his arms, which turned out to be relics of a rough upbringing and casual teenage street fights, not gang kingpin–inflicted war wounds like I'd imagined. And we talked about what he'd thought when he'd read my short-listed stories online.

"I re-read all of them at least twice," he said. "That's what kept pulling me to you. I wouldn't have risked it if it was just physical. Sex isn't worth getting on the wrong side of Ugly."

I elbowed him lightly. "So this is just platonic? You want to pick my big literary brain and that's all?"

"Let's not get carried away." A smile played on his lips. "Unless of course that's what you want. A nice platonic friendship."

"Hmm . . . I do need more friends."

He cupped my face, watching me intently. "So you want me to be your friend then?" His hands slid downward, fingertips trailing along my neck to my shoulders, pushing down the straps of my camisole. My pores were puckered with the chill of the waterfall spray, the thrill of feeling his hands on me, my chest rising and falling like a panicked bird's. But I was far from panicked.

"Sure," I said, standing, pulling the camisole over my head and stepping out of my shorts. "I'll be the best friend you've ever had."

We fucked slow and hard on that rock. And by the time it was over and we were catching our breath under the shifting stars of the fireflies, I knew that we were both in deep.

BITING INTO THE SUGARCANE

After that first time, Román and I didn't need to say anything aloud to know we'd be doing it all over again. And soon.

Two nights later, he called, and I was there on the front step again at two a.m., waiting. This time he took me to a hilltop where, after a short uphill climb, we came to a small plateau with a three-sixty view of ocean. Sparse village lights speckled the dark hills sloping down below us to the sea, endless and opaquely black, edged with white froth where it collided with the island. We stood looking out over it, considering the possibility of the sea and everything it could hold. Like with the first time, and like with nearly every other time to come, it felt as though we were communing with nature, drawing on its energy to feed the primordial way we couldn't help but take each other. That second time was even rougher and more carnal than the first, and it would always be that way with us. The softness, the gentle touches, the affection, those things came before and then after, never during. Simple skin-to-skin friction was never enough. Every sense had to be sated with a kind of urgency I'd never felt before. We licked, bit, clawed, grabbed, took one another savagely until we were completely enervated.

Laughing with Román afterward as we took stock of our respective grass burns, knee scrapes, the splinters that had dug into us, the stinging nettle we hadn't noticed rubbing us raw, I already knew this wasn't just some guy I was fucking. I'm not saying he was The One. But he was Something. Something more than the Ben Browns of the world.

We dressed and lay back on the crabgrass, temples touching, and like we'd done two nights before, we talked until it was nearly dawn, sharing our deepest fears . . .

"Dying before I publish a novel."

"Having to kill someone."

(I was relieved he hadn't already.)

Talking about our best childhood memories . . .

"Listening to Aunt Celia's ghost stories."

"Getting stoned with the other *barrio* kids."

And our worst . . .

"When no one turned up to my *quinceañera*."

"When my father left and my mother died."

As that night's conversation proved, and the conversation three nights later, then a week later, and on and on as our need for each other became increasingly insatiable and we saw each other with reckless regularity, Román and I were from different worlds, like Lady and the Tramp, crossing the divide thanks largely to our mutual lust and a shared love of books.

Román had read everything. He said it was how his English had gotten so good. Growing up, he'd pillaged the English and American lit sections of the National Library in Caracas. He knew everything written by García Márquez inside and out. Borges, Lorca, Allende, Ionesco—they were Román's old friends. And he didn't only read fiction. He knew all about the Spanish Civil War, about the Pinochet dictatorship, the Cuban Revolution, about Trujillo, Bolívar, Guevara, Castro, Zapata. I learned to hide my shock at how well read he was, at his effortless quoting of American, British, and even Trinidadian authors.

One night a few weeks into sleeping together, we were squeezed into the back of the Jeep sharing a joint. He'd exhaled and said, oh so breezily: "The free soul is rare, but you know it when you see it—basically because you feel good, very good, when you are near or with them."

I'd inhaled, held the smoke, coughed. "What?"

"Bukowski. You know him? An American poet. That line made me think of you."

Hardly what you'd expect of the guy who broke Mauricio's thumb without batting an eye. But that's the human animal for you—full of surprises.

No matter how in-depth or expansive our conversations, though, he avoided sharing the precise details of how he'd gotten involved with Ugly. "I had the skills Ugly needed and I was backed into a corner. I had no other options to get out." That was the most he ever said about it, and as one month of us sleeping together rolled into two, I learned to stop prying. At least I knew he wasn't a murderer and that he didn't enjoy what he did for a living, even if he happened to be gifted at it.

It was all blissfully addictive. The danger of it, the anticipation, the thrill of fucking him that never seemed to wane. I was sucking the sweetness straight from the sugarcane of life, just like Aunt Celia had instructed, and my teeth could rot and fall out of my skull because of all that sugar and I wouldn't care.

That said, I still couldn't ignore my guilt. It was always there, an acrid, unrelenting nasal drip that left an especially bitter aftertaste whenever I heard my parents venting about "Beelzebub." I turned, of course, to Aunt Celia to quell my guilt, because here's something you didn't know, and that I didn't know either until reading the memoir: Aunt Celia had married Mauricio knowing that he was a full-fledged criminal. Yup—*Mauricio*. And the whole damned family had known about it from the get-go, including my parents. So to justify my own wildly irresponsible relationship with Román, I kept sliding down the time tunnel to 1984, the year Mauricio had picked up Aunt Celia in that Miami nightclub and rocked her world with the finest booze, blow, and bourgeois lifestyle money could buy, while Aunt Celia lapped it all up and worked her womanly magic to get herself the trophy wife status she'd always aspired to. The year she married a criminal and no one in the family did a thing to stop it.

First thing I do after slipping on the pink diamond (three carats, thank you very much) is tell my parents there's going to be a flashy Miami wedding. No parochial backyard nuptials for this bride. I tell them we'll be flying the whole family up to the States for the occasion, taking everyone shopping for new suits and dresses—all on Mauricio. And my gown! Hoop skirts, beadwork, lace, corsets!

In this hubbub of sex, drugs, and wedding planning, no one, not even my *abuelo*, thought to ask what the groom did for a living. All anyone could think about was packing their bags for the big trip to the almighty USA. Even Celia didn't quite know what Mauricio did for work. When it had come up on the first or second date, he'd just said he was a businessman.

"*What kind of business?*"

"*The lucrative kind.*"

And the platter of lobsters or caviar or the bottle of vintage champagne, or whatever the hell it was, had been served and distracted them, and the whole question of Mauricio's livelihood was skated over. Until, three days before the entire Palacios family was scheduled to jump on a plane to Miami, two men snatched Celia in a mall parking lot, in the middle of the day, like it was nothing at all to grab a woman and toss her in your trunk. Which is what they did. Celia was taken to a warehouse where they unceremoniously burned her forearms with cigarettes and broke her wrist before taking her back to her car at the mall with one simple message for her husband-to-be: get the *fuck* out of Miami.

As I'd learned with absolute disbelief on my first reading, Mauricio had in fact been a smuggler back in 1984. A smuggler of drugs? Nope.

A smuggler of trafficked humans? Wrong again. He was a *honey* smuggler. Apparently raw honey was one of the hottest commodities on the international black market. Molasses-infused pseudo-honey being de rigueur in Miami food stores at the time, there was sky-high demand for the real deal. So Mauricio was part of a very small but very lucrative honey-smuggling operation bringing in high-quality honey from an apiary in Turkey, then selling tiny jars of the liquid gold for hundreds of US dollars to an exclusive Miami-based clientele. Of course they could've just set up a legitimate honey importation business, but apparently all the paperwork and regulatory hassle wasn't worth it. It was easier and more cost-effective to just smuggle the stuff in.

Frankly, I'd never heard anything more ridiculous, and although it was disturbing to know that Aunt Celia had been briefly kidnapped and even had her wrist broken by Mauricio's enemies, the fact that it was all because of illegal honeypots was, well, ludicrous.

My opinions aside, the fact was: Mauricio and his blushing bride were in danger, and they had to get the fuck out of Miami, just like they'd been ordered to do. The wedding was canceled, the gigantic dress was stuffed into a suitcase, and Mauricio and Celia skedaddled back to my grandparents' rambling old house in rural Venezuela. The day after they returned, the rest of the Palacios left, as scheduled, on their trip. After all, flights had already been booked and no one had told *them* to get the fuck out of Miami.

When that freeloading family of mine gets back to Venezuela from their holiday, they force Mauricio and me up the aisle of that dinky shack they call a church, where I'd already had to suffer through the sacraments of baptism, First Communion, and Confirmation. If I could've choked on the wafer when the priest stuck it on my tongue, just to put myself out of the excruciating fucking humiliation of it all, I would've. The reception is in my parents' backyard, under crepe-paper wreaths crafted by the industrious spinster hands of Milagros, a dismal quarter moon shining down on the cast still on my wrist.

So even after Mauricio's smuggler rivals had tortured Aunt Celia and ruined their wedding plans, she still went ahead and married the guy. And what really gave me hope: the whole Palacios family had accepted Mauricio, even knowing what had gone down.

After re-reading that chapter for the umpteenth time on a particularly guilt-ridden evening, I decided to sound my father out. How flexible would he be if Zulema or I were hooking up with a criminal?

He was standing over the stove, frying ye old corned beef with onions and diced tomatoes, when I brought up Aunt Celia's wedding and the circumstances surrounding it. I took it as a good sign that he was in stitches by the time I'd finished recapping her version of events.

"We couldn't believe it when Celia called to say the fancy Miami wedding was off." He wiped his eyes, gasping with laughter. "And that they had to leave the country because of rival honey dealers. I mean, *really*?

"She was so smug when she got engaged," he continued. "She must've called your Aunt Milagros once the entire time she was in Miami, then the second she got that ring, she called every *day* to gloat about her wedding plans. But, man, did Milagros enjoy that Miami vacation when the wedding was called off. I don't think I've ever seen her smile so much—from ear to ear."

"So what happened to Mauricio? How'd he turn out so . . . you know, like he is now, if he was such a *jefe*?"

Papá shrugged. "Even honey smugglers burn out, I guess."

I decided to put a feeler out. "Didn't it upset everyone that he was a criminal, though? The whole honey thing was stupid, but it was still illegal. Aunt Celia still got hurt because of it."

"The thing is," said *Papá*, nudging the sizzling corned beef with the spatula, "Mauricio is a good guy. He used to have so much more spunk. When we met him, it was all kind of *glamorous* to be honest, because *he* was so glamorous. No one really cared about the honey thing . . . I guess because it was so absurd."

He prodded the corned beef thoughtfully. "I think Celia just sucked the life out of him. I know you two were close, but Celia was a difficult woman. Hardly anyone could tolerate her except when she was on form with her storytelling and her jokes. Trust me, you don't know the half of what she put that man through when they got divorced."

"I got a pretty graphic idea from the memoir. But to be honest, Mauricio deserved it. She wrote about him cheating a lot."

"Mauricio had his indiscretions, you're right. But he was always in love with Celia. That never changed."

I raised a disbelieving eyebrow. "So why'd he have those 'indiscretions' if he was oh so in love?"

Papá patted my head like he used to when I was little. "*Amor*, the sooner you learn just how stupid human beings are, the better. Ever since old Freud came around, people like to think everyone has some deep-seated reason behind what they do, but the truth is, sometimes temptations crop up and people make stupid decisions. That's all there is to it. And that's all there was to Mauricio's screwups."

"So if I started seeing someone who was a criminal like Mauricio, would that same truth apply? Sometimes people just make stupid decisions?"

Fat hissed and spat in the frying pan. My father narrowed his eyes at me. "Why would you ask that?"

"No reason," I said airily. "Just asking for conversation's sake." But I couldn't meet his eyes.

Papá turned to face me squarely. I pretended to inspect my nails.

"You sure? No reason at all?" he asked.

"Yes, relax! It was just a hypothetical question."

I left that conversation more anxious than ever about what would happen if Román and I were found out. But I still held on to that teensy shard of hope—Papá knew that sometimes people did stupid things just because they couldn't say no to temptation. If there was ever a shoe that fit when it came to my choices with Román, that was it.

And then there was the other thing that gave me hope: honey smuggling was only the first of Mauricio's criminal endeavors. The manuscript revealed that the family turned a blind eye when Mauricio proved himself incapable of making a buck without the thrill of possible incarceration nipping at his heels. He was a born career criminal—not just for novelty honey crime either—and it all came to light in 1985.

Having only worked as a mediocre catalogue model in Panama City and then as a cocktail waitress in Miami, Celia's job options were limited. Mauricio was even less employable, his skill set centering entirely on honey smuggling. So Celia and Mauricio were living in Celia's childhood bedroom, much to Milagros's annoyance (she'd enjoyed being the only golden egg still under her parents' roof), and had to do chores around the house in lieu of paying *Abuelo* rent. It was a humiliating arrangement, especially for Mauricio, who had lost his red sports car, his chrome-and-glass Miami penthouse, and all the other luxuries of his honey gangster life, driving him into a slump of self-pity.

This cabrón *husband of mine. What the hell did I even marry him for? I should've kept my ass in Miami and made my own money instead of letting him sweep me off my feet. Now all he does is sleep all day, listen to sports on the radio, and harass me to bring his meals to the room because he can't even strap on a pair of balls big enough to face up to my parents.* Qué pendejo. *Only leaves that room once a week when I drag his ass out to do the chores my father asked him to do. Then he goes straight back to bed.*

What am I supposed to do with a dud like this? I'm twenty-one! I want to live, I want money and freedom and not to have to hear Milagros preaching about her goddamned Salvation Army work, like she's some martyr we should all be lighting candles to at night. So I take matters into my own hands, make a list of my and Mauricio's strong points: I'm resourceful, know how to write, can mix a mean cocktail, have a great ass. Mauricio: good with logistics, organized, well acquainted with the workings of the criminal underworld, great hair. I scrape together a list of more than twenty ideal jobs we could get ourselves—anything to get the fuck out of my parents' house. And when I re-read the list, I actually get excited that we're gonna get out of here. We can really do this if Mauricio would just get his shit together. I practically skip to that dank, depressing bedroom, the drapes always closed, the damn sports radio always droning in the background like a buzzing horsefly. Mauricio's in bed, como siempre. *I hand him the list—come, on, Mauricio, get excited about something again, get your ass out of bed for the love of Christ—but he crumples up the list and tosses it on the floor. I smack the motherfucker on the back of the head. I've started doing that a lot. Only way to get the anger out.*

"You don't like my ideas?"

Mauricio digs out a toothpick from somewhere beneath the sheet and cleans between his bottom teeth.

"I don't want to deliver letters just because you say I'm good at logistics. I'm not a damn mailman. Your ideas were stupid."

"¡Vete a la mierda!" I yell, kicking the bed because if I don't kick that then I'm gonna kick him. "A mailman is a knight in shining armor compared to you! You can't keep lazing around in bed all goddamned day like a puto koala bear!"

He stops picking his teeth, intrigued. "Why a koala?"

I can't help it. I smack the back of his head again. "They sleep twenty hours a day! You think I want to be married to a koala de la gran puta? *You think when this baby comes you can just feed it eucalyptus leaves?"*

"What baby!"

Hold your horses. That wasn't how Celia told Mauricio she was pregnant, because she wasn't. She wouldn't be pregnant with Ava for another eleven years thanks to Mauricio's low sperm count and occasional erectile dysfunction, a side effect of the coke he snorted "recreationally" until the early nineties. However, Celia knew that what Mauricio needed was a good kick up the ass to get him back to being the slick, flashy honey smuggler she'd fallen in love with.

It was the right move.

Mauricio threw his sheet off and leapt, *leapt*, out of the bed to swing Celia around in his arms. He was thrilled at the prospect of becoming a father. His spark was officially back.

Celia waited five weeks to tell Mauricio that she'd miscarried the imaginary baby. By then, he'd already set up his new business: breeding Orinoco crocodiles for the leather trade. Illegally, of course. Because that was the only way of doing business that gave Mauricio an entrepreneurial hard-on.

More on the illicit croc business later. Point was, the family knew all about Mauricio's new criminal venture, and no one made Celia leave him. So why couldn't my family accept Román and me being together too? Enforcing Ugly's blackmail wasn't all that bad. There were worse crimes a prospective boyfriend could commit.

(You know what they say—never underestimate the power of denial.)

LONG LIVE THE KING

E arly March. Nearly three months into our safe-housing sentence. The hedonistic decadence of the Carnival season was finally over— two unimaginably unproductive months strung together by nothing but glamorous fêtes, glittering masqueraders, moko jumbies stalking the streets on twenty-foot stilts, Blue Devils leering, mud-covered percussionists wielding bottles and spoons, steel orchestras beating their pans day and night in a musical orgy that sends rhythm reverberating right down into the bedrock of the island until it all culminates in the bacchanalia of Carnival Monday and Tuesday.

If it sounds like it'd flip you head over heels to be living amidst all of it, you'd be right. But at last the frenzy was over—at least for the island, if not for our houses crammed full of people. We were bang in the middle of Lent now, with sky-high fish prices and everyone gloating about how they'd given up chocolate, parading their diets as a Lenten sacrifice. And as the Season of Self-Righteous Waistline-Trimming crescendoed into the ever-climactic Easter Sunday, we were sailing along an unrelenting tide of illegals. Or rather—we were bucking and pitching over the tumultuous, shark-filled waters of our illegals, a deluge that had been steadily drowning us since long before Ash Wednesday.

For starters, there were the practical strains of higher utility bills and more mouths to feed that had forced us all to pick up the financial slack however we could. *Papá* was working between school pickups and on weekends now, using his minivan as an unregistered taxi. It was the kind of work he'd specifically wanted to avoid, knowing that the wrong kind of passenger could spell disaster for all of us, a passenger who might see him for the vulnerable illegal he was and take advantage of that. "Pulling bull," as the locals called taxi driving, also took him to parts of the island where he'd never normally venture: East Port of Spain and its ganglands, divided with invisible borders that, if crossed under the wrong circumstances, could leave you with a bullet in the head or worse. Yes—*worse*. *Mamá* had extended her working hours to a solid fourteen hours a day, with Zulema coming straight home from the Color Me Beautiful spa to help her. They were exhausted, their fingers and forearms aching with carpal tunnel from grooming other people all day into the night. As for me, I'd almost tripled my intake of translation projects, my days running nearly as long as *Mamá*'s and Zulema's as I scrambled to meet tight deadline after tight deadline. My novel, yet again, was shoved aside for lack of time and creative energy. It felt like running on a treadmill with the setting on max, gripping the arm rails and trying your best to keep up the pace so you wouldn't fall flat on your face.

Then there were the more human vexations that came with hosting so many illegals—strange men you felt uneasy around, people who'd finger our belongings like they were working out what prices they might fetch, bitches with attitude, lazy fuckers who thought they were at Ugly's Relocation Resort and came with expectations almost as high as the Manriques'. Worst of all was the complete loss of privacy—sharing the bathroom, the TV, the kitchen, having to be fully dressed and bra-clad at all times so you wouldn't catch some illegal lustily eyeing the outline of your nipples. The walls of the house seemed to bulge and throb with all the tense energy the illegal influx had brought. And all that got me through was Román. He was the paradoxical cure and cause of all my chagrin, the only thing that could ease my constant irritation at living in the halfway house he was imposing on us. It wasn't just the nights we spent together that served as an escape, both physical and mental, giving me the release of sex and good conversation, but smaller things that seemed to fill me with a burst of helium, allowing me to briefly but blissfully float up and away from my overcrowded house. Like when one afternoon, after giving a family of six our standard welcome speech and a stack of Jamaican patties, I was already seething at the two eldest children, teenage boys who'd asked between mouthfuls if there wasn't going to be "any proper fucking food" for them to eat after the patties. I'd told them no, there fucking wasn't because this wasn't a fucking hotel, which had earned me ample stink-eye from the parents, but when I locked myself in my room afterward, hoping to cool my temper enough to get back to the translation I'd been doing, I found a collection of short stories by Charles Bukowski on my desk. A page in it was dog-eared. I opened it to the page and read the line Román had said reminded him of me: "The free soul is rare, but you know it when you see it. . . ." And then the puerile disrespect of the teen brothers suddenly seemed funnier, fodder for a good anecdote I'd roll my eyes over when I saw Román next. Just the promise of seeing him was enough to get me through each day.

A week or so later, I got a call from him on the usual blocked number. It was around eleven at night.

"Hey," I said, knowing it was him. "The usual?" It was our code for fixing the usual two a.m. pickup time before heading to another of Román's seemingly never-ending lineup of isolated spots, all discovered in response to his city boy's hunger for nature that had led him to explore every cranny of his adopted island.

"I can't tonight," he said.

I frowned, confused. We never spoke on the phone, for safety reasons, even though he only used burner phones. He would only call to confirm "the usual," and we'd have our conversations face-to-face after expunging the invariable sexual craving that had mushroomed in us during whatever short time had elapsed since our last night together.

"Is everything okay then?" I asked.

"I just wanted you to know that I wish I *could* see you tonight."

"I wish I could see you too."

He was silent then and I felt that he was smiling into the phone.

"I'll call when I can meet," he said. "Maybe night after tomorrow."

"Sure."

That less-than-a-minute-long conversation had sustained my good mood for a solid two days after, even when an illegal decided to give herself a Brazilian in our bathroom, leaving the floor, toilet rim, and somehow even the sink dusted with shorn bristly pubes that she inexplicably felt no compulsion to clean up.

As for the rest of the family, I had no clue what their coping mechanisms were as we endured that steady flood of illegals. Sure there were some illegals who broke your heart and made you swell with unwarranted pride that you were able to help them in their time of need, but for the most part, I found myself increasingly thinking of how accurate Sartre's observation had been: hell really is other people.

Nevertheless, we slowly, inevitably became inured. To the clashing personalities, the shady characters, the disrespect, the nonexistent privacy, the enervating work routines. We even grew habituated to the most harrowing stories of destitution and deprivation, of abuse by the military and the *guardia*, the insinuations but never outright admissions of torture by the most haunted-looking illegals who landed up at our door. It took a lot to shock us now.

Or so we thought.

As we discovered on Easter Sunday, when everyone had congregated at our house for another of *Papá's* patriarchal lunches, we still had the capacity to be totally, utterly shocked by even the most unoriginal of family crises.

We were in a rare illegal-free period for that Easter long weekend, which was a relief to say the least. Well, it was a relief to most of us. Aunt Milagros, who was back to looking like she'd forgotten what a comb was, and had a stronger-than-ever *parfum de ashtray* trailing her, spent half of Easter lunch rambling about how she thought her illegals had been feeding information on her to Ugly. She was doing this, by the way, with Sancho's girlfriend Megan present. A big no-no. Thankfully Megan was out of earshot, eating on the back porch with Sancho, but my father still had to fake a violent coughing fit to get Milagros to shut the fuck up when Megan came to the table for a second helping.

"*¿Qué te pasa, hermana?* Have you forgotten Megan is Trini?" He chided Milagros when Megan had gone back out. "You can't talk like that in front of anyone outside the family."

Aunt Milagros was gripping her knife and fork in fists, leaning over her plate like she wanted to lunge across the table at him. "I'm telling you this last load of illegals in my house was acting strange! They're feeding back to Ugly, Hector. Why wouldn't they?"

"What would they even tell Ugly about you?" Mauricio scoffed through a mouthful of food. "That you pray ten times a day and go to a hundred Masses a week?"

Her face twisted into a knot. "Ugly might want to know about my work at the charity. About my connections in Venezuela."

"Ha! Catholic charity connections. Just what Ugly's interested in," Mauricio chortled, lifting a beer to his still-stuffed mouth.

"No more talk of any of this here today," said my father firmly. "Milagros, you need to relax. You're letting this whole situation get to you."

She harrumphed, scraped her chair away from the table, and went to the kitchen.

"You think she's okay?" I whispered to *Papá* as she walked away.

"Milagros has always been high-strung, always thinks everyone's out to get her. I wouldn't worry about it."

Who knows how differently things might've turned out if he had.

———

Along with Megan, who'd made the cut as we didn't have to feed any extra illegals, Fidel and his mousy, polite mother, Camille, had also joined us for lunch. Now nearly two years old, Fidel had sprouted the same thick, wavy hair as Mauricio, and had his father's pouty mouth and slanting eyes. Good thing Aunt Celia died when she did, because if Fidel had grown up and passed her in the street, she'd have known without a doubt that Mauricio had cheated on her in Trinidad and his ass would've been toast. After lunch, we were all ooing and ahhhing at Fidel's antics when Vanessa, out of nowhere, walked to the center of the porch and cleared her throat.

"Excuse me, everyone, I have something I would like to tell you all."

"Now, *mija*?" This was Mauricio, resting his teacup on the ground before standing.

I glanced at Sancho. He was like a hunting dog that's just heard a twig snap—eyes staring intently, not a muscle moving.

Vanessa nodded slowly. "Yes, *Papi*. Why not now?"

No one spoke or touched their coffee. All eyes converged on those big bouncy boobs as Vanessa took short, nervous breaths.

And then out it came. "*Estoy embarazada.*"

Embarazada? She was embarrassed? No, Anglophones: pregnant. As Vanessa blurted out the news, twisting her hands, tears smearing her makeup, I couldn't resist observing Sancho's reaction.

Fun fact: when pugs get worked up, their protuberant eyes sometimes pop right out of their heads.

I share that trivia because Sancho looked like a pug that'd gotten worked up. Like at any second, his eyeballs were going to catapult across the porch and hit Vanessa in the forehead.

Megan, meanwhile, had her face down in her mug, doing a poor job of hiding a smug smile at Vanessa's misfortune. It surprised me, actually, that her first thought wasn't that Sancho was the one who might've knocked up Vanessa.

Zulema, bless her, was the first to say anything. She went to Vanessa and hugged her. "*Felicidades*," she said. Vanessa grabbed on to her, bucking with a sob. Then Aunt Milagros and my parents, obviously touched, joined the group hug, murmuring condolences-cum-well-wishes like "A baby is always a blessing," and "It'll all work out." When Vanessa was released from their collective embrace, the twins rose from their seats and engulfed her in another hug, a sandwich of long Amazonian hair and peachy asses.

I stayed in my chair and watched the scene play out. I wasn't explicitly trying to be a bitch, but I was wary of Vanessa for two reasons: my illogical loyalty to Aunt Celia that made me feel guilty anytime I found myself enjoying a conversation with Vanessa, and because of the time I'd seen her and Sancho under the mango tree. If I got close to her, I could wind up caught between the two of them, embroiled in something I'd rather know nothing about. So I'd been keeping my distance, and felt it would read as distinctly hypocritical to now play the sympathetic older pseudo-cousin, wrapping her in a big phoney embrace while we all waited for her to proceed with the rest of the announcement: who the father was.

Papá was the one who eventually asked. "*¿Y el padre?*"

I would've bet a kidney that Sancho was the perpetrator from how red and bloated his face got at that question, like all the blood in his body had shot up to his head and it was going to rocket clean off his spinal column.

Vanessa wiped her tears, leaving swatches of bare skin on either cheek, like a window wiper had just cleared a dusty windshield. I leaned forward, a spectator at the Colosseum. Then Vanessa blurted out the one name no one expected, although in hindsight, the writing had been on the wall from day one.

"It's King De Oruña Willoughby!"

She dragged *Willoughbyyyy* out like a war cry, as though she were calling him back to her, crying out over the Atlantic Ocean that separated us from jolly old England, where he was merrily living in exile, totally ignorant of the spawn he'd left behind.

As Vanessa's wounded wail tapered out, Sancho jumped to his feet, hurling his coffee mug across the porch. "Well long live *el desgraciado* king!" The mug exploded against the wall, sending ceramic shards and splinters flying through the air and skittering across the tiles. We all ducked, dodging the shrapnel. Everyone but Megan, who was staring at Sancho in the very same way a bull stares down a *torero*, while he stared at Vanessa with nothing but heartache.

DANGEROUS ADDICTIONS

So what happened between Vanessa and the ever so charming King? Nothing that hasn't happened countless times before, ever since antediluvian man realized that any especially beautiful antediluvian woman was usually riddled with insecurity, struggling to mask the fear that she was dull or worthless without her looks. In the long tradition of his silver-tongued and handsome forebears, King spotted that Achilles' heel lickety-split and told Vanessa everything she wanted to hear, made her feel special, smart, unique, blah blah. She ate it all up. Even believed him when he gave her some story about how he'd been rendered sterile by an injury he sustained in the army. That's how she wound up pregnant. They'd gone at it like rabbits during King's ten-day sojourn at Mauricio's house, and not once had they used protection.

I learned all of this from the twins, who reported as a single journalistic organism, one sister seamlessly picking up from where the other left off, filling in every gap with what they'd individually gleaned from Mauricio's phone calls to Vanessa's mother, and of course, from what Vanessa herself told them.

I thawed more toward Vanessa after I found out what happened, tried to be thoughtful when she came around by switching off *Mamá's* electronic Glade air fresheners plugged in all over the house that triggered Vanessa's now sensitive gag reflex. Because let's be real—if I'd been her age and Román had cropped up, swearing he was infertile, telling me I was beautiful and unique as a snowflake, I would've probably let him knock me up too.

I'm sure you're wondering how King reacted to the news when Vanessa told him. Well, keep on wondering. Mauricio begged Román to track him down, and though Román did get King's latest address, nothing ever came of Mauricio's indignant letters—possibly because no one opens a mailbox anymore—and it became clear pretty quickly that Vanessa was on her own with that baby.

And Sancho? He was dumped on the spot after smashing the coffee mug in a flagrant declaration of his spurned love for knocked-up Vanessa. After the shock of the smashed mug had passed, Megan screamed at Sancho to go fornicate with himself, to put it euphemistically. Sancho didn't even respond. Didn't even follow her when she stormed out, her kitten heels click-clacking all the way out the front door, never to return.

Now he was on a dating rampage. I don't know if it was his way of having his wounds licked (literally) or of proving he didn't care about Vanessa (or for that matter, Megan), but whatever the case, he was on a hot streak. Anytime he came over for dinner, which was a couple times a week, regardless of whether or not we were looking after a batch of illegals, he would bring a different woman. It was like he was bobbing for them in a UN barrel: Indian, Chinese, white, black, Syrian, Lebanese, Carib, mixed. Name any race present in Trinidad and I can guarantee Sancho fucked it.

Some of the women were so attractive and educated that we only saw them the once—they couldn't possibly tolerate the self-destructive way Sancho was drinking to soothe his hurt pride. Others were so unattractive (think missing teeth, morbid obesity) that Sancho tossed them the second the rum goggles cleared.

So between the ones who were too good for him and the ones who weren't good enough for anyone, there was a rapid rotation of women passing through Sancho's house, and by extension, our house too.

"*Hijo*, we need to keep a low profile," warned my father. "We can't mix too much with the locals. How do you know these women won't report us? How can you explain the illegals staying with you and with us?"

"I tell them it's all family," said Sancho, waving a dismissive hand. "They don't know a thing. Think we've been here legally for years. Don't sweat it."

And then it was time for another drink. It was always time for another drink.

———

I asked Román for advice about Sancho one night. We were lying on a blanket at the bank of a jade-green river, listening to the groans of bamboo and other now familiar nocturnal sounds of the rainforest while sharing our usual postcoital joint.

"He won't listen to anyone," I was saying. "At this rate, he's going to drop dead of liver disease before he's thirty."

"It'll pass." Román paused, tapping his cheek to blow a series of smoke rings. "When male pride takes a hit, it hurts. The drinking is just temporary anesthesia."

I rolled my body onto his, nuzzled his neck. "I find it very hard to believe your pride was ever hurt by a woman."

"Everyone's had their heart broken," he said, running a hand along my spine, tossing the stub of the joint with the other. Then his face darkened slightly. "I do need to speak to Sancho, though. The women coming in and out of his house isn't good for business. I've been letting it slide but it's been going on too long now."

I pulled my head back to scan his face. "You're *just* going to talk to him, right?"

Román hadn't been looking at me while he spoke, was looking over my shoulder toward the river. "Of course I'll just talk to him." He shifted his eyes to mine now. "Once he listens and does what I say."

I propped myself up on his chest, anger tugging at me. "And if he doesn't listen?"

"I won't set out to hurt Sancho. But be realistic about our circumstances. It'll raise suspicions if I don't do my job properly. There could be conseque—"

I rolled off and away from him, reaching for my clothes. Feeling my temper writhing and spitting, and yet aware that I was putting Román in a difficult position, I knew the only thing I should do was distance myself, get dressed, get back in the Jeep, and cool it before I said or did something I'd wish I hadn't.

His fingertips stroked my lower back. "*Amor*, I won't do anything I don't have to. Easy with the drama."

I turned to glare at him. "Drama? You're talking about physically harming my *brother* and I'm being a drama queen?"

Román stood in one smooth movement. I stood as well. I wasn't going to cower under him.

"You knew what this was when it started, Yola. Don't make things more complicated than they need to be." That sobering Al Pacino voice. I fucking hated it sometimes.

"You think you're Sonny Corleone?" I spat. "What are you gonna do, smash his skull in with a baseball bat? Sancho's going through a hard time. Talk to the guy, he's not stupid. And don't you dare make veiled threats that you *might* hurt my brother and expect me to be okay with that shit."

Román's jaw clenched. I knew he was grappling with his anger. He didn't like to shout or yell or show he was upset. Thought it was a sign of weakness. Our stare-off went on for a solid thirty seconds before at last he exhaled, running his hands over the back of his neck.

"I won't hurt him."

"Promise me," I said.

He tugged his jeans on. "I said I wouldn't. Do you know me to be a liar?"

"No."

"Then don't ask me to make promises like some twelve-year-old. I'll talk to him, but so will you. Make it clear that there is no option but to listen to what I say."

Moments like that, when I got a real reminder of who Román was in relation to my family, the guilt would really get to me, shooting up like a geyser of heartburn. But by the time we pulled up at my house, though the guilt was still festering, my anger had waned— after all, Román had agreed to put his neck on the line for me with his lenience.

He pulled the handbrake up to look at me. I could see he wasn't worked up anymore either. I wondered if he was relieved in his own way for an excuse not to do his job the way Ugly expected. I slid across the seat to put my arms around his neck. He resisted for a split second before leaning in to kiss me.

"I knew you'd be trouble," he said as he pulled back. But he gave me a half smile.

"I'll talk to Sancho, I promise," I said. "I'll make sure he understands how dangerous his behavior is. It'll be fine."

"It better be."

In the end Román and I each had separate cautionary chats with Sancho. And fortunately, it worked. After three months of one-night stands, endless flings, and demented masochistic drinking, Sancho finally cooled down. Vanessa's stomach was now a big oval pod housing King's baby (which I hadn't yet had the balls to jokingly suggest she name Prince), her nose had broadened, dimpled saddlebags hung from her hips, and she was bloated as a bullfrog. Even her hugely engorged breasts had taken on a bovine look. Pregnancy just didn't agree with her. It was exactly the panacea Sancho needed. He stopped drinking from the moment he woke up and returned to the comparatively stable drinking routine of all functional alcoholics: from six p.m. until KO.

The stream of random women came to a halt, and he resumed twice-daily showers, much to the relief of his illegals, who'd been miserably tolerating the sour rum-and-sweat stink that clung to him like a remora fish. It was just as much of a relief to the rest of us, especially me. If Román had hurt my brother at his lowest point, I wouldn't have been able to stick around.

And therein lay my unresolvable conflict when it came to Román—the very man I'd have to give up if he pushed the limits of hardship inflicted on my family was the same man I couldn't bear that hardship without.

LOOSE SCREWS

ancho wasn't the only family member hit hard by the news of Vanessa's pregnancy. While Sancho was boozing and whoring it up for those three months, Mauricio was watching the twins like a hawk, terrified that another King De Oruña Willoughby would waltz into his home, gonads bulging, just waiting for the opportunity to impregnate another of his daughters.

"He even put latches on our bedroom doors so he can padlock us in when we go to bed!" Sequestered in her room at night, Alejandra reported on Mauricio's paranoia like a gossipy Anne Frank, texting me updates on whatever new security measures he'd taken. "He keeps the padlock keys on a piece of twine around his neck. He doesn't even take it off to sleep! *¿Qué carajo?*"

At a Sunday barbecue I asked him if it was a good idea locking the girls in at night like that—"What if there's a fire?"—and he said he'd rather the twins went up in smoke as well-secured virgins than have his house turn into a brothel full of pregnant teens. I didn't have the heart to tell him that the twins' hymens were about as intact as a piñata at the end of a Mexican birthday party. Lucky for Mauricio, though, none of the illegals who came to our respective households during the months following Vanessa's insemination posed any risk of seducing his daughters. All we'd been getting lately were more "dancers." Still, his paranoia persisted and Alejandra got calluses on her thumbs from texting me all night.

Aunt Milagros took the news of Vanessa's pregnancy just as badly as Mauricio. Worse, even. Not long after our eventful Easter lunch, where we'd already noticed the screws of her mind loosening, she was having coffee with *Mamá* and me. "It's such a betrayal of trust," she was saying, blinking furiously. The vague smell of old smoke around her was even stronger now, like she was using cigarette ash as talcum powder. "You let these people into your home thinking you're *helping* them, and then they go and do something like this, after everything we do to help."

"But Vanessa willingly let Kingsley put a bun in her oven. He didn't force himself on her."

Aunt Milagros rounded on me, eyes fiery. "Well, that's a fine view to take! Blame the victim! Blame the poor girl who's been seduced by a worldly, smooth-talking soldier!"

It was like trying to reason with a coconut. Anytime she brought up Vanessa's pregnancy (which was often), she'd flip out on anyone who didn't see eye-to-eye with her. Whenever she saw that growing belly at family gatherings, she'd shake her head in lament and clutch the crucifix dangling from the rosary beads permanently wrapped around her wrist. She just couldn't let go of the idea of another illegal stealthily seducing and knocking up one of our own. Then in May, while Sancho's liver was still screaming for salvation and he was hopping from woman to woman, we finally got to the bottom of why Aunt Milagros had been stinking of smoke for months.

Zulema, the twins, and I were at her house for a movie night, midway through a corny chick flick and a jug of frozen daiquiri mix, when I smelled smoke—fresh this time, not the stale day-old smell that had become Aunt Milagros's signature scent. One by one we all smelled it, sitting up and sniffing like a bunch of meerkats. I turned toward the smell, and there was Aunt Milagros in the doorway, a full ashtray in hand, a cigarette in her mouth. I guess it shouldn't have come as a surprise given the stink of her clothes and hair for the past few months—and come to think of it, her teeth and fingertips had taken on a yellow tinge too—but you have to understand, this was the woman who caught Zulema smoking when she was twelve and force-fed her a pack of cigarettes as punishment until Zulema threw up everywhere. Now she was sucking on back-to-back cigs like they were her sole source of oxygen. She blazed through half a pack that same night, right in front of us, without a care in the world for all our jaws grazing the floor.

When my parents saw her smoking at our family barbecue the following Sunday, they were equally shocked. It was so out of character for Aunt Milagros to sit there puffing away, aureoled in smoke instead of her usual saintly halo, that it was actually awkward to talk to her about it, as if she'd slipped into some act of senility and it would be cruel to point it out. My father was the only one who didn't feel awkward confronting her. While everyone was sucking ribs clean and Aunt Milagros was sucking on cigarette number eleven, he broached the topic.

"*Hermanita*, those things will kill you. You must be stressed. Talk to us, tell us what's wrong."

She gave a gravelly laugh, ashed her cigarette into a glass of water. "How to help? None of you seem the least bit concerned about what's going on under our noses. You can't help anything if you can't even see the problems we have to fix."

She took a hard drag on the cigarette, so hard all the fine lines around her mouth stood rigid, forming a miniature mountain range. When she exhaled, *Mamá* coughed pointedly and fanned the air in front of her even though Aunt Milagros was on the other side of the dining table, blowing smoke in the opposite direction.

"I'll help myself, thank you very much, Hector," said Aunt Milagros. "That's why I bought the gun."

At that, *Mamá* threw her hands up in angry disbelief, her pork rib clattering onto her plate. Everyone paused, faces smeared with barbecue sauce, fingers sticky, to gape at Aunt Milagros. A *gun*? She went on to tell us that she'd purchased an automatic air rifle. It was only a pellet gun, but according to her it looked like an AK-47, the real deal. She said it all very casually while puffing on her cigarette, unruffled by the shock on all our faces and by Sancho and Mauricio's tipsy sniggering.

"What are you going to do, Milagros? Shoot someone if you think they're suspicious?" asked my father, brow knit in concern.

"That's exactly what I'm going to do. I need to feel safe under my own roof and I can't trust the animals Beelzebub keeps forcing into my home. Remember, Hector, it's just me on my own in that house. I have no husband to protect me."

Papá dropped the subject. Even he couldn't withstand the discomfort of the spinster card being played.

At the next Sunday barbecue, when we were all on safe-house duty, one of Aunt Milagros's illegals told *Papá* that he'd seen her patrolling the house in the dead of night with the gun hoisted onto her shoulder, a lit cigarette clamped between her teeth. When this story was eventually relayed to me, I couldn't imagine it was true. Aunt Milagros prowling around the house like some linen-clad, rosary-wielding Rambo? But the next time I saw her, a living, walking pillar of smoke, voice husky with cigarette phlegm, I believed it.

I toyed with talking to Román, asking him to maybe leave Aunt Milagros out of the rotation for a while, give her a breather. After I heard the story of her prowling, I nearly did tell him. We were driving along the isolated Arima Road, no houses, no streetlights, only dark rainforest to either side of the slim ribbon of asphalt as we sped along it, Román's hand in its familiar spot on my thigh. I'd been on the verge of telling him then, had actually started—"There's something I need to talk . . ."—when he slammed the brakes, crossing my body with his arm to stop me lunging forward.

"Sorry," he said, whipping off his seat belt.

He didn't give me time to ask why he'd stopped. He was already out in the road, kneeling, scooping up what looked like an exceptionally large, round-bottomed guinea pig. I got out too.

"What is that?"

"An agouti. It's hurt."

I watched him take the quivering animal to the roadside, walk a few feet into the bush, and gently place it on the ground, covering it with a large fallen balisier leaf.

"Hopefully no predators will spot it. Didn't see any blood or anything so maybe it'll recover by morning."

When we got back into the Jeep and his hand resumed its post on my thigh, I squeezed it in lieu of telling him I'd never seen anything so sweet as what he'd just done. I didn't say anything about Aunt Milagros, either, because I saw the man he was—hardened and calloused by experience but not by nature. If I told him about Aunt Milagros, he'd want to help, and then I'd be putting him in a position where he'd have to counteract Ugly's orders. I didn't want him to have to deal with that on top of the angst he already felt over his job, putting him between a rock and a hard place like I'd done when Sancho was having his meltdown. Our relationship was complicated and dangerous enough. Why make things even stickier?

I said nothing and no one did anything, collectively turning a blind eye to the changes in Aunt Milagros, and hoping—if not fully believing—that the only collateral damage of her mental unraveling would be to her lungs.

With the way our familial luck had been since Aunt Celia's death, we should've known better.

SAME FAN, MORE SHIT

Though I'd decided not to discuss the conundrum of Aunt Milagros's precarious mental state with Román, my time with him was still a source of respite, from the stress of Aunt Milagros and everything else. With my family, all we spoke about was our situation, our illegals, our trials and tribulations. We'd become pathological complainers, especially because we couldn't complain to anyone but each other—no one on the outside could know what was going on. With Román, there was none of that. There were only childhood anecdotes, vigorous debates about the merits of this book or that movie or that dubbed-over nineties sitcom (though Román knew hardly any of those). Whenever an Executive Relocation Package apartment was available, we'd get to play house too. Fully stocked with everything to meet the affluent, high-paying illegal immigrant's needs, these apartments were handled solely by Román, so we were safe from the threat of Ugly. There, I could pretend that was what it felt like to wake up next to Román, to be his live-in girlfriend, to bitch about his dirty boxers on the floor, his hair wrapped around the soap, the fact that he never did the dishes—all those mundane aggravations that add up to domestic intimacy.

Lying on my back on the plush neutral-hued duvet of one of the exec apartments one night, inhaling the fragrant THC of local high-grade weed and watching as Román did back twists on the hardwood floor in his boxers, I marveled at how good it felt to step into this imagined life with him.

Would this fantasy ever really come true, though? Would Román ever be able to stop working for Ugly? Would we ever be able to actually take this thing we had into the realm of daylight and real life? The weed anxiety spread its thorny branches and I took another drag to shake it off, watching as Román lay supine, arms stretched out to the sides with one bent leg crossed over his body, exhaling and deepening the stretch. When he twisted the other way, his head turned toward me. I flipped over onto my stomach, arching my back into a posture I hoped would convey the wanton minx thing I was going for. He crooked a come-hither finger at me.

"I'm very comfortable here, thank you," I said with a toss of my head.

"I don't care. Get your ass over here."

"I don't want to interrupt your stretching."

"That's exactly why I want you here. I wanna see how limber you are."

"I'm *very* limber I'll have you know."

"You not gonna come down here and show me?"

"Not good to stretch unless I'm warmed up."

He leapt onto the balls of his feet. "Oh I'll warm your ass up." As I jumped up from the bed, letting him chase me until we collapsed back into the soft duvet, I knew then that it didn't matter what happened with us in the end. The future wasn't important when we had this present.

———

Shortly before daybreak, I tiptoed back into the house, shutting the door softly behind me so I wouldn't wake the illegals staying with us—a batch of men for a change: three guys in their late twenties planning to island-hop their way to Florida. Good luck, *hombres*!

As I made my way toward the bedroom hallway, past the pull-out couch and futon where the guys were sleeping, I noticed the dark outline of a figure sitting on the edge of our back porch. I froze, heart thudding.

Ugly?

I took two tremulous steps toward the porch doors, squinting through the glass panes. Then I saw the gray curls, the paisley shirt, the thin stream of cigarette smoke. Aunt Milagros.

As I eased the door open to go out to the porch, I glanced at my watch. It was going on four-thirty in the morning. Aunt Milagros started as I put a hand on her shoulder. Her air rifle was resting across her lap, a dozen cigarette butts scattered in the grass around her feet. "Hello, *querida*," she said, as though there was nothing out of the ordinary about her sitting with an automatic pellet gun on our porch at four a.m.

I sat next to her, coughing slightly as she blew a stream of smoke.

"What are you doing here, *Tía*? Is everything all right?"

"Ha!" She flicked the cigarette butt into the yard. I watched the glowing tip soar in an arc to land in the unruly grass that *Papá* no longer had time to mow. "Everything *is* all right. Not that any of you would know it."

"Huh?"

"All fast asleep with a bunch of strange men in your house. How do you know they're not just waiting to strike in the middle of the night? Who's keeping a goddamned watch here? Everything's all right because I came to make *sure* it was all right."

"Aunt Milagros, we've had illegals staying with us for like six months now. They've all been fine. We've never 'kept watch' and there's never been a problem."

"Oh *really*? So Vanessa isn't pregnant by some filthy illegal? I'd say that's a problem, Yola, wouldn't you?"

She lit up another cig.

I shrugged. "I wouldn't say it's a problem. Not my problem, any-

163

way. Vanessa thought Kingsley was cute, so she slept with him and got pregnant. What's the big shocker in that? Happens all the time."

Aunt Milagros squeezed her eyes shut and shook her head like a dog shaking water from its fur. For a second I thought she might stomp her feet and throw a tantrum.

"It doesn't happen all the time. IT DOES NOT!"

"Aunt Milagros! Shhh! Not so loud!"

She turned her face to me and her eyes were red, probably from a combination of exhaustion and all the cigarettes. "We cannot let these men run amok in our homes. We have to stay vigilant."

Nimble as an acrobat, she sprang to her feet and slung the gun strap over her shoulder.

"Everything is in order here." Her white linen pants quivered in the breeze as though shaking with laughter at her militant tone. "I'm going back to my house to do rounds until dawn."

She turned, walking briskly across the garden and around the side of the house, disappearing from view.

"When are you going to *sleep*?" I called out, forgetting that I'd shushed her only a second ago.

She didn't answer. I don't even know if she heard me. What I did know was that Aunt Milagros had officially lost her marbles.

––––––––

I was too unnerved by the state of Aunt Milagros to sleep. Aside from her linen and paisley armor, everything about her was completely warped—from the hadn't-been-combed-in-months cave-woman hair to the masculine stride and the smoke perpetually wafting around her like she was carved out of dry ice.

How could I help her without involving Román? I didn't know what to do. We'd already lost one aunt that year. I didn't want to lose another to a full-blown nervous breakdown or accidental suicide by pellet gun. I searched every corner of my mind for some way to soothe my anxiety, but only got more worked up. I remembered then that this wasn't the first time a pregnancy announcement had tipped Aunt Milagros over the edge. Maybe this was all just a symptom of her wishing she'd had kids herself, and it would all blow over, just a temporary blip in sanity. Because according to Aunt Celia's manuscript, Aunt Milagros hadn't taken the news of Aunt Celia's pregnancy too well either.

It was 1998 and Mauricio had made himself a millionaire again by breeding and skinning Orinoco crocodiles, critically endangered and therefore illegal to "harvest," yet renowned for the unfortunate blessing of having beautiful hides just perfect for crafting high-end suitcases, shoes, bags, wallets, and belts that were scattered to luxury stores all around the world, that inimitable Orinoco-croc sheen catching the eye of many an Arab princeling, British aristocrat, and brittle-boned supermodel.

Here we are—more money than the Pope. We could even build ourselves a teeny-weeny Vatican City, buy a penthouse anywhere in the world if we didn't have to stick around in this backwater to keep Mauricio close to the crocs. But at least there's not a bulb in our house that's not twinkling in a chandelier, not a bed without four posters and a velvet canopy, or a room without a Persian rug and priceless black-walnut antiques. Plus being stuck in this shithole town means we can rub my parents' noses in it after all the time we spent cleaning their gutters and mopping and sweeping and raking their fucking leaves in exchange for rent, like we were peasants on a hacienda *begging for charity from the* Patrón. *Let me tell you, those two are still as cold-blooded as when they abandoned me with the goddamned nuns. But who the hell cares, because now we're rich enough to found our own religion on the Rock of St. Mauricio and my parents will never be able to lord themselves over me again.*

This was the state of things when Aunt Celia announced that she was finally pregnant, having convinced Mauricio to lay off the weekly blow binges long enough to at least get his *polla* back in good working order.

Everyone's at my parents' house for dinner. All my brothers—Hector, good as gold like always, and Ignacio and Rubio, drunk like always. Milagros of course is there, boring us with her usual violin-accompanied whining about joining a nunnery if Prince Valiant doesn't appear out of thin air.

Before telling them about the baby, we figure we'll set the celebratory tone by giving out a few party favors. Gold watches. Cartier. We give them out and I see Milagros's face go from pink to red to purple like some tie-dyed chameleon. Then you know what the sanctimonious little bitch does? She takes one look at that watch and throws the thing clear across the table. If I'd been as flat-chested as she is, the pendeja would've cracked my fucking sternum. I'm about to throw a bowl of scalding soup in her face when I realize what'll really burn her.

I stand all martyr-like. "Oh, Milagros, I'm sorry you don't like the gift, but hopefully you'll be more pleased with my news."

I put a hand to my stomach and lay it on her—pregnant! Ignacio and Rubio jump up on the table and start carousing, and the soup bowls are clattering on the floor and Mamá and Papá are hollering at them to get down and stop stamping in the food and Milagros is just sitting there, breathing hard, and I'm watching her and I know it's coming.

Then KA-BOOM! She fucking BLOWS. Goes feral.

Starts screaming that a couple of crass, money-hungry criminals like us don't deserve a baby, and she's flinging cutlery everywhere, yelling that she won't stay in this house a second longer and she'll leave that same night, and Ignacio and Rubio are dancing some kind of lunatic jig on the table, spattering everyone with stew and beans, shouting that it's high time Milagros join a nunnery anyway because Prince Valiant ain't never turning up, and food is all over the place and crockery is tumbling off the table to shatter on the floor, and Hector is tugging at their pant legs trying to get them down from there, and Mauricio is pounding the table and laughing his coked-up head off, and Mamá is crying she's so happy for a new grandchild, and Papá has his head in his hands, and it's all fucking magnificent.

Aunt Milagros moved out the next day. Not to a nunnery, though Uncle Ignacio and Uncle Rubio would've shaved her head that same night to get her ready to be a novice if my father hadn't stopped them, but to a distant relative's home in Caracas, hours away. She cut herself off from her siblings and parents for six months, returning every letter and ignoring every phone call.

Still, moving to Caracas and not speaking to anyone for a few months was hardly the same as smoking compulsively, buying a pellet gun, and doing late-night patrols. I shivered at the thought of Aunt Milagros catching me sneaking out to meet Román. What would she do—shoot me?

———

The next morning I relayed my conversation with Aunt Milagros to my father.

"Okay," he sighed, "I'll deal with it."

"How?"

"I don't know."

Reassuring!

In the end, his big solution was to call Aunt Milagros and "have a chat" to try putting her addled mind at ease. He did call. But it was a big fat waste of time: two days after that futile conversation, Mauricio's entire household was awoken in the middle of the night by the screaming of one of their illegals' daughters. The little girl had gotten up to use the bathroom and was scared senseless by Aunt Milagros's face pressed against the window, gun barrel pointed at the glass. It was like a prison riot after the child screamed, with the illegals scampering around in an uproar thinking Immigration had come to haul them back to Venezuela, and the twins and Vanessa banging on their doors and rattling their windows, shouting for liberation, thinking the house must be on fire with all that ruckus.

I went with my parents and Mauricio to see Aunt Milagros the day after the incident. She showed no remorse. When she justified her actions, she had the same strangely militant attitude as when I'd spoken to her that night on the porch, as self-assured as Castro giving interviews from the sierras during the revolution.

"I have every right to patrol my family's houses and make sure things are in order," she said coolly. "Just because the men of this family have failed to look out for our family's well-being doesn't mean I will."

"Milagros, you're being ridiculous," snapped my mother. "Creeping around people's houses at night with a pellet gun is far from protecting our well-being. You could hurt someone."

"We're all very mindful of the risks of the situation, Milagros," *Papá* added gently. "Mauricio is even locking the girls' rooms at night."

Hearing that, Aunt Milagros slammed her hands onto the dining table. The glass ashtray rattled against the tabletop. "WE'RE ALL JUST SITTING DUCKS!"

She screamed it over and over, until her face was purple and *Papá* had to grab her by the shoulders to get her to hush.

Meanwhile, Aunt Milagros's illegals, a woman and her young son, a rare non-Venezuelan pair from the Dominican Republic, were out on her porch. Before the conversation took that crazy turn, Aunt Milagros had shamelessly informed us that she now locked all of her illegals outside during the day while she slept. She left them with a stocked cooler of food and water. Then in the afternoon when she woke up, she'd let them back in. All night every night, she patrolled her house, ours and Mauricio's, until morning, when the illegals were put outside again.

Back at home after our failed intervention, none of us could come up with a solution. Aunt Milagros had gone off the deep end and no one knew how to save her.

"Maybe we should have Beelzebub warn Ugly," suggested *Mamá*. "Milagros is a danger to those poor people staying with her. She has to stop housing illegals for a while."

"Good idea," said *Papá*. "I'll call him tomorrow on the emergency cell."

Román never got the call. *Papá* never got a chance to place it. Because less than twenty-four hours after our talk with Aunt Milagros, she shot that little Dominican kid who was staying with her.

Luckily it was only a pellet, and though she didn't hit anything major, she did bust a couple of ligaments in his shoulder.

No one was ever really clear on how the whole thing happened, but we did find out that the boy's mother went absolutely berserk after Aunt Milagros pulled the trigger. So did Aunt Milagros, but more in a PTSD sort of way. Seeing the boy clutching his shoulder that was spurting blood like a sprinkler system, Aunt Milagros dropped the gun and locked herself in her bedroom closet. That's where the police found her when they eventually turned up in response to a neighbor's call to report a gunshot and screaming.

Not long after, Aunt Milagros, the boy, and his mother were all carted away in the back of a police car. No ambulance ever came. The police dropped the mother and her son off at the Port of Spain General Hospital, accompanied by a police escort, and Aunt Milagros was left in a holding cell at the police station.

The shit had hit the fan. Again.

All of this was relayed to us by a woman who came to see my parents on the night of the shooting. Our illegals had just left that afternoon, so we were celebrating by binge-watching TV and eating Chinese takeout. I was munching on a spring roll when we heard a knock on the door. *Papá* groaned.

"*Por Dios*, Ugly must really be making a fortune! More illegals already?" He pushed himself up off the couch and went to the kitchen in his boxer shorts to grab some clothes off the airing rack that stood atop the now obsolete dryer.

"That's not illegals," I said to my mother. It wasn't Román's precise triple knock. We'd also never had a drop-off at night.

Mamá went to the window to peep out. *Papá* walked up behind her, wearing a clean but crumpled pair of shorts and a T-shirt. "Who is it?" he whispered.

"*No sé.* Some lady."

Papá opened the front door, and after some brief introductions, he invited the woman inside. Zulema was out with friends, but would've had a heart attack if she saw her: barefaced with wire-rimmed glasses, androgynously cropped gray hair, dressed in a completely asexual beige polo shirt and khakis. I could just imagine my sister whisking this poor woman into her lair and assigning her swatches of magenta, emerald, and midnight blue. *You're a Winter! I can tell right off the bat!*

The woman came in shyly, fiddling nervously with a wooden rosary bracelet on her wrist. It was clear she hadn't come on a happy errand.

My parents guided her into the living room, where I was wiping my spring roll–greased fingers on a napkin in anticipation of having to shake the woman's hand, but she just nodded at me and said, "Hello, hello," in a timid little voice, shifting her weight from foot to foot.

My father gestured to the couch. "Please, sit down . . . Bethan?"

"Yes, Bethan," she said with a feeble nod. "Thank you."

She sat. My parents sat. I kept sitting. We all looked at her, waiting for her to explain.

"Well," she ventured at last. "As I said, Mr. Palacios . . ."

"Hector, please."

"As I said, Hector, I work with Milagros down at the Sacred Heart Community Center, although we haven't seen her in a while. Something about having her hands tied with night work, I believe, and needing her days for rest?" If only Bethan knew that Aunt Milagros's "night work" consisted of armed patrols of her family's homes. "Anyway, you can imagine my surprise then, when out of the blue Milagros calls me up about an hour ago to say she was arrested. I'm sorry to have to tell you this, but she accidentally shot a child who was staying with her— the son of a friend, she said? The child is okay, but they're holding her at the police station down at Four Roads."

"*¡No lo puedo creer!*" Mamá pressed a fist to her chest and threw herself against the backrest of the couch. She'd always had a cinematic flair for drama.

"Oh Lawd," said *Papá* in his faux-Trini accent. He exhaled. "Why she didn't call we?" The usual nervous-tic Trini dialect.

"I'm not sure. She just asked me to pass the message along. She wouldn't give me your number, just the address. Sorry again to barge in, but I figured you'd want to know right away." Then she told us all the rest, about Aunt Milagros in the closet and the police taking her away. After she'd told everything there was to tell, she stood and smoothed the front of her khakis. "I'd better be going. I don't want to intrude any longer, but I didn't think you'd want to wait before finding out."

"We appreciate that you come all the way here," said *Papá*, standing as well. "Thank you so much."

Mamá was still steadily pounding her fist against her chest, eyes closed. I took her free hand and squeezed it, more to get her to stop with the theatrics than to offer comfort.

Papá walked Bethan out, but before she left, she turned on the front step and said, "Listen, I know Milagros's residential status here is a little . . . iffy. But I hope you know she was one of our best, most beloved workers down at Sacred Heart. We're going to do everything we can to keep her here and make sure this doesn't become a real prob- lem. I called one of our church brothers who's a lawyer. Hopefully he can help. Such a sweet woman. I'm sure this is all a terrible mistake."

"I'm sure it is," said *Papá*.

But he knew it was no mistake. It had been a catastrophe waiting to happen ever since the day Aunt Milagros bought herself that pellet gun.

We also knew why Aunt Milagros hadn't called us. In a moment of lucidity she must have realized that the less the police knew about all of us, the better.

As my father returned to the couch, switched off the TV, and put his arm around *Mamá*, it was all too clear that Aunt Milagros's fuckup was a thread that had been pulled from a very tenuous tapestry. What were the police going to ask the illegal mother and the kid who'd been shot? What would they find out about Aunt Milagros's irregular status and her safe-housing? Where would that lead next? Each of us was a link in a chain that went directly to our lead ball: Ugly. And, of course, Román.

This was going to be a problem—a big one.

A TIGRESS NOT TO BE FUCKED WITH

After Bethan's visit, there was no family meeting, no grand plan to liberate Aunt Milagros from her holding cell. We didn't do anything because we *couldn't*. We were illegal immigrants housing other illegal immigrants. Our hands were tied, our mouths gagged. Our only hope was Bethan, and she wasn't much help. All she told *Papá* the day after she came and the day after that and every day the following week until she stopped taking his calls was: "Our church brother is doing all he can." Which was apparently nothing.

Papá called various immigration lawyers, blowing money on consultations, but they all gave the same advice: Don't go to the police station. Don't do anything. Not unless we wanted to land up in that holding cell with Aunt Milagros.

I overheard my parents talking in the kitchen after one of those disheartening consultations. "No legal recourse and no loopholes. That's all he kept saying," said *Papá*. "He said if any of us gets caught living here illegally, we're out. Milagros doesn't have a chance and there's nothing we can do to help her. It's either prison or deportation for her."

I felt for him. I felt for Aunt Milagros.

More than anything, I felt for myself: I hadn't seen or heard from Román since the day before Aunt Milagros shot the Dominican boy.

The day after Bethan's visit, I didn't expect to see him. I figured he'd have his hands tied sorting out the Aunt Milagros mess. I expected to see him the day after, though.

And the day after. And the day after.

But nothing.

Seven days and nothing.

To anyone else, a week might seem like no time at all, but every day that I didn't see or hear from him felt slower than the last, like I was living in an hourglass filled with treacle. My mind ran rampant as one week trickled slowly, excruciatingly, into two and then three, with no way to contact him because his only regular cell phone was tapped by Ugly, and he normally called me from untraceable burner phones anyway.

At first I suspected that Aunt Milagros's breakdown had driven him away, then when there was still no word, my neuroses really started picking up speed, whirring gyroscopes of panic generating an un-bearable anxious energy in me. I convinced myself that it wasn't Aunt Milagros—that *I'd* done something to offend or repulse him. I picked apart every second of the last times we'd seen each other. Had he been quieter than usual? Did he hold my hand like he normally did on the drive home? Had he kissed me goodbye? I ran through each memory until they were smeared blurs in my mind, impossible to grasp with any clarity, drained of color and movement—grainy sepia stills splotched with hurt and confusion.

A month passed. Still no update on Aunt Milagros and nothing from Román. I was a woman possessed. When a new illegal turned up, now heralded by the doorbell ringing, never the triple knock, I practi-cally catapulted myself at the front door, tearing outside into the street to see if the Jeep was driving away. It never was. The new illegal(s), usually startled by my bat-out-of-hell sprint out the front door, would tell me the same thing: "He said to wait for him to leave then ring the doorbell." It was a kick in the crotch every time. I couldn't understand why he'd abandoned me.

Morning after morning I'd wake up, and for the briefest split second, I'd be fresh and ready to take on the day, but the tumor of pain in my chest would surface again in an instant, and I'd be heavy, leaden with missing Román. I stopped working on the novel altogether, not even bothering with the sporadic writing spurts I sometimes managed despite my hectic translation schedule. Shirking my duty to contribute to our already tightly stretched household budget, I told my translation agency I'd contracted dengue and couldn't work. All I did was stay in bed, crying, not caring that I wasn't earning a cent and that as a result our household forcibly became vegetarian whenever we were burdened with illegals. I fed my family the same dengue line—said my bones ached, I had fever, a rash on my stomach, headaches, whatever symptoms I could dredge up on Google. *Papá's* gentle questioning and my mother's less-than-gentle interrogations about my dating status made it pretty clear they didn't believe the dengue spiel, but when I stuck to my story, they played along, brought me soup and toast in bed, even offered to take me to the doctor, though God knows we wouldn't have been able to pay the bill.

It dragged on.

Then, strangely, I started to perk up. My misery was snowballing into something else, something less agonizing and easier to manage: rage.

I rolled around in my fury like a pig in shit. At least it felt better than moping day and night. And of course, anytime I felt that fury fading, I could always rely on Aunt Celia to keep up my angry momentum. She'd been no stranger to romantic frustration during her marriage, but had she let it get her down? Had she let Mauricio's bad behavior turn her into the soggy, crying lump I'd been for weeks? Hell no. When Mauricio started straying, she didn't wallow in heartbreak, she broke *him*. One of my favorite badass moments in her memoir went down when Mauricio was even more slick than in the Miami glory days, his renewed Tony Montana–esque swagger attracting the attention of every woman under fifty in that nowhere town. Heavily pregnant, Aunt Celia had clocked them eyeing Mauricio's Orinoco-croc boots, his tight imported Levi's, and ropes of thick gold chains. Still, she convinced herself time and again that no one would ever stray from a woman like her, least of all Mauricio, whom she'd stuck by through thick and thin, even during their days of penury when he wouldn't get out of bed for months after the demise of his honey empire.

After Ava was born, however, Mauricio started staying out for whole nights. Then whole weekends. Always "working." Celia would be pushing Ava along in a stroller for a walk to the park, and even with the jewelry draping her neck and wrists, even with the Parisian makeup and the Egyptian creams perfuming her skin, she felt as small and ugly as a garden gnome when she saw how other women eyeballed her. She was sure they were laughing at her, poking fun at the cuckolded wife of Mauricio the Crocodile Baron. Then she'd go back home all riled up. Ava would be dumped on one of her grandparents and Celia would attack Mauricio with full force. Her jealous rages got so bad at one point that all the knives in the house had to be hidden beneath floorboards, under flowerpots, behind various appliances. Everyone in that household knew Celia was capable of murder, and Celia was proud of it. She wanted Mauricio to know she might slit his throat if he ever dared come home stinking of another woman's nether parts.

And then one day he actually did.

After throwing a frying pan, two vases, and a water jug at Mauricio, who'd become adept at dodging flying objects, Celia chased him out into the street where anyone could see, wielding a hammer. Mauricio had never been one for beating his wife, so he didn't try to restrain her. He just kept on running, Forrest Gump style. They ran through the streets of the dinky little town center, with everyone staring delightedly. They ran through several backyards, through an artisanal market, and finally onto the border of a small coffee farm. There, Mauricio spotted a massive beehive and ran to it, raising his arms to keep Celia away. "Stop, goddammit, woman! STOP!" Ironically, given that he'd made his first fortune in a honey-smuggling racket, Mauricio was fatally allergic to bees. One sting and his throat would swell right up.

He figured if he stood beneath the hive Celia would back off, scream at him for a bit, then cool down, like she always did.

Wrong!

Celia hurled the hammer at the beehive and burst the thing right open. "Bull's eye!" she screamed, arms pumping victoriously. Mauricio was of course stung in the resulting swarm of angry bees, and would have died of anaphylaxis had the farm owner not saved him in the nick of time with an EpiPen he kept handy for his son, also deathly allergic, to peanuts.

Celia watched the whole thing casually from a near distance: Mauricio's face swelling as he gasped for breath, the farmer running to the house hollering at his wife to get the EpiPen, and finally the EpiPen being rammed into Mauricio's thigh.

Purged of her anger, confident that Mauricio wasn't going to die, Celia left him there on the coffee farm and went back to the town center, where she treated herself to a leisurely churro at the town's one little café.

None of the women in the town ever eyeballed Celia after that. None of the men did either. She'd earned her stripes and everyone knew she was a tiger. Or as she put it: *a tigress not to be fucked with.*

I had that tigress anger in me now. I wasn't going to feel sorry for myself or slip 'n slide down some bleak rabbit hole of heartache. If Román thought he could ghost me, well . . . maybe I wouldn't be nuts enough to throw things at him or commit murder by bee sting, but I'd keep my head high, stay nobly stoic in my misery.

And that's what I did. I translated almost compulsively to make up for my lapse in earnings, so at least I had the silver lining of a rapidly fattening PayPal balance—never mind that the bulk of it was spent feeding illegals—and did my best to keep working on the novel. Even in my lowest moments, I wouldn't let myself cry over Román anymore. Instead I watched reality TV marathons on my laptop. There was no better balm for my aching insides than the voyeuristic sadism of observing mentally unstable, emotionally unhinged Americans expose their basest selves for the sake of cheap entertainment like screeching monkeys tugging at their genitals and flinging fecal matter to entertain onlookers at the zoo—because, after all, things could always be worse. I could be a reality TV star.

That guilty pastime is exactly what I was indulging in one night from the comfort of my bed, watching some garish specimen of humanity blather into the camera about how she was "the realest, classiest person" in a household comprised of individuals all handpicked by astute producers for their collective lack of a fully developed prefrontal cortex, when I heard a scratching at my window. I froze, hit pause on the laptop. A spinster cat manifesting for me just like it had for Aunt Milagros?

Then a *tap, tap, tap*. I stared at the window, my ears ringing with pumping blood, heart like a bouncy castle with fifty fat kids jumping on it. It had to be Román out there.

I tried focusing on Aunt Celia. I pictured her chasing Mauricio through the street, watching with satisfaction as he was stung by bees. Where was my anger? How had it all drained away in an instant, leaving me full of nothing but pathetic, desperate hope? I went to the window, pulled back the curtain, and cracked the louvers open slowly, a small part of me praying it would just be Aunt Milagros escaped from her holding cell, a cigarette between her teeth, air rifle at her side. I could handle that. My heart wouldn't ache, my insides wouldn't hurt, my tongue wouldn't be incapable of forming a comprehensible word.

But no Aunt Milagros. Sliced up by louvers, unmistakable as the face of Christ: Román.

"Come outside," he whispered.

Rubbing my arms, trying to stop myself shivering, I knew it wasn't the cool night breeze that had given me the shakes. I crept through the living room, past the couch that held yet another sleeping "dancer," whose open suitcase had revealed actual clear heels and nipple tassels, and made my way out to the porch. Scanning the dark backyard, my eyes finally settled on him leaning against the mango tree, dressed all in black like the Sunday morning we'd met. The night was clear, cloudless, only the stars and melodiously noisy frogs watching on as I walked across the dew-dampened grass, trying to craft the perfect opening line, hoping to arrange my features into something resembling indifference. It was all for *nada*. By the time I got to the tree, I was tongue-tied as a tween swooning over her boy-band crush.

Immediately, Román pulled me into him, buried his face in my hair, slid his hands hungrily over my body like a blind man. "Yola . . ." It was a sigh.

I felt a flame lighting the wick on a stick of dynamite, on a Roman candle, on pinwheels—the fireworks were coming. Still, I pulled away, doing my best to keep my expression hard.

"I know you're mad," he said, taking my hand to press the fingertips to his mouth. I closed my eyes in spite of myself then drew my hand back.

"Where the fuck have you been?"

He kissed my cheeks, tried kissing me on the mouth but I turned my face away, hoping he wouldn't see how my nostrils were fluttering, my bottom lip quivering.

"I had to stay away," he said. "After everything with Milagros . . ."

"So it's because of *her* that you dumped me? Because it's too complicated for us now?" Jesus, I sounded like a child. I only realized I'd given in to crying when Román wiped my cheek, the tenderness of it making me feel as though a blood-pressure band were constricting my chest, squeezing tighter and tighter. "You could've at least explained yourself, Román. I didn't know what the hell happened to you or where you'd gone. I felt like a complete idiot."

"I'm sorry you felt that way, but this isn't a game. You think Ugly's gonna tap me on the wrist for seeing you? After Milagros, I was being

179

trailed constantly. Ugly holds me responsible. I had to protect you and myself. As for Milagros . . ."

I took a step backward, as if physical distance would help lessen the effect of his excuses. "Yeah, I get it, Aunt Milagros fucks up and I'm the one who has to suffer. You just do whatever the fuck you have to do. Who gives a shit about how I feel, right?" I'd had no one to talk to for weeks about how I'd been feeling. It felt so good to finally get it out. I couldn't stop. "You had a million different ways to let me know you were okay, that there was a *reason* you weren't anywhere to be seen. But you let me sit there like an idiot, waiting for you like a desperate asshole. Big bad surveillance expert and you can't figure out how to leave a note? *Eso es pura paja,* that's total bullshit and you know it."

Román grabbed my arm and pulled me back into the tree's shadow. His breathing was harder. So was mine. My wrists were clamped together in his hands, my balled fists useless and tiny. He jammed his mouth against mine. I wanted to jerk my face away but couldn't stop myself giving in.

"I couldn't risk contacting you," he said again when we'd broken apart. "What don't you understand? Ugly would kill us both. Don't be such a fucking child."

"Bullshit. You could've still—"

His mouth on mine. Opening, sliding my lips apart. The taste of his tongue. I pulled his lower lip between my teeth, bit down hard. He yanked his head back and touched a finger to his lip, checking for blood and staring at me like I'd lost my mind.

I crossed my arms over my chest. "It's not as easy as a quick sorry and a kiss. You don't know what the last two months have been like. I expected more from you."

His eyes bulged, the first time I'd seen his emotions get the better of him. "*Expected?* You can't have expectations in a situation like—" He cut himself short just as he'd begun to shout, then turned and pressed his hands against the tree trunk, his muscles shifting and slid-ing beneath his T-shirt as he rolled his shoulders back and exhaled hard through his nose. I didn't care if he was about to lose his temper. I'd been losing mine for two months.

When he turned to face me again, he'd composed himself. Usual cool, crisp Román. "Go to the San Fernando High Street tomorrow. Wait for me in a parking lot somewhere."

"You want me to drag my ass two hours down the highway to meet you? What the fuck for?"

"Listen!" Something in his tone made my mouth snap shut. "There are icebergs up ahead. What Milagros did was bad, not a boo-boo I can slap a Band-Aid on. Ugly wants repercussions. Just find yourself on the San Fernando High Street tomorrow and wait for me. Any parking lot."

I knew better than to stay on my high horse then. I'd never heard that kind of urgency in his voice.

"What time?"

"Doesn't matter. I'll know when you leave Port of Spain. Just do what I'm telling you."

Though I stayed stiff, he pulled me to him, pressed his mouth to mine one last time, and then left. Watching him walk away, I dragged my fingers through my hair, wanting to scream, chase him, beat him with my fists, let him pull me down onto the grass and fuck the anger out of me because goddamn had I missed him and already I was hating myself for not being able to hold back my rage when all I'd really wanted was to wrap myself around him. More than hating myself, I hated him for making me need him so badly that I couldn't help but be furious at his absence, couldn't help illogically dismissing his explanations and pushing him away—the one person I wanted more than anyone.

———

When I slipped back into the dark living room, the dancer was waiting for me, sipping a beer on the couch. I froze, caught red-handed.

"Don't worry, I won't tell," she said, waggling a pair of thin, severely arched eyebrows. She smiled a greasy smile. "Relax, *bruja*, I won't say a word. God knows I wouldn't kick Román outta bed."

"Listen," I croaked, "it's just that if my family knew, they—" But she didn't care what I had to say.

"There must be something about that tree," she interrupted, clearly enjoying herself, languidly running a two-inch teal-blue fingernail along the mouth of the beer bottle. "I saw your brother and that pregnant chick really going at it under there a few nights ago. I mean *really* going at it, doggy-style. Weird. Isn't she your cousin or something?"

And that's how I found out Sancho and Vanessa were fucking.

BACKHANDED FAVORS

Exactly like when I'd seen Sancho and Vanessa fooling around under the mango tree all those months ago, I opted to forget what the dancer told me. She'd be leaving in a couple days anyway; then there wouldn't be anyone left who knew about their little secret—not to mention my and Román's secret. Problem solved. In any case, Sancho and Vanessa were hardly at the forefront of my mind. The following morning, as Román had instructed, I wrangled the Datsun out of Zulema's custody and drove to San Fernando. By eight a.m., I was parked at a pharmacy, and within a few minutes, a pop of a horn called my attention to a dark-tinted black SUV driving into the parking lot. It stopped in front of the Datsun, idling. I hesitated, unable to see through the heavy tint. As much as I wanted to see Román (regardless of how angry I still was), I wasn't stupid enough to get into some strange car that I couldn't see into. I stayed put. My phone rang once from a private number then cut off. I knew for sure then that it was him. He must've used another car in case the Jeep was too easy for Ugly to track.

I opened the passenger door of the SUV, slid into the dark, leather-swathed interior, and let Román run his hand up my thigh. He leaned in to kiss me. As much as I'd planned to stay close-mouthed and icy, I couldn't help but let him.

"Thank you for coming," he said, pulling out of the pharmacy lot.

"Did I have a choice?"

He snorted. "As if you could ever be forced into doing something you didn't want to."

"So what's going on with Aunt Milagros?" I said tightly. "Every lawyer my father speaks to says not to contact the police station where they had her because of our status here—we don't have a clue what's going on, if charges have been laid or what."

I noticed as Román's knuckles bulged. He was gripping the steering wheel hard.

He ignored my questions. "We're going somewhere safe that we won't be seen. We'll talk there."

"Román—"

"It's a beautiful place," he said, cutting me off. "Somewhere I've wanted to show you for a long time."

Now I was really on edge. But I knew there was no coercing Román into talking about something until he was good and ready. So I sat back and took in the drive as we made our way out of the small city and into the wilderness of the countryside.

As we drove on for more than an hour, I started recognizing places I hadn't seen since we'd rocked up on the shores of Trinidad in that pirogue without the faintest idea what lay in store for us. We passed through La Brea, where two years ago my father had shared all of his recently acquired trivia about our new home.

"You see how the roads are lumpy and uneven? It's because of the asphalt overspill from the Pitch Lake that makes the ground shift all the time. See how it makes the houses wobbly and tilted?"

"And look!" he'd said, rhapsodizing over the sights like we were cruising through a Grimm Brothers–crafted Enchanted Forest. *"You see the stilts all the houses are built on? They're drill pipes from the rigs. This used to be real oil country."*

"Uh huh."

"Did you know the Pitch Lake is the largest natural deposit of asphalt in the world?"

"Neat."

The SUV rolled on past those same splintered houses teetering on drill pipes, past Cedros, where my family and I had alighted, and several other sleepy villages, until we came to Icacos—one of those mystical corners of Trinidad that people know of but where few have been. Its mysticism has been earned mostly because it is, to use a Trini expression, behind God's back, an unholy four-hour drive from Port of Spain. But there's another factor contributing to its mystical atmosphere: it is an infinite galaxy of coconut trees. There are so many coconut trees that when you're driving through them, it starts to feel like you've submerged yourself in one of those Magic Eye posters from the nineties—you know, the ones where you're supposed to see the hidden image of a dolphin but all you can see are colorful dots and squiggles? We drove through all those dizzying coconut plantations for what felt like forever, until we bumped along a dirt road that ended at long last on a dismal strip of beach looking out onto the faded blue outline of Venezuelan mountains, just across the Gulf. I understood now why the spot was special. *La Patria* was so close you felt you could reach out and touch it, could almost smell the tear gas clouding the streets of Caracas, hear the echoes of army batons cracking into protestors' skulls and the self-righteous bristling of Maduro's mustache as he looked out over it all from the balcony of Miraflores Palace.

Román took off his sunglasses and turned to face me. "Milagros is gone."

He said it so matter-of-factly I could only stare at him. "Are you telling me Aunt Milagros is dead?" I asked finally.

"No—though she nearly could've been."

"What!"

"She's not dead, just gone." He turned to look out at our homeland. "Back in Venezuela."

I stared out over the placid aluminum ocean like it would make my eyes telescopic, as if I'd be able to see Aunt Milagros on a distant mountain peak, her linen clothes flapping in the wind, cigarette smoke streaming above her to merge with the clouds.

"That was the best I could do for her, and I could get myself murdered for it. I did everything I could."

I tried to interrupt him, but he flashed a palm to stop me. "Ugly wanted her in the ground for putting his business in jeopardy. As in: throat cut, bullet in her head, dead, gutted and buried. Do you understand?"

I felt like a hernia had just ruptured in me. I clutched at my stomach.

"I got her out of here and she's safe," Román continued. "As far as Ugly knows, she's dead. But I had to tell you the truth because she can't contact any of you herself. It's too dangerous. I couldn't do anything better than that for her. She understood that."

I didn't know what to say. Poor, sweet, lost-her-marbles Aunt Milagros back in the hellhole of Venezuela. I know you're thinking, *That's better than being dead*, but my head just couldn't wrap itself around the idea of her actually narrowly escaping murder. I mean, we were illegal immigrants, but middle-class illegals. Middle-class people are conditioned to fear cancer, inflation, mortgage-rate spikes, greenhouse gases, pesticides, the rampancy of HPV, the incurability of premature baldness, the perils of fucking tooth decay. Murder is simply not on the middle-class person's list of quotidian fears—why the hell else did we leave Venezuela if not to eschew the disarmingly unfamiliar threats of murder, starvation, death-due-to-no-medical-supplies? So maybe my synapses just couldn't truly connect the dots of what Román had done for Aunt Milagros, or maybe I was in emotional shock, but all I felt was fury and a sickening sense of injustice that any of this had happened to Aunt Milagros at all.

Román was still talking. "Ugly said she couldn't be trusted in that state of mind. She could've led the police straight back to him. He insisted, Yola. Do you have any clue what could happen if Ugly ever finds out I betrayed him? Do you know the position I put myself in for you, for your family?"

I stayed tight-lipped, still reeling. Aunt Milagros was back in Maduro's near-dystopian abyss. She could easily be shot or stabbed for a cell phone, a bracelet, any trinket while walking the streets. Without a job or money, how could she pay the soaring black-market rates for basic food? What if she was hurt while making her way back to Caracas? Would a hospital have any supplies to help her? People were killing and blackmailing each other for sugar and diapers, far less real medical supplies and proper food. Román may have saved her from murder, but only to condemn her to a slower death.

And it was all Ugly's fault—and Román's. Forcing us to bring strangers into our homes, driving Aunt Milagros crazy from paranoia then punishing her for it. And to think Román wanted me to pat him on the back, to condescend to thanking him for not murdering my aunt.

He'd gone silent, was looking at me like he was eyeing a pit bull, not quite sure if or when I'd lunge at him. But what could I say or do that would make a difference now?

"Take me back to my car," I said quietly.

"Yola—"

"RIGHT NOW!" Something snapped in me with an almost audible crack. "You think you're some kind of Prince Charming because you didn't murder one of my relatives? Well, thank you very much for your magnanimity. Is that why you didn't come around? Because you didn't have the balls to tell me what you did?"

I knew I was being unfair, but together with my fear for Aunt Milagros's uncertain future, that sense of injustice that Román and Ugly were responsible at the root made me want to scream and gnash my teeth, shatter the windshield. The whole mess of it all only reminded me that we were helpless, that backhanded favors like the one Román had done Aunt Milagros were the most we could hope for in our position. And the only thing that made me feel better about that helplessness was to vent that rage at Román, no matter how ungrateful and illogical that made me.

His expression hardened the more I laid into him, until, by the time I was done, his face was a stone mask.

We didn't talk the entire drive back, as clusters of houses grew denser, as ramshackle produce stands morphed into air-conditioned grocery stores, as potholes became shallower if not sparser, children more clothed and less potbellied. Only when we got to the pseudo-urbanity of San Fernando did I feel collected enough to speak again.

"How could you do that to her?"

Román exhaled. I couldn't tell if it was out of exasperation or relief that I'd at least spoken to him. "Why do you have to be so hardheaded? What else could I have done to help?"

It was even more infuriating that I knew he was right—in our under-the-radar lives, all people like us Palacios had was the helping hands of our oppressors. Isn't that how it always goes? You have to be grateful for the employer who hires you under the table, even if it's doing bitch work for below minimum wage. You have to smilingly accept the boss's hand on your ass because any lip from you and all he has to do is put in a phone call to National Security to report that his housekeeper has no papers. Sure, Román had helped, but he was also responsible for creating the situation that had led to Aunt Milagros needing help in the first place. I couldn't bring myself to swallow my anger and kiss the oppressing hand just because it had the dual power to protect.

"I don't know, Román, I don't know what else you could have done. I don't know your world. But you could've come up with something better."

"Something better like what? Stick her in a top hat and magically pull her out in some suburb in South Florida? Venezuela was the only option there was. How can you sit there and be pissed when you know I had no other choice but to send her back there?"

I should've gotten out of the car right then, listened to the tinny little voice in my ear telling me he'd done all he could, should've pulled the door open and dropped and rolled out of the moving SUV right there on the San Fernando High Street before I said something I'd regret. But I didn't.

"You and the same old record: *I didn't have a choice. I work for Ugly and beat people up and stalk them for a living because I have no choice.*" I spat every word at him. "You knew exactly what you were sending Aunt Milagros back to, so why don't you take some accountability for your actions for once?" And then, because I was an irrational fucking bitch: "You're a piece of shit, just like Ugly, except what makes you worse is you're doing this to your own people. You're the reason families like mine had to leave, you're why my whole entire life is in chaos, you're the reason people all over the world look at us like refugee scum when a generation ago we were the richest country on the continent, you're why everything has gone irrevocably to shit. Because the people in charge are opportunistic fucks like you who pat themselves on the back thinking they're fighting the good fight for the socialist Bolivarian dream when all they're really doing is personally benefiting from shitting all over broken, helpless people. Exactly like you do."

––––––––––

At the pharmacy parking lot I whipped off my seat belt and was about to get out of the SUV without another word, but Román grabbed my arm.

"What now?" I was already regretting what I'd said to him, knowing I'd crossed a line, but was still too upset, or maybe just too stubborn, to take any of it back.

"I can't believe you don't see how much I've risked for you," he said. His tone was softer than I'd ever heard it, but I was just too damned angry. I pulled my arm away and got out of the car.

I frothed with a confusing combination of rage and regret the whole way up to Port of Spain. I cried until my head throbbed and my face was a swollen, mottled mess. I wasn't only crying for Aunt Milagros, but for the bitch-slap of reality that my family and I were among the most vulnerable of vermin in this country. I'd thought of us as cockroaches before, hiding in the shadows. But we were worse than that, because at least a roach had a hard shell. The fuck did we have to protect us?

By the time I got home, though, my shock and anger had cooled, gelling into a dry, hard crust of regret. Because with a clearer head, I realized that things were definitively over with Román. I knew the pride he had, the love of country he'd revealed while we lamented Venezuela's fall from grace over many a shared joint, the two of us stoned, misty-eyed with homesickness. I'd taken that patriotic pride and shat all over it. And I'd done it even though I could see how hurt he was that I wouldn't acknowledge what he'd risked. No, he wouldn't be with me after that. However much I tried to justify my outburst, it wouldn't be good enough, and I'd never be able to take it back.

———

Though I could hardly pull another dengue stunt and mope in bed all day, I gave myself one week to abandon hygiene, grooming, and healthy eating as I mourned Román's now inevitable disappearance from my life—at least in a romantic capacity. While scarfing cheese puffs in two-day-old pajamas, I tried not to keep replaying the harshness of what I'd said to him, cursing my inability to thwart all those genetically wired impulses that allow pop culture to accurately peg Latin women as "feisty," "fiery," and "mothafuckin' crazy as shit." How could I not have seen past my instantaneous emotions to recognize that Román had risked his life to do right by me and my family? I'd made my own bed of pure shit and now I had to lie in it and breathe in the stink.

On day seven of unwashed hair, too few showers, and too much junk food, I began the grueling process of getting myself together, turning to familiar salves: writing and Aunt Celia.

I clutched Aunt Celia's manuscript like a talisman. I don't know how else I would've survived the pain of pushing Román away. Because Aunt Celia had done the very same thing when she divorced Mauricio in the late nineties, experiencing the same conflicted, guilt-riddled suffering I was feeling. So I slipped into the story of Aunt Celia and Mauricio's divorce like it was a vat of numbing cream—like if Aunt Celia could justify divorcing a man she loved, I could justify what I'd said to the man I loved. Or maybe I read it over and over because I hoped Román would come back to me in spite of what I'd said to him, just like Mauricio never left Aunt Celia, proposing to her almost annually with extravagant rings, even though she always took the ring and always said no.

Just before Aunt Celia divorced Mauricio, he was almost definitely fucking every single woman who crossed his path. The bee-sting incident had only cooled his loins for a hot minute. Ava was less than a year old when Celia's suspicions spiked. Mauricio had called one day to say he'd be gone overnight to do a big croc-hide shipment. Celia said sure, no problem, and hung up. Then, obeying her woman's intuition, she dug through Mauricio's belongings until she found the one thing that told her exactly where Mauricio would be: chicken feathers stuck to the sole of his leather boot. She scooped up the baby and drove straight to the fowl farm where María (the former cold sore–afflicted beauty queen Mauricio had tried hiring as the new nanny) lived with her brother's family. María's brother had been selling chickens to Mauricio as croc food from day one, so Celia knew exactly where to go. She found the farm in darkness except for a light burning through the window of a small annex round the back of the main house, where María lived. She crept up to the lit window, and when she peeped through, there was Mauricio balls deep in that failed pageant queen whose skyward giraffe legs were almost scuffing the ceiling while Mauricio pounded away.

Celia didn't do a thing. She went home calmly. The next day she paid a few unscrupulous friends of Uncle Ignacio's to beat Mauricio senseless. Which they did.

Believing the beating to have been arranged by rival crocodile breeders, an oblivious Mauricio went on screwing around as he saw fit—which meant every day, often with different women, even more often with Beauty Queen María. Celia was beside herself. But the angrier she got, the more she kind of felt like screwing too. She'd scream at Mauricio and throw things at him and once even stabbed him in the thigh with an ice pick, but then after every fight, they'd screw, screw, screw. It shouldn't have come as a surprise then that when Ava was barely over a year old, Celia accidentally got herself knocked up with Alejandra.

That was the last straw from Mauricio. It *really* pissed Celia off that she was pregnant again. It was time for Mauricio to face the music. She set his car on fire. Smashed his entire collection of expensive watches. Fed his leather shoes to stray dogs. Put red wine in a spray bottle and spritzed his suit collection with merlot. Mildly poisoned his food so he suffered constant diarrhea, nausea, cold sweats. Then when she still wasn't satisfied, she told him she was filing for divorce and kicked him out of the house, which, as it turned out, is when Mauricio spent the week at his parents' home in Isla de Gato, a visit so productive it yielded Vanessa nine months later.

Despite Vanessa's conception, which Aunt Celia would never discover, Mauricio did appear truly devastated upon his return from Isla de Gato. He couldn't understand why Celia would break their family apart. She told him she didn't love him anymore, just to hurt him. She said the way he talked, walked, smelled drove her crazy, turned her stomach, made her sick. She called him a scumbag, a loser. She said she wished she'd never taken that shot with him back at the nightclub in Miami, that she wished Ava had a decent father, that she should abort the baby in her belly so it wouldn't have to grow up with Mauricio for a dad.

The one thing she never told him was that she'd seen him cheating with María.

Though Celia divorced him, dragged his name through the mud, and humiliated him in front of the judge, Mauricio never moved out.

Celia, still very much in love with her now ex-husband, never wanted him to anyway.

So maybe I could blame my irrationality on genetics—maybe that was just our feisty, fiery, mothafuckin'-crazy-as-shit Palacios way.

———————

My regret piqued when Román informed my parents of Aunt Milagros's true fate. I wished he hadn't. Because all of a sudden, Román the Villain became Román the Hero. Beelzebub became Christ Reborn.

Mamá: "The way he put himself in danger to protect crazy Milagros . . . he's a saint."

Alejandra: "I knew a guy that hot couldn't be all bad."

Mauricio: "A true *venezolano*! I knew it the minute I met him, that he'd never harm his Bolivarian brethren. *¡Viva la República!*"

Papá: "I will be forever indebted to him. God bless Román. *Que Dios le bendiga.*"

Everyone: "*¡Que Dios le bendiga!*"

It was further proof that Román did care about me and, by extension, my family, risking his own skin just to reassure my parents that Aunt Milagros was safe.

He also stuck his neck out to give *Papá* a warning: Ugly would be making all of us compensate for Aunt Milagros's near-fatal error. Things were about to get even more interesting for us Palacios.

THE BEST EVER AD FOR SUPERGLUE

By the time Ugly came a-calling, I was ready to crawl on hands and knees begging Román's forgiveness. I would've found a way to take him aside whether or not my family and Ugly were there, just for any chance to apologize. But when Ugly turned up on the day Román had forewarned, he was alone.

I was in the porch watering the ferns and orchids that hung in wire baskets when I heard Ugly knocking on the front door and announcing himself.

"Hector! Come out, come out wherever you are! Ha! Ha! Ha! Don't make me huff and puff and blow down the house. Ha! Ha! Ha!"

Prick.

I watched through the glass-paned doors as my parents let him in and led him to the living room. A second later my mother told me to wake Zulema. "Ugly wants to speak to everyone," she explained tersely.

When Zulema and I went to the living room, Ugly was sitting on the couch with his legs crossed like a dandy, clad in an absurd denim suit and holding a curved cane that seemed to be a bent piece of iron rebar.

Seeing my sister and me, Ugly spread his arms in greeting. "*¡Qué placer!* My Spanish really getting good, eh?"

Zulema, the daft bobblehead, complimented his accent. I sat in the chair farthest from Ugly and said nothing. We were all there—my parents, Zulema, and I—but Ugly wasn't in any rush to get down to business. Once we sat, he withdrew a neatly constructed joint from his jacket pocket, which he lit with a heavy gold lighter. After what felt like a decade of him lazily smoking, Ugly dropped the joint filter into his empty teacup and leaned back against the couch, folding his hands behind his head. He was right at home, the shitbag.

"So, ladies and gent, you all aware that Milagros cause a bit of a problem for me and my operations, yes?"

"Yes," said *Papá*. He cleared his throat loudly like he usually did when about to tell a lie (I'd figured this out as a kid because he'd clear his throat compulsively when telling my siblings and me about Santa Claus and the like). "And we haven't seen Milagros yet. At the police station, they do not tell us where she has been sent or if she is there. We're very worried."

Ugly flashed his movie star's smile. His mouth stretched clear across his face to meet his ears, each bearing a large diamond stud. That wide, angular grin made him look like an alligator.

"Milagros well taken care of," he said. "She just fine. But don't expect to hear from her anytime soon."

Now Ugly's grin was so wide his face looked like it'd been sliced clean in half.

"How you ain't going and tell me where my own sister gone?" said *Papá*, giving it his all with the fake indignation, the damned dialect tic cropping up like it always did. He leaned forward in his chair to drive a finger onto the coffee table. "I DEMAND you tell me where Milagros is."

"Hector!" Ugly laughed. "I ain't have to tell you a fucking thing, my man. I could bring Milagros in front your face and slit she open from her chinny-chin-chin right down to her hairy Catholic cunt and you wouldn't be able to do a thing about it. So it best you think before you go making *demands* like you forget who the fuck I am."

Mamá made the sign of the cross and started up with the chest-pounding. "*Ay* Milagros." I had to hand it to her: it was a credible performance. Even I sort of wondered if *Mamá* had somehow forgotten Aunt Milagros was safe in Venezuela.

Ugly chuckled. He was flicking his lighter open and closed, squinting at the flame shooting up then disappearing again, like it was the most fascinating thing he'd ever seen. "Calm yourself, Yasmin. Milagros just fine. Forget about Milagros."

While he stared at the flame, his smile never wavered. His eyes were two red slits. With those eyes and the reptilian grin, he genuinely looked demonic. I almost couldn't bear to look at him.

"Forget about she and worry about all-you own selves. Maybe I getting soft, but usually I'd have shoot every one of you between the eye for what Milagros do. Imagine—nobody come to warn poor old Ugly that Milagros gone mad. Nobody even think, *Hmm, now how this crazy bitch could mess up Ugly business?* Very disappointing. We had such a good run of things since Celia kick the bucket."

He stood and tucked the lighter in his pocket, then drew a handgun from a holster hidden in his jacket. He held the gun and contemplated it the same way he'd looked at the flame—up close, squinting hard.

"Fire really something special, eh?" he said, almost to himself, while examining the gun from all angles. "You could do so much with it. Cook a food. Light a fire to cozy up. Burn down house. Make a little ball of lead fly in a straight line till it end up in somebody skull."

My father got up from his seat while Ugly was saying all this. His shoulders were thrown back, head held at that alpha male angle it took on when he was leading a family meeting or sizing up one of our new boyfriends. Every muscle in my body was suddenly taut. Could he really be insane enough to square up to Ugly? *Mamá* was staring intently at *Papá*, fist glued to her chest, face like a frightened rabbit.

Ugly hadn't picked up on *Papá*'s confrontational stance. He seemed as relaxed as could be. He even tucked the gun back into its holster and grabbed hold of the cane, resting his hands atop it like some genteel old fogey.

"I going to give all-you a chance to make up for how you let me down with Milagros," he said smoothly. "I am a businessman first and foremost, after all. Things could usually be rectified in dollars and cents for me. If we consider things that way, what Milagros did only increase the interest on Celia's debt. Naturally, all-you now have to pay that interest."

Saying this, he slowly raised the cane to aim it directly at my father like a professor singling out a student with a pointer. *Papá* was unfazed. Maybe he thought we had a stronger leg to stand on because Román had two-timed Ugly. Like Román would keep us safe just as he'd kept Aunt Milagros safe.

But Román wasn't there.

"How is it that Celia's debt not paid yet, Ugly?" My father's chin was lifted, defiant. "Since November we are keeping people in our houses for you. It is July. This have to come to a stop sooner or later."

Ugly howled and hooted. He was tickled pink by that one. "It continue as long as I say, *amigo*! And I could tell you one thing—it most likely to be later rather than sooner!"

"I think the debt is paid already." My father walked forward until he and Ugly were squared off, separated only by the rigid horizontal cane between them. "Enough is enough."

"I go agree to disagree on that one, Hector. I also go have to ask you to take a seat." He prodded my father once, lightly, in the chest with the cane. "Because you in my personal space and I don't fucking like it."

Papá didn't move. Ugly exhaled as though disappointed in him. Then in one coordinated movement, Ugly lowered the cane, withdrew the gun, and aimed it smack in the middle of my father's forehead. Almost point-blank range. We heard the bullet slide into the chamber with a neat little click as Ugly took off the safety.

There wasn't a breath in that room.

Papá took two steps backward but didn't sit.

"Thank you, Hector. Now without any further interruption, here how things going to work from now on."

He re-holstered the gun and perched himself on the couch, folding his hands across the curve of the cane. He then proceeded to tell us about his latest entrepreneurial venture: a gentlemen's club.

For those not up to speed on their sex-trade jargon, "gentlemen's club" is a euphemism for strip club. This explained all the dancers who'd been staying with our households. None of them had come to escape Maduro's bullshit. They came for a specific job opportunity: to work for Ugly in his soon-to-be-opened strip club.

With all the bizarre aplomb of someone pitching to a panel of investors, Ugly informed us that strip clubs were illegal in Trinidad, even though there were a few tucked away behind Chinese restaurants and various seedy establishments. The problem, he said, was that these strip clubs were strip-clubs-cum-brothels. A lap dance could easily turn into a fingerbang or a blow job or whatever the guy had the cash to pay for. While gesturing dramatically with the cane, Ugly explained that he had loftier ambitions for his business.

"My club go be like all the global strip club franchises, like Spearmint Rhino. No mattress in a back room. No groping up the dancers. No *nastiness*. This going to be the highest standard of gentlemen's club. Class, style, exclusive. Not just anybody could get in neither. Only the cream of the crop could cross my threshold to feast they eyes on the most beautiful Latin women in the world." His eyes glowed red, his tongue darting feverishly between the corners of his mouth to wet his lips. "It go be like in Prohibition, when everybody want to go the speakeasies, where you went to see and be seen. This go be the start of an underground *empire!*"

He raised the cane with a triumphant flourish then looked around the room as though expecting applause.

Mamá cleared her throat. Zulema looked slightly confused. *Papá*'s face showed nothing but contempt. I was begrudgingly impressed that

199

Ugly knew about Prohibition and speakeasies and international gentlemen's club franchising.

"So where do we come in?" asked *Papá*, weary.

"I have the dancers," Ugly replied, pulling another premade joint from his jacket pocket. "All you go be staff. And to be clear, your services to be provided free of charge."

So that was our punishment for Aunt Milagros: in addition to safe-housing, we'd be unremunerated strip-club workers.

My father's face resembled nothing so much as a scorpion pepper, red and engorged with fury. He cleared the few feet between him and the couch to stand over Ugly. "If you think my daughters go work in a dirty strip club, you mad! I will NEVER allow it!"

Before I could even process the stupidity of what my father had done, Ugly had driven the curved handle of the cane into the base of my father's nose, breaking it in one clean shot. *Papá* stumbled backward, hands over his face. My mother was on her feet, screaming. Zulema and I leapt up from our seats openmouthed but no screams came out. Ugly had gotten up, was taking slow steps forward, eyes locked on to my father. Blood streamed over *Papá*'s mouth and chin. He was disoriented, dazed by the blow. Ugly raised the cane. I shrieked as it came down on the back of my father's skull. *Papá*'s knees buckled; he fell forward into a kneel, cradling the back of his head. Fat drops of blood splattered from his nose onto the tiles. *Mamá* started forward to run to him, but Ugly pointed the cane at us and tutted.

"You see what I have in my hand?" asked Ugly evenly.

We didn't answer.

"I said *you see what I have in my hand*?"

We nodded, knowing better than to risk no response.

"This is a rebar that come from a house my father try to build when I was a schoolboy." He lowered the cane and walked in a slow circle around *Papá*, who was still kneeling and hunched over. I think he was concussed. He didn't move or say a word, but his body swayed slightly like at any second he might flop to the side or flat onto his face.

"My father was a good, hardworking, honest man. He always tell me be kind. Tell me respect people, think about they feelings. That how my father live he life. He work hard, save up, and finally he have enough money so he could build a nice big house. And you know what happen when that house halfway up? My good, kind, respectful father get rob by a man who not so good or kind or respectful. Not once or twice, but all the time. When them bad-john see he start to earn money, he get rob every fucking payday, and if he try to hide the money, he get beat and I get beat and my sisters get drag in a alley by these men who know it don't do any good to be kind and have respect. My father lose every cent. We lose the house. We lose everything.

"I gone to that half-finish house and take a good look at the future my father lose. The future *I* lose. Then I pick up this piece of rebar from the construction site like a souvenir of everything we lose—a reminder of why I never going to be kind or have respect for no-fucking-body. I make up my mind then and there—kindness and consideration only make you weak. People in the town where I grow up say they could see it in my face the day I gone for that rebar and decide to never be weak like my father. They say my face turn ugly from that day, that all the badness in me come through the pores and twist up my whole face. I never care. I tell them, good, call me Ugly. I could survive ugly in life. Better ugly than weak. If you weak you take licks like a dog and anybody could take away everything from you.

"So when people like your pappy Hector here feel he could play on my good nature, which allow me to give all-you Vene cunts all kind of different way to repay the debts and fuckups of your family members, you could understand why I cannot tolerate that type of disrespect. That would be *weakness*. And it don't have no room for weakness in this life. Not my life."

He'd made a full circle to stand in front of *Papá*, who was groaning and trying to straighten up, blinking hard to focus.

Ugly tapped the cane on *Papá*'s shoulder. "Get up, Hector." He

201

pointed the cane at *Mamá*. "Yasmin, get the man some water. This conversation not over. He have to wake his ass up."

My mother ran to the kitchen.

Satisfied that he'd made his point, Ugly sat on the couch. He gestured for Zulema and me to sit back down. We did. Zulema was crying, but I found myself looking Ugly straight in the face. Anger pushed out my fear. I wanted him to know how much he disgusted me. I wished I were stupid enough to launch myself at him and claw his eyes out. Lucky for me, he didn't look back at me. He crossed his legs, waving one foot in its white snakeskin brogue, and stared at my father as though daring him to try defying him again.

Mamá blew into the room with a glass of water and kneeled beside my father, murmuring to him. Ugly, meanwhile, was lighting up his second joint.

Finally *Papá* managed to move my mother aside, and even with two instant black eyes, a busted nose pouring blood, and a probable concussion, he stood up with his chest puffed out like a gladiator.

"We won't do it. You hit me as much as you want. My daughters are not strippers."

"¡Puta madre, Hector!" shrieked my mother. "SHUT UP!"

Ugly sniggered. "Take your wife advice and shut your mouth, Hector. Because I ain't go hit you again, but I go shoot every fucking tooth out your head if you feel you going to disobey me."

"I am trying to do the best for my family," said *Papá* stiffly, his voice all nasal and weird from the broken nose. He was fucking insane. Or maybe it was the concussion messing with him.

"And that exactly why you should do as I say, *amigo*." Ugly stayed unnervingly cavalier while he finished his joint. "I understand your resistance to working in my gentlemen's club. I not unreasonable, Hector. Not unreasonable at all. But if you don't work there, if *any* of your family members feel they not working there, I can promise, hand on heart . . ." He put his hand on his heart. ". . . that I go personally gut each and every one of all-you myself. I go sell your organs to recoup my unpaid debts from Celia, and send your skinned hides directly to your father. Maybe he could use them for a lampshade, or to upholster a couch, I ain't know. I believe his address is Calle Principal, house 104, San Antonio Parish, Libertador Municipality—that right? So you make your decision whether or not you want to disobey what I telling you. That up to you, Hector. But I assume you not stupid enough to make the wrong choice."

Then, smiling as always, Ugly stood, hooked the cane over his arm, and left.

———

The following morning, Ugly left us a little something, I guess to prove that his threats weren't empty and that he did indeed know a thing or two about gutting and skinning living things.

Mamá was the one to discover it when she was heading over to the annex.

Attached to our front door with inexplicably powerful superglue was the grotesquely skinned head of Aunt Milagros's unnamed spinster cat, its mouth rigidly open and stuffed with a balled-up note.

My father, sister, and I ran outside at *Mamá's* screams. *Papá*, lurid violet bruises beneath his eyes, shielded the hideous cat head from my mother's view, and Zulema and I took her into the house, where she beat her chest and wailed. Meanwhile *Papá* dug the note out of the cat's mouth and read it aloud, his voice still unnaturally nasal. In neatly printed lettering, it said: "Make the right decision for your family, Hector—Best wishes, FEO."

Papá tossed the note and tried prying the cat head off our door. The thing wouldn't budge. That superglue *worked*. Eventually he called Sancho to bring over his tool kit and give him a hand. Then *Papá* inspected the house's perimeter and found that the cat's organs and innards were scattered around our porch, black and shifting with flies. He gathered it all in a trash bag while we watched, gagging, from the living room. Further inspection revealed that other severed cat parts had also been superglued all over the place. The stiff tail was stuck to one of the porch pillars, a hind leg stuck onto the groin of a garden gnome like a disproportionately large, fluffy erection. On the front bumper of *Papá*'s minivan, the cat's forelegs were arranged side by side like Frankenstein arms, its white paws like dainty debutante gloves—in any other circumstances it would've looked pretty funny.

When Sancho came, he and *Papá* made the rounds again, trying to remove all the cat bits. No luck. It was the best ad for superglue I'd ever seen. Eventually they Googled how to loosen even the strongest superglue. Turned out the answer had been under their noses all along: acetone. *Mamá* had liters of the stuff in her annex for acrylic manicures. So they doused the festering skinless cat head in acetone and went around the house anointing the various cat parts until our home was no longer a feline necropolis. With their work finally done, believe it or not, everyone went back about their business: *Mamá* to the annex, Zulema to the spa, and *Papá* to his new gig as a part-time Spanish tutor. Proof that once enough shit went down—blackmail, breakdowns, beatings—you just got desensitized to it all. There'd be no wallowing over tortured cats at the Palacios house.

Anyway, that left Sancho and me alone. He was at the kitchen sink scrubbing the acetone smell off his hands when I spotted my opportunity to tackle him on Vanessa—I'd never confronted him after that dancer had told me she saw the two of them at it under the mango tree.

"So," I asked, sidling over. "How are things with the ladies? Been a while since you brought anyone around."

"Not in the mood for women's whining and bitching these days."

"Vanessa doesn't whine or bitch? Because you're obviously in the mood for *her*."

Silence. The faucet gushing water. Sancho's face reddening by the second.

"Mmm? Isn't that weird that you'd be sleeping with Vanessa if you're not in the mood for women with all their bitching and whining?"

He closed the tap and leaned over the sink, staring into it like he wanted to jackknife down the drain hole and disappear. I was enjoying myself. "Also weird that you'd be sleeping with Vanessa seeing as she's pregnant for another guy. If she even *is* pregnant for that douchebag King. Sure it's not your baby?"

Sancho turned to jam a finger into my chest. "Shut the fuck up, talking about shit you know nothing about."

"Relax," I laughed, swatting his hand away. I'd been affectionately needling Sancho my whole life. His bark had no bite. "I'm just trying to tell you I know about you and Vanessa. That dancer chick Andrea saw you and her under the mango tree. She told me about it."

"Yeah? And she told *me* about you and Román under the mango tree."

Fuck. Didn't see that one coming.

"Ohhhh, so you don't like it when people call *you* out, do you?"

"It's . . . it's over anyway . . ." I started sputtering.

"Don't worry," he interrupted. "I know Román's not all bad. We talked before, a heart-to-heart sort of thing when I was going through that rough patch. He was actually pretty decent about it, tried to help me out. And he did save Aunt Milagros. Look, I won't say anything, but you need to shut your mouth about Vanessa. And she's not pregnant with my kid. We never actually slept together until after she was pregnant."

Relieved as I was that Sancho would keep my secret, I couldn't help making a face. "But she's pregnant with someone else's child. That's so . . ."

"Whatever, man. In Amsterdam pregnant prostitutes get good money just for being pregnant, and . . ."

I waved my hands in his face. "Nope, no. Just stop. It's weird and you know it."

He shrugged, but now I could see that he was embarrassed. I felt bad. "So do you love her or something?" I asked, just to change the course of the conversation.

"Or something," he snorted. But his cheeks were flushed. Whoa boy.

"Sancho, she's not even eighteen. You just turned thirty."

"I like her."

"But . . ."

"Yola, I *like* her. Drop it. It'll work out."

I doubted it.

THE PINK PIE

Not long after the cat incident, Román called a meeting of the Palacios houses to brief us on our new "assignment" at the strip club. I found out about the meeting a few days beforehand and was racked with insomnia all over again. There was the torment of being blackmailed into the choppy unknown of the sex industry for starters, but what really kept me awake was Román. I'd have to sit there surrounded by my family pretending to be completely normal, without giving the slightest hint of how badly I wanted to make amends for letting that red mist of fury overtake me in the car that day.

I had no idea how I was going to get through it.

Finally, the night before the meeting, I wrote him an apology letter, planning to slip it to him somehow. In it, I didn't push for any reconciliation, knowing I didn't deserve that, and knowing also that Ugly would be watching us more closely than ever with Román *and Papá* now in his bad books—a reconciliation would be too dangerous. So I just stated the facts of how ungrateful and unreasonable I'd been despite what Román had risked to save Aunt Milagros. All I could hope for was forgiveness.

The meeting was on a Saturday just after midday, the heaviest, stickiest time of day in the rainy season. Grossly hot, the sky a suffocating tarpaulin of black cloud. The entire family was gathered at Mauricio's house waiting for Román to turn up. My insane father had asked him if Ugly were coming so he could confront him about the cat. No, it would just be Román. So Fidel was there too, since Saturday was just another day of servitude for Camille and there was no risk of Ugly coming to threaten the kid again. Vanessa was playing with him, practicing for when her baby came in a couple months. Sancho was playing with Fidel too. Watching the three of them on the floor stacking building blocks, it was plain as day that there was something between Sancho and Vanessa.

Sipping my G&T, I idly wondered if Sancho would adopt Vanessa's baby. Though it was only lunchtime, we'd all had a drink already. (Sancho was on drink number four.) Everyone was edgy, especially my father and Mauricio, praying Ugly wouldn't force their daughters to strip. Sure, Ugly had said he only needed staff, but if he changed his mind, what the hell could we do but don our G-strings, bend over, and spread 'em?

I was just as nervous as they were, but that was strictly Román-specific. I didn't have the headspace to panic about the strip-club stuff *and* him. Folded into a tiny square, the letter was a hot coal in my pocket. I kept flitting to the bathroom to re-read it for the thousandth time, constantly on the brink of flushing it down the toilet. Why would he want a letter from me after how I'd acted? He'd probably tear it up in front of my face. I only stayed put after *Mamá* snapped: "You're driving me crazy! Up and down, up and down like a yo-yo!" So I sat, knees jigging, rattling the ice cubes in my second G&T. Waiting. Torture.

Then a knock on the front door.

Mauricio opened up and Román stepped into the house. I felt that lecherous cartoon wolf in my chest, pounding the table and whistling. Román looked *good*—wearing his standard jeans and T-shirt, but something was different. Could his shoulders be even broader? Was he taller? My mind was playing tricks on me, making the unattainable look even more appealing—the proverbial red apple gleaming waxy and full of saccharine promise on the Forbidden Tree.

There were sunny hellos all around for Román the Savior of Aunt Milagros. All eyes were on him. But when he lowered his sunglasses, the only place he looked was at me. He walked to the center of the living room and sat on an ottoman directly opposite my seat on the couch. My stomach was more than in knots—it was one of those giant rubber-band balls that's impossible to unravel. As he sat, our eyes locked like a couple of Lego blocks snapping into place. My cheeks flushed. I had to drop my gaze or I'd give myself away to the family.

"Thank you for coming, everyone," he said in the dry tone of a company director kicking off a shareholders' meeting. "I know things are sticky right now, but it's all going to be okay once you do as instructed. I want to clarify first off that you will all be floor staff only. Waitressing, bartending, and so on. No stripping." He paused to look around the room, waiting for any questions. When no one said anything, he continued: "The club is called the Pink Pie."

Sancho snorted. "The Pink Pie? Doesn't leave much to the imagination."

"I know, I know," said Román, turning his palms up to show that the name hadn't been his choice. "Anyway, the Pink Pie is where you'll be working, but as far as the rest of the world knows, you'll be picking up extra work at the Grosvenor Square Freemasons' Executive Lodge."

Then he went on to explain it all. The Pink Pie would be hidden behind the front of an exclusive lodge. The highbrow businessmen and politicians or whoever would walk shamelessly in the front like they were going to attend a lodge meeting, and coming in through the back would be streams of Latina strippers—and all of us. No one would investigate or disturb an exclusive lodge, particularly one whose members were the cream of the political and corporate crop. By keeping the client base exclusive and catering to the local police and regiment as well, Ugly's club would stay protected from the long arm of the law and from politicians' meddling.

The club would be open Thursdays to Sundays. We were all to work every night, from seven p.m. to four a.m., including Ava and Alejandra.

"But we have school!" Ava protested. She was in her final year, at the top of her class. She didn't fuck around with her studies.

"Everyone has to work," said Román. Then, more sympathetically: "I'll see if I can get you Thursdays and Sundays off. Don't get your hopes up."

The only ones who'd come into work later than seven were Mauricio and my father, who could come when the club opened at eight. Mauricio would be working as a valet. My father would be the on-call maintenance guy. The rest of us would be bar and waitstaff, so we had to come early to set up before opening time. Seven p.m.—not a minute later or the general manager would report back to Ugly immediately.

After he'd finished briefing us, Román stood and took a slip of paper from his back pocket. "This is the address." He handed me the paper. I looked up at his hand and remembered the feel of its rough palm running over my most delicate skin. I took the paper, felt his index finger lingering on mine. *I still want you*: that's what that finger said. Then he stepped back, clearing his throat and leaving my finger burning. Just like whenever he'd press his thumb to my lip and I'd feel it for hours after, like a tingling jellyfish sting.

"Ladies, you'll all have uniforms," he said, addressing everyone. "But please come wearing black heels and a black bra. You'll need that as part of your uniform. Yasmin, you won't need a uniform, but you must dress in appropriate business attire. Gents—white shirts and black trousers, please. This isn't a casual establishment. Make sure your appearance is sharp. Ugly is catering to Trinidad's elite, so we have to deliver. Any sloppiness will be reported by the manager and there will be consequences." He shoved his hands into his back pockets. "That's it, really. Yola has the address. Be there on Thursday night at seven. Questions?"

No questions. My parents and Mauricio even looked pleased, they were so relieved that no one would have to strip.

"Right," said Román, putting his sunglasses back on. "I'll try to work it so there are no drop-offs for the next week or so, at least while you're adjusting to the new work schedule. Though I can't make any promises."

Papá went to him. "Thank you, Román. I also wanted to thank you in person for Milagros. . . ."

Román motioned brusquely for my father to stop talking. *Papá* gave an acquiescent nod as Román then turned and walked to the door. My palms were instantly clammy—he couldn't leave! The letter! As he pulled the door open, time slowed, everything moving molasses-like. I had to stop him.

He'd already stepped outside when I sprang to my feet. "Wait!"

Now all eyes were on me, all eyebrows raised. Román froze in the doorway but didn't look back. "Yes?"

"I . . . I have a question. Sorry, it only just came to me."

Sancho was staring at me wide-eyed, trying to tell me to shut up; I was showing the whole family my hand. I ignored him.

"I, um, I'd rather ask you privately, though," I added.

"Yola, you can ask right here in front of everyone. I don't see why your question should be private," said my mother snippily. *Verga*. She'd smelled a rat.

"No, no, not *in private*," I said, fudging for the right phrasing. "I just want to ask something about the uniforms, and well, it's embarrassing. Can we just step outside for one second, Román?" I chewed the inside of my lip. If he said no, that was it, he was done with me. I was unforgiven. Now and forever. But if he said yes . . .

"Sure." He jerked his head toward the front yard.

A moment later the front door was shut and we were alone on the front step. I snatched the letter from my pocket.

"Román, I'm so . . ."

He pressed a finger to his lips and motioned for me to follow him onto the front lawn where we'd be out of earshot and could speak privately (thank God for whatever shoddy architect had designed Mauricio's living room without front windows). I handed him the letter. The air was so moist and warm I could see the paper already softening into waves as he unfolded it. Rain was going to come busting out of those clouds any second.

Thankfully, Román was a fast reader. In half a minute, he'd folded the letter and put it in his pocket. Followed by the pure agony of silence. He said nothing, just looked at me expressionlessly through the black of his sunglasses. I was going to have to apologize in person too.

I let it all come spurting out like hot blood from a fresh wound. "I'm so unbelievably sorry. I was wrong to say what I did. I know how much you risked and how unfair my reaction was. And the things I said. I know I can't take them back but I . . . I'm truly sorry. I didn't mean any of it, Román."

He took his sunglasses off and hooked them onto the collar of his T-shirt. Looked at me impassively. "I appreciate the apology."

I bit my lip. "I know there's no way we could ever start up again but . . ."

I couldn't speak anymore. A tear crept with humiliating slowness down my cheek. His expression softened then. He brushed the tear away gently, let me lean into his hand.

"Yola . . ." His voice had tightened, and I knew then, at least, that this was hard for him too. I looked up at him, wishing I could figure out what to say to get things back to where they'd been, but knowing that they never would be. And then every moment split into a dreamlike dichotomy of past and present: Román lowered his hand, surreptitiously scanning our surroundings before loosely linking his fingers in mine, and I was there in the pain of the present, but also in the Jeep driving along the coast, sliding my fingers across the car seat to interlace them with his, laughing and singing along to whatever lyrics we knew to "Gimme Shelter" and "Back in Black."

In a wildly reckless moment, Román pulled me against him and I was back to reality on Mauricio's front lawn, throat painfully constricted with restrained tears as I heard Román breathe in the smell of my hair like he was taking a final olfactory snapshot of the coconut-scented shampoo he once told me he loved. But I was also lying against him on gritty sand blanched bone-white by the moon as he buried his face in my hair. *"You smell like an island . . . like salt and coconut."* I'd laughed: *"The salt smell would be the ocean right over there and the coconut smell would be my shampoo."* He'd shaken his head and breathed me in. *"No, it's you. You're my island."* As we stood apart now, facing each other, his professional veneer back in place lest some family member should suspiciously crack open the front door, you'd never think he was capable of that sentimentality. Anyone else would just see the scarred forearms, the cage fighter's build, the former street urchin's toughness. No one would see what I knew of him—the dry humor, the unpredictable acts of tenderness that turned my insides to honey, the way he'd take his shoes off in the bush just because the earth under his bare feet made him feel grounded. His little idiosyncrasies like the holes in his socks that I always teased him about. His love of *Archie* comic books because they were one of the first things he'd managed to read cover-to-cover in English as a kid. His habit of keeping crackers and guava jam in his Jeep for a quick bite so his fingertips often had a faintly guava-sweet scent.

"Yola?"

He'd been telling me something but I hadn't heard a word of it.

"Sorry, what?"

"I was saying this is hard for me too, but it's too dangerous now for us. Do you remember I once told you Ugly wasn't a trusting man? Well, he has an associate, they call him Mongoose. He's keeping tabs on me now—not today—but he's broken into my place, taken a look around, thought I wouldn't notice. Ugly thinks I was slipping and distracted to let the Milagros fuckup happen. And he was right. I was distracted." He sighed and lifted a hand as though about to stroke my face, but dropped it. "I need to be careful. So do all of you—Mongoose might be checking up on all the clients under my purview now. Call it Ugly's new quality-assurance measures. You need to watch yourself, okay?"

I nodded, swallowing back the tears I couldn't allow to fall—not if I didn't want my family wondering what was wrong with me when I went back inside—but I didn't give a fuck about this Mongoose character monitoring us now. We were more than used to living with permanent whiplash from always looking over our shoulders. All I cared about was that this was the last time Román and I would be speaking privately to each other. Our last one-on-one conversation and it was on Mauricio's lawn under the guise of a Q&A dialogue about strip-club uniforms. There'd be no goodbye kiss, no last-hurrah sex, no opportunity to at the very least have the harrowing, tear-soaked breakup talk where everyone cries and then yells and then cries some more and it's awful and takes hours but at least by the end of it you're so emotionally sapped that you're ready to go home and grieve in peace.

All I got was a two-second hug and a warning that some guy called Mongoose might soon be stalking me.

"It's better this way, Yola." The gentleness of his tone only made it all the more painful, shoved me headfirst into that vertiginous cleaving of past and present, where I was suddenly giddy with those very words, *"It's better this way, Yola,"* once said full of impish teasing as I squealed à la Damsel in Distress in Román's arms, being carried naked to the edge of a flat green river, to be tossed right in. *"It's better this way, Yola, trust me, none of this one toe in, adapt to the temperature shit. Come on, I'll jump in with you. One, two . . ."*

"I know it's better this way too," I mumbled, a guttural rumbling from the rain clouds pulling me back to the present.

"Are you okay to go back inside?" he asked. "They might get suspicious if you stay out here too long."

I nodded, but I wanted to stay outside as long as I could, drag out every single second even if it meant holding back the tears and doing all I could to stop myself throwing my arms around him and begging and pleading, doing all the things your gut screams at you to do when you know you're facing the firing squad and it's all coming to a bitter, bloody end.

"I'm okay," I whispered tightly.

"They're going to want to know what secret question you had to ask. Tell them you wanted to ask about uniform sizing, you were worried about how skimpy they were. Say you were embarrassed about some specific body part to make it sound credible."

I nodded again, mute.

A glance at the house, then he took my hand, pressed it to his mouth, eyes closed. Saying goodbye.

Then he left.

The yard swam around me. With a thunder crack, in a perfect display of pathetic fallacy, the clouds split. I stayed alone on the grass, letting the rain soak me through for a long moment, washing away the few tears I couldn't hold in. Then I went inside, a ventriloquist, parroting off the lie Román had told me to tell, numb with the realization that it was really over between us.

RODENTS IN MANGO SEASON

The official split with Román left me a productive cadaver, translating, working out, writing, only managing to sleep thanks to sheer emotional exhaustion. Through the haze, I noticed an unobtrusive man in unobtrusive clothes standing unobtrusively on our street. I noticed him again a few days later. Same exact clothes. Same air of intentionally standing around doing nothing. My father noticed the man too, lingering at one of the schools where he dropped kids off. Then outside one of the houses where he tutored. *Mamá* saw him watching her in the grocery parking lot, Zulema on the street opposite the spa where she worked. I knew it was Mongoose, keeping tabs like Román had warned.

My father reported it to Román, and Román explained why Ugly was imposing more checks and balances.

"He says it's nothing to worry about," *Papá* told us over dinner. "This Mongoose guy is just a supervisor to make sure there are no more Milagros-type incidents."

"Totally gives me the creeps!" declared Zulema. "At least we never knew when Román was following us around. This other guy, like, *sucks* at his job."

I had no opinion. Not on that or anything else. Forming an opinion was too draining. All I had energy for was functioning on autopilot.

Until late one night, while watching infomercials for wonder products all conveniently priced at US$19.99, I knew with absolute certainty that someone's eyes were on me. Splayed across the couch in my habitual T-shirt, I drew my legs into my chest and straightened up, muting the television. Glancing at the windows to my right and the porch doors to my left, I realized my first classic-crime-victim mistake: I'd left the overhead light on so the glass panes showed nothing but a reflection of my own tense face. I got up and pulled on the cord dangling from the ceiling fan. With a click the living room went black and the porch doors transparent, showing the man standing on the back porch, looking straight in at me.

I clamped a hand over my mouth to stifle . . . something . . . although I was too startled to scream.

It was Mongoose, standing with a mango in his hand. He must've gotten it from our tree—it was laden; every day was punctuated by the soft thuds of overripe mangoes falling onto the grass, attracting manicous and rats that sent my mother and sister into absolute fits when they scurried across the back porch, claws clicking against the tiles, narrow snouts dripping with mango juice. The irony wasn't lost on me that now a man named after a large rodent was also on the porch, lightly tossing the mango up and down, eyes fixed intently on the porch doors. Intently on me. I needed to get to the switch so I could turn on the porch lights and make the glass panes opaque to him. But that meant getting up, walking toward the doors, and letting him watch me as I did it.

A long, tense moment stretched by in which my brain was too clouded by fear to signal my arms and legs to move and switch that light on or run down the hall and wake my father, or just . . . do something. It was exactly like when Ugly first appeared in our backyard all those months ago. The shock of the moment simply paralyzed me.

Seeing that he'd been spotted, no doubt delighted like every voyeur fervently hoping to get caught, a slow smile twisted Mongoose's face, showing unevenly spaced milk teeth set into glaringly scarlet gums. A narrow tuft of hair just beneath his lip twitched as he smiled, its pointed tip flickering up toward me like some tiny hairy phallus. And then he raised the mango to his mouth, and I saw that he hadn't picked it from the tree, ripe and whole and sunset-orange. He'd taken it half-rotten from the ground. The skin was speckled black, pocked with gaping fleshy holes, rough-edged where it had been pecked by birds or gnawed by squirrels. He lifted that rotting, filthy fruit to his mouth and sank his tiny square teeth into it. The juice sluiced his chin as he kept the mango against his mouth, sucking obscenely on the soured flesh of it, mouth puckering hard as though pulling on a nipple. It snapped me out of my momentary paralysis. I ran to hit the switch and illuminated the back porch. I could still see out but he couldn't see in anymore. He hadn't even moved, was still sucking on the mango, eyes still fixed to the door. I turned away just as he brought his free hand to his crotch.

In the bedroom hallway, I pressed myself against the wall, my body slowly slumping down until I was crouched, panting, skin crawling with what I'd seen, with the way his eyes had felt on me. I wanted to shower immediately, scrub my skin clean.

When I'd gathered myself, I went to my parents' bedroom, moving quietly to the nightstand to pick up my father's cell phone. In my room, I sat at my desk and skimmed *Papá*'s contact list until I came to Román's emergency number, hesitating before pressing the call button. Ugly had tapped the line for starters, which I knew thanks to Román, and I didn't know how Román would even react to me calling him—I'd never done it before, not on this number or any other, to avoid Ugly knowing I had any sort of direct relationship with him, even just in his capacity as blackmail enforcer. But my father had enough on his plate without me filling him in on Mongoose's stunt, and I had to do something—there was a man sucking lasciviously on rotten fruit while

219

stroking himself on my back porch. I couldn't exactly tuck myself in and sail to sleep knowing he was out there.

Román picked up after one ring.

"Yes, Hector?" You'd have thought it was nine a.m. on a Monday from the alert clarity of his voice.

"I'm calling to report a problem with Mongoose." I kept my tone formal and dry.

A pause. I'd thrown him. "Who is this?" Smart.

"Yola." I hesitated, adding, "Yola Palacios," for more credibility in case Ugly listened in.

"What's the problem, Yola?"

I told him what had happened like I was making a complaint to a cable technician, with no familiarity whatsoever. When I was finished, Román was silent for a long moment.

"Thank you for the report," he said finally. Though his tone was curt, his voice was gruffer than usual.

I deleted the call from *Papá*'s call log and returned the cell to his nightstand, already knowing I wouldn't tell my parents anything about what had happened. I had to spare them feeling the way I did at that moment.

As soon as I got back into bed, prepared to spend the night awake, listening for any sounds of forced entry into the house or heavy breath-ing or juice being greedily slurped from a mango outside my window, my phone rang. Private number.

Román didn't give me a chance to say hello. "He'll be dealt with, Yola."

I wanted to cry with how badly I wished he were there with me right then, shame-faced as I was for feeling that way because you're not supposed to be that patriarchy-constructed, twenty-inch-waisted, flailing Disney Princess needing to be rescued by her prince, but god-damn did I want him there all the same, beating up mango-slurping baddies and keeping me safe.

"It was scary," I said, because I couldn't bring myself to say what I really wanted to: *I'm scared. I'm shit scared and I want you to come over immediately and kill that pervert lurking outside my house.*

"I *promise* he'll be fucking dealt with."

The following day, I'd find myself shaking off a shiver whenever my mind skipped back to the moment I saw Mongoose watching me, like when you see a spider and swear you can feel the tips of its eight legs creeping over your skin for ages afterward. And the following night, I couldn't help getting up out of bed every hour to peek between the louvers. But no matter how many times I felt as though he were there staring at me with a fruit pressed up into his inflamed red gums, he never was.

None of us would ever see Mongoose again.

A couple of days after the incident, illegals were dropped at our house. I let them in, set them up, and when I went back to my bedroom, Román was there. Oddly, I wasn't startled to see him—after our conversation over Mongoose, some intuition had told me to expect him. Just as, by that same intuition, I knew exactly what would happen when we saw each other.

He was sitting at the edge of the bed and was on his feet as soon as I shut the door. Without hesitating we crossed the room, meeting in the middle, mouths colliding, the two of us stumbling toward the wall until my back was pressed up against it, legs hoisted up around his waist.

He had to hold me up afterward, my knees were trembling that badly.

"I thought we couldn't see each other," I said between breaths.

"Fuck it. I'd rather be around to make sure you're safe after what happened with that *hijo de puta*." He pulled back, lowering his gaze to mine. "We were careful before. We'll keep being careful now."

"What if Mongoose sees us?"

"He's no longer an issue."

"Román, what did you—"

He brought a guava-jam-sweetened finger to my lips. "I said he's no longer an issue."

I pulled his finger into my mouth, tasted its sweetness. Tasted all the sweetness of him.

STRIP-CLUB
STREET CRED

In a stroke of genuine irony, our strip-club servitude at the Pink Pie began on August 1, the day of the Emancipation Day holiday in commemoration of the abolition of slavery. On the grand albeit secret opening night, my father drove me, Zulema, and *Mamá* to the club for seven o'clock sharp, as instructed. On a quiet side street off Trinidad's bustling equivalent of the Vegas Strip, Ariapita Avenue, we pulled over at a quaint gingerbread-style house with delicate fretwork, a spired roof, and jalousie windows. In the well-tended front garden, a sign read "The Grosvenor Square Freemasons' Executive Lodge" in swirly gold letters. There was absolutely nothing—not a decibel of music, not a glimmer of a red light—to hint that it was really an illicit strip club. Even the private parking lot at the side of the house, with a guard booth and a gate bearing the same gold-lettered sign, looked completely legit. Seeing the club's innocuous façade, my nervousness waned. Even *Papá* seemed less tense when he saw it wasn't some dingy hole-in-the-wall with clients masturbating in the window and dead-eyed strippers tying off their veins on the front steps before their shifts.

"*Suerte*, ladies." He kissed my mother goodbye in the front seat, craned his neck around to give Zulema and me a smile of encouragement. "Remember, if there's anything that makes you uncomfortable, do not do it. Don't let anyone force you into anything you don't want to do."

Mamá rubbed the back of his neck. "Everything's going to be fine. You heard Román. It's just normal work."

I was impressed at how together she was. I'd expected her to be pounding at her chest and gnashing her teeth at the degradation of working in a strip club, but I guess she was also so relieved by the club's charming exterior that she could almost convince herself she was heading to work at an elegant little patisserie.

Zulema, *Mamá*, and I walked up a path lined with pink periwinkles, leading us to a covered verandah furnished with dainty wrought-iron tables and wicker chairs. You could just picture a little old biddy sitting there sipping her tea and eating her crumpets if it weren't for the whirring security cameras following us eagle-eyed from above the heavy wooden front door.

With a courageous flourish of her freshly blow-dried, extra-bouncy hair, *Mamá* marched up to the door and knocked. It swung open almost instantaneously. A brick wall of a man stood in the doorway, dressed in a sharply tailored suit. He didn't say a word, just motioned for us to enter like one of those Frankenstein-type butlers from old horror movies.

Inside, I looked around at the high ceilings, the sleek recessed lighting, the chandelier, the leather couches, a glass coffee table with magazines arranged in fan-like displays. I'd expected lamps draped with red silk, naked women splayed on velvet chaise longues, Japanese businessmen smoking opium while fondling themselves. Instead I felt like I'd just walked into the lobby of a posh attorney's office.

The mute doorman pointed us to a tall receptionist's desk made of well-oiled oak at the far end of the room, where a woman in a snug skirt suit was beaming at us. We walked across the room to the desk, our heels echoing on the hardwood. The woman was a petite little thing of indiscernible race, with voluminous curls and a face full of makeup. She had the distinct look of a stewardess.

"Welcome, welcome!" Her once-over was so subtle and swift I *almost* missed it. "You must be the rest of the Palacios! Sancho and the other girls just arrived too. Though, remember, you're meant to get dropped at the side of the building next time. There's a fire exit back there for staff." She climbed down from her tall leather stool and walked out from behind the desk. "I'm Breanna."

We shook hands, introduced ourselves. Breanna had a helluva grip on her. That grip said she was not to be fucked with and she wanted us to know it.

After introductions, Breanna led us deeper into the house. It was infinitely bigger than it appeared from the outside. We followed her small, wiggling behind down a short flight of stairs, then along a narrow passageway that led at last to an enormous door that stretched all the way up to the ceiling. Above the door there was a security camera, and next to it, a security pad. Her back shielding the pad, Breanna entered a code and we heard a latch unclick. She pushed open the immense door with some effort, and we followed her into another reception area, except this one *did* look like what I'd expect of a strip club. The floors were carpeted in black and the walls were painted hot pink, trimmed with gilded crown molding. Hanging from every wall surface were gold-framed photos of bizarre erotica: buxom women mummified in cling wrap, gimps choking on ball-gags, naked nymphs lying spread-eagled, a close-up of a bright pink tongue licking a dirty gray pavement, a topless girl in a Stetson riding a cow while three large-breasted women lay on their backs squirting milk into their mouths from the cow's swollen udder.

There was a receptionist desk as well, with a desktop computer, a phone, and a cash register, but it was unmanned. In the wall to the right of the desk, there was an open doorway, blocked only by heavy, pink velvet drapes. On either side of this curtained doorway stood two huge juiced-up men like the one who'd let us in. They were also wearing monkey suits. Muffled music and chatter seeped out from behind the drapes, but Breanna led us away from the men and the doorway up a flight of stairs to the left of the receptionist desk. Up we went, pausing on a landing where Breanna pointed out the bathroom for "the girls" and us. Then finally we got to where we were going: the dressing room. If you've never been in the dressing room of a strip club, let me tell you: it's an experience. It was like someone sprinkled estrogen into the atom bomb and then dropped it right onto that sweet old colonial house. The dressing room was an absolute explosion of girly *everything*. Underneath wall-to-wall mirrors framed by rows of blazing lightbulbs, a long countertop wrapped all the way around the room's perimeter, its entire surface covered in spilled powders, creams, self-tanner, bronzing wipes, false lashes, tampons, eyelash curlers, vaginal wipes, washes, douches, perfumes, mouthwash—every single product ever manufactured for the enhancement of a woman. The floor was just as disastrous, scattered with balled-up lingerie, crumpled costumes, thigh-high boots lying flaccid, and garish pink and animal-print suitcases splayed open full of still more products.

Then of course, there were the strippers.

Some were in panties, some just in bras, but most were completely buck naked. It was the most surreal thing I'd ever seen—even more than Aunt Milagros in military mode. Tits and ass everywhere. Anywhere you turned there was a differently sized and colored nipple. Vaginas abounded, and I never knew until that moment how rich God's vagina tapestry truly was. You think of one generic vagina when you think of the female form: the neat Barbie-doll puss, hairless, compact, everything tucked away. I just so happened to have that puss myself, so I'd thought everyone else did too.

Wrong!

There was all kinds of action going on below the belt that I had no clue about. The only thing uniform about all those vaginas was the hairlessness. No one had so much as a landing strip. I wondered if

Mamá was seeing the same business potential I was—did she realize she was standing knee-deep in prospective waxing clients?

But my mother wasn't even scoping out the room. She was listening to Breanna, who was telling her that she was going to be the "house ma'am."

"What is that?" *Mamá* was asking when I tuned in.

"You see that table over there?" Breanna pointed to a far corner of the room. There was indeed a table there, and behind it on the wall, a shelf stacked with beauty products. "There should be everything there that you need to take care of the girls. Your job as house ma'am is to make sure everyone meets Mr. Ugly's standards—nails and hair should always be done, *everything* should be hair-free, and if any of the girls looks a little pasty, there's a spray-tan machine there too. You know how to give a spray tan, right?"

"Um." *Mamá* looked bewildered.

"We'll figure it out," I said, knowing my mother must've been completely overwhelmed. She was looking around the room like she'd just been plopped into the aftermath of Chernobyl. I could see in her face that she had not been mentally prepared to ever witness so much nudity at one time.

Breanna, on the other hand, was clearly a hardened veteran of the strip-club biz. Unfazed, she put her hand on the small of *Mamá*'s back and guided her through the maelstrom of naked women, open suitcases, and scattered stripper heels, to the table that was to be *Mamá*'s, the house ma'am's, new post. My mother sat at the table, still looking lost, while Breanna pointed out a few other things, opened up drawers to show her what went where, and so on. Then she left *Mamá* to it and skipped back through the bedlam to Zulema and me.

"Right," she said, chipper as a cheerleader, "you two are going to come with me to the manager's office to get your uniforms!"

"Who's the manager?" asked Zulema. "Ugly?"

Breanna covered her mouth daintily to laugh. "No, no. Mr. Ugly has too much on his plate for that. The manager is Gordy Griffin. We all call him the Captain—well, he asks us to, anyway."

We left my mother unsupervised with the strippers and followed Breanna up still more stairs to the manager's office. It was your standard office, with filing cabinets, a flat-screen monitor showing all the security feeds, and a large metal desk with a computer. I even spied a fancy coffee machine, and there was a printer going in the corner, adding to the officey feel. Seated at the desk, leaning right up to the computer screen and squinting hard at an Excel spreadsheet, was the guy I rightly guessed to be the manager. As he noticed us, he jumped up from his chair. Though he was good-looking and built enough to be a *Magic Mike* extra, with chiseled features and a pristinely groomed, right-on-trend beard, I took one look at his shiny metallic suit and decided he was a dick. He came bounding forward, showing aggressively white teeth, and vigorously shook our hands as we introduced ourselves.

"Welcome to the Pink Pie, ladies! Breanna, thanks a mil, honey. You can go back to reception now—only another half hour to go before the doors open! Lots to do! Lots to do!"

"Yessir, Cap'n."

Breanna turned to leave the office, but Gordy yelped suddenly like he'd been kicked in the shin and ran to stop her. "Wait! I almost forgot!" He scurried to the printer, took the sheet of paper that had been printing when we walked in, and handed it to Breanna.

"Solid message here, sweetheart. Solid message."

She looked at the page, and I could see the exact moment where she masked her annoyance with a cheery smile. "Thanks, Cap'n! I'll file it with the others."

"Now, don't just file it and forget about it."

"Oh, of course not." An awkward moment. Then she left.

When she walked out of the room, Gordy turned to us with a big dopey grin and jabbed his thumb over his shoulder.

"I do that kinda thing all the time. Find motivational quotes to give to my staff. Management 101. You have to pinpoint people's weaknesses then give them the tools to overcome them. This is only me and Breanna's second night working together, but I can see that girl's weaknesses a mile away. I've already found three quotes to help her. It's gonna make a big difference to her life, let me tell you."

"That's great," I said.

"It really is," he agreed.

He grinned at us. We smiled back. We all stood there grinning at each other like idiots for another minute before Gordy snapped out of it and went to a closet for our uniforms. He handed me a hanger bearing a black miniskirt and a black blazer with "The Pink Pie" embroidered over the breast pocket in hot pink writing.

"You're on reception, Yola, so this is what you'll be wearing. Zulema." He handed her a hanger holding a black waistcoat with the same pink logo, a pair of pink sequined panties, and pink fishnet tights. "You're waitressing, so this is your uniform."

Zulema, horrified, took her hanger.

"There we go!" he said, standing back to grin at us some more. "Now, just to be clear, you can call me Gordy or you can call me Captain. Whatever you like. Personally, I prefer Captain, so call me that. It's from my days in the Coast Guard. Old habits, you know."

He bobbed his head up and down almost violently, those Hollywood-white teeth glaring at us. He obviously wanted us to ask about the Coast Guard, but I seriously couldn't get it up for this guy. Zulema was also too flabbergasted by her uniform for small talk, so we didn't say anything. He eventually gave up and sent us down to the dressing room.

In any case, we'd find out that same night through the stripper grapevine that his Coast Guard days were literally that—a few days—though he looked for any opportunity to persuade people that he'd served for years. When he was sixteen, he'd gotten "someone" (Ugly) to get him a fake birth certificate to prove he was eighteen so he could join the Coast Guard. It all worked, and he got into the Coast Guard even though he was underage. Then after eleven days protecting the seas and shores of Trinidad, he turned seventeen, and his mother mailed in a birthday card with a big glittery 1-7 on the front. When the Coast Guard secretariat opened the mail to check that there was no anthrax or whatever in the envelope, they discovered Gordy's secret, and he was out on his ass and banned from ever joining Trinidad's armed forces again. That's when he'd started working for Ugly and how he'd ended up general manager of the Pink Pie fifteen years later.

So there you have it.

———

Back in the dressing room, preparations were in full swing, the strippers primping and glamorizing, chattering and squawking with raucous laughter. *Mamá* was painting one naked girl's nails and chatting. She looked like she was actually enjoying herself.

I tried to find a private corner of the room to get changed, but it was a waste of time. In the end, I stripped down like the rest of them and donned my uniform. I was mortified. The skirt was about the width of a headband and looked even more obscene when I stepped back into my black patent heels. Glancing in the mirror, all I saw was *leg*, a never-ending highway of bare skin. Then I put on the blazer. That wasn't so bad. It fit well, looked good over my black T-shirt.

I looked over at Zulema. She was wearing her uniform, but she could've just wrapped herself in pink dental floss and called it the same thing. Her huge breasts were busting out of the scant waistcoat, and the sequined panties were, well, sequined panties. As for the pink fishnets, there's probably no sluttier item of clothing on the planet. I had to stop myself laughing. She was a caricature of a hooker. I went over and gave her a little hug. "You look hot, *marica*, don't worry," I said, holding in a laugh at the misery in her face.

"This is, like, so humiliating," she moaned.

"Don't be silly." I waved a hand across the room. "You fit right in!"

———

We hung around in the dressing room awhile longer, both afraid to go out and learn what our new jobs required of us. Meanwhile *Mamá* was having a whale of a time, blazing through the strippers, painting their nails, spraying their hair into place, rubbing them down with tanning wipes, applying their false lashes, finding scissors for the strippers on their periods who needed to cut off their tampon strings (tricks of the trade!). So much for being prudish. To look at her you'd think *Mamá* was *born* for house ma'aming.

Creamed, tanned, powdered, douched, the girls were wriggling into their different costumes now as opening time drew nearer. There were a couple French maids, a nurse, a football referee, a Swiss milkmaid, half a dozen slutty schoolgirls in crotch-skimming tartan skirts, while some girls kept it simple in lingerie and netted dresses. With all the genitalia packed away, I realized then why *Mamá* was so at ease—we knew more than half of the strippers! I looked at the girl who was bent over with her ass cheeks pulled apart while my mother, the woman who raised me, sprayed fake tan into her ass crack. The girl had been at our Christmas lunch! I scanned the room and saw that *all* the girls who'd been at Christmas lunch were there. There were tons of familiar faces! I pointed it out to Zulema, and we went around the room saying hi, chatting with the girls who'd slept on our couch and shared our bathroom, until our little reunion was interrupted by Gordy busting in through the door, an unnatural grin plastered to his face.

"Ten minutes, ladies! Ten minutes and I need you all out on the floor!" Gordy pointed at Zulema and me. "You two need to be at your posts! Ten minutes, just ten minutes till opening!"

His eyes ran down my body. "That T-shirt isn't part of the uniform. You need to wear your *exact* uniform, Lola."

"Yola," I said, looking down at myself then back up at him. "But there was only the blazer and the skirt."

"That's the uniform! Hurry up and get that T-shirt off—I still need to brief you on reception. Ten minutes till opening!"

He stayed right there while I took off my T-shirt and put the blazer back on. Now it was Zulema's turn to laugh at me. The blazer had just one dinky little button in the middle to keep it together. My entire bra and stomach were exposed.

Where was a noose when you needed it?

I didn't dare glance in a mirror, but with the room covered in them, it was impossible to escape my reflection. There's no other way to say it—I looked like a whore, but being so exposed also made me feel weirdly confident, like I could do whatever I wanted, and screw whoever judged me for it. Maybe those demure jeans and T-shirts had been holding me back all these years from being the ball-busting sexual free spirit I was meant to be. I had a sudden flash to Aunt Celia's memoir, remembered all the sequined minidresses, skimpy hot pants, and camel toe–highlighting spandex jumpsuits she'd described from her disco days. *Verga*, she really did have all the secrets to not giving a fuck. Who'd have thought dressing slutty would make you feel so liberated? Maybe there were things to be learned from strippers after all.

"C'mon, ladies. Let's hustle!" Gordy was calling me and Zulema over, flashing us his zircon-studded watch.

Zulema was sent through the pink drapes at the reception area. Sancho, as bar manager (good luck with your inventory, Ugly), would be showing her the ropes.

Gordy stayed with me at the reception desk. As it turned out, despite my Jezebel's work attire, my job was actually going to be a proper receptionist job and then some. Like a normal receptionist, I had to answer the phone and take table bookings and so on. Then things got a little more strip-club-centric. I was in charge of checking the stripper roster on my computer and making sure everyone turned up for her shift. Gordy organized the roster, and every stripper had to work at least three nights a week. If someone was a no-show or late, I had to call her up to see where she was, then report it to Gordy. The strippers also had to pay a house fee at the beginning of each shift—one hundred dollars—so my job was to get the cash from each of them as they came in, then check their names off the list on the computer to record that they'd paid.

"At the end of the night, you'll also be tallying up all the dances the girls have done. The girls have to pay a house commission of ten percent for every lap dance they do. There are doormen inside with clipboards who take note of the dances each girl does. At the end of the night they'll hand you the clipboards, and then you tally up what each girl owes the house and you get the money from her before she leaves at the end of her shift. Everything needs to be entered into the system so we can keep track."

I was amazed. I'd expected some grotty one-room club with cum stains on the furniture and downtrodden drug-addict strippers looking for quick cash for their next fix. But Ugly hadn't been kidding around—this was some first-world shit. I also couldn't believe how ingenious it was to own a strip club: your employees actually had to pay *you* to work there. Even if no customers came, the house would still make money because the strippers had to pay the house fee just to be able to work. Hats off to all the exploiters of the world who'd come up with the strip-club system.

———

So there I was, tits, stomach, and legs on display, waiting for our customers to arrive. The strippers, all freshly minted by *Mamá*'s magic and trussed up in their cheap costumes and lingerie, streamed past me and through the pink drapes. The doormen eyed them all up and down, but didn't say anything. Then one stripper was stopped. The doorman grabbed her by the arm.

"What the fuck?" she yelped.

"Hand it over."

"Hand what over?"

"Give it to me."

The doorman yanked her gold purse from her hand, unzipped it, and took out a plastic straw that had been melted shut on either end.

There was white powder in it. The doorman took the straw, pocketed it, and let the girl's arm go.

"No drugs at the Pink Pie."

She called him a *pendejo*, but he only laughed, tapped her on the ass, and sent her through. Then he gave me a wink. "What's your name, sweetie?"

"It's definitely not sweetie."

He and the other doorman cackled, not meanly. They left their posts and came to introduce themselves. They were like Tweedledee and Tweedledum, huge matching black men, visions of virility. They called themselves by their last names: Hazel and Harrison. I liked them. They didn't stare at my meager cleavage for one thing, or at my bare legs. I guess there was no need when there were women traipsing around almost naked. We chatted away until Hazel got a warning in his radio earpiece that our first customers had arrived, then they returned to their posts and put their game faces back on.

When the heavy door finally swung open, Breanna was there, smiling obsequiously as she held the door for a group of older men in suits. Each of them looked familiar—I was sure I'd seen them before in newspapers or on political posters stuck to lampposts. They looked perfectly at ease. This clearly wasn't their first time in an illegal strip club. They stopped at my desk and reached for their wallets to pay the cover charge, but as I'd been instructed, I told them there was no cover. This earned me a few corny pickup lines and an offer to get taken home later that night, which I politely refused.

I understood then how Ugly's business would work: he'd let the politicians, oligarchs, and policemen have the time of their lives for "free," so they wouldn't ever raid or shut down his place, and Ugly would still make a killing off the dance commissions and the bar. Brilliant.

As Hazel and Harrison held the pink curtains apart for the men to enter, electronic dance music pumped alluringly out to the lobby, tantalizing with the promise of tits shaking rhythmically, of asses clapping in time to the beat.

Not long after, another group came. Then a third and a fourth. Customers were pouring in. More politician types and men who looked like they referred to themselves as "serial entrepreneurs" and "self-made."

Between greeting customers, I played solitaire on the PC and chatted with Hazel, Harrison, and the in-transit strippers en route to the dressing room to freshen up or change outfits. They each had the frazzled air of a daycare teacher sapped by having to entertain small children all day. Except that unlike daycare teachers, they were all understandably a little bit drunk.

Zulema came out once around two a.m. "It's, like, *crazy* busy in there! I can't keep up with the drink orders. My feet feel like they're going to fall off from walking in these heels all night and . . ." and on and on she went until she paused for breath and pulled a wad of hundred-dollar bills from her bra. "At least the tips are pretty fricking amazing! Sucks for Vanessa—she's stuck in the back room on glass-washing duty. Total downer. The guys in there are, like, *throwing* money at us."

That's when I realized that even though Zulema and the twins had wound up in the pink fishnets and sequined undies, I was the one with the shitty end of the stick.

––––––––

Before I knew it, it was four a.m. Once the club was officially closed and emptied of customers, the lights brightened, the music was switched off, and all the strippers filed past me, back up the stairs to change into their regular clothes. While they did this, the doormen from the main floor (floormen?) came out and handed over their clipboards. Again, I was surprised by how orderly the whole system was. Every clipboard held a spreadsheet with each girl's name at the top of a column. Below her name, there was a tick entered for each dance she'd done, and next to the tick, the time of the lap dance was entered. My job was to count the ticks then work out the total each girl owed in commissions.

I sat there with a calculator, clacking away, entering the due amount in another spreadsheet. When I'd only just finished tallying up the totals fifteen minutes later, the girls came down the stairs and formed a line right up to my desk, each pulling a wheelie suitcase behind her and holding a little purse bursting with cash. These were seasoned strippers. They knew they had their dues to pay.

The first girl wasn't one of our illegals, so I didn't know her. But she was Latina, so I spoke to her in Spanish. "Name?" I asked.

"Charity," she said.

"Two hundred and seventy-five."

"*Coño.* That shit ain't right. I didn't do that many dances."

"Says here that you did." I showed her the four clipboards.

"That ain't right!" She jabbed one of the clipboards with a bright pink claw. "I never did no dance at three twenty-seven! I was on break then. I called my sister. Check my phone. Take a look at my call log. Three twenty-seven my ass." She started digging through her purse for her cell phone.

One of the floormen, Branson, walked up. Hazel had told me Branson was the head floorman, so he had to stick around in case any of the strippers contested the clipboard entries. He was a big motherfucker. Even bigger than Hazel and Harrison. Which is saying something. And he had a face like he was just looking for any excuse to knock someone the fuck out.

"What's the problem here?" he asked, his voice a gravelly devil-sounding thing. Charity looked up from her purse and quaked.

"You write that I do a dance at three twenty-seven," mumbled Charity in stilted English. "I didn't."

I was amazed at how much of her confidence had instantly been drained by the switch to her second language.

Branson took the clipboard with his name at the top and gave it a cursory glance. "Says here you did."

236

"But—"

"I don't make mistakes. Pay your fee."

He put the clipboard down and stared at her. Charity couldn't hold that gaze for even half a second. She handed over the money. I put the cash in the register and noted in the spreadsheet that she'd paid her commission. The next girl sauntered over. She had that news anchor thing—big hair, big smile, deep dimples.

"Scarlett," she said, flashing me those dimples.

Scarlett was a big earner. By the looks of her chart she'd burned more calories lap-dancing that night than she would have at a Zumba class.

"Seven hundred and sixty," I told her.

"*¡Puta madre*, Maribel! You did well tonight, *mami!*" hollered someone a few girls back in the queue.

Maribel? Then I realized I'd been dealing with their stage names. Scarlett/Maribel had no problem paying her fee. She knew she'd raked it in. Her breast implants had paid for themselves tenfold. Good for her. Most of the girls weren't that easy. Almost everyone had to be put in her place by Branson's demon stare. When I was finally done collecting commissions and the strippers had all gone home, Branson relaxed. His face looked less homicidal and his sociopath's voice was gone. He was just a normal guy, tired and ready to clock off work.

"I've worked in strip clubs before in Texas and London," he told me. "Same shit everywhere. Those bitches never want to pay up. They don't know we have cameras in every inch of this place. All I have to do is look back at the night's footage to shut 'em up. Every night they gonna test my patience, Yola, you wait and see."

"I have your back, Branson, don't worry," I joked.

He laughed. "I like you. We're gonna get along just fine."

"I think so too, Branson."

"Call me B."

"Okay, B."

After that first night, we all went home with a little more swag in our step. Hell, we were illegal aliens, safe-housers working for a crime lord for the past eight months, and now officially strip-club workers. Though two out of three of these "accolades" had been forced upon us, no one could deny it now—we Palacios had street cred.

IT AIN'T ALL
BOOTY-POPPING

We fell into the Pink Pie work routine pretty easily. Within weeks, the staff felt like family. Gordy, or the Captain as he kept trying to get us to call him, was the only thorn in our sides. He was always bitching about something or other. If there was so much as a rogue hair floating around on the carpet, he'd be down on hands and knees inspecting everything, proselytizing the importance of impeccable cleanliness.

"He's terrified of Ugly," Harrison explained. "Thinks he's going to come in for an inspection any day."

It's not that Gordy was a bad guy, just a tool. No one could muster up respect for someone who referred to himself in the third person as Cap'n while strutting around in metallic suits and shiny silk shirts. Then there were the motivational quotes—good God! Because he thought I took too long to tally up the dance commissions, he printed out a sheet of quotes on efficiency and work ethic that he cut into strips, one for each quote, and then gave to me along with a pack of thumbtacks and a small bulletin board.

"Put up the bulletin board then stick these quotes on it. They'll really make a difference once you read them every day and *absorb* them. It's all about positive affirmations. That's how you get ahead. I mean, look at me—positive affirmations got me where I am today."

I nearly told him a salary would've been much better incentive to boost my efficiency than a bunch of quotes about work ethic, but instead I just let him talk and grin at me with those phenomenally white teeth. As soon as he walked away, I threw the quotes and bulletin board in the garbage.

Hazel, Harrison, even Branson, and the other floormen got quotes printed out for them too. During staff meetings Gordy would roll the quote sheets up like scrolls and hand them out like he was awarding diplomas.

"Now listen, Branson, don't go throwing this away. I got you some great quotes on positivity. It'll really help improve your interpersonal skills."

"Is that right?"

"They've been complaining about you, you know, the girls. It'll be good for you to work on how you deal with people."

"Is that so?"

That's all Branson ever said to Gordy, giving him the old Satan stare.

We all tolerated Gordy that same way: with grunts, monosyllabic replies, and gritted teeth. Even the strippers paid him the same one-worded lip service when he gave them motivational speeches, sharing his tips on the "art of conversation," and on and on, one pointless pearl of wisdom after the next. The only employees who gave Gordy any backtalk were my mother (who I think Gordy even became a little afraid of), Sancho, and the one other barman, a guy who called himself Chill. Gordy was always going on about how heavily Sancho mixed drinks and how slowly he balanced the register at closing time. He never seemed to realize that my brother was already drunk when he turned up for work and only got steadily drunker as the night went on. I didn't know if Sancho tweaked the bar inventory and drank through the club's supply or if he walked with his own flask from home, but either way, it was pretty obvious to me that someone that drunk would never be a speedy worker. Gordy must've had blinkers on not to notice. Or maybe he really was just as stupid as he looked.

Whatever the case, as soon as Gordy started prattling on about boosting productivity, Sancho would invariably interrupt him and start spewing inconsequential crap until Gordy inevitably accepted defeat and left Sancho in peace, working at his usual snail pace.

Chill, the barman, had a different strategy. He liked to use Gordy's motivational nuggets to launch tedious intellectual debates until Gordy couldn't stand it anymore and eventually fucked off, just like Chill had planned from the get-go. An example: one night Gordy called an "urgent" staff meeting. We sat around in the fully lit club on the pink-velvet couches and armchairs. Like in any bar, nightclub, or strip joint, there was a real sadness to the room under bright lights. You could see the ringed water stains on the black cocktail tables and the tiny rips in the carpet where spiked heels had hooked on loose threads. At the center of the main floor, the circular stage with its silver pole had a starkness to it. All lit up, it looked more like a dais for a guillotine.

Once everyone was there, Gordy wasted no time in singling out Chill as the reason for the staff meeting. Chill had apparently told a customer to back off Alejandra after the customer had tried forcing drinks on her.

"Now, Chill, nothing is wrong with protecting the well-being of your coworkers. But as you know, every customer who walks into this establishment is a man of high standing who expects to be treated a certain way. We can't very well have staff telling them to 'back off' anyone. It's a gentleman's prerogative if he would like to buy a lady a drink, wouldn't you say? Besides, that drink purchase would've been money for the house. Having said that, Chill, what we need to remember is . . ." A collectively stifled sigh as we all waited for the quote. "It is not your aptitude but your *attitude* that determines your *altitude*."

Chill stuck his thumbs through his belt loops and rocked back on his heels. We settled in for the debate.

"Gordy . . ." he began, running a hand over his chin.

"You know you can call me Captain."

"Right, sure. Listen, Gordy, do you know the importance of assertiveness as a behavioral quality in the man of African descent? Do you understand the centuries—*centuries!*—of oppression endured under the thumb of the white man, where all the African man could do or say was 'yessuh' and 'nosuh'?"

"Um."

"Do you understand why it is critical for me, a man of African descent, to feel liberated and respected enough in society to be able to assert myself and protect another minority from abuse by the oligarchy?"

"Chill, you know very well that the customer who complained was black."

"Yes, I knew exactly who he was: a black oligarch. Same oppressor, different coat of paint!" Chill's nonprescription hipster glasses were practically steaming over. "And even though I know what strings he could pull, I still asserted myself to protect another marginalized person. Because that's what we are here—the marginalized, the oppressed, the—"

"All right, all right, for godssake, forget the whole thing. Just don't speak to the customers unless spoken to, okay?"

"Yessuh, Cap'n, suh."

With our collective disdain for Gordy and our shared amusement at our varying Gordy-deflection tactics, we staff at the Pie were all pretty tight. The strippers, of course, were also part of our work family. We hung out with them while getting ready for our shifts, and they'd chat with the twins and Zulema at the bar on slow nights. They couldn't get enough of *Mamá* and her beauty expertise. Most of them even ended up becoming regular clients who showed up at the annex for manis, waxing, and the rest of it. They fawned over Vanessa, whose belly now had the same diameter as Pluto. They'd pull up her top and slather her stomach in cheap-smelling lotions, rehashing their own gruesome pregnancy and birthing stories.

At first it shocked us to learn that a lot of the strippers had children, boyfriends, husbands, families who'd joined them from Venezuela and other neighboring countries. But later on, I couldn't understand why we'd been shocked at all—strippers were like anybody else. They just liked to earn a living shaking their asses, spreading their everything, and sweet-talking men. That's right: they *liked* what they did for a living. At the Pink Pie there were no victims of human trafficking, no desperate addicts, no wholesome-yet-busty university students scrimping and saving to pay their tuition. We had good old-fashioned career strippers. Every one of them just loved getting men to pay cash to see her naked. End of story. As far as they were concerned, their bodies and charm were useful commodities for earning a living without actually having to *give* themselves to anyone and without the on-camera permanency of porn.

I didn't think how they chose to use their bodies was bad, though I knew stripping wasn't for me. Not because of the nudity, but because of having to cajole strange men (usually assholes) into paying to see me naked. Night after night, plastering on a smile, enduring the customers' greasy lines or, worse yet, the arrogant insults and brush-offs if you weren't to their taste. It took a thick skin, a cool temper, and a proclivity for endless small talk. So take note, any of you out there considering a stint in stripping: it ain't all booty-popping and getting champagne sprayed on your tits.

———

The weeks passed, and we worked our four nights a week at the Pie, slept when we could, and continued to work our day jobs in a state of permanent exhaustion. I have no clue how the twins managed with school, since their request to take off Thursdays and Sundays was predictably denied by Ugly. As for Vanessa, you couldn't help feeling sorry for her working all those long nights eight then nine months pregnant. She was kept in the back room of the bar at all times. Her looming stomach horrified Gordy, whose sole desire in life was to run the most seamlessly perfect illicit strip club possible. If he so much as saw Vanessa peeking out from the backroom, there'd be a staff meeting and a lecture about upholding the company brand. Of course Chill used this as a launchpad for diatribes on women's rights, but it never made a difference. Gordy wouldn't budge. He couldn't wait for Vanessa's due date so she and her belly would be out of his hair.

Sancho seemed to hate having Vanessa there too. He was genuinely worried about her being on her feet washing dirty glasses all night. The more pregnant she got, the more blatant Sancho became in his attentiveness. It was sweet. But I was pretty sure that soon the whole family plus the rest of the Pink Pie employees would be in on their secret.

I hadn't spoken to Sancho about his relationship with Vanessa since that time in the kitchen, so at our Eid al-Fitr family dinner, I waited until he went to the bathroom then positioned myself in the hallway to tackle him when he came out.

"Hey," I said, startling him as the bathroom door opened. "I see things are getting sort of serious with you and Vanessa now."

Sancho screwed his face up, belched. "What?"

"Things are serious. It's pretty obvious. You're always fussing over her."

"She's pregnant. Everyone fusses over her."

"Not like you."

"Okay, so what?" He picked at something between his teeth, and then oh-so-breezily: "I guess I love her, so why wouldn't I fuss?"

"You *love* her?"

Had I been a pug, my eyeballs would've been on the floor.

"Yeah, I guess."

"So what does that mean, Sancho? You guys are gonna be together publicly now?"

"Dunno." He shrugged. "I'll figure it out."

He burped again, and with that final flourish, he was done with the conversation.

I talked to Román about the Sancho-Vanessa romance a couple days later. We were spending my night off at one of the unoccupied exec apartments, lounging in bed together while Román sprinkled organic local weed into a strip of hemp paper. My skin still damp from our romp, I watched him deftly rolling the joint onto the tip of a cigarette—a roll-on, the Trinis call it—and run his tongue over the edge of the paper to secure it.

"I mean, I have no issue with Vanessa really—not anymore, anyway," I was saying, "but is Sancho really going to raise a kid that isn't even his? He's a raging alcoholic for starters. Oh, and let's not forget the fact that she only just turned *eighteen*. How long are things really going to last between him and a teenager?"

"Hmm . . . I don't know, *flaca*, I think you should be a little more optimistic."

He sat back against the headboard and lit the roll-on, then reached over and pulled me to lie stomach-down across his lap, sliding a hand over my bare ass and grabbing a handful. I reached up and plucked the roll-on from his mouth.

"Focus!" I laughed. "I'm seriously worried about what's gonna happen when she spits this kid out."

I crawled across his lap to sit next to him, and we passed the roll-on back and forth a couple times in comfortable silence.

"You're overthinking it," he said finally. "Sancho knew what he was getting into. Maybe he sees raising Kingsley's kid as some kind of moral Everest he wants to climb."

"Please," I snorted. "I highly doubt Sancho's concerned about enhancing his moral fortitude. And what about the age difference?"

"What about it? Look at us. You're twenty-four, I'm thirty."

"Oh c'mon. A six-year difference is normal. Twelve years isn't—especially not when one person is barely a legal adult."

He squelched the last of the roll-on in an ashtray on the bedside table, then turned to nuzzle my neck and inhale the coconut shampoo I always used now because I knew how much he loved it.

"Who knows," he whispered huskily, "you could be saying you're twenty-four and you're really eighteen. Could be one of those jailbait girls."

"Mmm, you're right. But then you'd be a pretty shitty surveillance expert."

He looked at me with mock indignation. "You saying I don't know how to do my job?"

"That's exactly what I'm saying."

"No, no, no," he said, shaking his head, "I can't let that kind of disrespect slide. I take great pride in my work, Yola. I'm sorry but you're gonna pay for that."

He pulled me across his lap as effortlessly as if I were a blow-up doll and raised a hand warningly above my ass. "Sure you wanna call me a bad surveillance expert?"

I propped my chin in my hands, playing cavalier. "Pfft. Bad? More like the worst."

His hand came down with a smack. I yelped, laughing.

"Be careful, Señorita Palacios. You forget I'm a dangerous man."

"Prove it."

And he did. Until nearly daybreak, when it was time to roll up the fantasy of us being a regular couple with a regular life living in our regular apartment, tuck it in my pocket, and return to my inescapable life as another cog in Ugly's wheel of illegal enterprise.

CHE

It was September. We'd been working at the Pie for just over a month, and despite the chronic fatigue, I actually enjoyed my unpaid job. Even Gordy grew on me just because it was so fun to make fun of him, especially when he took to making up his own nautical-themed quotes: *"The sea is like life. Sometimes it's rough."*

Deep.

He'd also bought himself a laminator and had taken to laminating the quotes he distributed nightly, presumably in the hopes of deterring everyone from throwing the quotes away. Now his office was plastered wall-to-wall in laminated A3 pages showing nonsensical nautical quotes in flowery fonts. Not to mention the immense laminated scroll above his desk bearing the mission statement of the Coast Guard.

The man needed therapy.

The only person Gordy never inundated with quotes, laminated or otherwise, was Vanessa, whom he'd always considered a lost cause. Lucky for her, she'd finally got Ugly's go-ahead for a maternity leave of sorts after Gordy submitted warning after warning that having a pregnant woman around was bad for the club's image. And boy did she need it. Her morning sickness had persevered right through to her final month. Her joints ached, her feet swelled. She had hives on her stomach and thighs. "I look and feel like a troll," she told me one night in the dressing room, nearly in tears.

"You look great, don't worry," I said, though the well-distributed bodily thickness that had worked in her favor before had certainly turned against her, and even her bump wasn't cute because the baby was lying sideways, making her look impossibly wide.

Not that any of it deterred my brother. He really must've been in love with her. As soon as she went on leave, Sancho stopped bothering to be discreet about his feelings for her. He was compulsively on his cell phone, his lifeline to Vanessa, and whenever he wasn't working at the Pie or his regular job bartending at the casino, he'd be at Mauricio's house massaging Vanessa's feet, playing cards with her, making her fruit smoothies. He'd even taken her to her last doctor's appointment, according to Alejandra. It was all pretty endearing, so I took Román's advice and kept my doubts about their relationship to myself.

Nevertheless, I had to admit—I did feel a touch guilty to be tacitly supporting Sancho and Vanessa's love affair. It somehow felt disloyal to Aunt Celia. That wasn't the only reason I felt disloyal. With so much going on—the Pie, translating, finishing up my novel draft, sneaking around with Román—I'd been thinking about her less and less, hardly ever dipping into her memoir. Lately I'd begun to worry that if I didn't start reading again, her memory might eventually disappear just like she had. So on the rare occasions that I found myself with nothing to do, I'd pick up the manuscript and re-read it for hours, always stopping before the final chapter. Though I'd had the manuscript for months now, it had become some strange form of masochistic pleasure-delaying restraint to deprive myself of the ending. It was like I was saving a vintage cognac to be drunk on a special occasion. Or maybe it just felt like reading the last chapter would be the same as finishing the story of Aunt Celia altogether. The final goodbye, when there'd really be nothing more of her left, when I'd have nothing more to get from her. So to keep her at my fingertips, I would re-read from the very beginning, and with Germanic discipline, always leave the last chapter untouched.

One day in late September, I was nestled into bed doing exactly that—reading my permitted portion of the manuscript and reconnecting with Aunt Celia. I'd only woken up around lunchtime, after my shift at the Pie, but by mid-afternoon, after revisiting Aunt Celia's acts of domestic violence, I had to venture out in search of food. To my surprise, the house was empty. I checked the wall clock in the kitchen. *Papá* should be on school runs, taxi-driving or tutoring (I couldn't keep his schedule straight with our wacky working hours), but I'd expected Zulema and *Mamá* to be home since they'd both stopped working Fridays and Mondays to recover from their Pie shifts. Zulema's tips supplemented her income, and once the strippers found out that *Mamá* wasn't paid to be their house ma'am, they started paying her full price for her dressing-room beauty services. (See what I mean about strippers? Hearts as big as their implants.)

Then I saw the note stuck to the fridge door: *Vanessa's baby is coming!!!! We're at St. Clair Medical! Meet us there!! xoxoxoxoxo Zu.*

———

At the hospital I had no trouble finding my family. The excited babble of a half-dozen Latinos awaiting a new baby was unmistakable, billowing out from the waiting area through to reception. As I walked toward the Spanish cacophony, a wisp of a receptionist leaned over her desk and waved at me, gold bangles tinkling on her avian arm.

"Miss! Ex-cuse! You part of the crowd in there?"

I nodded.

"Tell them keep it down! Is a hospital in here, not a fiesta!"

Ignoring the xenophobic fiesta jibe, I carried on toward the noise. They were all in there, every last family member. With Aunt Celia's rage at Mauricio's philandering fresh in my mind from the manuscript, I admit that I did feel more than a twinge of annoyance at the fact that we were all gathered for the daughter Mauricio had conceived on the side. But then, seeing my father's face shining with anticipation, my mother aglow with excitement while munching on kale chips (the strippers had introduced her to super-healthy organic snack foods, so you never saw her without a kale chip or a black-bean brownie now), there was really nothing else to do but jump on the bandwagon. After all, a new baby was always something to be celebrated—even if the pretentious douchebag father was on the other side of the world, oblivious to the kid's birth, the mother was a teenager in love with an alcoholic twelve years her senior, and the grandfather was currently in a wildly disheveled state, looking like he stank of booze and cat piss, slurring at whoever cared to listen that he was going to be an *abuelo*. "*Abuelo* Mo-Mo! That's what he'll call me," Mauricio was saying to *Mamá* while she crunched down on her kale and nodded along, humoring him.

I gave my family a collective wave to the usual "*Hola Yo-laaaa*" greeting, then grabbed a chair beside the twins, who were in their school uniforms hunched over a giant stork-shaped card, scribbling congratulatory messages.

"Hey," I said to Alejandra while she drew a giant heart in the card, "where's Sancho? Stuck at the casino working?"

Alejandra rolled her eyes. "Please, you really think he'd miss this? He's in the delivery room."

"Seriously?" I couldn't believe Sancho was actually voluntarily present at something as gruesome as childbirth. Growing up, he'd always been queasy at the sight of blood, fainted whenever he got an injection.

"He insisted," said *Mamá*, who'd been eavesdropping. "It shouldn't be too long now. She started pushing a half hour ago."

"Just a half hour? But haven't you all been here for ages?"

"*Ay*, Yola, don't you know when a baby is coming, the mother always has a foot in the grave? It's important for us to be here from early on to give her and the baby our positive energy."

I stared at my mother as she gestured with her hands to show that there was positive energy radiating from her. What the actual fuck was she talking about? She was letting those strippers fill her head with all kinds of bull.

"So," I said to Alejandra, "no one was shocked about him being in the delivery room? Everyone knows Sancho freaks over blood."

She shrugged. "Nope, not really. We expected him to go in. Not like we can't all see that they're together. He like *lives* over at our house taking care of her."

She pulled on her pink chewing gum, stretching it out like a long tongue before slowly pulling it back into her mouth with her teeth. Then after a few moments: "What *did* surprise everyone was that he's paying for the delivery, plus he said he's going to adopt the baby and raise it with her. I think they're even going to get married."

Alejandra knew the key to any twist was *timing*.

I, on the other hand, was not so hot with timing. I just couldn't keep it in. Like projectile vomit shooting up out of me, a hideously inappropriate "ARE YOU FUCKING SERIOUS!" at the top of my lungs. It came out in English too, so all the other nice Trinis waiting for their loved ones, tolerating my noisy family and drunk Mauricio, turned to give me the evil eye. Like a shot, the receptionist flew into the waiting area, pointing a finger in my face like a gun barrel, her gold bangles rattling indignantly.

"All-you need to keep the blasted volume down in here! This is a hospital!"

I raised my hands in surrender and apologized. If only she knew how warranted my outburst had been.

When the receptionist left, both my parents came to loom over me. They could not *stand* scenes in public. My father stood stony with his arms crossed while *Mamá* hissed her chastisements. "What kind of language is that to use in a hospital? Shouting like some streetwalker! You'd think you were raised in a *barrio!*" *Papá* chimed in with "*Precisamente*" and "*Exacto*" while she ranted.

They were so busy cutting me down to size that they didn't notice two things: Mauricio laying himself down on the ground with a dreamy drunken smile, sprawling out as though making a snow angel. And Sancho running red-faced down the hallway, grinning wider than I'd ever seen, even at his drunkest.

"It's a boy!" he cried breathlessly.

My parents spun around, their anger obliterated by excitement. Mauricio was cheering and whooping like he was at a football match, pumping his arms and legs in the air, looking like a giant overturned beetle. At that, the receptionist came stalking back in, but when she realized what the commotion was about, she left us to celebrate. Even if she'd tried to shut us up, it would've been useless. Sancho's joy was infectious. And here's what was weird: with all that collective happiness, it suddenly didn't seem crazy at all that Sancho would adopt Vanessa's baby. It didn't seem crazy that we were all happy for her even though she was Mauricio's outside child. It felt as though Sancho and Vanessa had planned this baby all along. It all just *fit* like a perfect puzzle. I'd never experienced it before, the contagious joyfulness of a brand spanking new life.

When at last I got my hands on my brother, I squeezed him tight. "I'm so happy for you," I said.

I meant it.

He gave me a wet smack on the cheek. "I have a *son*, Yola."

A fat tear rolled down his cheek and I felt myself choking up too. I guess that meant I was an aunt.

Vanessa's son was a perfect nine-pounder with big round cheeks, chubby thighs, and the most exquisitely teeny toes. Adorable as he was, every time I looked at him, I was struck by the depressing thought that we'd been under Ugly's thumb long enough for a cluster of cells to morph into an actual human being. Ten whole months since that fateful Sunday barbecue.

Mauricio had begged Vanessa for the privilege of naming the baby, and shockingly, she agreed. So of course the kid wound up with the name Che. We visited almost every day just to ooh and aw at Baby Che's spit bubbles and gurgles and squidgy wet baby farts. We couldn't get enough. And we weren't the only ones—visitors rolled in and out of there around the clock, including everyone from the Pie. *Papá* even started getting antsy about so many people popping by.

"What if the police catch on?"

Mamá flapped a hand at him. "Catch on to friends visiting a new baby? Relax! Here, have a chickpea cookie."

Luckily, none were illegal visitors. Román saw to it that Mauricio's household got a breather, even if it meant the rest of our houses were at illegal capacity, and in a stroke of good fortune, Gordy told Vanessa she was off-duty indefinitely, until she "got her physique back into an acceptable state." A real gem, that Gordy. As for Sancho, no time off from the Pie. Ugly told Gordy to relay the message that if Sancho didn't report to work as normal, he might have a hard time carrying the baby with two broken arms. When he wasn't at the Pie or the casino, Sancho was in full-on daddy mode, changing diapers, rocking the baby to sleep, crooning lullabies, the works. Equally shocking: he was dry as a bone—not a drop of liquor in him—and all he did was talk about how perfect his "son" was. He referred to Che as his child so freely I might've even wondered if the whole thing with Kingsley was a mix-up and maybe Sancho really had been the one to get Vanessa pregnant. Alas, there was no mistaking that high-born brow, the fair Willoughby skin, the aquiline nose of that aristocratic Castilian ancestry. I could've spotted that little Prince De Oruña Willoughby anywhere. But Sancho didn't care who the hell Che looked like. He was seeing the world through glasses so rosy he really could have thought a turd was a peacock, tail feathers and all.

The only person left out of the new-baby hubbub was Vanessa's mother. When she'd tried to get on the plane to leave Venezuela, the *guardia* asked if she had five hundred US on her. They might as well have asked if she had five hundred pounds of bullion. Who in Venezuela had *five* US dollars, far less five hundred? They refused to let her travel without the money, along with more than half the other passengers. Maduro was using any tactic he could to stop the whole country jumping ship. So Che's grandmother had to stay put, because unlike my wayward family, she had no desire to either embroil herself with the criminal underworld or find herself a man with a boat.

Vanessa didn't seem bothered. I don't think she had the energy to care about a damn thing other than Che and surviving on a few hours of scattered sleep a day. She was like any new mother. Cried a lot, looked blissfully happy one second, then as if she were going to kill herself and everyone around her the next. She was covered in vomit, snot, and liquid black shit from sunup to sundown. And you know what? It made me like her even more, forcing me to let go of any vestigial resentments I'd tried my best to harbor on Aunt Celia's behalf.

It wasn't Vanessa's abject fatigue and fluctuating emotional torment that did it. I'm not a sadist. It was seeing her be a mother. Through all of the terrifying postpartum changes happening to her body that she'd never expected (and that I was equally horrified to learn of), she sucked it up, never complained, and did it all like a champ. I guess it shouldn't have surprised me. After all, she was only seventeen when she'd made up her mind to get out of Venezuela, then traveled to Port of Spain alone through pure determination—and with a lot of help from her Lycra-clad curves. Then, of course, there was the other thing that made it impossible for me not to like Vanessa: Sancho was happier than he'd ever been. Not to mention stone-cold sober. How could I dislike any girl who'd achieved that? I even found a quiet moment to congratulate her on it while she was sterilizing bottles one day.

"You've really been a blessing for Sancho," I said. "He hasn't been so dried out in as long as I can remember, and he's never been this way over anyone before. So settled and happy. His track record with women has always been sort of . . . tumultuous, at best."

She smiled weakly, eyelids heavy with sleep deprivation. "Really? He's always been so great to me. He's the real blessing. I don't know what I would've done without him."

She dropped her eyes abruptly, her lip trembling.

"You okay?" I asked gently.

She wiped a fat tear. "Sorry, hormones," she said with a watery laugh. "I'm just really glad you and I are cool. When I first got here I used to worry that you sort of . . ." She trailed off with a shrug.

"Didn't like you?"

We shared an awkward laugh.

"Listen, it was never about you, Vanessa. Your dad was the one I was pissed at. I shouldn't have made you feel bad. It's just Aunt Celia and I were close, you know?"

"I get it. I always heard she was a sort of—*legendary* woman. My mother was terrified she'd find out about me and find a way to make our lives hell."

I shook my head. "She wouldn't have hated you. Aunt Celia would've liked anyone with the balls to smuggle herself out of a country alone and raise a baby she didn't expect."

It was the truth. If there was one thing Aunt Celia had taught me to respect, it was a woman who could stand on her own two feet.

THE CAPTAINCY
BEARS FRUIT

About a month after Che was born, a few interesting things
happened. First, I turned twenty-five. I had no time or energy to
commemorate the milestone, but a bouquet of white anthuriums was
on my bed when I crawled home exhausted from the Pie at six a.m. on
the morning of my birthday, along with a signed first edition of *Love
in the Time of Cholera*, which Román knew was my all-time favorite
García Márquez novel. Needless to say, the man knew how to keep me
head-over-heels.

Second, Sancho asked me to be Che's godmother. We were sitting
at Mauricio's dining table playing rummy while Vanessa and the
baby napped. It was that time of the afternoon when the clouds turn
cotton-candy pink and flocks of screeching green parrots come in to
roost. I was shuffling the cards, looking at the light coming in through
an open window, a fat shard of diaphanous rosy gold. Then I realized
Sancho was looking at me with this boyish grin.

"What?" I asked, instinctively covering my mouth. "Something in
my teeth?"

He chuckled and shook his head.

"What then? I hate when you do that, sit there laughing to yourself with some stupid little secret."

"Vanessa and I want you to be Che's godmother."

I stopped shuffling. "Me?"

"Yes, you."

"But . . . why?"

Sancho blew into his second cup of herbal tea in twenty minutes. (He guzzled the stuff now. You'd never see him without a steaming travel mug.)

"You're the family bitch so no one will ever mess with Che if you're his godmother."

"What!"

"Shush! The baby!"

"Sorry—but *what*? I'm the family bitch?"

Sancho reached over to clap a hand on my shoulder. "It's a compliment, *chama*. Aunt Celia left an opening and you got the job."

I thought of the twins, Zulema, *Mamá*, and even Aunt Milagros back in Venezuela, and realized that yes, by God, I *was* the new resident bitch of the family. *Mamá* was a close contender but she'd never shown her catty side to Vanessa because she'd never cared for Aunt Celia. All I could do was graciously accept my new title. That's when I noticed Aunt Celia's urn was no longer at the center of the table. Just heaps of baby stuff plus Sancho's teapot.

I scanned the room until I found her—relocated to the bottom shelf of an inconspicuous side table.

That's how it was. You died and stayed the center of attention for a while, until the next big thing came along. Then you were tucked away, a memory no one would forget, but ultimately out of sight and out of mind. I felt a pang in my chest and promised myself to keep re-reading the manuscript so Aunt Celia would never be relegated to a dusty corner of my memory like she had been in her own home.

———

Not long after Sancho awarded me my godmother/head family bitch title, the third interesting thing to happen was this: the Pink Pie was booked to host a birthday party for its most highbrow, high-ranking guest yet.

It was four-thirty a.m., after another night of strip-club indentureship. The club was empty and the strippers had paid their dues—everyone had gone home but us staff. Gordy had gathered us all on the main floor, a large room decorated black and hot pink, with plush booths along its perimeter where the lap dances were given, and a pole-equipped stage at its center. It was separated from the bar area by a dramatic arched doorway hung with a floor-length curtain of glittering black beads that lent an air of mystique, like Mata Hari might be back here shaking her stuff instead of all of us, red-eyed and exhausted. We sat around on the velvet seats, checking for any fresh suspicious stains the evening might have yielded, struggling to stay awake as Gordy launched into a motivational monologue. I nodded off at least twice and had to be woken with a jab to the ribs from Sancho. Finally, after blabbering about first impressions and taking pride in your work and God knows what else, Gordy got to the crux of the thing.

"Only a couple hours ago, I received the momentous news that tomorrow night, we at the Pink Pie will be exclusively hosting our most distinguished guest to date. The attorney general himself, to celebrate his fifty-eighth birthday, will be joining us along with a party of his fellow government ministers. . . ."

Chill began clapping with stupendously sarcastic vim. "Isn't that just perfect," he said. The rest of us snickered. Gordy, not quite sharp enough to figure out whether Chill's ovation was sincere, smiled uneasily.

"Yes, it's a big deal. It really is—and another prime example of why you must all listen when I encourage you to always be on top form. As it turns out, the AG's personal assistant was here a few months ago and called me personally this evening to book a table for the AG's birthday celebrations tomorrow night. Imagine if things had been sloppy when he came in? If my standards hadn't been upheld? Well, thankfully, my captaincy of our ship has borne fruit. Not only will the AG be coming in tomorrow, but I've informed the AG's assistant that regardless of the late notice, we will happily close the club so that the AG can have the Pie to himself and his friends for his own private birthday festivities. I'm told Mr. Ugly himself will even be joining the AG, who I believe is his close personal friend."

What a surprise. Ugly and the attorney general, best buds.

"Needless to say, you must all be at your very best tomorrow despite the very short notice. I expect everyone to come in an hour early to ensure that the club is spick-and-span." Gordy turned to my father. "That applies to you as well, Hector."

My father nodded grimly. The bags under his eyes hung gray and curdled.

"Waitresses," continued Gordy, addressing Zulema and the twins. "I want top-class makeup, and Yasmin, I'd like you to have them spray-tanned and with their hair properly styled."

"I'm not a hairstylist," said *Mamá*. "You think I'm some kind of one-stop shop? The services I offer are specialties. You need—"

"All right, all right!" Gordy waved his hands to shut her up. "Girls, you need to go get professional blow-dries then. None of this half-done nonsense."

Zulema, Ava, and Alejandra all had their hair pulled back into neat ponytails. Clearly that wasn't going to cut it for the Most Honorable Attorney General. The three of them stared at Gordy blankly. I think they were sleeping with their eyes open.

Gordy carried on, nitpicking at each and every person until he was finally satisfied an hour later.

"Please remember everything I've told you tonight, and most importantly, let's show Mr. Ugly and the AG that even at a moment's notice, we deliver top-class service! The best of the best! Off you go now, get your rest. Tomorrow—or should I say, *tonight*—is going to be a busy one."

Just as we were all sleepily peeling ourselves off the chairs and couches, Gordy called me and Branson over. "I need to see you both upstairs. We have to go over the books, make sure the commission payments and dance records all match up in case Ugly plans on reviewing everything while he's here. He's a meticulous man, as you know."

Branson shook his head. "Gordy, I'm so tired I can't see straight. We'll do it when we're back this evening. We'll be coming in early anyway."

The vein running along the center of Gordy's forehead was suddenly turgid and thick, pulsing grossly, distorting his clean-cut handsomeness. "It must be done right fucking now! There's no *time* later! Don't you realize that in less than . . ." He looked at his watch. "In less than twelve hours we need to be back here, dressed and ready for the *attorney fucking general*! NOW LET'S HUSTLE!"

It took two hours to finish reviewing all of the club records. After crawling back home in rush-hour traffic, I finally fell into bed with the mid-morning sun burning through my curtains.

Less than nine hours later, we were all right back at the Pink Pie, preparing for a birthday soirée we wouldn't soon forget.

FROM THE PINK PIE TO THE GINGERBREAD HOUSE

Just as Gordy had ordered, we'd all come to work an hour early. Sancho was the last to arrive, as usual, at eight minutes past six. I knew this precise detail because we'd been ordered to go straight through to the main floor for a staff meeting before taking up our posts. The only person not required to attend was *Mamá*, who was administering spray tans and applying makeup and doing whatever else was needed to get the strippers ready for the attorney general's viewing pleasure. She had her hands even more full than usual—Breanna had ushered in an extra two-dozen strippers fresh from South American soil, all specially flown in for the AG. They were career strippers like our girls, no doe-eyed newbies, but it still meant *Mamá* the House Ma'am was operating on all cylinders.

While the rest of us waited those eight minutes for Sancho to roll in, I took in the festive décor. I had to hand it to Gordy—things did look very birthday-of-an-attorney-general-appropriate. The framed nude photographs on the walls had been festooned with gold balloons and streamers; every cocktail table was draped in gold cloth and a banner saying "Happy Birthday!" was stretched across the top of the beaded doorway between the main floor and the bar area.

When Sancho walked in, Gordy threw his hands into the air with much melodrama. "It's eight minutes after six, Sancho! I said *an hour* early. That means six o'clock, not eight minutes past, not ten past, not half past—it means *six!*"

Sancho ran his tongue over his front teeth, sucking them hard. "Guess my watch is slow."

"Just sit down!" Gordy pointed a stiff finger at an empty chair. With everyone now present, Gordy went over the protocol for the night. It's worth noting, for the sake of my own personal amusement, that he was dressed in a gold silk shirt underneath an obscenely tight ivory suit that perfectly matched his teeth, which he'd obviously whitened even more for the occasion, because they were near fluorescent. Maybe that suit was cutting off circulation to his more delicate parts, but while he spoke, Gordy wouldn't stop fidgeting with his crotch. Everything he said came out blustering and flustered. His nerves were out of control. Strutting back and forth in his stupid getup, he stressed the importance of sterling customer service, an accommodating attitude (what sort of behavior were we expected to accommodate?), and on and on. When he was finished going over all the dos and don'ts of the night, he turned to me.

"Go up to my office. Your formal uniforms are up there—yours and the waitresses'. Take them to the dressing room and all of you hurry up and get changed."

"Formal uniforms?" asked Zulema.

"Yes! Formal uniforms! Formal fucking uniforms! What's the problem?"

About these formal uniforms. First, recall the description of the waitress uniforms: open waistcoats save for one tiny button, fishnet tights, sequined panties. And my uniform: a bra, an open blazer, a miniskirt the width of a strip of duct tape. Now picture all of that in gold, and of course, gold sequins. Whatever image you've come up with of that flesh-baring, glittering fiasco of a costume, that was our "formal" uniform. To clarify: my entire blazer was gold sequins. My miniskirt was gold lamé. (Just imagine what liquefied metal would look like if it were spray-painted directly onto a woman's ass.) For Zulema and the twins, the gold versions of their uniforms weren't much different than the originals. My skirt and blazer definitely felt tighter. I could hardly walk, just wiggle. So once I was dressed, I wiggled down the stairs from the dressing room, wiggled to my desk, and wiggled up onto my tall stool to wait for the attorney general's arrival, which I anticipated would be tantamount to the second coming of Christ as far as Gordy was concerned.

By ten, the club was still dead, gold balloons bobbing forlornly in the cold currents of the air-conditioning vents. With every passing hour that the attorney general wasn't there, Gordy looked like he was getting closer to an aneurysm. He was up and down the stairs, back and forth between every room, chewing his nails, smoothing his beard, tugging at his thick gangsta rapper–style chain, adjusting his poor suffocated ballsack in that mercilessly tight suit. Then at last, when he happened to be pacing in front of my desk, interrupting my game of solitaire on the computer, some radio chatter came through. I watched as Gordy grew rigid and pressed his earpiece deeper into his ear. Hazel and Harrison, also hearing the radio, became alert.

"It's time," said Gordy softly, turning to look at me, eyes aglow. "It's *time*!" He swung around and pointed at Hazel and Harrison. "It's time! Man your posts!"

Hazel and Harrison glanced at each other. They were already at their posts. Gordy didn't care. Gordy just wanted to yell and run and go nuts. Which he did until we heard the telltale beeping of the security pad just beyond the door.

"He's here!" hissed Gordy, buttoning, smoothing, then unbuttoning his jacket.

I stood behind my desk, arranging my face into an expression of perfect docile stupidity, just what our customers liked.

Breanna pushed open the heavy door and in they poured. Behind her was the attorney general, whose face I easily recognized from the news as one of the island's rare white politicians. He was a hulking man with a barrel belly and a dashing white stripe in black hair that had been coiffed into a tall, square do. Like all politicians who came into the Pie, he had remarkably smooth, pudgy hands. I could tell from his bearing and the way he kept his fleshy fingertips pressed together that he thought of himself as a modern-day pharaoh. To me he was just a spoiled fat-boy lucky enough to have a friend who became prime minister. Gordy, however, was eating that pharaoh shit up, fawning over the AG and the stream of sycophants flooding the reception area, pumping their hands, grinning deliriously. By the time Breanna finally shut the door and escaped to the front desk, there must've been four dozen men packing the reception area, all dressed in their Sunday finest for the attorney general's birthday celebrations.

Once the security door was closed, Gordy addressed everyone. "Gentlemen," he said, flushed and sweaty with exuberant pride, "Most Honorable Attorney General, allow me to welcome you all on behalf of Mr. Ugly to the Pink Pie. My name is Gordy, and it is my privilege to have you here with us this evening. Should you need anything at all, you need only ask any of our fine, friendly staff, like Yola over here, our lovely receptionist."

Ninety-six curious eyes turned to stare at me.

"Welcome to the Pink Pie, Your Honor." I bowed obsequiously behind my desk, batting my eyelashes. There were tips to be made after all.

"Thank you very much, miss," sneered the AG. "Although 'Your Honor' isn't quite right."

His cronies chuckled smarmily.

"My apologies," I said, bowing again, putting on the full geisha act. "Your . . . Majesty?"

266

At this, the room erupted into roars of laughter, the AG slapping his big belly with glee. "I like this girl, man!" He threw an arm around Gordy. "If this is what you have on offer at the front desk, I can't wait to see what other goodies you have for me inside!"

"Oh, just you wait . . ."

Gordy blathered on, but the AG wasn't listening. He was taking a wad of hundred-dollar bills out of his jacket pocket. He whipped two bills out from the roll and waved them at me. I took them, giving another geisha curtsey.

"Thank you," I said.

"I hope to see more of you later," he replied, baring his teeth. My skin went clammy as I wondered what it must be like to feel the immense weight of that belly over you, that big soggy body thrusting away. I lowered my eyes, afraid that he'd see my revulsion. The lowered gaze worked. He handed me another hundred-dollar bill. I knew he'd like the blushing damsel thing.

All weak men do.

———————

Moments after the AG and his entourage were led through the pink curtains, I heard Hazel and Harrison's radios going again. Listening intently, Hazel snapped his fingers to call my attention and mouthed, *Ugly is here.*

Oh God.

Thirty seconds later, I heard the *beep, beep, beep* of the security pad. The door opened to a gale of laughter from Breanna. Ugly followed her through, looking smug as hell at his own hilarity. I was about to deliver a mechanical "Welcome!" but the words caught in my throat. Walking through the door behind Breanna and Ugly was none other than Román, slick in an impeccably tailored gray suit, eyes fixed on me. I forced myself to look away, already feeling my cheeks reddening, a smile tugging at the corners of my mouth at the pleasant surprise of seeing him there. Fortunately Ugly was too distracted by his flirting with Breanna to notice while I recalibrated to robotic receptionist mode.

Ugly strode up to my desk, adjusting his neon-yellow ascot (presumably selected to match the neon-yellow pinstripes on his black suit). "Well, well, if is not little Miss Yola. Aren't you something to see."

"You're too kind." I gave a simperingly sardonic smile, squirming as he smacked his lips, his eyes lingering on my exposed bra.

"Quite the little morsel."

Pressing my lips together, I smiled so hard my cheeks hurt, not trusting myself to respond without saying something that could cause me and my family serious harm.

Giving me a final once-over, Ugly returned his focus to Breanna. "Why you don't take me on through to the main room, sweetheart? I sure the AG would like to see a little more of you anyway."

He offered Breanna his arm with exaggerated gallantry. She took it and walked with him through the curtains. But before they'd disappeared from view, Ugly paused to holler over his shoulder. "Román! What you waiting on, man? More breast in here than a bucket of KFC!"

"Be there in a minute. I need the bathroom."

"A'right but don't stick, man."

Román waited until Ugly was safely through the curtains, then leaned against my desk. I smoothed my hair back from my face with a glance at Hazel and Harrison. They were talking to each other and weren't paying attention to us.

"This is some little number, huh?" I joked, giving a subtle shimmy of my shoulders.

But Román's expression was hard as concrete as his eyes flitted to Hazel and Harrison then back to me.

"Listen," he said, so low it was barely audible. "When the time comes, go straight to the fire exit at the back of the dressing room. Go out the exit to the back alley. Take your mother with you if she's in the dressing room. There'll be a Jeep waiting. Do not hesitate when the time comes, Yola, just go straight to the fire exit and down to the alley. No detours, understand me?"

My mouth went dry.

"What are you talking about? Román . . ." In my confusion I'd forgotten to whisper, but he gripped the back of my hand once, so hard I nearly winced, to get me to stop talking.

"Dressing room fire exit. When the time comes. Do not forget, Yola."

"But . . ."

Román straightened up. "Just do as I said," he said again, still low enough that Hazel and Harrison couldn't hear.

I watched the back of him as he passed between Hazel and Harrison, acknowledging each with a nod, and then disappeared through the pink curtains. Unable to run after him without attracting dangerous attention, I let the cold, portentous dread of his instructions trickle through me.

Gordy had introduced silver, gold, and platinum chips that customers could buy and give to the strippers in exchange for protracted lap-dance sessions. Silver for fifteen minutes, gold for a half hour, platinum for a full hour, with a whopping 20 percent house commission when the girls cashed in their chips at the end of the night. Now he was flitting out from the main floor every fifteen minutes to replenish the AG's ceaseless stream of dance chips, leaving me no choice but to stay fixed at my post.

That meant there was no way to tell my parents about Román's warning, and I for shit sure couldn't venture into the main floor to glean more information from Román or to at least pass his warning along to my siblings and cousins. Not unless I wanted Gordy to use the AG's gold party streamers to hang me from the rafters.

All I could do was sit on my ass while my nervous tension mounted. In an attempt at being proactive, I conjured up a mental image of the dressing room. The fire exit was just behind *Mamá's* spa station—the usual big metal door with a pushable bar across it. Aside from that, I could only keep my eyes on the pink curtains, willing Román to come back and tell me what was going on. But there was no sign of him or of anyone else in my family, everyone too busy tending to the needs of the AG and his homeboys.

By two a.m., the best I'd managed by way of escaping my post was one bathroom break I begged for while Gordy manned the front desk. I tried carrying on up the stairs past the ladies' room, to hopefully reach *Mamá* in the dressing room, but Gordy was gripping the back of my blazer in an instant, wanting to know why I hadn't stopped on the landing to use the bathroom.

"I need a tampon from the dressing room," I lied.

"Get back to your station! I'll get it!" And he'd shot upstairs, returned at reception half a second later with a tampon in hand. I'd dutifully gone to the bathroom to pretend to use it. Other than that, there'd been no opportunity to leave my post.

At nearly three-thirty, I chugged an energy drink, hoping the cocktail of toxic chemicals and caffeine might trigger an idea. I was drumming my fingers on the desk, scheming in that ADHD way that energy drinks make your brain work, when a burst of loud feedback came crackling through Hazel and Harrison's earpieces. Jittery from the drink, I jumped at the sound of it. "What the hell was . . ."

Hazel and Harrison had shot through the pink curtains like a pair of unleashed attack dogs. I leaned over my desk, trying to see through the swaying curtains, then shimmied down from the stool and wiggled over to the doorway. Heavy EDM pulsed louder as I stepped through the curtains to the bar, my eyes adjusting to the dim violet lighting. It was like entering the darkened womb of some beast, swallowed by the echoing electro bass of its heartbeat.

The stillness of the room told me something had just happened— some of the AG's buds were sitting at the bar, strippers draped over them, but all rigid, necks craned around to look at the beaded fringe doorway to the main room. Chill was behind the bar and had been in the middle of drying a glass but was now motionless as a statue, frowning intently at the doorway while the beads rustled against each other, freshly disturbed by Hazel and Harrison. Then the music shut off abruptly, and without the buffer of the sound system, the noise of a scuffle in the main room jumped up by several octaves. Men's voices shouting. A glass shattering. A woman screamed. Others squawked in response. I kicked my heels off and wiggled as quickly as I could to the bar, wishing I could rip off my constraining skirt.

"Where's Sancho?" I shouted to Chill. The ruckus in the main room was growing louder and more chaotic by the second. My siblings were in there. My cousins. Román. My hands went numb. I clenched and released my fists, trying to get the feeling back.

A thud in the main room, then the heavy clattering of furniture being knocked over. More shouting, shrieking, cussing. The guys at the bar had thrown the strippers off them and were speed-walking past me, back out to reception. They were getting the fuck out of there. Whatever was happening couldn't be good. They knew it, I knew it.

I reached over the bar to grab Chill's arm. "Where's Sancho?"

He dropped the glass he'd been drying, letting it shatter, and ran out from behind the bar. "I'm getting the hell outta here!" He shot past me and out through the pink curtains.

"Chill!" I tried snatching his shirtsleeve but he was too quick. I turned to face the main floor head-on. I wanted to barrel through those sparkling black beads, make sure everyone was okay, but fear and common sense held me back—it sounded like a full-fledged riot was under way. The strippers still in the bar area were moving in a single cluster toward the doorway, like moths sussing out just how dangerous a flame might be. I took a few steps forward, heart in my mouth. Sancho and Zulema. The twins. Román. I couldn't just run away.

Then bursting through the glittering beads and the tremulous amoeba of strippers, I saw Sancho with my sister and cousins behind him. Alejandra was shrieking, bright fresh blood pouring from a gash at her hairline. Ava was gripping her sister's gold waistcoat, dragging her roughly. "Come on! Come *on!*" she screamed. The four of them ran toward me and in that split second I realized: *When the time came!*

Sancho was running toward me, yelling. "Upstairs! The dressing room! Move your ass!"

I tugged my skirt up above my hips and *ran*, glancing over my shoulder only once, just as a chair hurtled through the beads. Two men brawling tumbled out after it. The strippers scattered, screaming. I saw Scarlett's ankle buckle in her clear heels. She collapsed into the brawl, a fallen gazelle. More screams, a high-pitched howl as Scarlett caught a fist or a foot or God knows what, the other strippers swooping in to pull her out of the tangle of beefy limbs punching and kicking.

A gunshot from the main floor turned everything momentarily into a film still. Everyone and everything stopped moving for a single endless second—all heads turned toward the shot's echo reverberating deafeningly beyond the glittering black beads, all breath held in that moment of fear. Then that evanescent moment split starkly from complete silence to a tumult of screams, crashing furniture, the raging of my own blood in my eardrums as we continued running, whipping the pink curtains back as we ran across reception, past my desk. Men's voices boomed just beyond the security door: "ONE! TWO! THREE!" and what sounded like a battering ram slammed into the door with walloping thuds. Christ, they were coming for us—it had to be a roundup of illegals, a bust of the Pie. Adrenaline and the energy drink surged through me, propelling me like some superhuman force so that I bounded up the stairs to the dressing room, taking them three by three, not feeling the burning in my lungs, in my legs. I could've run to the moon, hurdled over treetops.

The others tore up the stairs behind me, Zulema stumbling in her heels so Sancho had to drag her by the arm to stop her lagging behind, Alejandra screeching that she couldn't see with all the blood pouring into her eyes from the cut on her head.

After the mayhem of the main floor, the dressing room was eerily quiet. The eye of the storm. With all the strippers downstairs, the only one there was *Mamá*, filing her nails and drinking a detoxifying kefir one of the strippers had made for her. Seeing the state of us as we burst through the door, she jumped up, accidentally overturning her table and sending the bottle of kefir flying.

"Alejandra, your head! *¿Qué te pasó?*"

"We have to get out of here!" bellowed Sancho.

"Where's your father?" yelled *Mamá* as Sancho barreled past her, knocking the shelves of beauty products onto the floor to shove the fire exit open. *Mamá* clutched Sancho's shirt. "What's going on? Sancho, tell me! We need to get your father!"

Sancho grabbed her shoulders. "It's a raid! We need to get out of here or we're all going to be arrested!" He pushed her out through the fire exit and motioned for us to follow. "Come on! Hurry, hurry!"

"What about *Papi*?" yelled Ava as she ran toward Sancho.

"He'll be fine, we can't wait for him! Come on!"

Pelting across the dressing room, I snatched a pair of discarded sweatpants off the floor and pulled them on awkwardly, hopping from foot to foot while I ran. Sancho was shouting at me, but there was no way I was going out into the night bare-assed. Just as I was through the exit, at the top of the fire-escape stairs, I stopped and looked back. *Papá, where are you?* There was a strange taste of pennies on my tongue. My sweat smelled sharper. *Come on, Papá.* Then Sancho's hand was on my arm, tugging me out the door, slamming it shut behind us.

"But Papá!"

"No time, Yola! Román said to get the fuck out right away, no waiting around!"

We clattered down the metal stairs to an alley behind the club. An immense army-green Jeep was idling, waiting for us. Sancho pushed me through the open car door. My sister and cousins were already inside, cowering together on a second backseat row beside *Mamá*, who was leaning over the seat shouting rambling questions toward the back of the driver. Then as I clambered into the Jeep, Sancho following and slamming the door shut behind us, I saw who my mother was yelling at.

Aunt Milagros. Shrouded in cigarette smoke, hands gripping the steering wheel.

———

The second Sancho and I got in, Aunt Milagros flicked her cigarette out the window and the Jeep screeched away from the back of the club, racing down the alley like it was a Formula One track.

"Aunt Milagros!" I didn't know how else to react, or what else to say. There were too many questions—for starters, what the fuck was she doing there and how had Román known that she would be?—and I was still reeling from the raid too much to put anything into words. But Sancho had leaned forward to stick himself between the front seats and was interrogating her.

"How did you get here? What's going on inside? Why are you here, Aunt Milagros? Why aren't you in Venezuela? What's happening? How did you get this car?"

"Not now!" she yelled. "Light this for me!" She tossed a cigarette and lighter that hit Sancho in the face just as the Jeep ramped over a deep gutter running across the alley, sending us flying up out of our seats and slamming back down with shrieks from Zulema and the twins. I squeezed my eyes shut and gripped the armrest, too light-headed to do anything else. The metallic flavor in my mouth and strangely acrid smell of my skin only made me dizzier. More now than ever, with Aunt Milagros there like an action-hero phoenix risen from the ashes of Venezuela, everything felt wildly surreal—melting clocks oozing over walls and spindle-legged hundred-foot elephants strolling past wouldn't have surprised me in that moment.

The Jeep charged up to the mouth of the alley, which led onto the bustling Avenue. SWAT cars and TTPS SUVs were flying up the busy main road, swerving between the traffic. Horns and sirens ripped through the party music pumping from the bars and nightclubs while curious partygoers spilled out onto the pavement to see what all the commotion was about. Careening onto the Avenue, the Jeep went in the opposite direction of the police cars, away from the Pie. I glanced behind me at the second backseat row. Zulema and Ava were huddled together, looking about as shocked and dazed as I felt. *Mamá*, on the other hand, despite seeming almost savage with fury when we'd got into the Jeep, screaming questions at Aunt Milagros, now looked as though all the energy had been siphoned out of her. Her face had ossified into a hard mask of fear as she held a shirt against the deep gash on Alejandra's forehead. The white shirt was tie-dyed dark crimson as blood seeped through it, wetting *Mamá*'s palm.

"*¿Mamá, todo bien?*"

Her eyes were blank. She wouldn't look at me. "Your father's still in there. I left him in there."

"Román is in there too, *Mamá*. He'll take care of *Papá*. He won't let anything happen to him. I know it, don't worry. We can trust Román."

She flashed me a look, her eyes scanning my face. I went red, about to lower my eyes when suddenly she leaned forward.

"MILAGROS! We have to go back for Hector!"

I looked ahead to see Aunt Milagros's face in the rearview mirror, smoking the fresh cigarette Sancho had lit for her. "We can't do that, Yasmin."

Mamá dropped the bloodied shirt to grip the back of my seat, leaving a palm print of dark red on the leather. "I'm telling you to go back for my husband! GO BACK!"

Aunt Milagros didn't shift her gaze from the road. She was weaving between cars at a frightening pace. "We cannot go back. Sit down. Hector will be okay."

Mamá made a sound between a wail and a growl and threw herself back against the seat. Zulema wrapped an arm around her, but she shrugged it off roughly and snatched up the bloodstained shirt, pressing it against Alejandra's wound so hard she winced. Her eyes seared into the back of Aunt Milagros's head, her chin trembling, and I could see how badly she wanted to burst into tears. But she wouldn't cry. Never. She kept her eyes on Aunt Milagros and sat silent as a stone.

"Aunt Milagros, please," I said. "We need to know what's going on. How did you get here? Where are you taking us?"

"We're heading to a safe house. You can't go back home tonight, but everything will be okay." She took a long drag on her cigarette and exhaled so the rearview mirror was clouded with her toxic fog. "I'll fill you in on the rest when we get to where we're going." Sancho kept plying her with questions anyway as the Jeep sped along the highway heading east. She kept batting them back with the same dry reply: "Everything will be fine." Eventually, Sancho gave up and we continued in a heavy silence punctuated only by my mother's angry sighs, like a bull blowing hard through its nose, scuffing its hooves in the dirt before charging.

All I could think about was *Papá* and Román. Were they safe? Román was in the main room—had he been shot, bludgeoned, beaten? A harrowing reel of images unspooled itself in my mind's eye, each more graphic than the last. Román sprawled across the black carpet on the main floor, shot and bleeding out, being trampled by the spiked heels of fleeing strippers. Román's face battered and swollen, his skull dented in like crushed papier-mâché. And *Papá*. He wasn't in the main room, but had he been picked up in the raid and thrown into jail by Immigration? Had he been humiliated and roughed up by police, dragged out of the Pie by his hair, shackled in handcuffs, tossed into a cell wondering where we'd all gone, why we'd left him, if we were all right?

———

After forty minutes of driving, we took an exit into an urban commercial district that quickly turned residential and spacious, then rustic and run-down. It was a Saturday night, so the rum parlors' doors were flung open, some already festooned with frayed silver tinsel and red-gold-and-green fairy lights though it was only early November. It reminded me of what the previous November had brought us—Ugly's reign—and only added to my growing pessimism for what might have befallen *Papá* and Román.

Paying no mind to our Jeep speeding past, customers lolled and boozed on Rubbermaid chairs on the chipped pavement. No Prosecco being popped, no electro-house music wafting from recessed speakers. I watched them, village men and women out in the humid night wearing flip-flops and old T-shirts, drinking cheap liquor, but having a better time than all the glammed-up, snooty Prosecco drinkers back in Port of Spain.

Finally the village we were driving through ended abruptly at a dirt road shadowed by tall pine trees on either side. No houses, no streetlights, nothing but darkness and the sound of our tires rolling over dirt. We bobbled along over dusty stones and potholes, hanging on to whatever we could to stop from being tossed around. The Jeep tore past a clearing in the pine trees at the roadside, occupied by an imposing samaan tree that stood like a night watchman. Then a trick of the mind: the dark outline of a body swinging beneath a thick bough. I pictured my father, eyes bulging, tongue out, face purple. I rubbed my eyes. It was only a shadow. But my skin stayed clammy, the rusty taste in my mouth more acute than before.

Just beyond the samaan tree, the road veered left, the Jeep groaning as it climbed a steep incline. Eventually, after we had driven so far up the hillside my ears were popping, the pines to either side of us began thinning and the road evened out, widening into a broad driveway that led to a large house with a curious gothic steeple rising up out of its center. It was warmly lit, with pink bougainvillea bushes and fuschia ginger lilies bordering a spacious wraparound porch. Large silver chimes hung from the eaves, glinting in the soft glow of security lights as they knocked together, tinkling. Everything about the property was cozy and inviting. I felt like Hansel and Gretel must have when they finally stumbled upon that gingerbread house in the forest.

We drove up the long driveway, crunching over white pebbles that presumably served as ostentatious gravel, until at last Aunt Milagros brought the Jeep to a halt, hunching over to light another cig before turning to look back at us. "This is the safe house. You'll be in good hands here."

"You're not getting out?" asked Sancho.

"No," said Aunt Milagros through a mist of freshly blown smoke. "But you need to get out. I don't have time for this."

"What about my father and Mauricio?" said Sancho. "They're still—"

Mamá had simultaneously piped up from the back, talking over Sancho: "Milagros, you said you'd explain when—"

"Dammit!" Aunt Milagros had swung around in her seat, glowering. "GET OUT! I said there's no time! What don't you understand? OUT— ALL OF YOU, NOW! I need to go back for Vanessa and the child!"

Mamá sat back, her face bloodshot with rage, lips pressed together, but Sancho gripped Aunt Milagros's shoulder. "Vanessa and Che aren't safe? But they're at home."

Aunt Milagros's face was unreadable. "I'm bringing them here," she said, giving no indication of whether it was for their safety or not.

"Not without me." Sancho wedged himself between the front seats to climb onto the passenger side. Aunt Milagros shrugged and turned forward.

"Fine," she said. "The rest of you—move!"

We obeyed like a herd of drugged sheep. The second we got out, the Jeep was immediately in action again, peeling out of the driveway, spraying white pebbles in its wake. We stood watching its taillights shrink into distant red specks in the darkness. When the Jeep was out of sight, Ava turned to me.

"What's going to happen to *Papi* and Uncle Hector?"

The fear in her face made her makeup fade away. She no longer looked like a strip-club waitress, just the frightened teenager she was.

Not knowing what to say, I looped my arm around her waist and gave her a squeeze.

"It's a raid," said my mother icily, still staring down the driveway. "The National Security Ministry has done it before—a whole island-wide crackdown on illegals. Your father and my Hector are probably being deported as we speak."

Ava's face crumpled. "What are we supposed to do without our father here? How will we pay the rent or buy food, or—"

"Don't do that to yourself, Ava," I said, surprised at the convincing evenness of my voice. "Mauricio's going to be fine. *Mamá*'s only guessing at what's going on."

"But what if someone shot him accidentally or something at the club? You weren't on the main floor, Yola. It was terrible! Look at what happened to Aleja!" Ava was sobbing into my shoulder now.

"Don't think about that. It'll be okay," I said firmly. "Whatever happens, it'll all be okay." Though I had absolutely no clue if it would.

Then a clinking of chimes and a "*Yoooo hoo!*" from the house got all our heads to turn in unison.

Magnificent as ever, wrapped in a crushed velvet robe as she swanned down the front steps: Veneranda Manrique.

The witch in the gingerbread house.

IN FREE FALL

"*Bienvenidos!*" Veneranda swept across the white pebbles in her robe, Cinderella at the royal ball. Vicente had also emerged in a burgundy smoking jacket, a rotund Hugh Hefner scuttling down the stairs on bandy legs, gut heaving with every step as he came alongside Veneranda to greet us.

"So good to see you all!" purred Veneranda, flitting from person to person, bestowing on each of us an air-kiss. "My goodness, look at the attire you ladies have got on. Heavens!"

Vicente was at the rear, following up Veneranda's kisses with a warbled "Grand to see you." We shook hands with him numbly.

Everyone duly greeted, Veneranda waved a hand toward the house. "*Por favor*, do come inside."

We stood there like a bunch of deaf mutes, gaping at the Manriques. Why in the hell had Aunt Milagros sent us to *them*? If we were confused before, now we really didn't have a goddamned clue. It was like having Alzheimer's. Other people seemed to know what was going on, and all you could do was go with it and give up trying to figure out your ass from your elbow.

The house was even bigger than it looked from the outside. Vaulted ceilings, vast windows looking out over hills lush with virgin rainforest, and furnishings straight out of *Architectural Digest*. The Manriques took us from the porch to a spacious living area, then a grand dining room leading onto a kitchen brimming with stainless steel and marble. Another luxuriously furnished sitting room off the kitchen led to a long hallway warmly illuminated by crystal chandeliers.

"That's the guest wing, where all our . . . well, I suppose you could call them refugees . . . stay," said Vicente, pointing down the hallway. "You'll be there too. Our private wing is to the other side of the house. No need for you to worry about that, but if—"

"Hang on, hang on." This was *Mamá*, squeezing the bridge of her nose. "I thought *you* were the refugees and we were the safe-housers? Can someone please, for the love of Christ, tell me what is going on?"

"Oh my," sniffed Veneranda.

"Steady on," said Vicente, hoisting his jowly chin upward. "There's no need to take that tone. And I'm afraid we haven't been privy to the details of whatever is afoot this evening, other than your need for urgent protection from Ugly. It's simply been requested of us that we afford you the comfort of our home as shelter, in keeping with our usual line of work. So I'll thank you kindly not to take that tone again, Yasmin. You are in *our* home now, after all."

A terse silence. All I could hear was *Mamá's* strained breathing.

She was about to blow.

"Listen," I said, hoping to break the tension, "how about we all sit down and try to relax until Aunt Milagros gets back."

My mother exhaled by way of agreement. The Manriques shrugged and nodded.

"Good, let's all take a second to breathe," I continued. "*Mamá*, maybe you can use the phone here to try calling *Papá*?"

There hadn't been time to grab our things when we made our hasty escape. We had nothing but the clothes on our backs.

Veneranda raised a finger like a bejeweled sausage link. "I'm afraid this is a phone-free household. Too risky to go setting up landline accounts. And we shouldn't use our cell phones on a night like tonight, just to be safe. Ugly can track anything. Not worth the risk."

Mamá blinked at her, seething. "So what do you use to communicate—carrier pigeons?"

"Oh goodness, Yasmin, no need to be so snippety!"

"No need at all," gurgled Vicente, chins wobbling.

"Of course we use prepaid cell phones, but tonight we can't take the risk of Ugly tracking any calls. What if Hector is in Ugly's custody and he gets a call from you? What *then*, Yasmin? Ugly's people would find us in no time. No, no. We're very well acquainted with proper security practices, given the work we've been doing. For years now, I'll have you know."

I was curious to hear what that work was. I knew *Mamá* was too. All the Manriques had ever told us was that they were hoteliers who'd gotten on Maduro's bad side. But we also knew they were gagging for us to ask so they could gloat more. We wouldn't give them the satisfaction. So we shut up and let them lead us back out to the porch. Then we all sat in silence, everyone except the Manriques, who took the opportunity to point out all of the architectural merits of their home, though we were an unresponsive audience.

———————

About an hour later, we heard the distant grinding of tires over pebbles. *Mamá* was the first to leap up from her seat and run along the porch to the front of the house. The rest of us followed, breathless, to stand beside *Mamá*, who was watching the approaching Jeep like a siren waiting for a ship. It was blasting up the long driveway, almost skidding over the small stones. Then it was in front of us, the driver's door flung open. Mauricio got out. His face was red, sweating, hair flattened wetly to his forehead. My heart dipped—no one else had come with him.

He jogged up to my mother. "Vanessa . . ." he said, almost collapsing onto *Mamá*, his head flopping forward. She held him upright by the shoulders, bending to look into his face.

"What happened, Mauricio? And where is Hector? Why isn't he with you? Calm down and tell us everything." *Mamá*'s voice, though strained, was gentle. But her hands were gripping his shoulders so tightly they looked like gargoyle claws.

Mauricio just kept shaking his head, muttering Vanessa's name until my mother gave up and shoved him. And I mean *shoved*. "TELL ME WHAT THE HELL HAPPENED!" Mauricio stumbled backward over the pebbles. *Mamá* was seeing red. I grabbed her arm to stop her lunging at Mauricio and she spun around so roughly her chignon came loose, sending dark hair whipping around her face. She was a banshee in that split second, a thing of raw, fear-fueled rage. I held her with my gaze like I was soothing a bucking mare.

"You're not helping, *Mamá*. Stop it."

She looked at me. I didn't know what to expect. Then her chest rose and fell in two great heaves, as if a bellows were hidden under her starched cotton dress. And then, finally, *Mamá* let herself cry. She wrenched her arm from my grip and covered her eyes with her hands, sobbing all the tears she'd pent up for years, since the day we'd been forced out of our homeland and driven into living as clandestine personae non gratae without rights or security—all because Maduro refused to give up his twisted dream of a corrupt socialist utopia. She wept for Venezuela. She wept for her husband. She wept for all of us, caught in the slipstream of Aunt Celia's deal with our very own devil.

I caught Zulema's eye, jerked my head toward *Mamá*. With a complicit nod, Zulema took her post at our mother's side and put an arm around her trembling shoulders. I turned now to Mauricio for an explanation but was stopped by a sparkling, doughy hand on my shoulder.

"We ought to go inside. The girls are frightened by this whole *display*," said Veneranda under her breath, rolling her eyes disapprovingly toward my mother.

I looked at the twins clutching each other, eyes like anime characters, enormously oval and glistening with tears. I nodded at Veneranda and made my way back into the house. The twins followed, silent and phantom-like, shoeless in their gold fishnets and sequined uniforms. Mauricio and the Manriques trudged inside behind them. But *Mamá* stayed where she was, sobbing loudly into her hands with Zulema there for comfort.

———

Gathered around the marble-topped kitchen island, we listened while Mauricio composed himself enough to tell us what had happened.

"I was in the Pie parking lot valeting when Milagros came. I didn't know what to say when I saw her—I was shocked, but she wouldn't explain a thing, just told me to go straight home, get Vanessa, and wait for her there. Said she'd come for us as soon as she could. And . . ." He paused to gulp air, chin wobbling. "And I did what Milagros said. But when I got home, the house was a wreck. The front door was on its hinges and the gate behind it was all twisted, like someone tried prying apart the wrought iron to get in but couldn't manage it. The burglarproofing all over the house was like that; on all the windows the metal was twisted and bent. I unlock the front gate and go in, and I find Vanessa . . ." He hesitated and glanced at the twins.

"It's okay, *Papi*," said Ava, each word sounding fragile as glass. "Go on."

"I find Vanessa on the floor in my bedroom. I heard the baby crying, so I knew where she was. She'd locked the door; I had to kick it in. She's facedown on the floor and there's all this blood. She'd been shot. I saw the two holes in her back. I saw them." He put a fist to his mouth, holding back tears. "She was alive, but unconscious. Che was wrapped up in blankets next to her. Her blood was all over him. And there were bullet holes in the windowpanes. I turn her over and her face is gray, gray like Celia's was when I found her. And the blood was . . ."

Veneranda rested a hand on his shoulder. "Consider the girls, please. What did you do? Did you take her to the hospital?"

285

"I . . . I didn't know what to do . . . The baby was screaming and Vanessa was breathing but I couldn't wake her. What was I supposed to do? I didn't know. I . . . I . . ."

I wanted to knock his fucking teeth out. Typical Mauricio. Too weak to think clearly enough to take his own daughter to the hospital.

"But Milagros came with Sancho and they took Vanessa and Che to the hospital with my car. She gave me the Jeep, told me to follow the GPS, and . . ." he looked around at all of us, ". . . and I'm here now."

"Did she say *why* people went to the house?"

Mauricio shook his head at me.

"What about my father?" I pressed. "Is he okay?"

"I don't know. I don't know what went on in the Pie. I just left when Milagros told me to."

I wanted to ask about Román too, was choked by the question, nauseated by how badly I wanted to spit it out. "Was anyone else hurt that you know of? Anyone else we know?" I asked at last.

Mauricio shrugged listlessly. I exhaled hard through my nose, wishing I could shake him by the shoulders and slam his face down into the marble countertop just for a way to vent my frustration. But what would that change anyway? Whatever had happened, or was happening, was unchangeable now.

"I'm going to lie down," I said. "I need a minute."

I lay on my back on the top bunk in the bedroom the Manriques had assigned to me, Zulema, and the twins. I was sick with fear for my father and Román after hearing what had happened to Vanessa. What was going on? Why would she be attacked at home by gunmen? The events of the entire night were a nonsensical jumble.

The door creaked open. It was Alejandra, the cut at her hairline freshly bandaged. She crept up the bunk ladder to lie next to me. We lay side by side staring at the ceiling.

"I wish my mother was here," she whispered.

"Me too."

GOLGOTHA

Around midnight Aunt Milagros called Veneranda's unmarked cell phone: she'd be at the house by morning. Vanessa and the baby were at the hospital. Vanessa was alive but in critical condition, in the intensive care unit. The baby was okay. Then she hung up.

"Nothing about Hector?" asked *Mamá*.

Veneranda shook her head. *Mamá* thumped her chest and continued crying. She couldn't stop now that the floodgates were open. Obviously I didn't expect Veneranda to say anything about Román—why would she?—but I couldn't help croaking out the question.

"Did she mention Román at all?"

The room went still as I asked it, everyone eyeing me with suspicion.

"No, she did not," said Veneranda, a penciled-on eyebrow raised accusingly.

I locked my eyes on to a Persian rug hung on the wall. Maybe everyone could see the disappointment on my face. Maybe not. I didn't care.

Though I'd been literally at the edge of my seat when Aunt Milagros called, I now slumped back down into the fat leather couch, deflated of the little hope the ringing telephone had brought. I found myself consumed by pessimistic despondency. Again our fate was unhinged and unpredictable, as it had been since long before Ugly, when the Bolivarian Revolution first bared fangs tipped with the gangrenous poison of leftist populism and sank them deep into the sturdy, warm flesh of my home, so that now Venezuela was just a necrotic limb of the continent and we didn't have a single place to turn, except to a pair of twats like the Manriques. I felt with absolute certainty that wherever we were going as a family, it would always be this way for us—we were collectively hoisting the cross of our unwanted status, marching ahead with dogged determination as though heading along the Yellow Brick Road to Oz in all its brilliant Technicolor glory, daydreaming of living out in the open with all the state-sanctioned rights of real live citizens, when really we were on the straight and narrow road to Golgotha. If *Papá* wasn't deported or accidentally shot that night, if Vanessa made it through, they would only be transient triumphs until the next disaster came our way, until some other loan shark with a penchant for eighties glam-rock fashion came knocking at our door, until National Security caught up with us, or any number of other scum came to leech off our defenselessness. It would always be something.

Four a.m. The bed shook as Zulema tossed and turned on the bottom bunk. Ava and Alejandra, wrapped around each other like twin fetuses atop the duvet of the double bed, were murmuring in their sleep as though having a conversation. My eyes watered with fatigue, but I couldn't sleep. Any sound, no matter how slight—the rustling of a sheet, the creaking sighs of the wooden house—made me bolt upright, straining to hear a car driving across pebbles.

I counted sheep, tried *Mamá*'s stripper-given tips on "finding the peace of my inner sanctum," even recited the rosary just for the soothing effect of the repetition, but nothing could stop me panicking at the thought that *Papá* and Román had suffered the same misfortune as Vanessa, catching a fatal bullet or blow in the mêlée at the Pie, or being hauled away by National Security. With masochistic vigor, I thought of all the small things I loved about them—*Papá*'s belly laugh; the guava-jam smell of Román's fingertips; *Papá*'s off-key singing while he gardened; the way Román would always pull over when we spotted a fruit-heavy tree at the roadside and make me try whatever local fruit it bore—star apple, pomerac, soursop, barbadine—watching eagerly to see my reaction. Were those the little things that were now destined to fade into sepia-hued memories like the many things about Aunt Celia that I'd already forgotten just over a year later? Small, unremarkable details that merge together to create each uniquely complex human being, but that are the very first to slip into oblivion, until the person becomes just a cardboard cutout, everything they once were simmering down to a concise epithet: A Wonderful Father, A Loving Wife, A Bitchy Aunt, A Workaholic, A Jokester . . . That's how everyone is eventually remembered. The multisensory memory of them is stripped down layer by layer: first smell (the scent of their skin, hair, favorite perfume), then sound (a laugh, signature sneeze, timber of their voice), then the more insubstantial details of how they look begin to soften and blur—the shape of an ear, the lines in a palm, the depth of a dimple—slipping in fat droplets through the sieve of your memory and you can't do a thing about it. I couldn't stand the thought of losing *Papá* and Román that way—first in the crushing blow of hearing they were dead, then slowly, through inescapable evanescence as time went on.

So I lay awake, but with my eyes shut, zooming in on the details I didn't want to forget, whispering a rosary I didn't believe in but knowing that prayer, however empty it felt, was my only way of doing something that made me feel less helpless.

AUNT MILAGROS'S RAT

Faint sunlight brightened the room. I climbed quietly down from the top bunk and made my way along the hallway. The kitchen was empty, but the smell of fresh coffee told me I wasn't the only one awake. Hearing muffled voices, I wandered through to the porch.

Sitting at a claw-footed bronze table over still-steaming coffee were my mother and Aunt Milagros. A blanket around her shoulders, *Mamá* was drawn, decades of anti-aging moisturizer and months of drinking the strippers' detoxifying kefirs and organic collagen-boosting elixirs undone by a night of unbridled crying that had left her looking withered as a dried apricot. Aunt Milagros stood and opened her arms to me, but I didn't move, trying to interpret the look on her face. To decipher whether the turn of her mouth, angle of her eyebrows, meant she was about to tell me what I'd been dreading all night.

She walked toward me, pulled me into her, rubbing her hands roughly over my back. "It's okay, *chama*, your father's safe."

Instantly my shoulders dropped, jaw slackened, every muscle that had been tightly knotted for hours unwinding, loosening, lungs spreading like wings as I drew a deep breath of relief.

She stepped back, cupping my face. "He's absolutely fine." And then her eyes dropped for a fraction of a second. Fuck. It wasn't all good news. "He's not hurt, but he was caught up in the raid. He's at a holding center now . . ."

"Holding center or deportation center?"

She dropped her hands from my face. "Deportation center."

I understood why *Mamá* looked like such a wreck. Even worse than when Princess Diana died, a clear memory though I was only five, because it was the first and only time I'd seen *Mamá* cry, for the woman she called her "style icon."

"They're not going to take any action against anyone yet," said Aunt Milagros. "There's still a lot of processing to do with all the dancers they picked up. Even the local staff are being held there, so no one is being tossed onto a boat back to Venezuela just yet."

Not being chucked back to Venezuela—*yet*. About as reassuring as being told at point-blank range that you're not going to be shot in the head *yet*.

"Let's be positive, Yola. I'm confident that through my connections we can get Hector asylum here."

Her connections? I shook my head then, realizing that it made absolutely no sense that Aunt Milagros had all of this information to begin with.

"How do you know what happened to *Papá*? How are you involved in all of this?"

"Why don't you get yourself a cup of coffee and I'll tell you everything."

———

As soon as I was back in the kitchen, the burst of relief I'd felt that *Papá* was okay—tempered as it was by knowing he'd been caught—was quashed by my fear for Román.

I'd have to find some way, *any* way, to ask Aunt Milagros if she knew of his whereabouts. She had to know something, given that she'd been there waiting for us in the Jeep, exactly where Román had told us to go. Steeled by the knowledge that Aunt Milagros obviously had secrets of her own interactions with Román to reveal, I decided to flat-out ask what I needed to. Fuck whatever eyebrows it raised or questions it led to.

Making my way back out to the porch equipped with the prop of hot coffee that I couldn't possibly swallow, not with the lump of anxiety in my throat over Román's well-being, I saw that *Mamá* had come inside and was lying on the couch with the back of her hand across her eyes. Her cheeks were wet.

I leaned over her, touching her shoulder gently. "*Mamá* . . ."

"I'll be fine," she said without moving her hand from her eyes. "I just need to get my thoughts together."

"Want me to stay with you?"

"No, go talk to Milagros. There's a lot to be filled in on. I need my time to think."

———

On the verandah with Aunt Milagros, I immediately tried segueing into the right line of conversation to find out if Román had been hurt: "So Vanessa and Che are okay?"

"They're keeping Vanessa in ICU until she's more stable," said Aunt Milagros. "But she's young and strong. They're cautiously confident that she'll pull through this, and keeping an eye on Che for signs of emotional trauma, but physically he's fine."

"And . . ." I faltered, sipping at the coffee. "And was anyone else we know hurt? The doormen or the manager . . . Román . . . any dancers?"

Aunt Milagros took a moment before answering, watching me almost slyly.

"No, no one else was majorly hurt," she said at last. And again, I had the sensation of my muscles softening, loosening, my lips parting as I exhaled in quiet relief.

"That's good to know," I said, trying to sound casual, and then wanting to veer the conversation into safer territory: "Does Mauricio know about Vanessa and Che?"

"He left to go see them just before you came out. Sancho, bless him, he's been pacing those hospital hallways all night—from Vanessa's bedside to Che's cot and back again." She sighed through pursed lips, shaking her head. "I thought Román had all the houses monitored in case of anything . . . It was exactly the scenario he wanted to avoid. There was so little time to plan the raid. Less than twenty-four hours from the time the AG decided to have his party at the Pie. There wasn't much Román could put in place to protect all of you in that time frame, especially since he was in Venezuela that entire day . . . and there must've been a leak, someone who told Ugly I was back in Trinidad, or that I was the informant. Could've been anyone . . . a rat in Special Forces, the pilot, I don't know. So they hit the Palacios houses hard. Exactly what we were afraid of, but—"

I squinted at her as she talked, as baffled as if it was the reincarnated and reassembled spinster cat sitting there telling me it was an informant working with Román against Ugly.

"I'm completely lost," I interrupted. "What are you talking about— Special Forces? You and Román were working together? Start from the beginning."

So she did.

Here's what happened after Aunt Milagros lost her shit, shot the Dominican kid, and was smuggled back to Venezuela by pirogue.

As instructed by Román, she lay low and got a discreet job in Caracas, working with a Catholic NGO called the Roman Catholic Army Against Human Trafficking, or RAT (because RCAAHT isn't exactly a workable acronym). RAT's senior members were keen to get as much intel as possible from Aunt Milagros. They knew all about Ugly and his liaisons in Caracas—turned out Ugly was responsible for half the sex slaves trafficked out of Venezuela, some of whom had survived it all and clawed their way back to Caracas, which is sure saying something about how desperate they were. Back in Venezuela, they turned to RAT to rebuild their lives. They all cited a man named Ugly as the boss behind their ordeals, though they'd never seen him in person.

At this point, Aunt Milagros interrupted herself to say, "Román wasn't involved in any of that. He just arranged the paying relocation clients." I could've sworn she said that for my benefit, from an almost imperceptible shift in her tone, but I stayed poker-faced and she continued with her story.

Aunt Milagros's intel brought her deep into RAT's inner circle. She was the first person they knew to have had firsthand dealings with Ugly. It was RAT's first real stab at building a case it could bring to the Venezuelan or Trinidadian authorities, to get them to stop turning a blind eye. Aunt Milagros helped connect crucial dots, filled essential information gaps, until finally all RAT had to do was get tangible evidence against Ugly. Testimonies were one thing, but witnesses could always be snuffed out or bribed. Indisputable proof was what they'd need to campaign to bring Ugly's operation crashing down—a fat enough file had to be bait for *someone*, whether it was the Trinidadian or Venezuelan police or even Interpol. So when it came down to it, what RAT really needed was a rat.

"I knew Román was the man for the job," she said. "He did risk his life to save mine, after all."

I thought of the countless times I'd wished I had some way of reaching Román other than the Ugly-compromised number. "How'd you actually get in touch with him, though, to get him on board without Ugly finding out?"

Aunt Milagros tapped the side of her nose. "RAT has its own intelligence network, *bruja*."

So Aunt Milagros reached out to Román and he was indeed at the end of his tether. "He told me he was through with Ugly. He'd hated working for him for years, but it was either work for Ugly or Ugly'd see to it that Román never worked for anyone again. We were his only lifeline."

Román was just the Golden Egg that RAT needed. He had all the intel on the illicit Pink Pie, its laundered income, and its illegal stripper recruitment strategies—three easy ironclad charges. So things steamed ahead, and RAT, having an ingrained mistrust of Venezuelan authorities, got Trinidad's Anti–Human Trafficking Unit on board. Román fed the Unit spoonful after spoonful of information on the Pie's systems of money laundering, recruitment, and daily operations, garnished with copies of bank statements from the Cayman Islands, nabbing himself full amnesty from the T&T government for his cooperation.

Ugly's legal coffin had been built. All they needed were the nails to hold it together: the files and security footage from the Pie.

With charges in place and warrants signed, the Unit had been in the process of devising Operation Pie Smash when Román learned of the good old attorney general's birthday soirée, thanks to Ugly's urgent orders for Román to go immediately with the light-aircraft pilot on his payroll to collect the host of extra dancers for the auspicious occasion. Only hours later, Román was on the ground in Caracas, drawing on his links in the seedy *caraqueño* underworld to source two dozen high-grade strippers willing to do a twenty-four-hour turnaround in Port of Spain.

"That's how I got involved," said Aunt Milagros. "Román wouldn't be back in Trinidad with Ugly's shipment of fresh meat until a couple hours before the raid, so he couldn't put anything in place to get all of you out of the Pie when it all went down. Plus he didn't trust anyone but me to help him without selling him out to Ugly."

In Caracas he made contact with Aunt Milagros, who slipped herself onto the plane under the guise of stripper manageress, without RAT or anyone other than Román ever knowing she'd left the country.

"Couldn't he have just called us, though, from a burner phone or something to warn us and then we could've made our own escape plans?" I asked.

"*Por favor*," she said with an eye roll. "And have one of you slip up and give something away? Or have your father or Mauricio come up with some elaborate *Charlie's Angels* escape plan that would've gotten you all shot or arrested?" She tutted and shook her head. "Too dangerous, Yola. We had to keep it simple. The fewer people who knew, the better."

She tilted her chair onto its back legs like a classroom delinquent as she lit a cigarette and wrapped up her story. "Anyway, that's how everything fell into place so beautifully—busting the Pie, rounding up the illegal dancers, gathering all the financial and operational records, the security footage. Arresting Ugly and the AG to boot was just a bonus the Unit could've never seen coming."

It was the wildest thing I'd ever heard—Aunt Milagros an informant on Ugly, turning Román, jetting over here at the drop of a hat amidst a planeload of strippers. She knew it was wild too, was watching me with just the faintest glimmer of self- satisfaction, sucking the cigarette hands-free and blowing smoke through her nose. Part of me wished Aunt Celia could've seen her: the woman she'd always called a meek church mouse, the cowering virgin terrified of life. And now here she was grabbing life by the balls, mounting it and riding it hard. I could picture Aunt Celia gripping Aunt Milagros's hand: *Finally! The sister I was meant to have!*

"So," I said, about a thousand questions chambered at the tip of my tongue, "why'd Ugly keep all those records anyway? Why leave a paper trail and keep security footage and all of that?"

"Román said Ugly's paranoid. Thought the manager would skim off the top if everything wasn't meticulously recorded for Ugly's review. And the footage," she paused to give a little snort, smoke barreling thickly from her nostrils, "that was just plain smart—think of all the men who went in and out of there. Cameras in every inch of the place. That's golden blackmail fodder if Ugly ever needed it. And Román knew all about it, where everything was stored and filed in the club. He was a godsend."

And there we were again: Román. As mildly reassuring as it had been for her to say no one else we knew had been majorly hurt, I couldn't ignore that question still clawing at my insides—where was Román now?

She seemed almost to be waiting on me to ask more about him as she stretched her arm out over the table to flick the butt of her cigarette, dropping a lump of ash into her empty coffee mug. Letting her words—that Román had been a godsend—hang heavily in the air.

I gave in: "And you said Román wasn't hurt in all this?"

"He's fine," she said, taking a final drag before crushing the cigarette under her shoe. I nodded slowly, working my ass off to appear neutral, and sensing that Aunt Milagros had more to say. Luckily she continued before I had to ask. "Should be on his way to Spain as we speak. He's not safe here now Ugly knows he was the rat."

"Oh." Could she hear the disappointment? "Makes sense."

Aunt Milagros was considering me carefully, tapping an upended cigarette packet to draw out yet another one. "It does make sense," she said, almost cautiously, as though afraid of treading on my feelings. "He needs to stay safe. He'll be a key witness against Ugly when it all goes to trial."

"Mhmm." I ran my finger along the rim of my drained mug. I didn't want to look at her.

"Spain is a great place for a fresh start," said Aunt Milagros, cupping the tip of a fresh cig, flicking a silver Zippo open to light it.

"Yup, Spain sounds great." There was a humming in my ears. My vision was blurring wetly. I pushed my chair back. "Be right back. I have to pee."

————

I sat on the lip of the porcelain tub, holding my face in my hands. I didn't want to cry or scream or throw things. I felt none of the usual impulses of my temper. I simply felt empty. Disemboweled. Exsanguinated. Like all of my organs had been scooped out, my veins and arteries pulled out one by one like threads, and I was just skin. Hollow. *But he's safe. He's safe. He had to leave. Ugly would kill him otherwise.* As useless as telling yourself *It won't hurt, I promise* as a train hurtles toward you, about to plow you over, crush your bones into the steel tracks. Because no matter what, hearing Román was gone hurt, would keep hurting. Of course I was relieved that he was okay, but still . . . he was gone. Maybe not permanently, not six feet under, but out of my life all the same. It felt puerile to be so upset, wishing he were there when I knew how dangerous Trinidad was for him now, when I knew he'd have had no way to warn me beforehand that he was leaving. But I was devastated anyway. Would I ever see him again? How would I see him? When?

A pounding on the bathroom door jarred me out of my wallowing.

"Yola, I'm totally about to pee my pants here!" Zulema. "Can you open up? I'll pee in the sink if I have to! I'm like bursting!"

She didn't notice the look on my face as I opened the door and she flew in, slamming the door behind her with a "Thankyouthankyouthankyouuuuuu!" but when I passed the hall mirror, I was taken aback at how sallow I suddenly looked, like I hadn't seen sunlight in a month. I had to pull it together. Román was safe. That was all that mattered. And *Papá* was unhurt. I had to focus my energies on that now: on taking care of *Mamá* and figuring out the next steps to get *Papá* out. I'd wait until later that night to let myself ache over Román, to immerse myself in the warm, spongy memories of us, because now I felt certain that that was all I'd ever have of Román again—memories.

Later, before the Manriques emerged—we remembered from their days as our "guests" that they'd reliably sleep until nearly ten in the morning—Zulema, *Mamá*, and I got the scoop on how they'd gotten involved in everything.

"Boy, was that a shocker," Aunt Milagros grunted. "Who'd have thought those posh snobs would have been working with illegal refugees for eons."

"Seriously? Those two?" Zulema gaped.

"Turns out they weren't hoteliers at all. They're as blue-blooded as it gets, millionaire philanthropists. They had to leave the country when Maduro found out they'd set up a network of halfway homes across Latin America for refugees and *Opositores* on the run. Their assets were frozen and they had to get out ASAP, hence how they ended up at your house. Luckily they had more than enough money left in offshore accounts to buy this place and keep fighting the good fight."

I was flabbergasted. "How'd you find out about all this?"

"RAT knows about the work they were doing—are still doing for refugees. They dealt with them a lot when they were still in Venezuela."

The Manriques, bleeding-heart humanitarians? There was an oxymoron if ever there was one. If the Manriques were a couple of regular Harriet Tubmans weaving an Underground Railroad across Latin America for our compatriots, then who knew—maybe Ugly was the Dalai Lama mentoring orphans in his free time. Anything was possible.

————

We stayed clustered around the house shyly that day, embarrassed that the Manriques, our former nemeses, had seen us at our worst the night before. They were hospitable, laid out great spreads of food, gave us one-size-fits-all beige scrubs apparently kept on hand for refugees with no possessions and which made us look like prison inmates, and were, I guess, kind in their own way. But just as Stalin could kiss and coddle Soviet babies for postal stamp photo ops on the one hand and then implement genocidal famine on the other, our munificent custodians were still Vicente and Veneranda—as bounteous in their vainglory as in their magnanimity. Generous as they were, they still found insidious ways to needle, self-aggrandize, and berate, driving the bamboo shoots of their smarmy do-goodery under all our fingernails. So it goes without saying: things were tense, especially as we awaited updates from Aunt Milagros, who'd been reaching out to her contacts for information on my father's status via a burner phone, calling her RAT comrades to see what they could do to help.

By that evening, we had a better idea of where things stood, with us and the other in absentia family members—it wasn't all roses.

First: Aunt Milagros got confirmation that Ugly had indeed found out, probably from the pilot, that she was alive and in cahoots with Román. That meant we couldn't ever go back to our house, as Ugly's people would be on the lookout, which, I realized with such a powerful wrench of the gut that I felt I'd been hit with a wrecking ball, meant I had no way of ever getting Aunt Celia's manuscript back. I could have kicked myself for hanging on to the final chapter like it was the last drop of some magic Celia-conjuring elixir. Why hadn't I read it when I had the chance? Why hadn't I at least scanned and uploaded the whole fucking thing? I comforted myself that at least my near-complete novel draft was safely nestled in the fluffy white cloud of Dropbox, accessible wherever and whenever. I asked Aunt Milagros if there was any way someone could bring the manuscript to me; it was right there on the nightstand, I could picture it, that chunk of Celia's consciousness and memory immortalized in warm, familiar pages curled at the edges from being re-read dozens of times, but:

"No one can go to the house and then come back here, Yola, it would lead them right to us. I'm sorry, but consider all of your things in that house gone."

Second: *Papá* wasn't going to be deported. At least not for a while. As Aunt Milagros learned from RAT, the director of public prosecutions wasn't going to let Ugly slip away this time—he wanted full depositions from every single person who'd been arrested at the club. That meant sourcing court interpreters, conducting and transcribing the actual interrogations, translating those transcripts, and holding everyone at that detention center until the DPP's office had everything it needed. And with the glacial pace of Trinidadian bureaucracy, not to mention the frequent long weekends due to almost fortnightly public holidays, there was no risk of *Papá* being deported anytime soon, giving Aunt Milagros ample time to brainstorm with RAT and get them working with the UN Refugee Agency to hopefully build a compelling asylum application for my father and all of us to relocate to another country far from the reaches of Ugly's henchmen. It wasn't the ideal scenario, especially not for *Papá*, but at least we knew he was safe, and Aunt Milagros was confident that his and our horizons would be sunny once she and her RAT comrades put their heads together with the UN folk.

Third: as Mauricio learned via indiscreet hospital staff that morning when he went to visit Vanessa, Sancho would've fared better had he stayed behind at the Pie with my father. Although the police never responded to the reports of gunshots at Mauricio's house, possibly because Ugly's gunmen had seen to it that they wouldn't, but more than likely because they just couldn't be bothered, the Port of Spain General Hospital had dutifully reported Vanessa's bullet wounds, and a couple of officers had actually shown up to prepare a report of how the shooting had happened and interview the ER doctors who'd tended to her. With Vanessa heavily medicated, dipping in and out of a dense morphine-induced sleep, there was only one person those docs could point the police to for an explanation: Sancho. Sober, but panicked into absolute stupidity, he fumbled and bumbled, not saying anything about Ugly or the Pie, but not saying anything comprehensible either. His substandard English and visible panic were tantamount to a yellow Star of David in Nazi-occupied Poland: a glaring beacon for the authorities in charge to fuck with you and send your ass packing. Within minutes of Sancho's nervous blathering, they were grilling him about his residential status and demanding to see ID. Sancho and Vanessa were now waist-deep in shit—Vanessa still convalescing, Che in the temporary care of social services, and Sancho either in a police station holding cell or already deported. As soon as we found out, Aunt Milagros asked her RAT colleagues for advice, but it was a whole other ball game compared to *Papá*'s case. Mostly because Sancho didn't have time on his side. "Deportation happens quick here," Aunt Milagros informed us after getting off the phone. "He might be on a flight or boat to Venezuela by morning."

———————

Knowing where everyone stood post–Pie raid, we discussed what to do next over a tension-fraught dinner—"Roast lamb, imported from New Zealand, and *pommes de terre dauphinoise*. We like to feed our guests well. No frozen mass-produced foods like Jamaican patties and what have you." As we tucked in, we decided that while we waited out *Papá*'s internment and said our prayers for Sancho and Vanessa, because there wasn't much else we could do for them at that point, we would come up with the best possible relocation plan for our family. It was more fantasizing than brainstorming, since we wouldn't have much say in where we wound up if the UN Refugee Agency really did come through, but at least it was a way to feel like we were doing something proactive. Mauricio, completely abandoning his former Communist ideals, suggested the most farcical plan of all: "We go back to Caracas to get Vanessa, Sancho, and Che if they all wind up deported, then we go to Florida and apply for asylum there! Camille can get work in some millionaire's house in Miami, and bring Fidel. He and Che can grow up to be little *yanquis*. The US is where our future lies!"

He was ignored en masse.

The twins, drawn by some Darwinian magnetism to high concentrations of equally hot women, suggested Brazil. Zulema, who was completely content in her life in Trinidad, thought we should stick with what we knew best and go all the way to, "like, San Fernando, which is like, totally a whole hour and a half away from Port of Spain and Ugly's *compinches* would totally never, like, find us there." *Mamá* shut her down with a vitriolic eyebrow raise that said: *Get real, bitch.*

Still in my fatalistic funk and wretched with longing for Román, I couldn't see how anywhere we went would be any different. There was no utopian immigrant-loving Candyland out there for us. The whole world was just a patchwork of plutocracies wanting to protect their own, all the same wolf underneath ideologically different sheep's clothing. I let them hash it out while the Manriques added their two cents with an air of magisterial omniscience, but unless we could find a country to give us actual residency papers or asylum, I knew we'd be on an uphill Sisyphean trek to nowhere with our Maduro-faced monkeys on our backs, like every unwanted refugee before us who'd crawled under an electric fence, or ridden the high seas in an inflatable dinghy, or walked thousands of miles with stars in their eyes only to wind up in shit and misery all over again.

———————

Later that night, we were riveted as the ten o'clock news unveiled the Ugly case, which had exploded in the media because it had already led to the immediate dismissal of a string of government ministers who'd been recorded frequenting the Pie. The most popular leaked viral clips were of the minister of finance tossing fistfuls of bills at an upside-down stripper (Scarlett) with legs blithely spraddled as she worked the pole, and of the ministers of energy, health, and education guffawing at the *applauding ass cheeks* of one especially buxom dancer (Charity) who rolled her eyes and yawned, full of ennui, as she twerked. It was a spectacular shit show and Ugly was gonna fry for it.

I'd have said karma had come around, but if karma were actually a thing, wouldn't I feel some kind of satisfaction at Ugly's downfall? Wouldn't *Papá*, Sancho, Vanessa, and the baby be gathered around the living room with the rest of us? Would Román be on the other side of the Atlantic? There was no karma. Life was composed of the random and the absurd. And I was exhausted by all of it.

I THEE LIBERATE

As I'd predicted, by three in the morning I was in my usual insomniac posture. Supine, staring with dry, aching eyes at the burls in the wood ceiling. My mind couldn't rest. I wasn't worried about *Papá* or Sancho. Aunt Milagros seemed assured that *Papá* would be okay, and even if Sancho was deported, he was so changed since the birth of Che, so relentlessly optimistic that I knew he and his new little family would be fine. It was the ache over Román leaving that was a feral animal, snapping and howling at me so I couldn't ignore it.

How could I go back to life without him? It would be like never tasting salt again, never seeing in color, never feeling the sun on my skin. All I saw rolling out ahead of me was a stretch of gray.

Hungry after hours of grim musing, I got up and went to the kitchen in search of something to eat, then out to the verandah with a cup of herbal tea and a pack of biscuits, pulling my sheet around me like a cloak to stave off the mountain chill. I nestled into a plump-cushioned love seat at the far side of the verandah, overlooking the swooping green bowl of the valley below, blew on my tea, and prepared to slip down the chute of my memories with Román. I decided I'd force myself to think of every single one, from the first day we met—that lingering electric touching of hands—to the first time he'd shown up in my room and kissed me. To the firefly fireworks, the white anthuriums, the dark rivers, hidden waterfalls, the moon-washed beaches, all those furtive nights together, our jokes, the feel of his teeth on my skin, the roughness of his scarred arms under my fingertips. I indulged deeply, like an addict having one last binge, going right to the brink of heroin-induced coma before going cold turkey.

———

My tea gone cold, biscuits untouched, I was languorously running the fingers of my memory over the time Román had shown me a leatherback turtle dragging its prehistoric heft up onto the sand to lay eggs, when I heard the crunching of feet over white pebbles. Pulse racing, I gently put the mug on a side table and lowered my feet to the floor. I didn't know whether to stay put and hide or to chance peering around the side of the house to see who was walking up the driveway. Could Ugly's people have found out where we were hiding so soon?

Now heavy footfalls were coming up the front steps of the verandah. I stood slowly, gripping the sheet around me as though it were a magic cape that would somehow make me invisible. I was still as a fly trapped in amber.

A figure shadowed in darkness rounded the corner as I held my breath, legs trembling, threatening to fold beneath me.

And then the man took another step forward, and though I couldn't see his face, I knew it wasn't one of Ugly's henchmen.

I bounded forward, the sheet falling away from my shoulders and rippling in the air behind me with exquisite theatricality as I—with equal theatricality—leapt up to lock my legs around Román's waist and kiss him like he was a war hero fresh from the trenches. Román—not in Spain sipping a Rioja and flirting with flamenco dancers, but here, holding me, crushing his mouth onto mine, and tasting and smelling and feeling like everything I loved most in the world.

When at last I broke our kiss to catch my breath, my lungs and heart felt like they'd spontaneously combust with joy. I hopped down, arms still around his neck. "Aunt Milagros said you were gone!" I breathed, light-headed.

He ran the back of his hand along my jaw. "How could you think I'd leave you?"

"Well, she told me everything that happened. About RAT and all of it. She said you had to leave right away. Won't Ugly's people be looking for you now?"

"*Claro*, but I know how to keep myself hidden when I want to, and besides," he paused to tuck a strand of hair behind my ear, "I couldn't leave without seeing you first."

"So you do have to go to Spain." My heart dipped. He'd come to say goodbye.

"I'm going to Spain, yes. It's the safest place for me. But let's talk first."

He led me back to the love seat and we sat. I felt as though my insides were shrinking, everything growing smaller and calcifying into hard little knots of dull pain. Seeing Román, feeling the smallness of my hand in his, the taste of him fresh on my tongue—and now I'd have to tell him goodbye, a proper gut-wrenching farewell. I chewed my lip to stop myself from blurting out that I understood things had to end and that he had to go, that long-distance would never work, that I loved him and I understood.

"It's a good thing you were out here," he said, clasping my hands in his. "Saved me having to break into the house and wake you."

I tried to smile.

"So," he began, "ever since I started working with Milagros and RAT, I knew there'd be a time in the near future when I'd have to get out of here, and I've been putting things in place for that. For myself and for you."

He reached into his back pocket slowly. Years of being conditioned by cheesy romantic movies kicked in and suddenly my fear of heartbreak was gone—I could practically picture the Tiffany-cut solitaire diamond winking at me, saw myself squealing with the cookie-cutter thrill of unexpected betrothal, Zulema coloring my whole wedding beautiful, the cans clattering behind the "Just Married" car.

Instead, what he pulled out was a red passport, "ESPAÑA" emblazoned across the front. He flipped to the back page and turned it to show me my own face looking back at me, emotionless and pallid under the fluorescent overhead lighting of the hole-in-the-wall I'd gone to for my passport photos. I didn't know how he'd gotten the photo—my Venezuelan passport was back at our house—but there it was, next to the name Rocío Sánchez. Born in Andalucía, Spain. Age twenty-four.

Román pressed the passport into my hand. I gaped at it, more thunderstruck than if he'd whipped out a diamond. Because a diamond may cost a fortune, but a flawlessly forged EU passport is priceless.

"I want you to come with me to Spain. Whole new identities, whole new lives."

"Román . . ." I traced the Spanish coat of arms with my finger. "How did you get this?"

"My connections," he said, smiling. "So, what do you think? I have an old friend over there, owns a tapas bar. I'm thinking I could invest, expand the business with him, even start a chain. And you could keep translating, finish your novel."

I was still slightly lost for words but already feeling a stirring of excitement for a whole new beginning, one where Román and I could be together openly, live together, have a life together without Ugly hanging over us. It was so close, so *real*, that I felt almost drunk on the idea of it.

"Of course I want to come," I told him. "I just . . . what about my family? Everything is so up in the air."

"I know," he said, rubbing my arm reassuringly. "I know. But Milagros has a lot of pull in RAT, trust me. She'll have them working with the UN people around the clock to get your family amnesty somewhere safe—Costa Rica maybe. Or who knows, they might even wind up in

Spain too. She thinks you should come with me, and I promise, Yola, it's not like you'll never see your family again. You'll always be a phone call or a video chat or a plane ride away."

"Hang on," I laughed. "You told Aunt Milagros about us?"

He shrugged. "We've been working together for months." And then, looking mildly bashful (a highly unusual look for him), he added, "She's a sharper woman than I thought—she actually confronted me about it. Suspected there was more to my saving her from Ugly and said you'd always acted funny if my name came up."

"*Verga.*" I shook my head in amused disbelief. Would Aunt Milagros ever cease to surprise me?

"Anyway," said Román, "take a day to think about it."

"A *day*? Can't I have a little more time? It's not that I don't want to come—obviously I do. It's just a huge decision."

"Sorry, *flaca*, the longer I stay in this country the more dangerous it is for me. I can't risk hanging around."

"Of course, I understand." I exhaled. One day to decide whether or not to start a new life on the other side of the world.

"I'd better get going," he said, standing.

I got to my feet and slipped my arms around him. "I wish you could stay."

"Me too." He was wearing an impish smile. "I have something for you before I go, though."

I followed him to an unremarkable black sedan with windows tinted an impenetrable black, parked far along the driveway so no one would hear it pull up to the house. He opened the driver's door and leaned over to get something off the passenger seat. When he turned back to me, he was holding the one thing better than a diamond ring, better than a Spanish passport, better even than Maduro's head on a platter with a red apple gleaming in his mouth: Aunt Celia's manuscript.

I snatched it like a starving child offered a loaf of bread. "Román! How did you . . .?"

"I got it right before the raid, when all of you were already at the Pie.

I didn't know how things were gonna go down, and I wanted to make sure you had this in case of anything. I know what it means to you."

What he couldn't know in that moment was how much *he* meant to me.

———————

I took the kettle off the stove just as the boiling water set it rattling, before it had a chance to scream and wake the house. I felt an intense kinship to that kettle, on the verge of blowing my top and screaming with the excitement of what Román had proposed and of having Aunt Celia back, at least in her paper reincarnation.

Holding a cup of Sencha tea—*"from the Japanese ambassador, a dear friend, most recognizant of the work Vicente and I do"*—I curled up on the same seat where Román and I had sat not fifteen minutes before, and flipped to the last chapters of the manuscript.

At last, the end—or at least the end until the bucket was kicked out from under Aunt Celia.

My thirties and early forties didn't belong to me. I dedicated everything, every breath, every second to those two little girls. Everything became about making sure they grew up strong and smart enough to not make the same mistakes I did, falling for a two-bit honey smuggler who can't control the impulses of his polla.

And then Ava and Alejandra got older, grew strong and beautiful like their mother. My two elegant little queens, already fluent in English thanks to the ex-pat schools, more eloquent than the Queen of England. None of that Benitez whining that makes Mauricio one of the most sniveling little worms around, I don't care what he says about making all the money and being the king in his castle. These girls are Palacios through and through. They have our fuerza, *without whatever genetic hiccup gave us holier-than-thou Milagros.*

But those two beautiful Palacios daughters of mine go off to secondary school and I realize coño, *here I am with all these years behind me spent doing nothing for myself. Now I spend all night pacing on the Persian rugs and staring at my face getting older with every fucking second in the gold-framed mirrors, and I can't sleep, it's like the plague in* One Hundred Years of Solitude *and soon I'm going crazy in this fucking castle Mauricio built us, trailing around the house like a zombie every night, wishing I could sleep outdoors in a hammock strung up between the palms like we used to do as kids, because I can't stand the stink of it anymore—the stink of dirty money from killing all those crocodiles. So much* puto *money and why did we have it all? Why did we fritter it away on STUFF? That's how it goes with money. You have it, so you start to buy, buy, buy. Then when you have everything you need, when all the flurry of commerce is over, you're left with this hole that gapes bigger every day. What to do? So you scratch the itch: you buy, buy, buy some more. Because you've had the same living room décor for two years—time to upgrade! Because your kitchen appliances don't have the newest features—upgrade! A never-ending carousel of consumerism. Then because you keep spending, you have to keep on EARNING. Those fucking crocodiles were never going to get a break. Mauricio had to keep slaughtering them, skinning them, and making more money to buy more stuff.*

They say opium addicts are always chasing the dragon, that first perfect high. Maybe that's what I've been doing too, chasing after those golden Miami days when Mauricio got me my first piece of jewelry, the first time I ate in a Michelin-star restaurant, first time I tasted real blow not cut with baby laxatives. But that first perfect high is never coming back—trust me, I've spent enough money to know it. And what else is there for me? Keeping a house, raising kids? How is that enough? Orangutans spend their lives spitting out kids, building nests, putting fruit and insects on the table. Shouldn't I want more out of life than some saggy-titted orangutan? How am I supposed to tell my girls to want a little more out of life than STUFF and housework when I'm just Mauricio's glorified concubine? And not just the twins—my nieces too. (Maybe not Zulema—she'd better find herself a Mauricio. Girl has a face like a movie star and a brain like a puff of cotton candy. At least she'll benefit from some of my tried and trusted seduction tactics when she's old enough for me to tell her.)

But that Yola, she's a bright one. Tells the best lies I've ever heard out of any kid that young. She was only ten years old when she told me she wanted to be a writer. "I like how you tell stories, Aunt Celia. It's amazing how I can picture the whole thing—even if the ghost stories are pretty scary. I want to be able to tell stories like that too. So people can see the story and feel scared or whatever I want them to feel. That's what writers do, right?" I wanted to hold her, squeeze her hard and tell her chama, *you can be a writer, be whatever the fuck you want, just don't tie yourself down with some asshole who wants you to do nothing but breed and swan around looking pretty. Let your soul roam wild, find a partner who lets it roam, makes it soar.*

Next to that paragraph, scribbled in her handwriting, were several messy notes:

*For Yolita—Be whatever the fuck you want.
**For you, Yolita. Never forget to let your soul roam.
***~~For the young woman who inspired me to~~ For Yola.

I swallowed back tears as I realized she'd been brainstorming dedications. The manuscript hadn't only been for her. It had been for me all along.

———

I read on to the year it all changed. The same year the rest of us Palacios had come over to Trinidad, and the year Mauricio's croc-skinning empire would come crumbling down, its bitter end heralded by the ominous ringing of the ivory telephone at Mauricio's bedside in the middle of the night. Police raid. Crackdown. Disaster. They had to leave that same night with nothing but a couple of suitcases of cash. Just enough cash to pay a shady guy to relocate them to Trinidad, and just enough time to make a deal to get the twins fake residency permits for a series of wild payments Celia never thought Mauricio would be unable to make. She never imagined that he'd fall into the same depression as when he lost everything in Miami, and that in middle age he wouldn't have the energy to bounce back; that he'd settle for working double shifts at a crappy casino, earning squat, leaving Celia to handle their debt to Ugly alone.

When she realized she couldn't count on Mauricio, she didn't cower or turn to anyone for help. She decided she'd somehow pay it on her own, make jewelry to start and then find an agent to sell her memoir for hundreds of thousands of dollars once it was finished. She'd do it to give herself more purpose in life than an orangutan, so she could prove to the twins that she didn't need their father's honey or crocodile-skin money.

So I can show Yola that she can make a living off of words, that you don't have to live enslaved to anyone or anything—not a prick husband, not a boss, not a grinding nine-to-five that bleeds all the creativity from your soul with the misery of half-hour lunch breaks and daily commutes and clocking in and answering to superiors and filling in fucking request forms for annual vacation.

The last lines she wrote were these:

Why can't I do it alone? What's the worst that could happen?

I looked out over the valley below, gently brightening under a hazy dawn sun. The worst really had happened, and if Aunt Celia could've foreseen it all, maybe she wouldn't have called Ugly's Caracas contact and signed a year of our lives away without even knowing it.

But would it have been better not to have lived the past year? If I erased the past twelve months from my life, that would mean erasing

Javier and the Jotas, erasing our wild drunken Christmas with all the illegals, erasing Baby Che, erasing the Pink Pie and all the crazy shit I'd seen there—erasing Román. As difficult and scary as things had been at times, I wouldn't trade the past year for anything. Wasn't that what life was all about anyway? The shit hitting the fan with projectile force, splattering you head to toe in fecal matter, but rolling with it, living in the moment and drawing whatever sweetness you could from that shit-covered sugarcane?

I stretched my legs out, joints stiff from sitting cross-legged while I read, and put the manuscript on the cushion beside me. The Spanish passport was next to it. Tantalizingly red. I flipped to the page with "Rocío's" photo and stared at it, feeling the weight of the passport, the weight of owning a document that unlocked borders instead of closing them off. It was like holding a wand, and all I had to do was wave it in the face of some narrow-eyed suspicious immigration officer and with a sprinkle of that European Union fairy dust, he'd be smiling at me, welcoming me across the border, no questions about the duration and purpose of my stay, no demands to see my return ticket, my tourist visa, proof of funds to support myself during my trip, my police record, my academic transcripts, my family tree, a fucking blood sample. Román could've said, with this ring I thee wed, but instead he'd told me with this passport, I thee liberate.

Even so, would I actually have the balls to go to Spain with Román? I'd never lived in a different country from my family. Or in a country where I knew literally no one. What if Román and I broke up and I was stuck living alone on a translator's fluctuating income, with an unfinished novel manuscript and no familial security blanket? I could stay in Trinidad, work on the novel, and wait with my family to head to Costa Rica or wherever, safe at last with the protection of asylum. It would be easy. Spain held the promise of adventure, but I knew, having been well acquainted with the vicissitudes of adventure ever since crossing the Gulf of Paria in that pirogue with my family, that that wasn't necessarily a good thing. Choosing Spain would be cut-

314

ting the familial umbilical cord, delving into a world of unknowns, of possible fuckups and mishaps and everything going wrong, of disaster and disappointment.

Yet somewhere deep in my viscera I felt that Spain held the promise of more than just tumultuous adventure. It was my sugarcane—full of the sweetness of passion, possibility, travel, new people, new experiences, a life I could shape with my own two hands, with a partner who *did* make my soul soar—and what if it was these moments, full of fear and excitement and doubt and not-knowing, that you had to bite down hard and sink your teeth into to get at that sugar?

The breeze picked up suddenly, rushed through the bristles of the pines surrounding the house, skimming urgently across my skin. I wished I could hear Aunt Celia hissing in the wind, telling me what to do. But Aunt Celia wasn't here. There weren't even any unread words of hers left to lap up.

And in that moment the realization struck me. I no longer had to mourn the void of Aunt Celia. I didn't need to ask what she thought about Spain because she'd already told me the answer I should give Román, and it all lay in one question.

What's the worst that could happen?

ACKNOWLEDGMENTS

You might never have met the Palacios family without Susan Armstrong, my wonderful agent. I am immeasurably grateful for the time and effort she put into this book. Not only did her shrewd editorial notes transform the manuscript but they also helped me to grow so much as a writer. The support from everyone at C&W, particularly Emma Finn, who was instrumental in the editing process, has made this journey such a joy.

Heartfelt thanks to Zoe Sandler at ICM, who championed *One Year of Ugly* stateside and buoyed me with her enthusiasm for the Palacios' story.

Thank you to my fantastic editors, Ann Bissell at The Borough Press and Dawn Davis at 37 Ink, together with their talented teams, for helping me to put the final polish on the manuscript. I cannot adequately express my gratitude for their belief that this story should be shared with the world and for making a lifelong dream a reality.

My husband, Stephen Mackenzie, was essential to the creation of this novel in so many ways: fuelling my creativity with endless nature excursions; providing ample inspiration for Yola and Román's hot-and-heavy romance; listening for hours as I blabbed about every scene and character and plot challenge. He's always been a believer in my words and the most supportive partner imaginable. Thank you. I love you.

I'm fortunate in that my life has been full of supportive friends and family. Kimberly Joseph, my best friend of two decades who found time to read, re-read, and compile notes on three drafts of the manuscript during her daily commute. The brilliant Summer Hughes and incredibly talented author Breanne McIvor, who also read the earliest drafts of *One Year of Ugly*. These three women, the book's very first audience, are who gave me the courage to put the manuscript out there.

I can't fathom weathering the rocky road to publication without the support of my tightknit little writing group comprised of Breanne, myself, and the poetic powerhouse Andre Bagoo. Their friendship has been critical to my development as a writer and to helping me produce this book.

Thank you to my in-laws, Lou Ann and Ken Mackenzie, who helped Stephen and me so much with our newborn son while I was completing my final edits. Without those extra hands, *Ugly*'s publication date might have been somewhere circa 2050.

In terms of building the real meat of the Palacios' story, I must thank those Venezuelans living in Trinidad who spoke with me in such detail about their experiences. Without your willingness to discuss your challenges and those of your families and friends back home, this novel would be void of any depth or purpose. Thanks to your candor, I hope I was able to portray at least some small part of the hardships you have endured and continue to endure, and that anyone reading this book—particularly Trinidadians—will come to consider the plight of the Venezuelan people with greater compassion.

Lastly, the two people who started it all: my parents, Christian and Debbie de Verteuil, who nurtured my love of storytelling, literature, and creativity in every possible way. My gratitude, love, and respect for these two sensational human beings are boundless.

A final note on my mother, Debbie, whom I lost over a decade ago. She is the real inspiration for the overarching message of *One Year of Ugly*. I watched her spend her very short life yearning to pursue her artistic impulses but locked into the grind of nine-to-five employment—yet somehow, in spite of it all, she managed to slap on a smile and fill her children's lives with laughter and lightheartedness. Seeing that, I refused to let life pass me by in a blur of commutes, complaints, and soul-numbing work. It motivated me to write so that I could make people laugh, make people hope, make people think about what it would be like to step out of their comfort zones and pursue a dream that is just a little bit crazy.

So, to my mother: you are the person I am most grateful to above all, for inspiring the message of this book and for all of the happiness of my creative little life.

AUTHOR'S NOTE: ONE YEAR OF UGLY

As in most works of fiction, the story of *One Year of Ugly* is built upon countless true stories. In this case, the stories of Venezuelans fleeing their homeland to settle in a place that is far from an idyllic refuge: Trinidad.

In 2016, the year in which the novel is set, there was no existing asylum policy to support refugees despite the fact that Trinidad and Tobago has received more Venezuelans than any other country in terms of population percentage. Arrest, deportation, and detention were constant fears for refugees, with the government maintaining a hard-line stance toward Venezuelans in hiding. Raids were conducted frequently on known Venezuelan "hot spots" and workplaces, refugees were given no access to protection or public services, and the criteria for anyone hoping to regularize their status were near impossible to meet.

It was in this tense, turbulent atmosphere that the stories of the Venezuelans in Trinidad came to my attention. First, through my work as a legal translator. The rapid spike in Venezuelan legal documents coming across my desk was the first sign of the Venezuelan influx.

Then, the changing nature of the translation requests—beyond the standard certificates of birth, marriage, death, and divorce, I began to see a new type of document with alarming regularity: power of attorney granting custody of young children to family and friends in Trinidad. This is what stirred me to imagine how the everyday middle-class person copes with the steady crumbling of his or her homeland. What would I do to get my own child out of a country that is falling apart? How would that change the way people perceive my family and me? What new risks would be inherent in our daily lives that we would otherwise never be exposed to?

The second way in which the "Venezuelan situation" fixed itself firmly to the fore of my imagination was through plain sight. The streets, bars, offices, salons, groceries, malls, and movie theaters were steadily swelling with a whole new demographic. It was impossible not to notice. Equally impossible to ignore: the local response to the new ethnicity in our midst, to the Spanish ringing out alongside our own Trini dialect. That more than anything is what drove me to write this book. I couldn't believe the prejudice, hostility, and flagrant xenophobia expressed by so many of my fellow Trinidadians toward the wave of Latin migrants. The comments I've heard are as vicious and myopic as what you'd hear at any far-right rally against exactly the immigrant demographic Trinidadians usually fall within. The irony was absurd!

Thus *One Year of Ugly* took shape, and though the subject matter is heavy, in that exile, exploitation, and the collapse of Venezuela constitute major themes, I wrote the book as a comedic novel because there is nothing that makes even the heaviest subjects more accessible than humor.

Then, of course, there is the other immeasurable value of comedy: it engenders hope. Laughter really is the proverbial panacea, and with the overarching message of *One Year of Ugly* being one of glass-half-full optimism, humor allows my characters to remain full of wry hope no matter how grim their circumstances. Humor is what helps my protagonist weather the many shit storms that assail her family, and it is ultimately what teaches her the core lesson of her time in Trinidad: life will hit you for six but you've got to roll with the punches and suck the sweetness out of it however you can. The first step is finding a way to laugh at yourself and at whatever challenge you're struggling through.

And so I hope readers will also have that takeaway from the novel—that you'll come away from it with a renewed thirst for life, knowing that no matter what form of ugly crosses your path, there's always a way to laugh through it.

ABOUT THE AUTHOR

Caroline Mackenzie is a freelance translator living in her native Trinidad with her husband and son. She studied in the United Kingdom for four years on a National Open Scholarship, earning a BA in French and Spanish studies from Sussex University and an MSc in scientific, medical, and technical translation from Imperial College London. Upon returning to Trinidad, she began writing more extensively, with her short fiction appearing in literary publications around the world. In 2017 she was shortlisted for the Commonwealth Short Story Prize and in 2018 she was named the Short Fiction winner of the Small Axe Literary Competition. *One Year of Ugly* is her first novel.